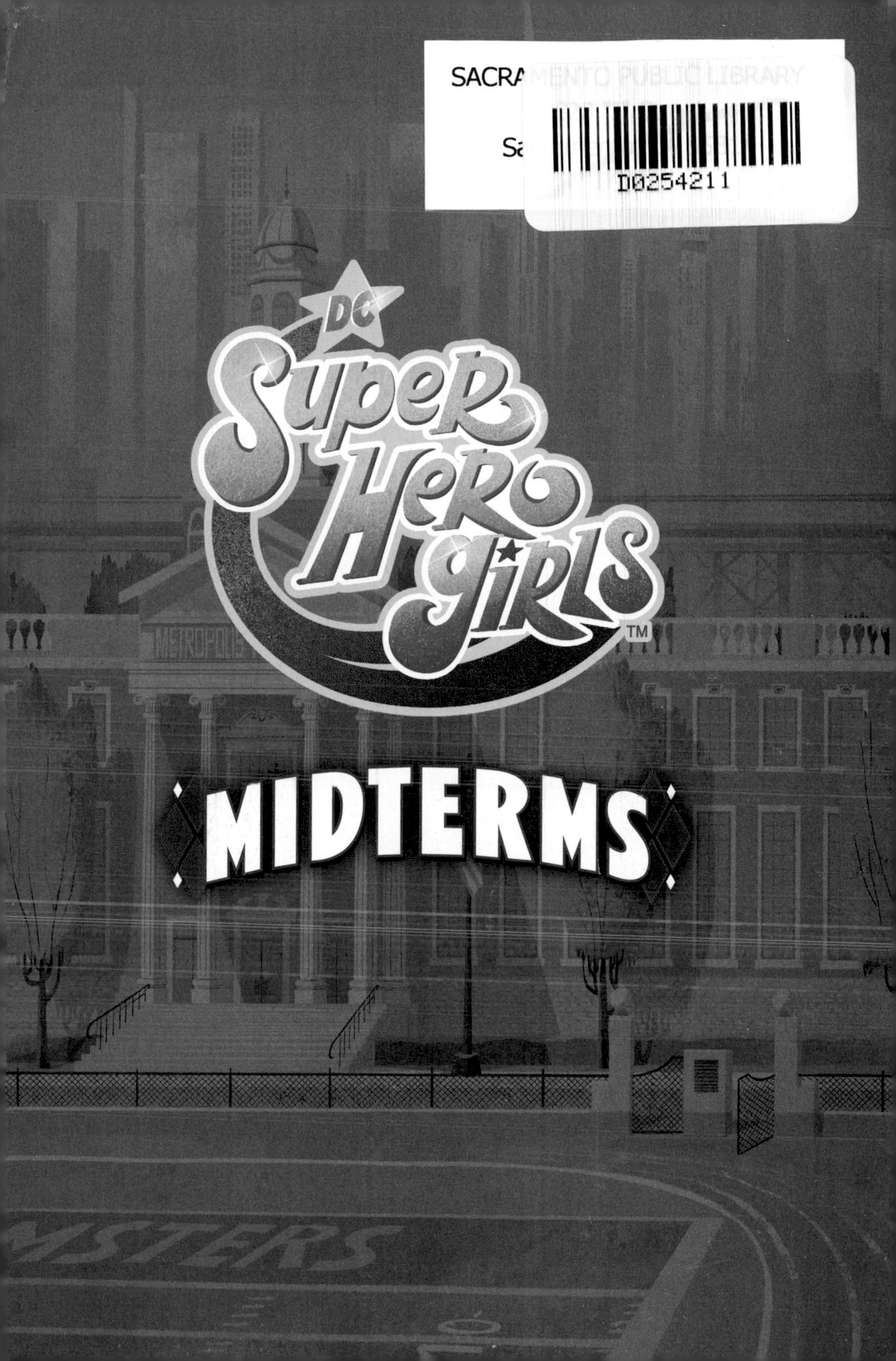
DC
Super Hero Girls™
METROPOLIS
MIDTERMS

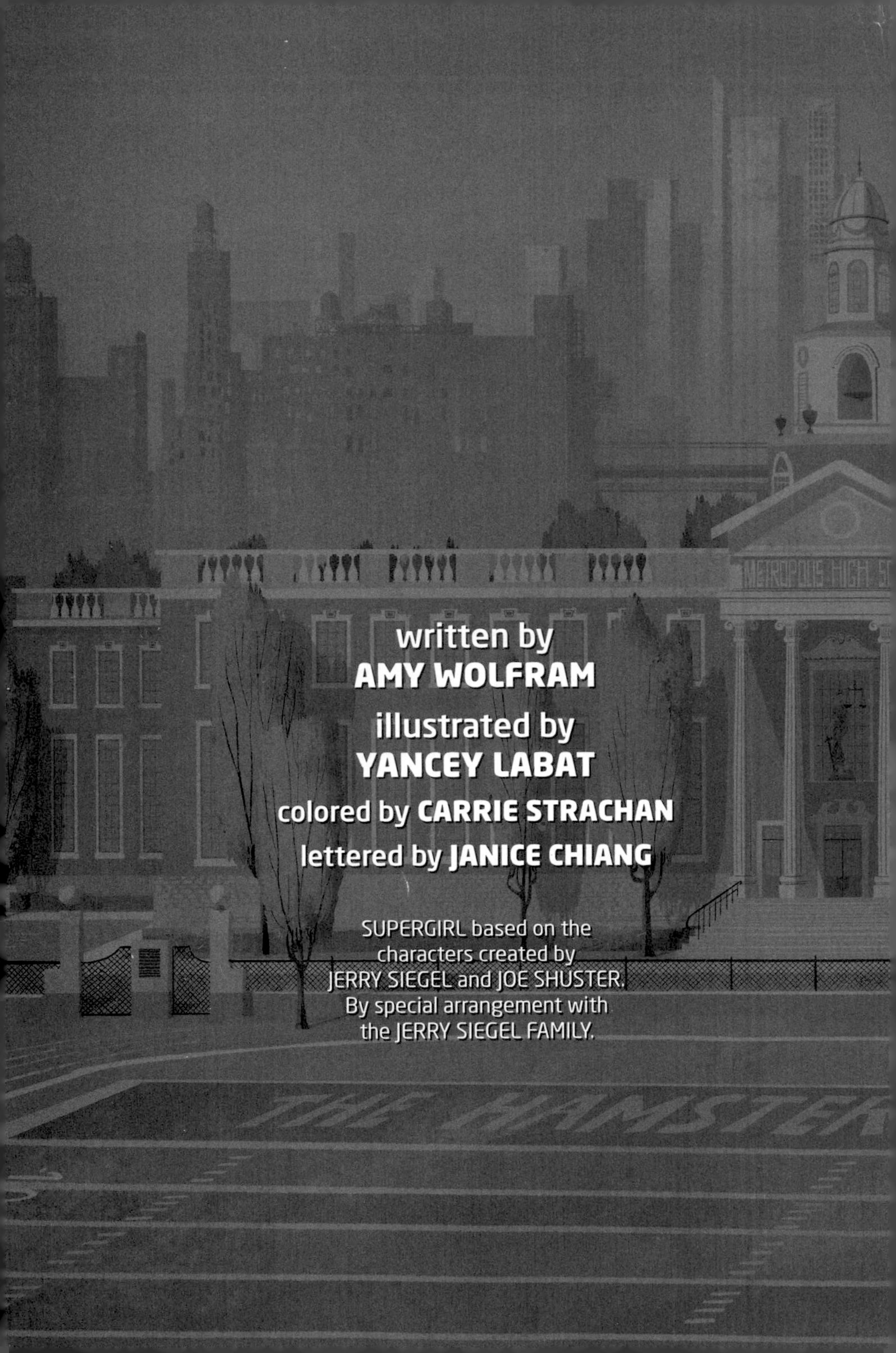

written by
**AMY WOLFRAM**

illustrated by
**YANCEY LABAT**

colored by **CARRIE STRACHAN**

lettered by **JANICE CHIANG**

SUPERGIRL based on the
characters created by
JERRY SIEGEL and JOE SHUSTER.
By special arrangement with
the JERRY SIEGEL FAMILY.

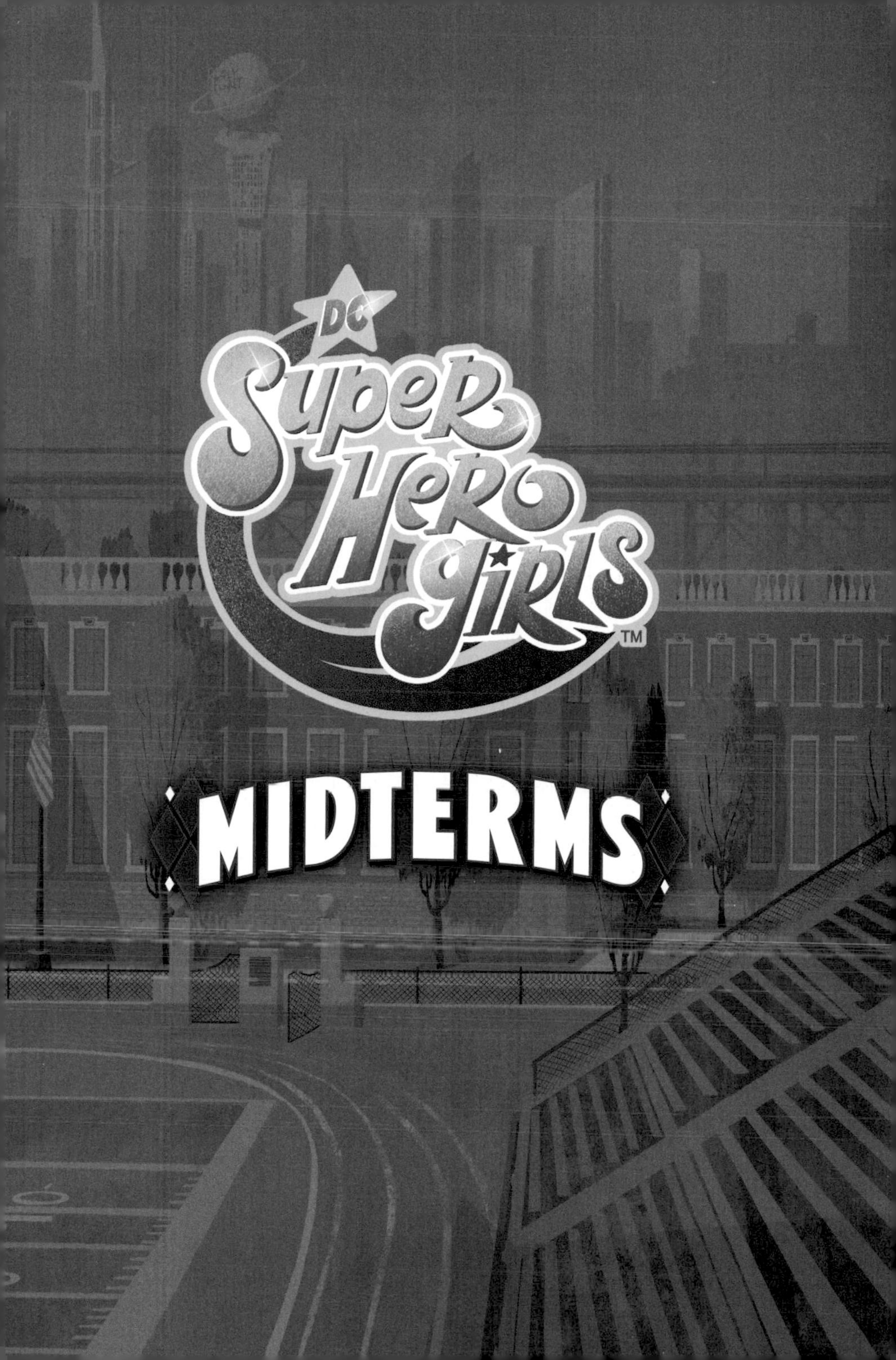

DC Super Hero Girls™

# MIDTERMS

KRISTY QUINN Editor
STEVE COOK Design Director - Books
AMIE BROCKWAY-METCALF Publication Design

BOB HARRAS Senior VP - Editor-in-Chief, DC Comics
MICHELE R. WELLS VP & Executive Editor, Young Reader

JIM LEE Publisher & Chief Creative Officer
BOBBIE CHASE VP - Global Publishing Initiatives & Digital Strategy
DON FALLETTI VP - Manufacturing Operations & Workflow Management
LAWRENCE GANEM VP - Talent Services
ALISON GILL Senior VP - Manufacturing & Operations
HANK KANALZ Senior VP - Publishing Strategy & Support Services
DAN MIRON VP - Publishing Operations
NICK J. NAPOLITANO VP - Manufacturing Administration & Design
NANCY SPEARS VP - Sales
JONAH WEILAND VP - Marketing & Creative Services

PEFC Certified

This product is from sustainably managed forests and controlled sources.

PEFC/29-31-337  www.pefc.org

*DC Super Hero Girls: Midterms*

Published by DC Comics. Copyright © 2020 DC Comics. All Rights Reserved. All characters, their distinctive likenesses, and related elements featured in this publication are trademarks of DC Comics. DC logo is a trademark of DC Comics. The stories, characters, and incidents featured in this publication are entirely fictional. DC Comics does not read or accept unsolicited submissions of ideas, stories, or artwork.

Printed at LSC Communications, Crawfordsville, IN, USA.

7/24/2020. First Printing.

DC - a WarnerMedia Company

DC Comics, 2900 West Alameda Ave., Burbank, CA 91505

ISBN: 978-1-4012-9852-4

Library of Congress Cataloging-in-Publication Data
Names: Wolfram, Amy, writer. | Labat, Yancey C., artist. | Strachan, Carrie, colourist. | Chiang, Janice, letterer.
Title: DC super hero girls : midterms / written by Amy Wolfram ; art by Yancey Labat ; colored by Carrie Strachan ; lettered by Janice Chiang.
Other titles: Midterms
Description: Burbank, CA : DC Zoom, [2020] | Series: DC super hero girls | "Supergirl based on the characters created by Jerry Siegel and Joe Shuster. By special arrangement with the Jerry Siegel family." | Audience: Ages 8-12 | Audience: Grades 4-6 | Summary: Karen Beecher, Lois Lane, and Harleen Quinzel are the top three students on the leaderboard at Metropolis High, and the upcoming midterms will determine who is the best in the class, but each girl must first face trials from their real lives.
Identifiers: LCCN 2020020206 (print) | LCCN 2020020207 (ebook) | ISBN 9781401298524 (trade paperback) | ISBN 9781779506108 (ebook)
Subjects: LCSH: Graphic novels. | CYAC: Graphic novels. | Superheroes--Fiction. | Competition (Psychology)--Fiction. | High schools--Fiction. | Schools--Fiction.
Classification: LCC PZ7.7.W6 D34 2020  (print) | LCC PZ7.7.W6  (ebook) | DDC 741.5/973--dc23
LC record available at https://lccn.loc.gov/2020020206
LC ebook record available at https://lccn.loc.gov/2020020207

# table of contents



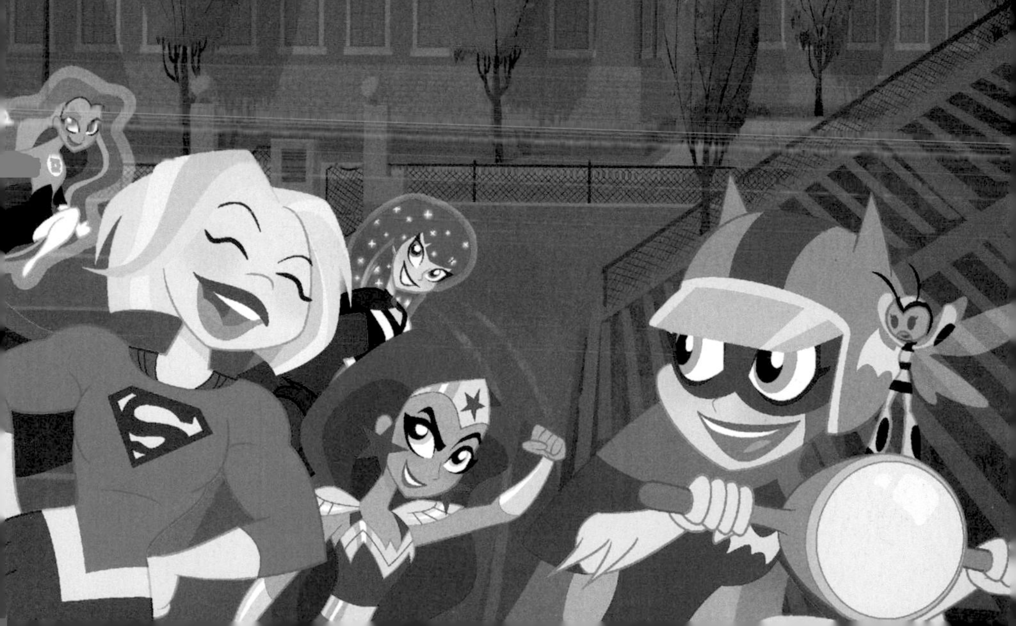

# chapter one

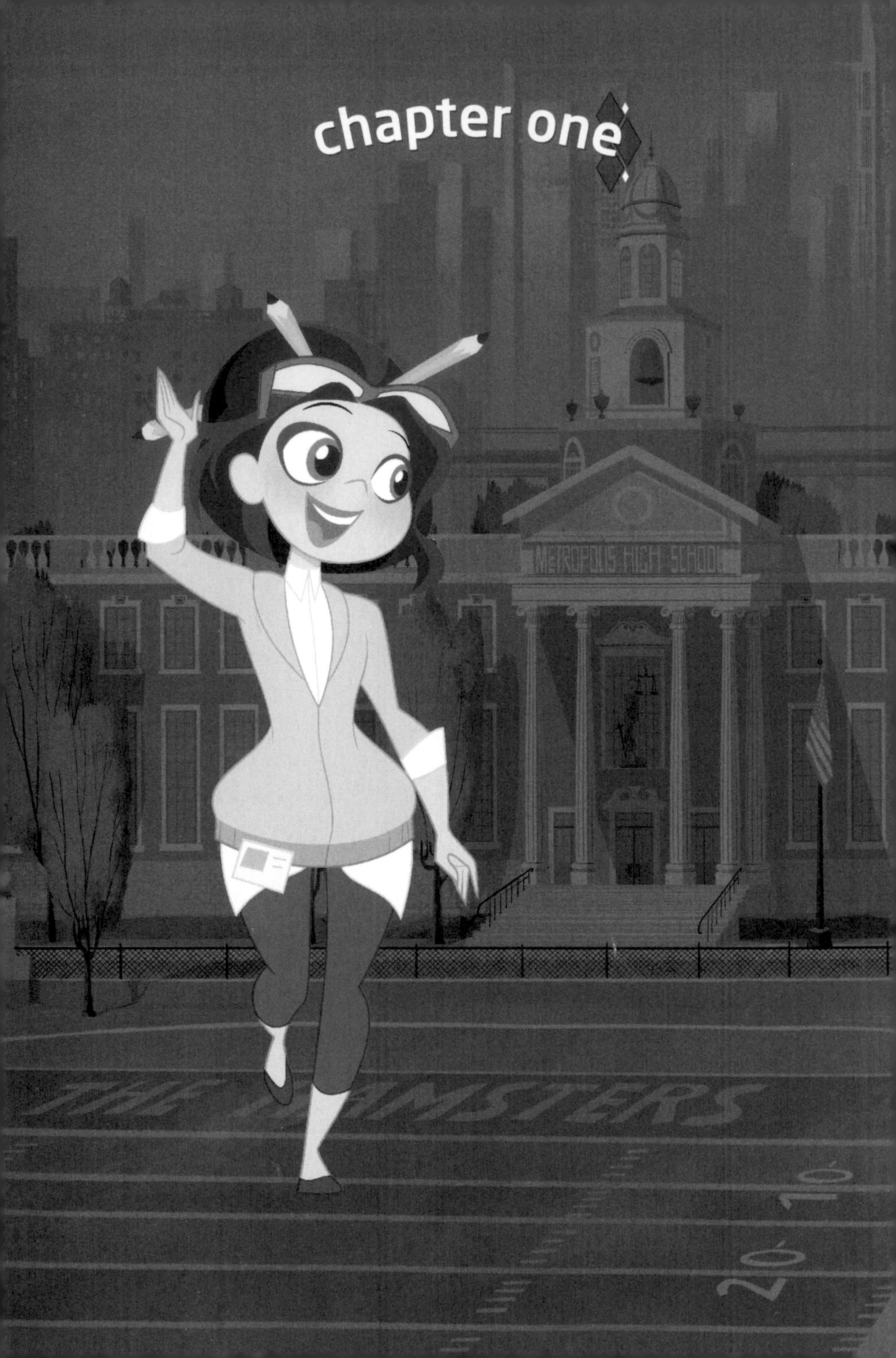
METROPOLIS HIGH SCHOOL

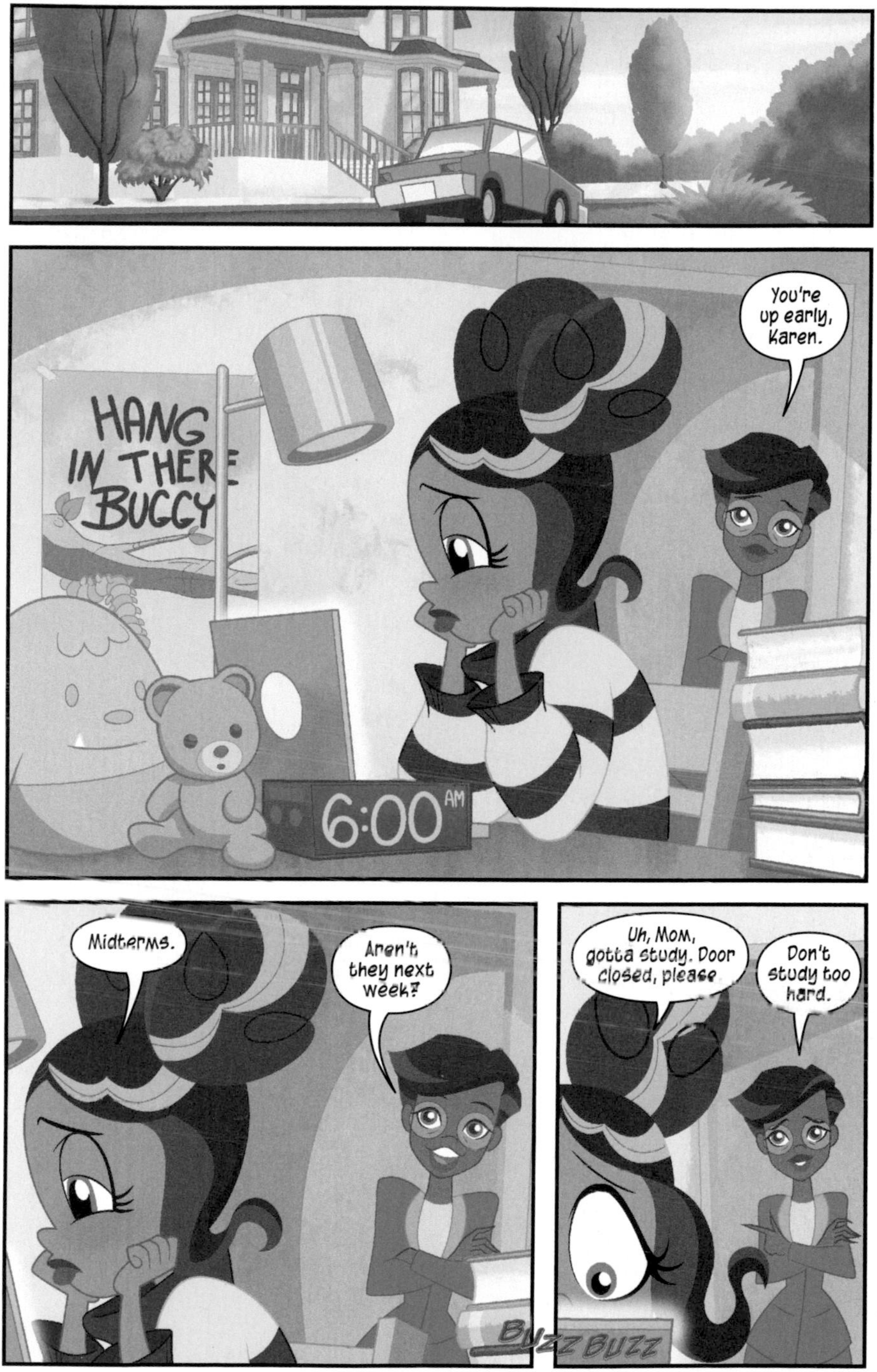
HANG IN THERE BUGGY
6:00 AM
You're up early, Karen.
Midterms.
Aren't they next week?
BUZZ BUZZ
Uh, Mom, gotta study. Door closed, please.
Don't study too hard.

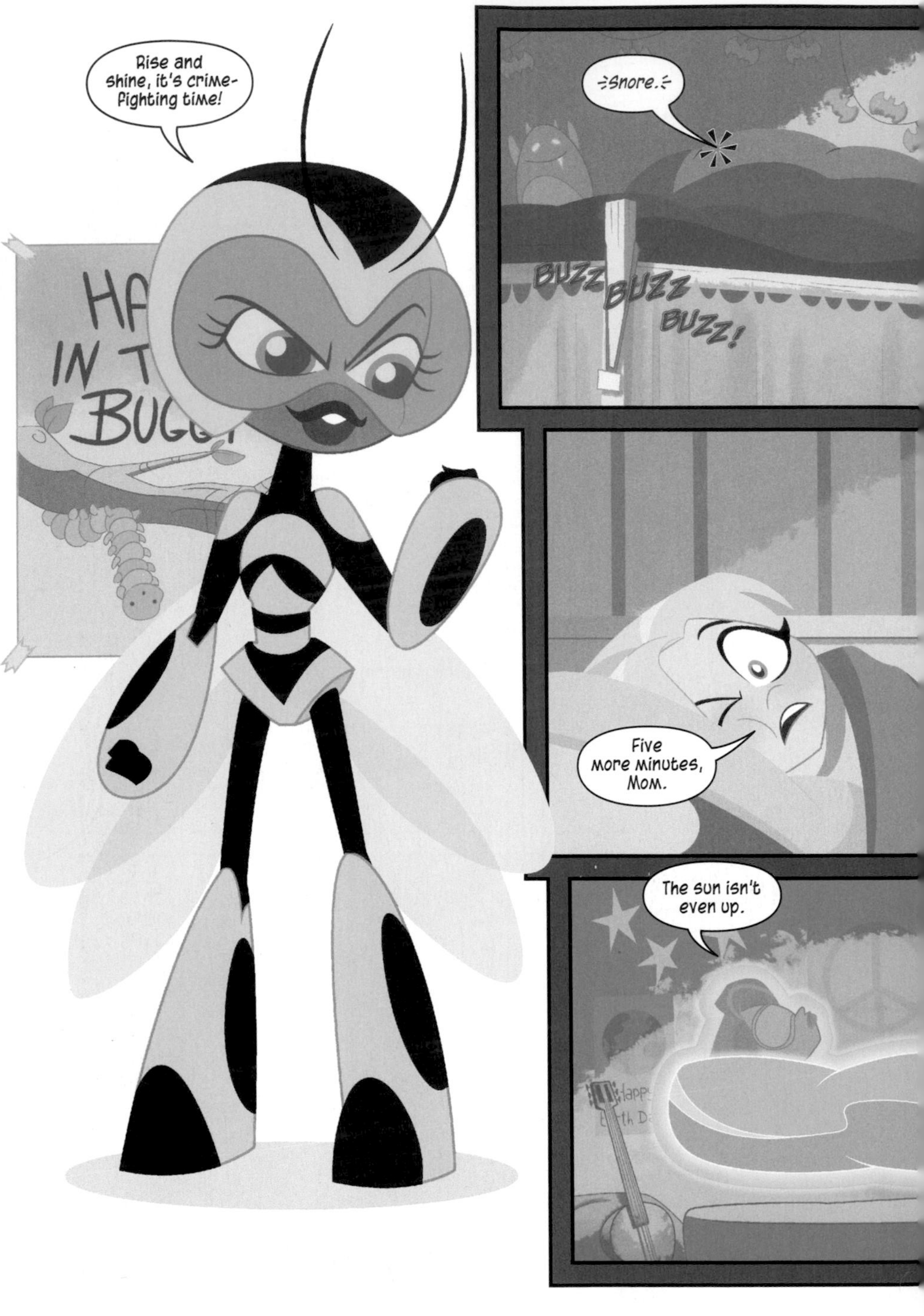
Rise and shine, it's crime-fighting time!
=Snore.=
BUZZ BUZZ BUZZ!
Five more minutes, Mom.
The sun isn't even up.

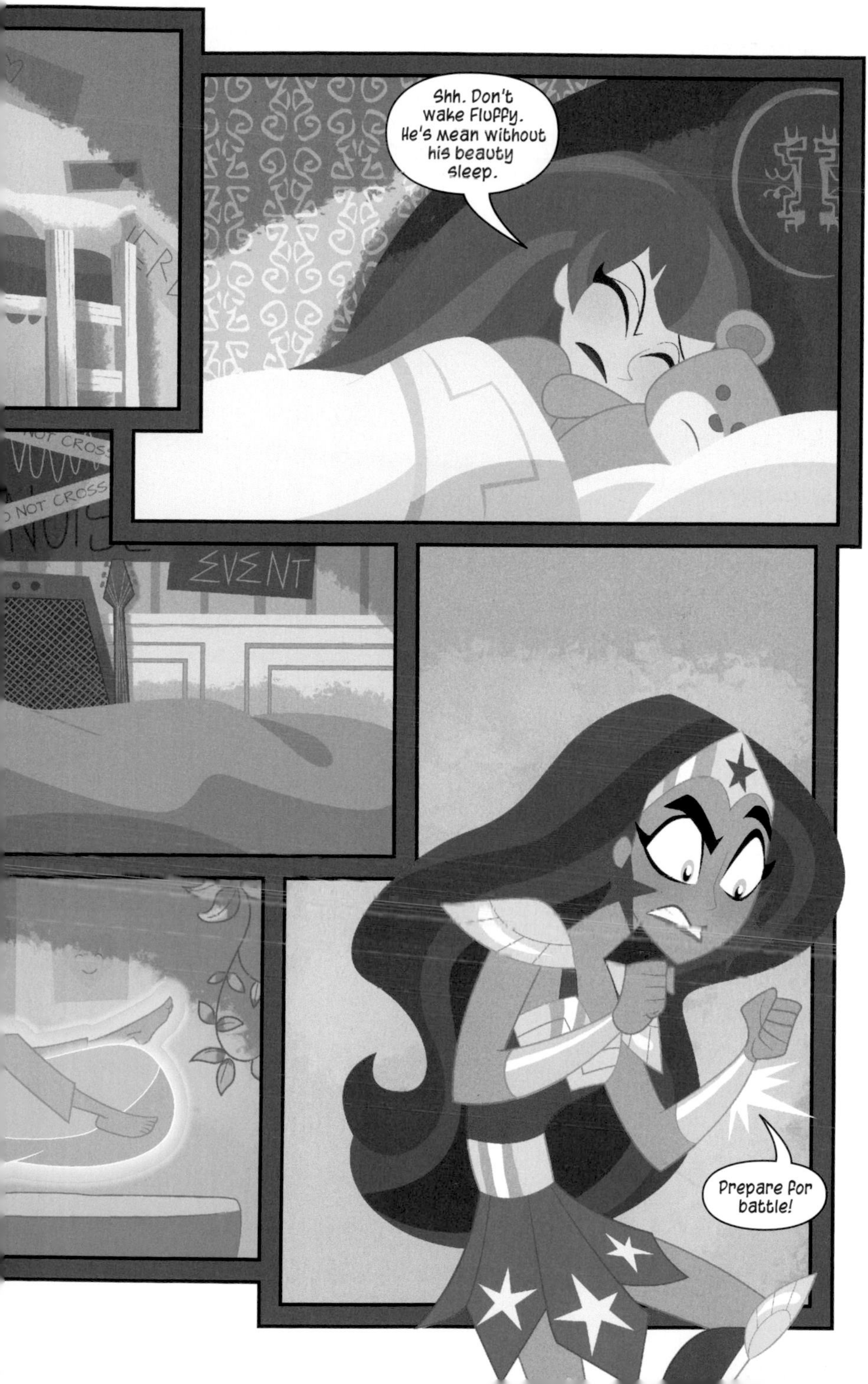
Shh. Don't wake Fluffy. He's mean without his beauty sleep.
EVENT
Prepare for battle!

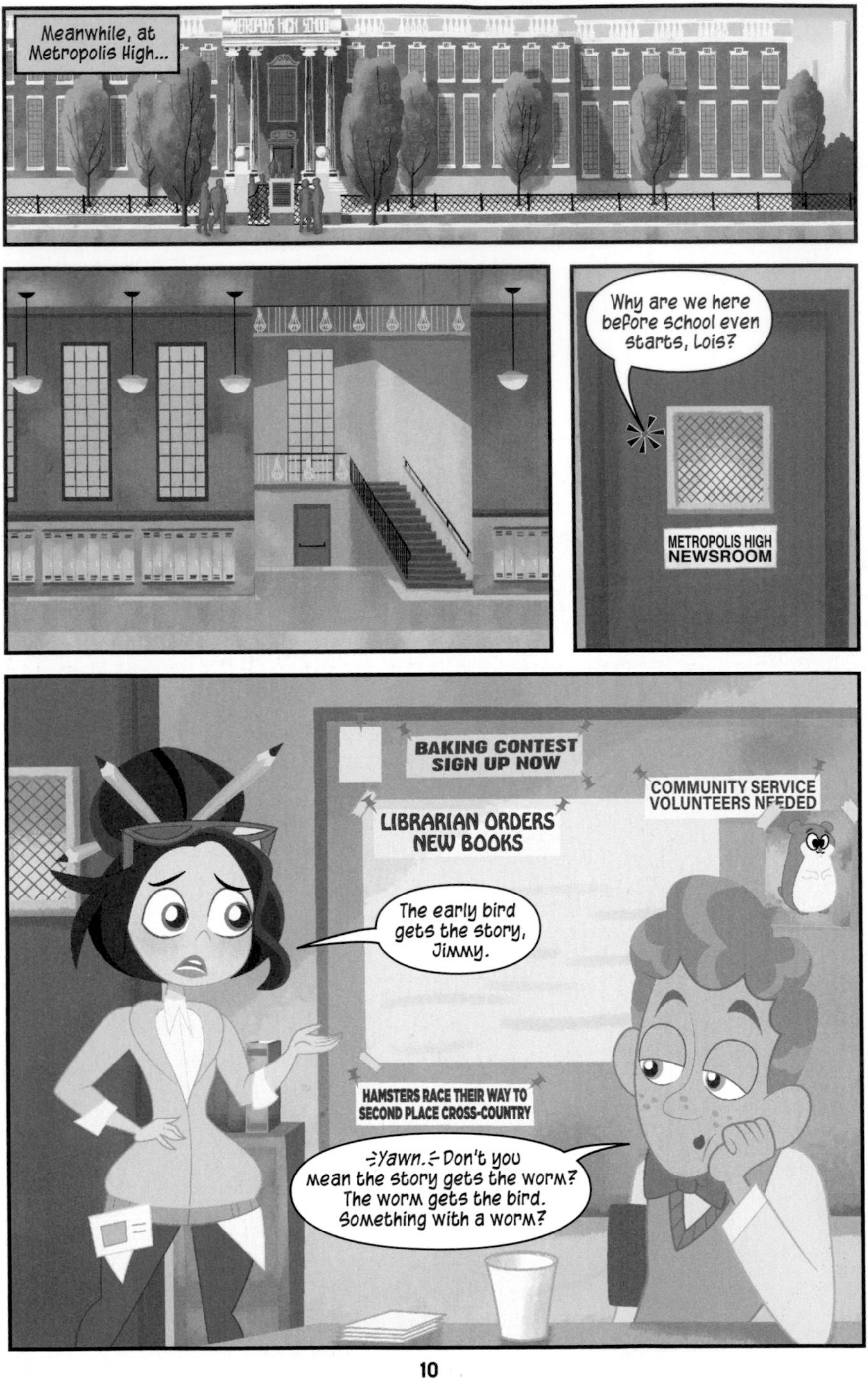
Meanwhile, at Metropolis High...
METROPOLIS HIGH SCHOOL
Why are we here before school even starts, Lois?
METROPOLIS HIGH NEWSROOM
BAKING CONTEST SIGN UP NOW
COMMUNITY SERVICE VOLUNTEERS NEEDED
LIBRARIAN ORDERS NEW BOOKS
The early bird gets the story, Jimmy.
HAMSTERS RACE THEIR WAY TO SECOND PLACE CROSS-COUNTRY
Yawn. Don't you mean the story gets the worm? The worm gets the bird. Something with a worm?

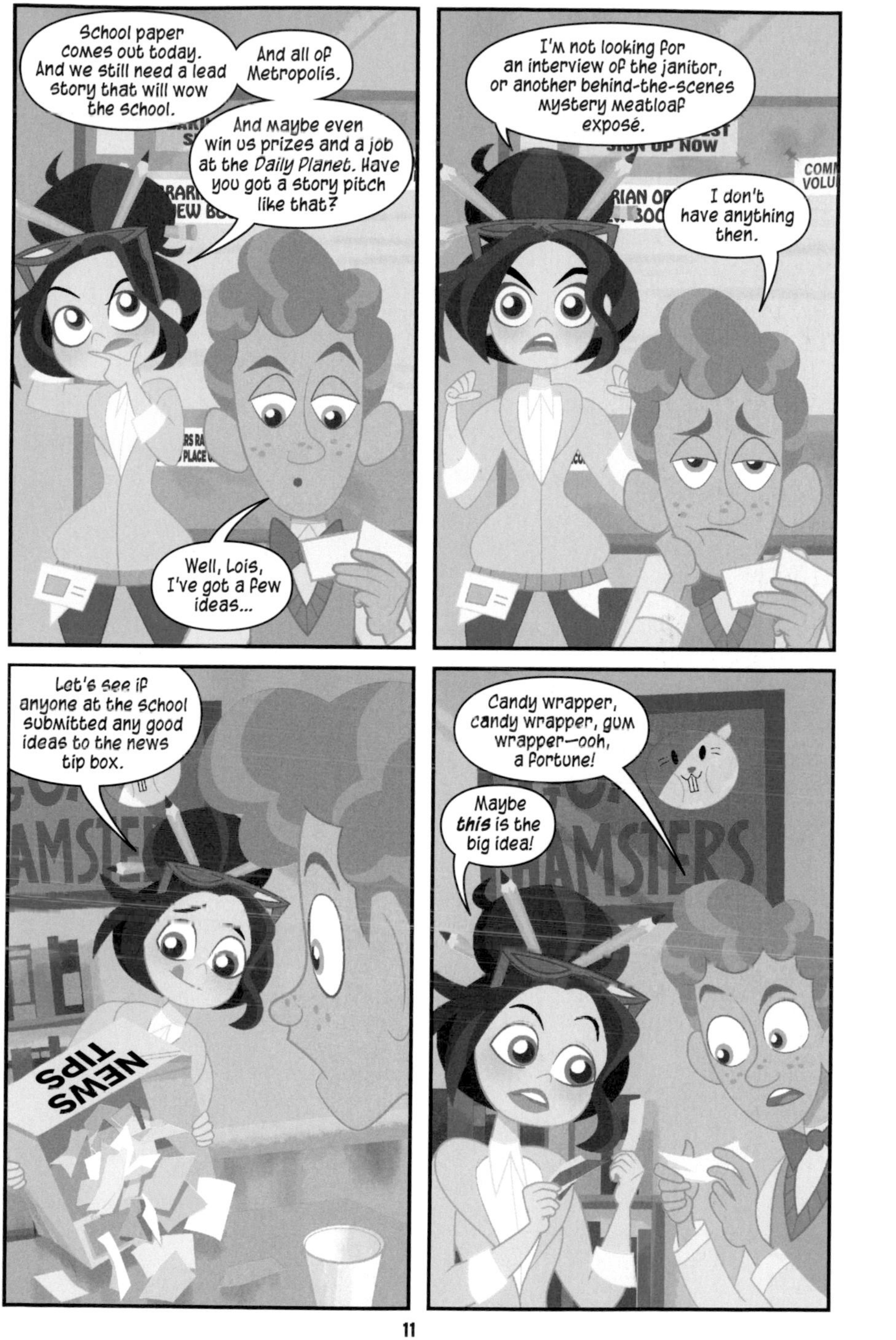
School paper comes out today. And we still need a lead story that will wow the school.
And all of Metropolis.
And maybe even win us prizes and a job at the *Daily Planet*. Have you got a story pitch like that?
Well, Lois, I've got a few ideas...
I'm not looking for an interview of the janitor, or another behind-the-scenes mystery meatloaf exposé.
I don't have anything then.
Let's see if anyone at the school submitted any good ideas to the news tip box.
NEWS TIPS
Candy wrapper, candy wrapper, gum wrapper—ooh, a fortune!
Maybe ***this*** is the big idea!
HAMSTERS
SIGN UP NOW

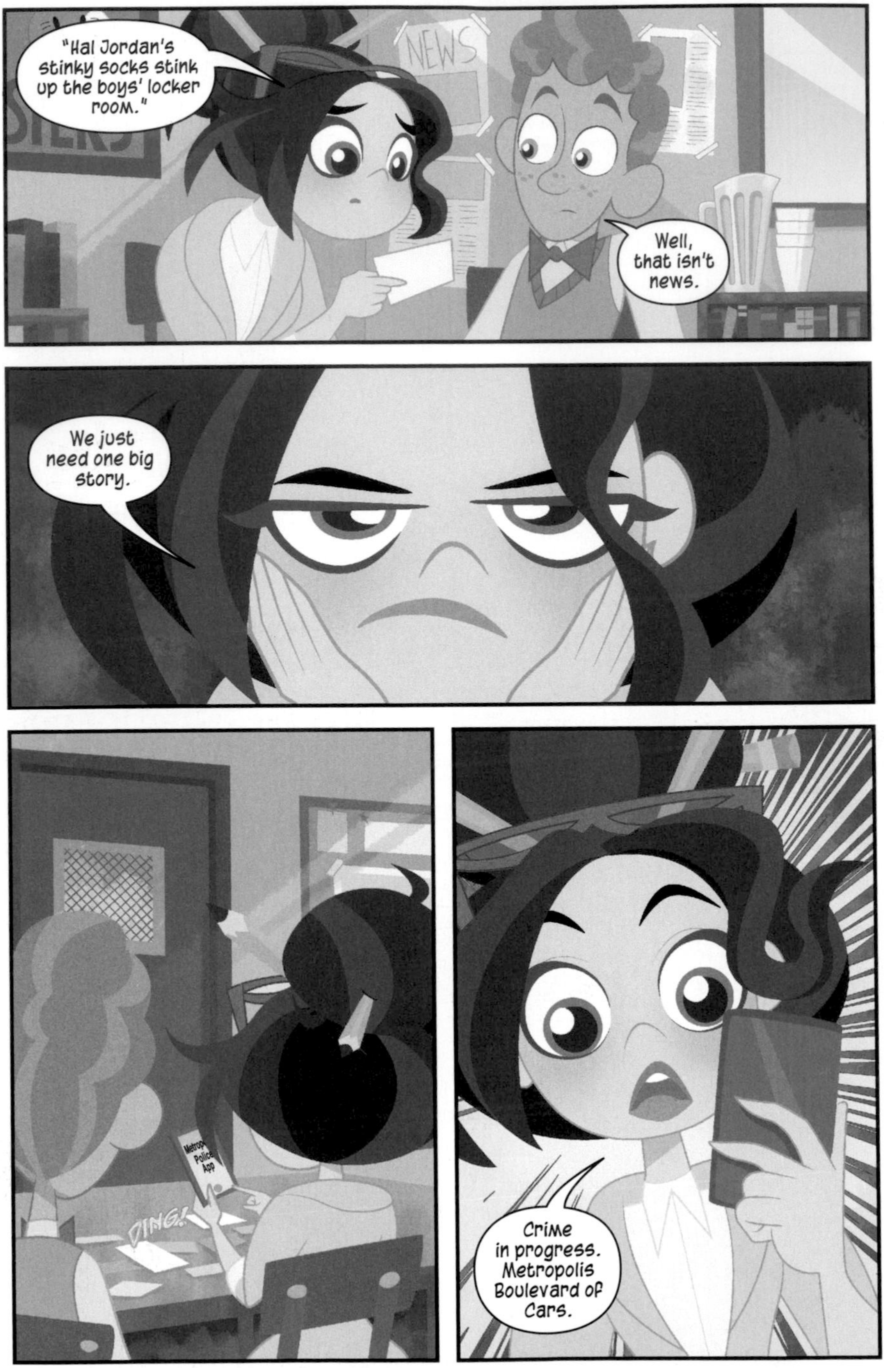
"Hal Jordan's stinky socks stink up the boys' locker room."
NEWS
Well, that isn't news.
We just need one big story.
Metropolis Police App
DING!
Crime in progress. Metropolis Boulevard of Cars.

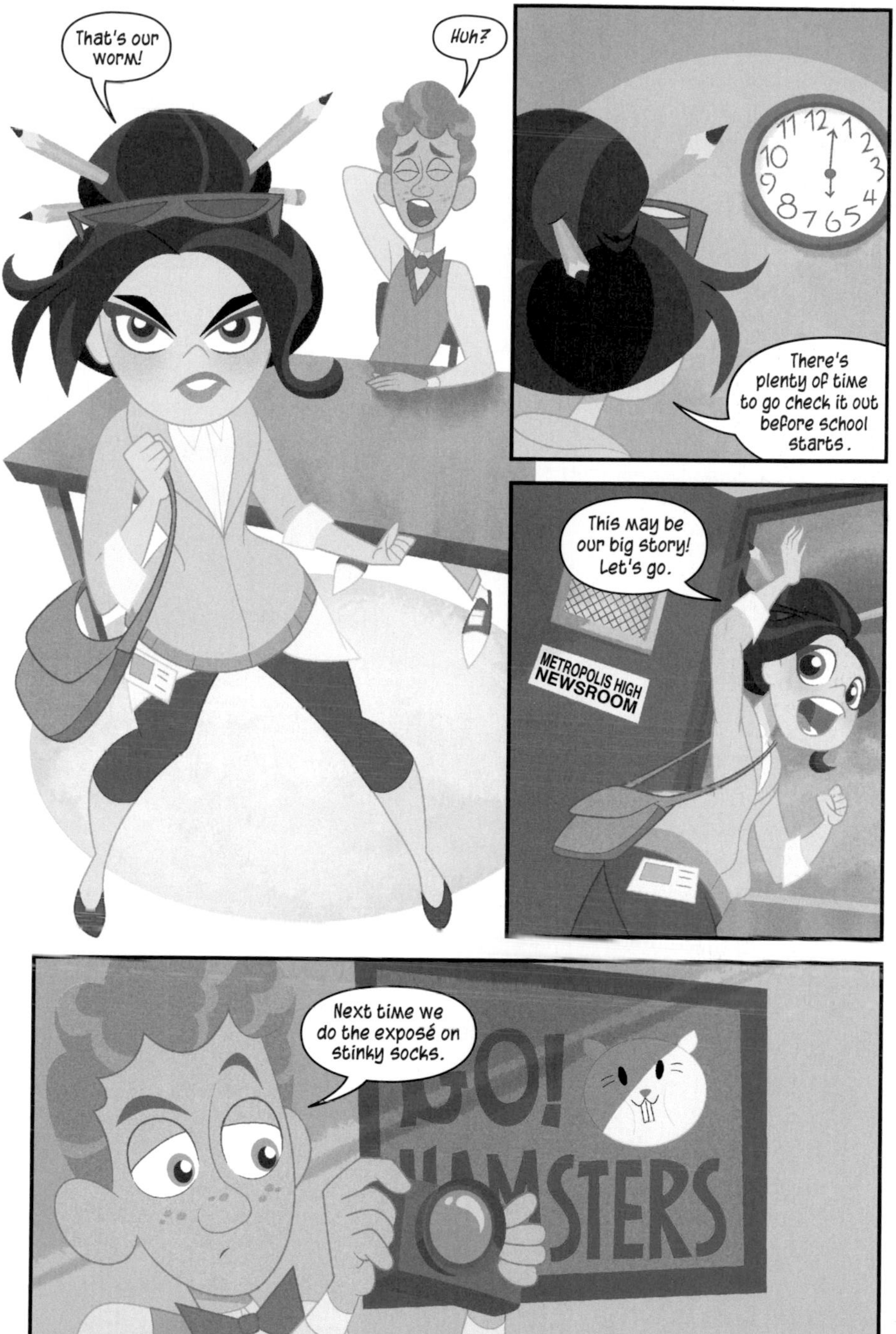
That's our worm!
Huh?
There's plenty of time to go check it out before school starts.
This may be our big story! Let's go.
METROPOLIS HIGH NEWSROOM
Next time we do the exposé on stinky socks.
GO! HAMSTERS

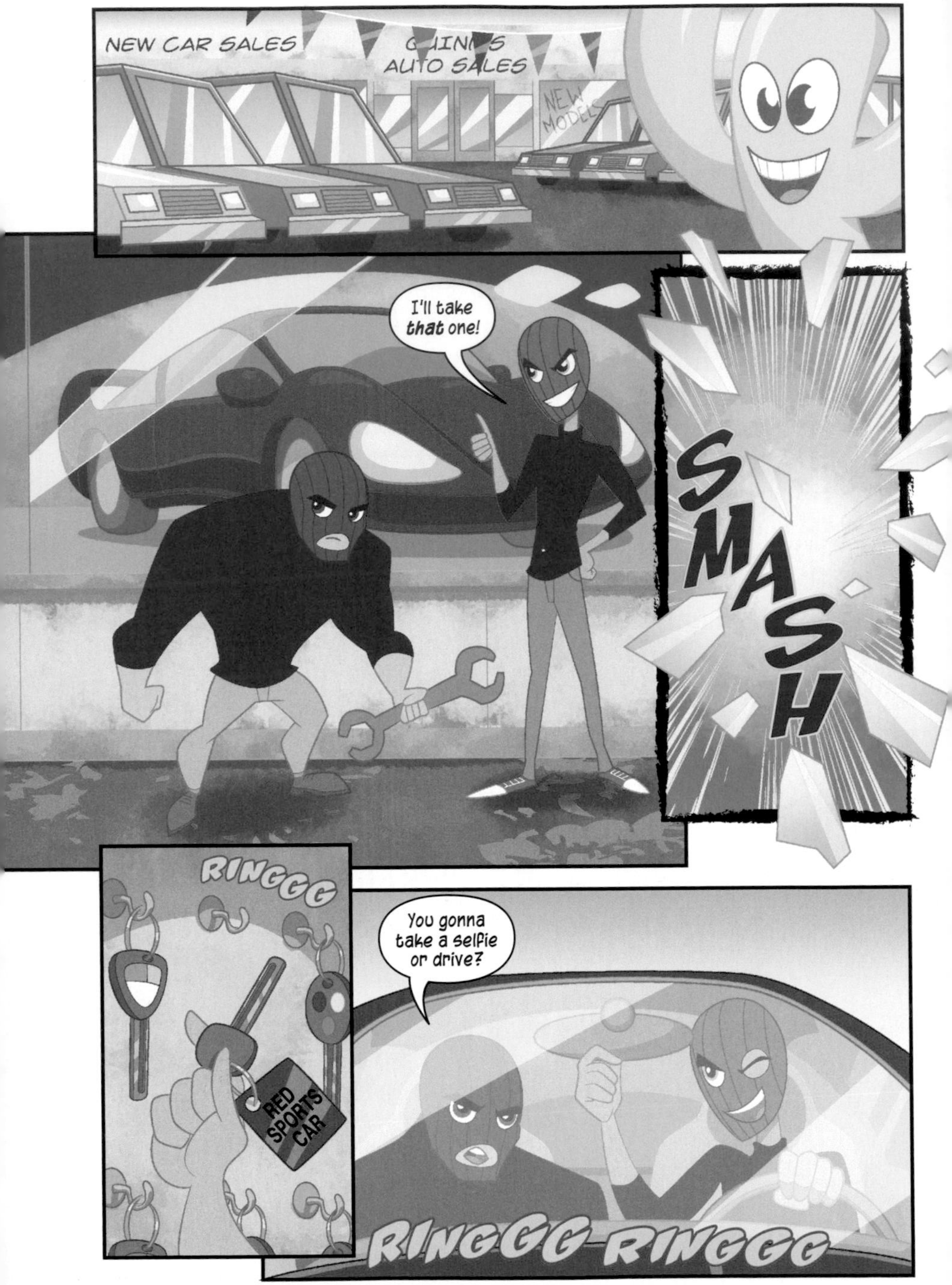
NEW CAR SALES
AUTO SALES
NEW MODELS
I'll take **that** one!
SMASH
RINGGG
RED SPORTS CAR
You gonna take a selfie or drive?
RINGGG RINGGG

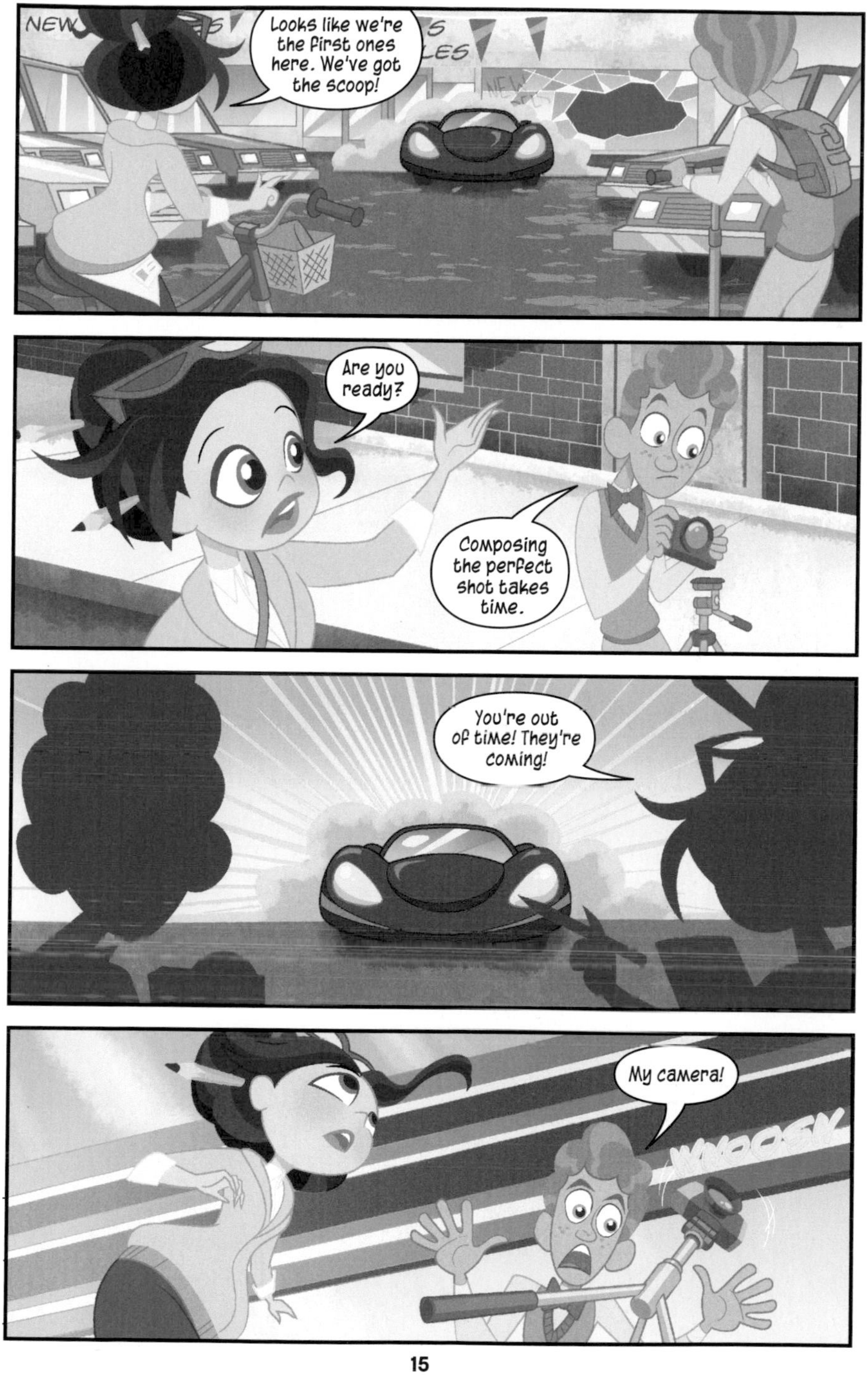
NEW
Looks like we're the first ones here. We've got the scoop!
Are you ready?
Composing the perfect shot takes time.
You're out of time! They're coming!
My camera!
WHOOSH

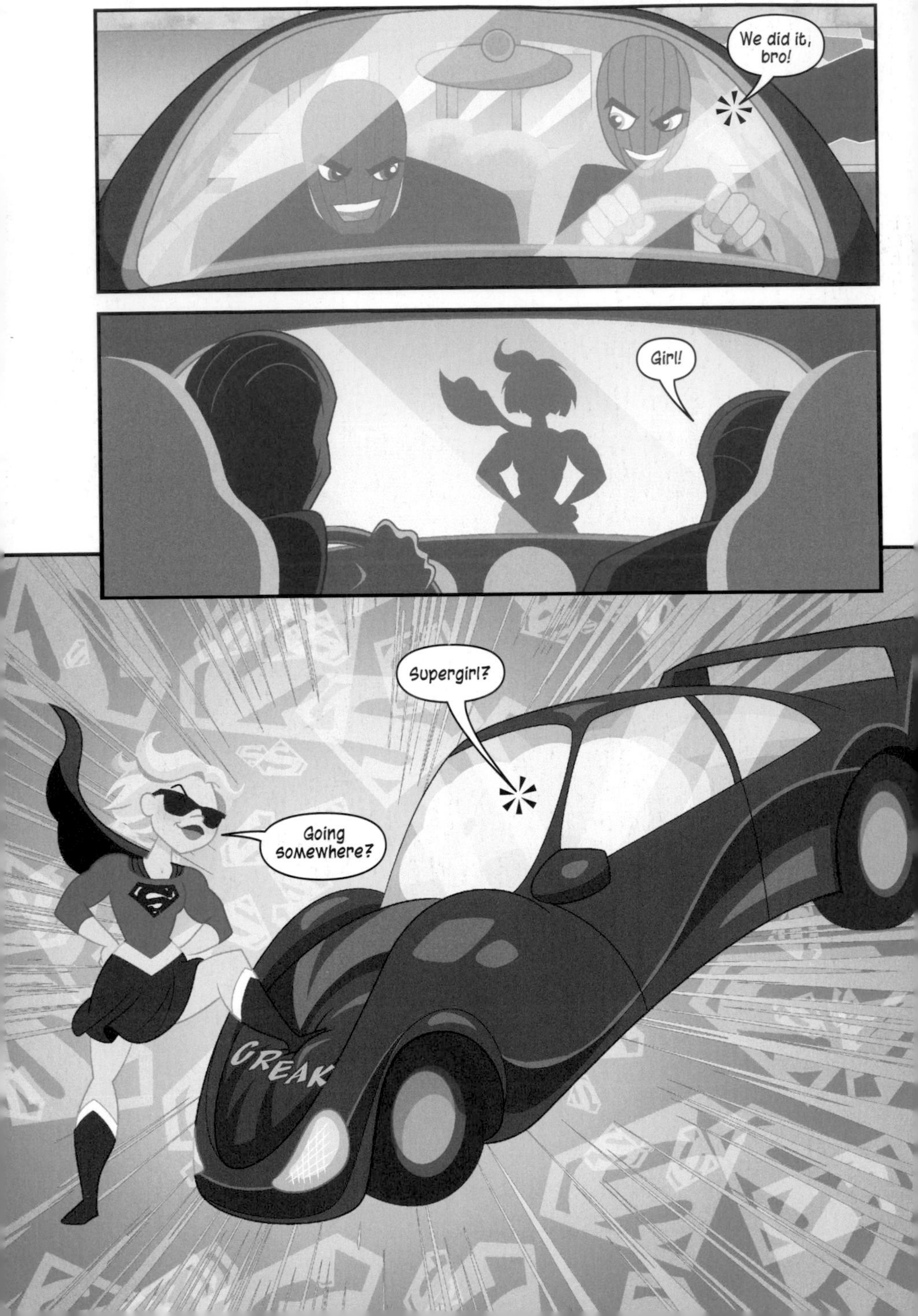
We did it, bro!
Girl!
Supergirl?
Going somewhere?
CREAK

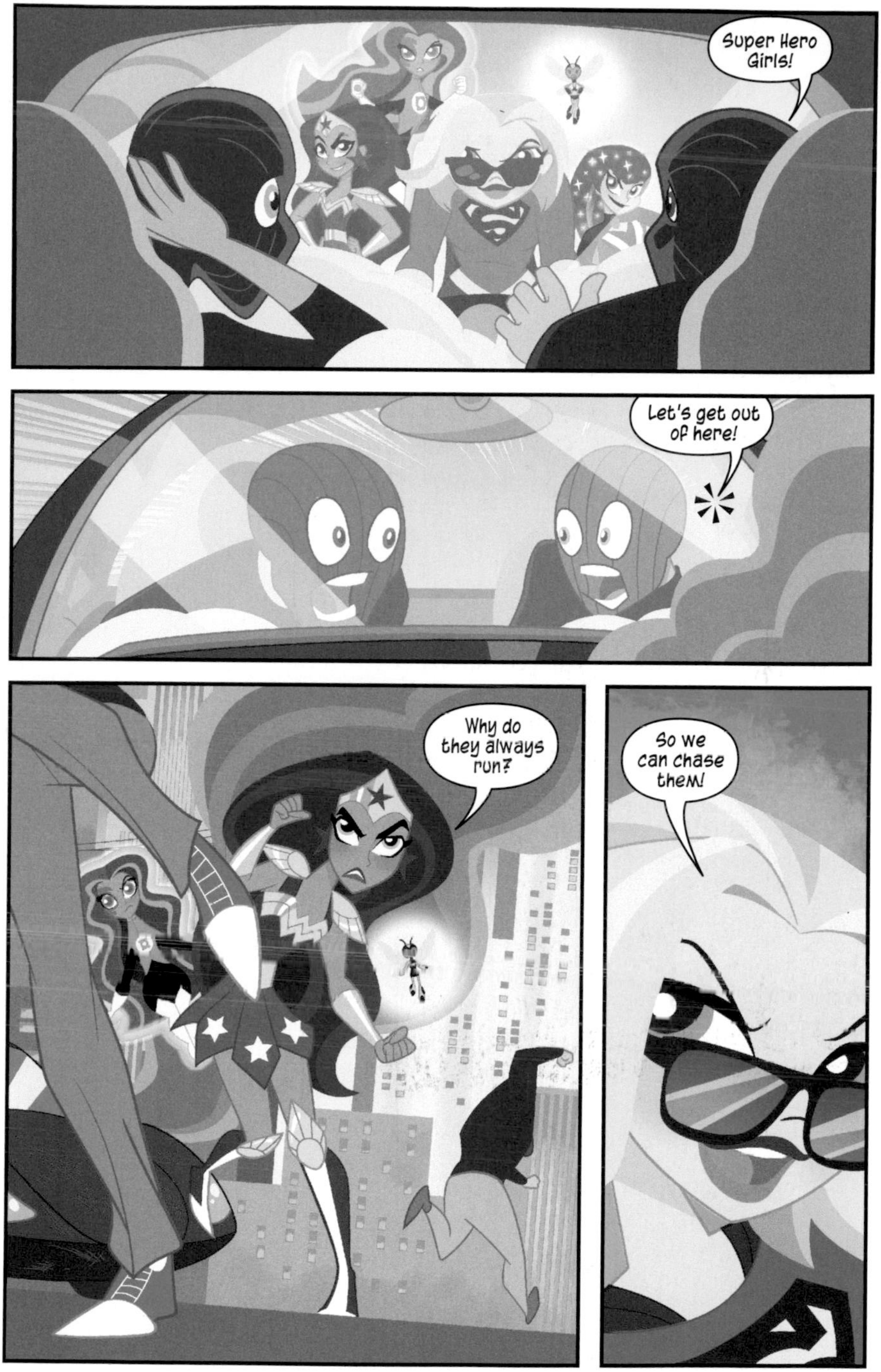
Super Hero Girls!
Let's get out of here!
Why do they always run?
So we can chase them!

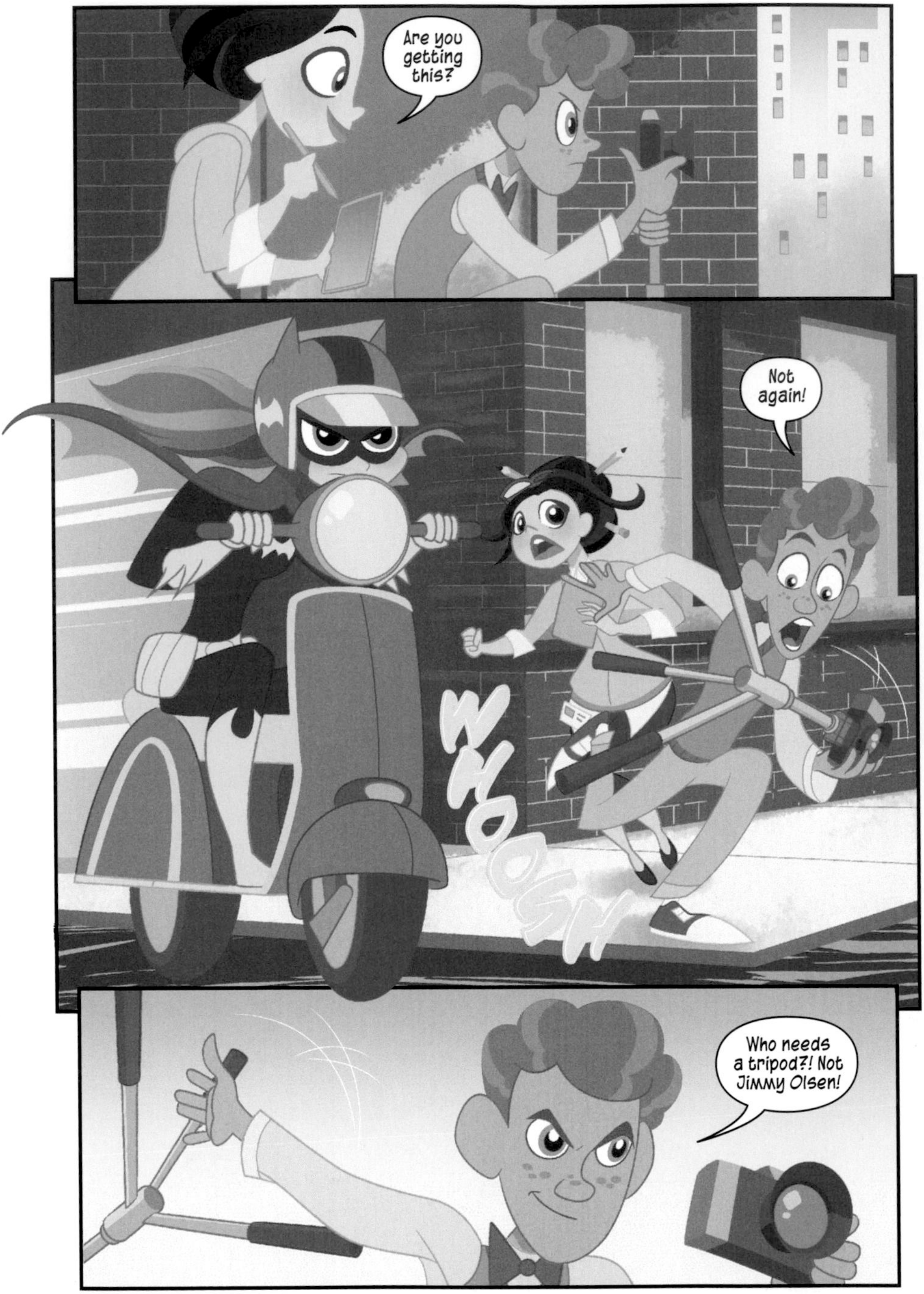
Are you getting this?
Not again!
WHOOOSH
Who needs a tripod?! Not Jimmy Olsen!

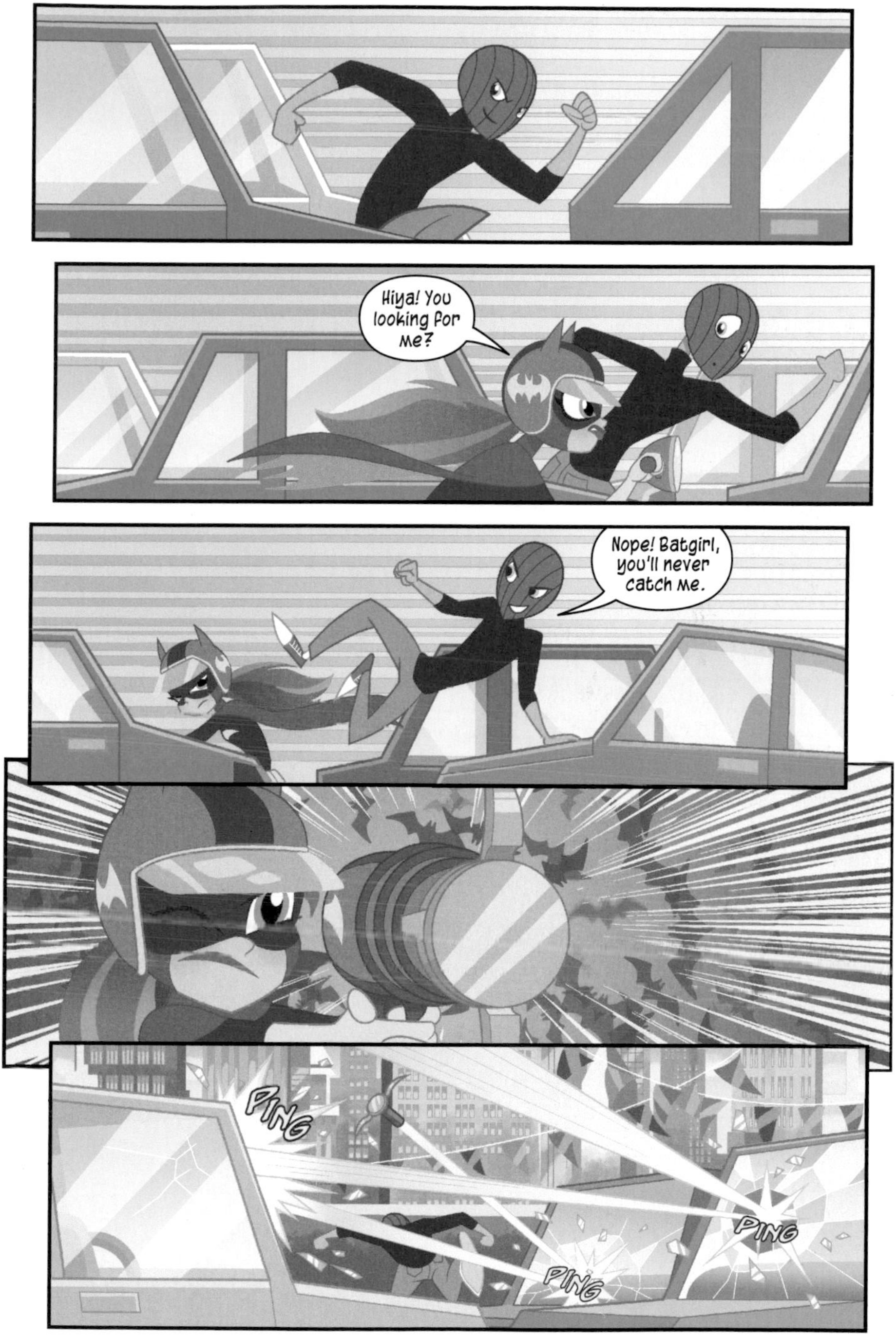
Hiya! You looking for me?
Nope! Batgirl, you'll never catch me.
PING
PING
PING

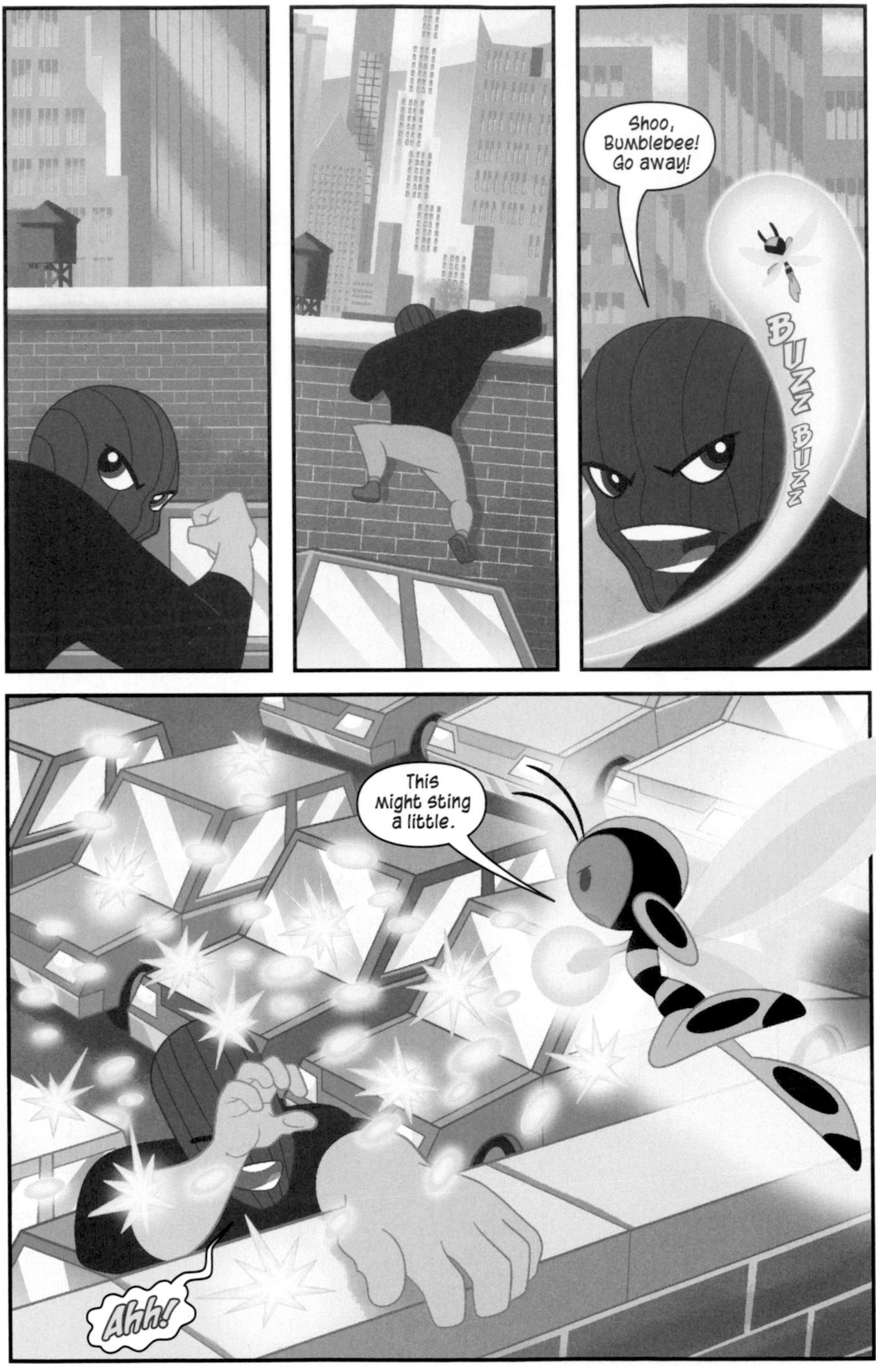
Shoo, Bumblebee! Go away!
BUZZ BUZZ
This might sting a little.
Ahh!

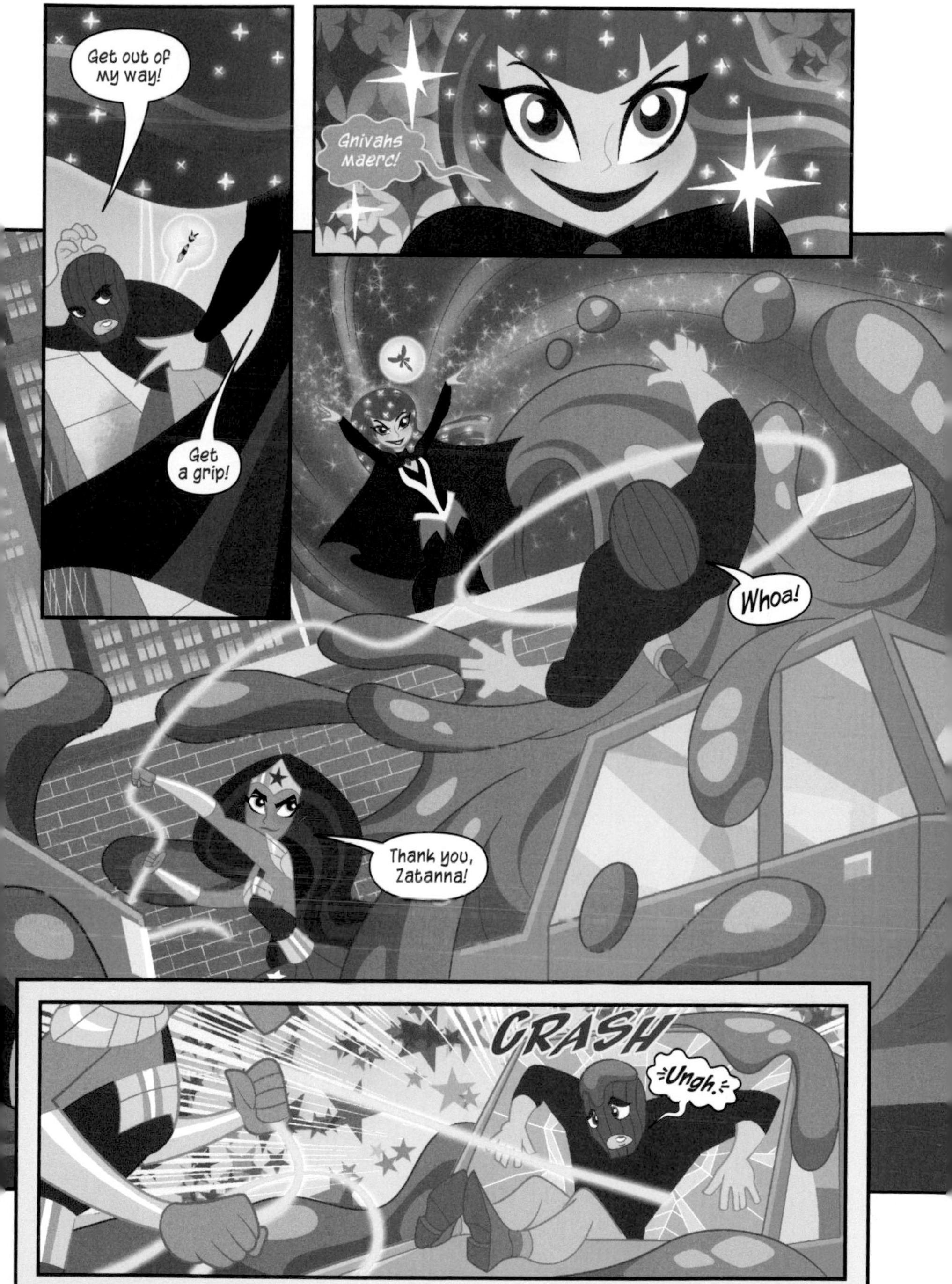
Get out of my way!
Gnivahs maerc!
Get a grip!
Whoa!
Thank you, Zatanna!
CRASH
Ungh.

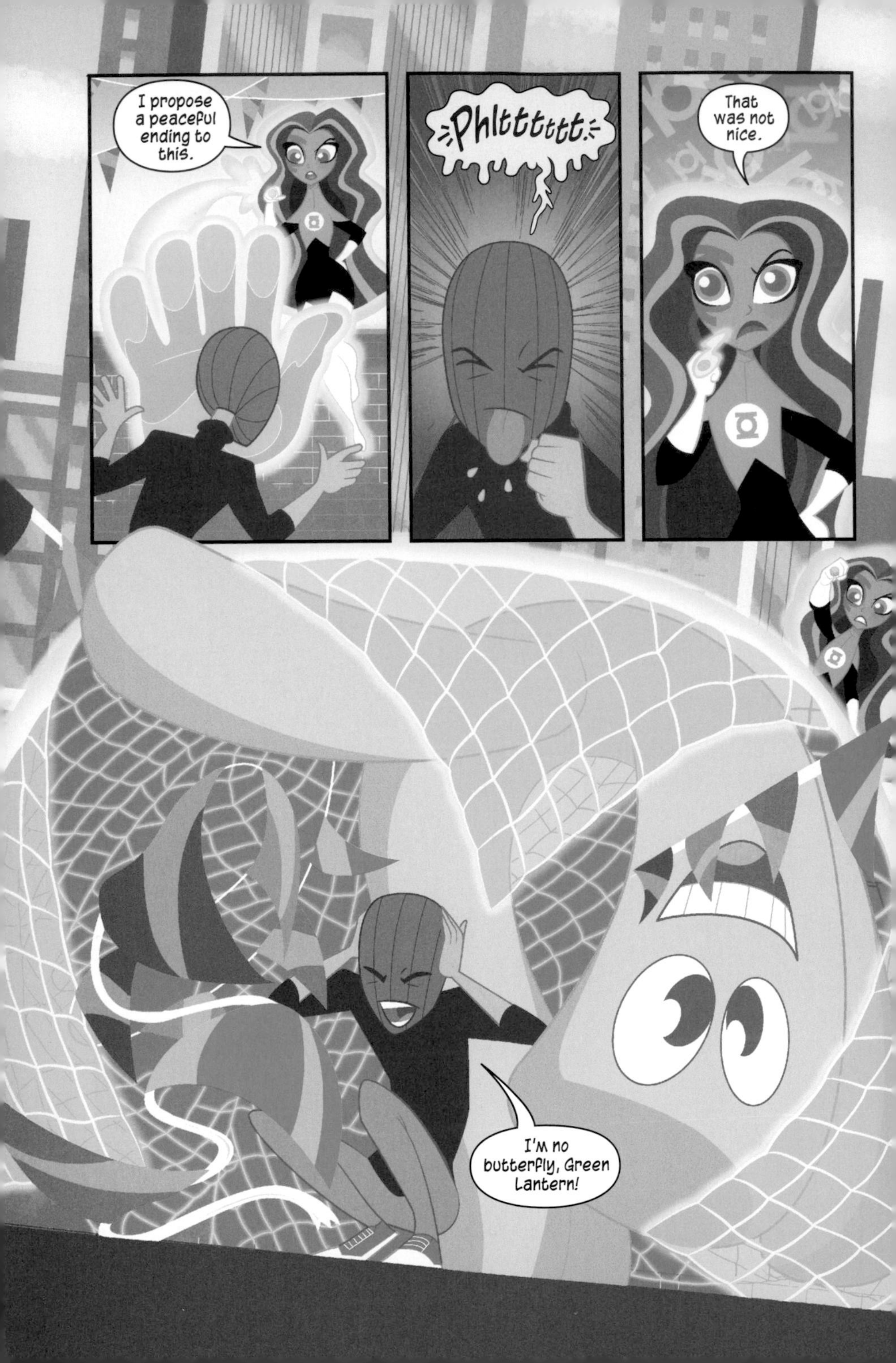
I propose a peaceful ending to this.
Phltttttt.
That was not nice.
I'M no butterfly, Green Lantern!

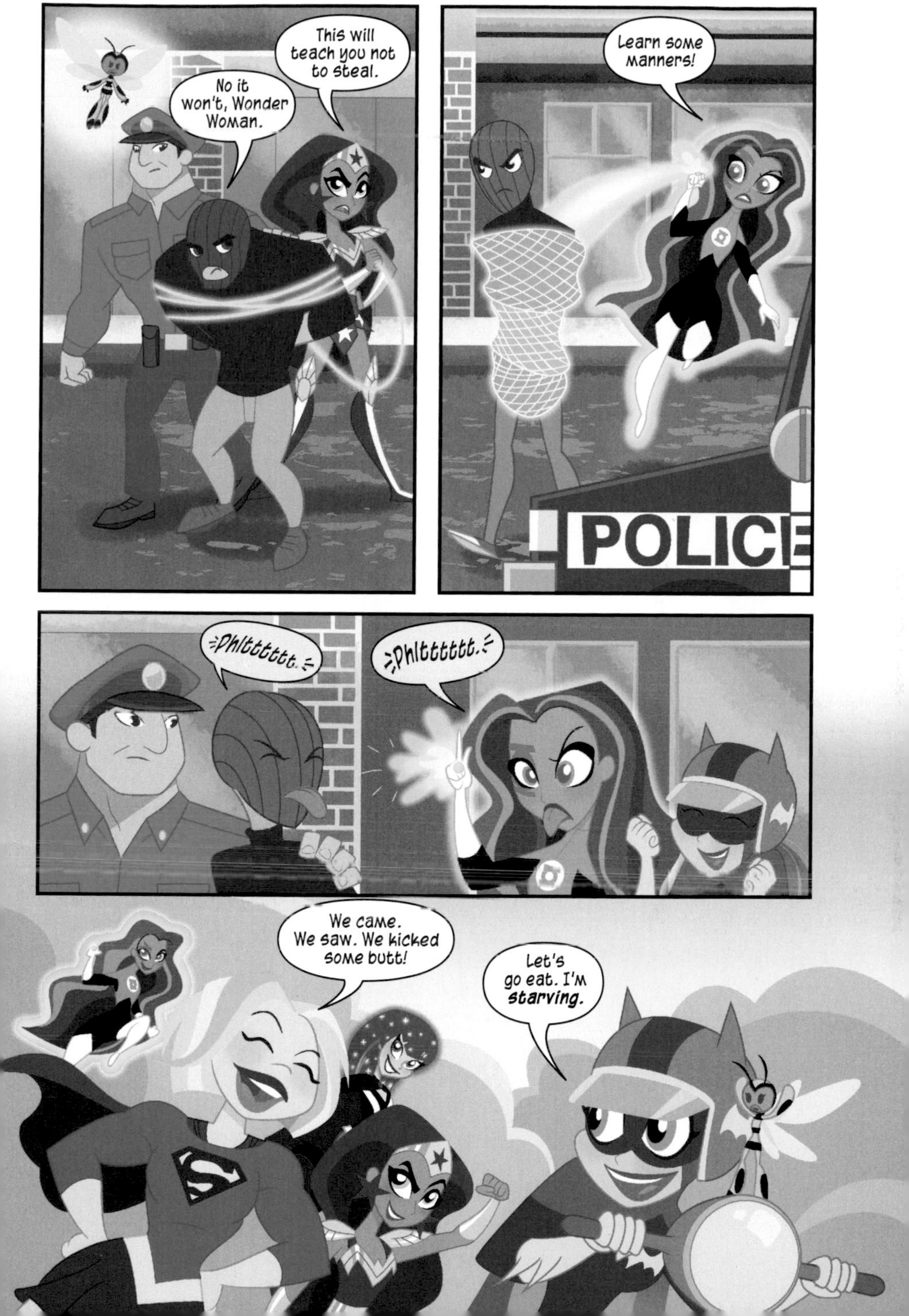
This will teach you not to steal.
No it won't, Wonder Woman.
Learn some manners!
POLICE
Phltttttt.
Phltttttt.
We came. We saw. We kicked some butt!
Let's go eat. I'M *starving.*

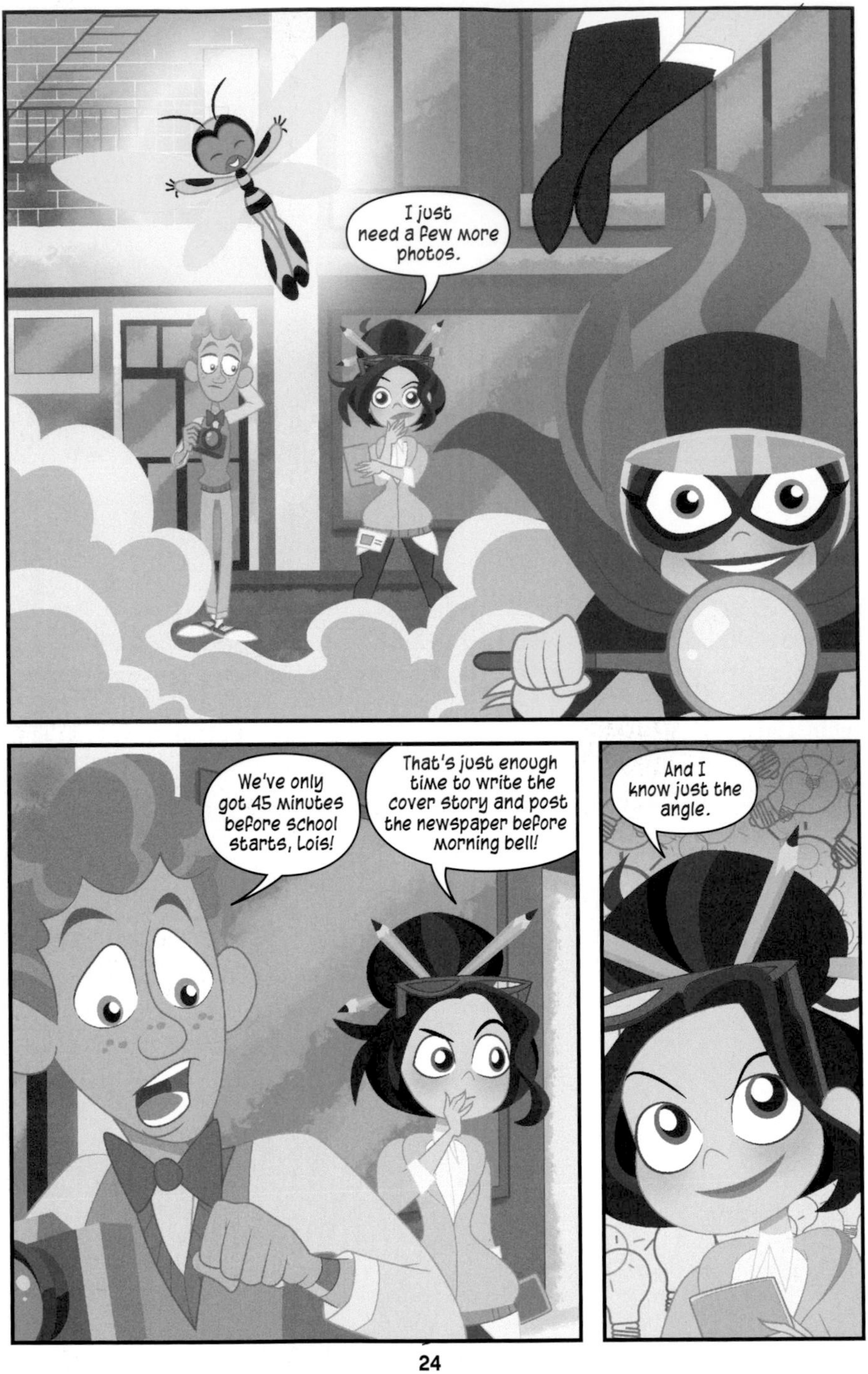
I just need a few more photos.
We've only got 45 minutes before school starts, Lois!
That's just enough time to write the cover story and post the newspaper before morning bell!
And I know just the angle.

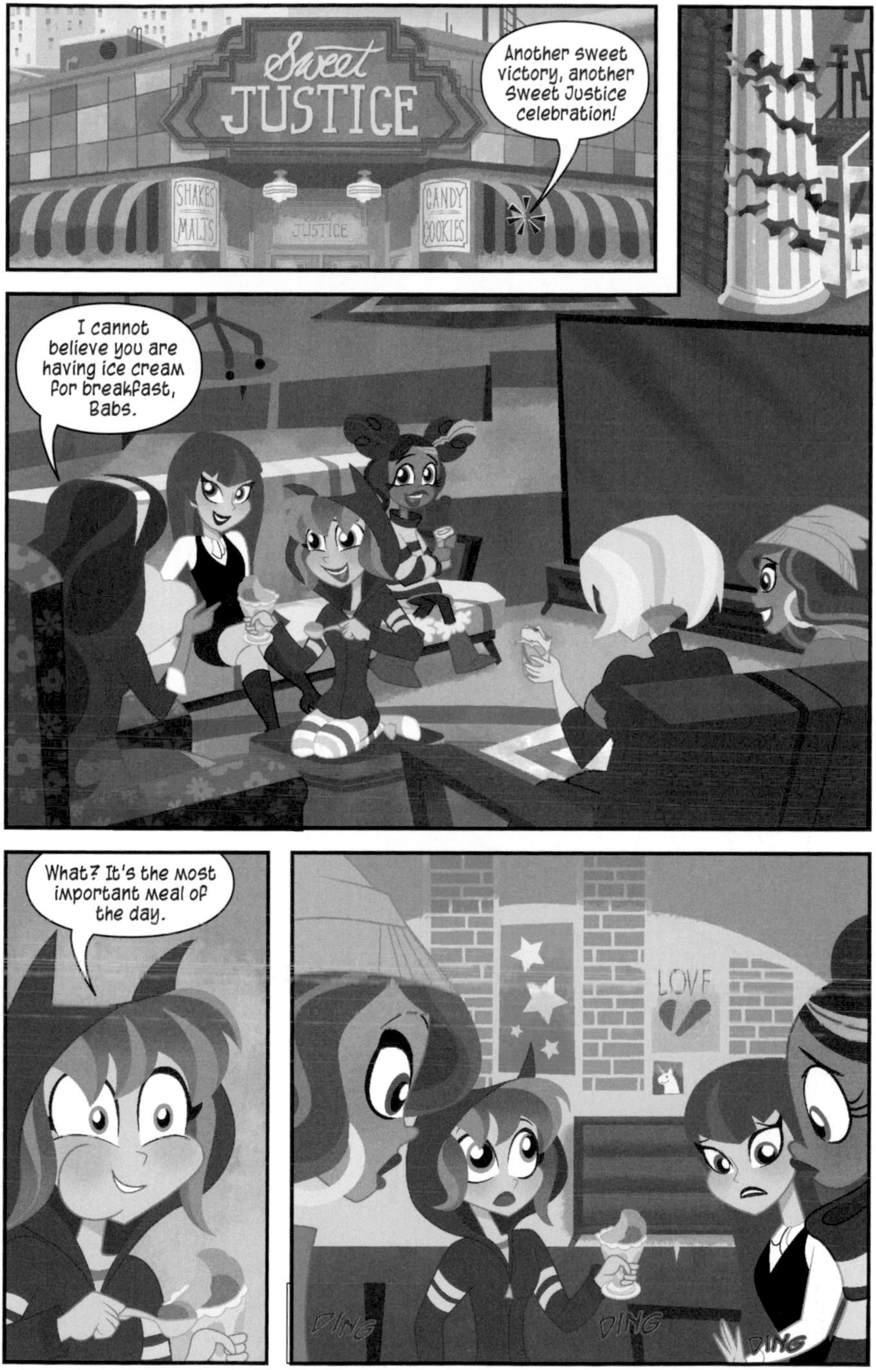

Sweet JUSTICE
SHAKES MALTS
JUSTICE
CANDY COOKIES
Another sweet victory, another Sweet Justice celebration!
I cannot believe you are having ice cream for breakfast, Babs.
What? It's the most important meal of the day.
LOVE
DING
DING
DING

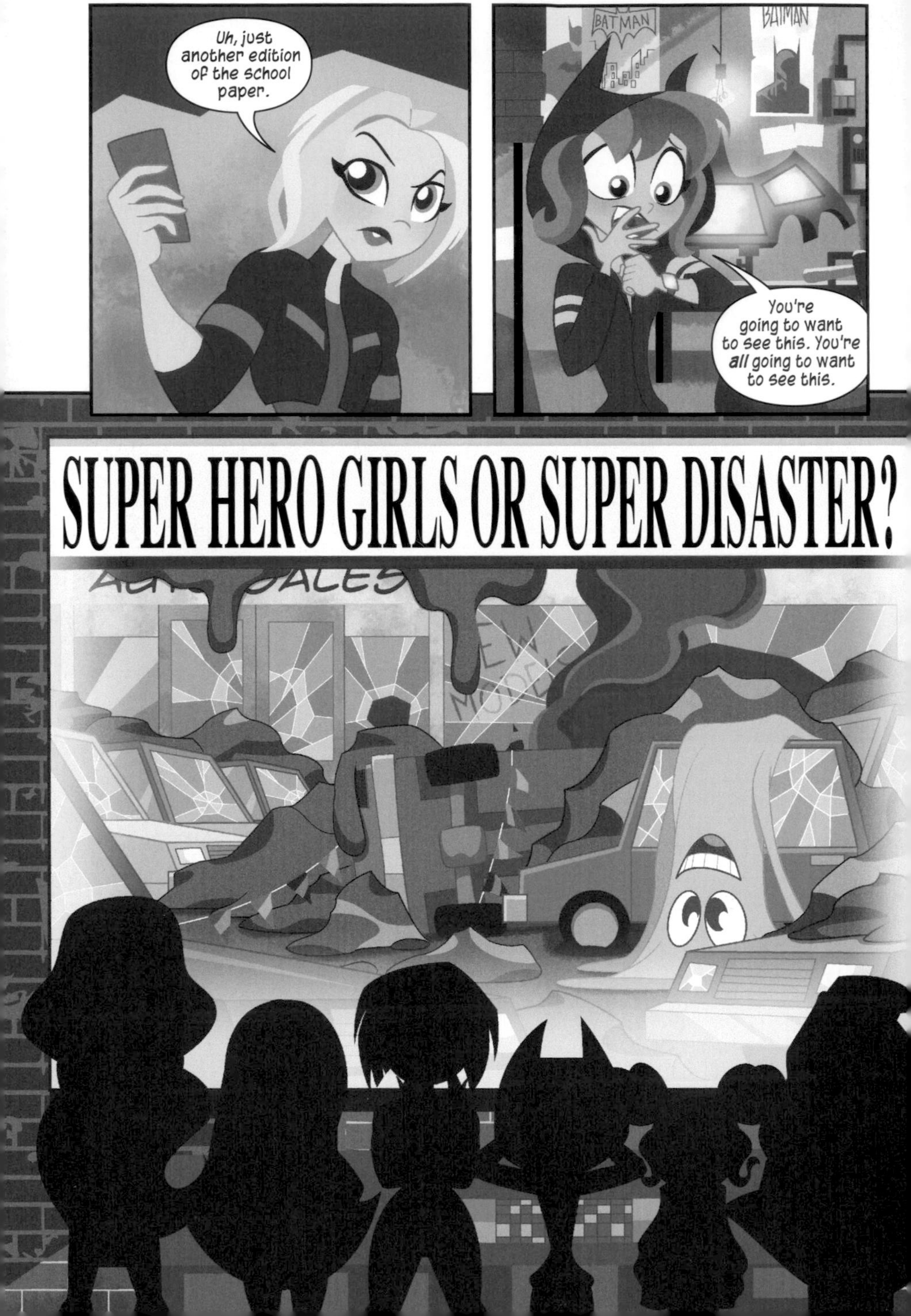
Uh, just another edition of the school paper.
BATMAN
BATMAN
You're going to want to see this. You're *all* going to want to see this.
SUPER HERO GIRLS OR SUPER DISASTER?

# chapter two

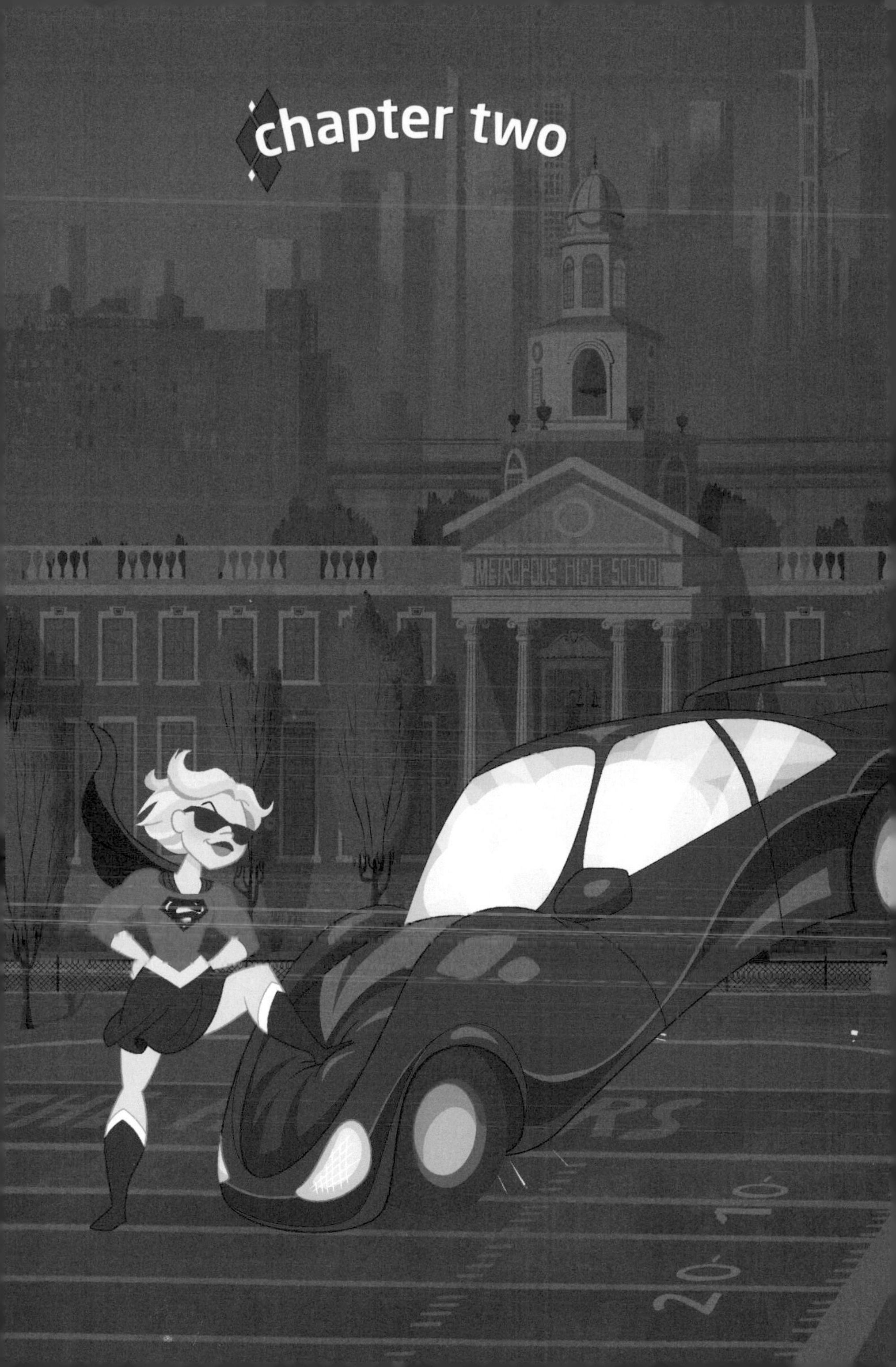
METROPOLIS HIGH SCHOOL

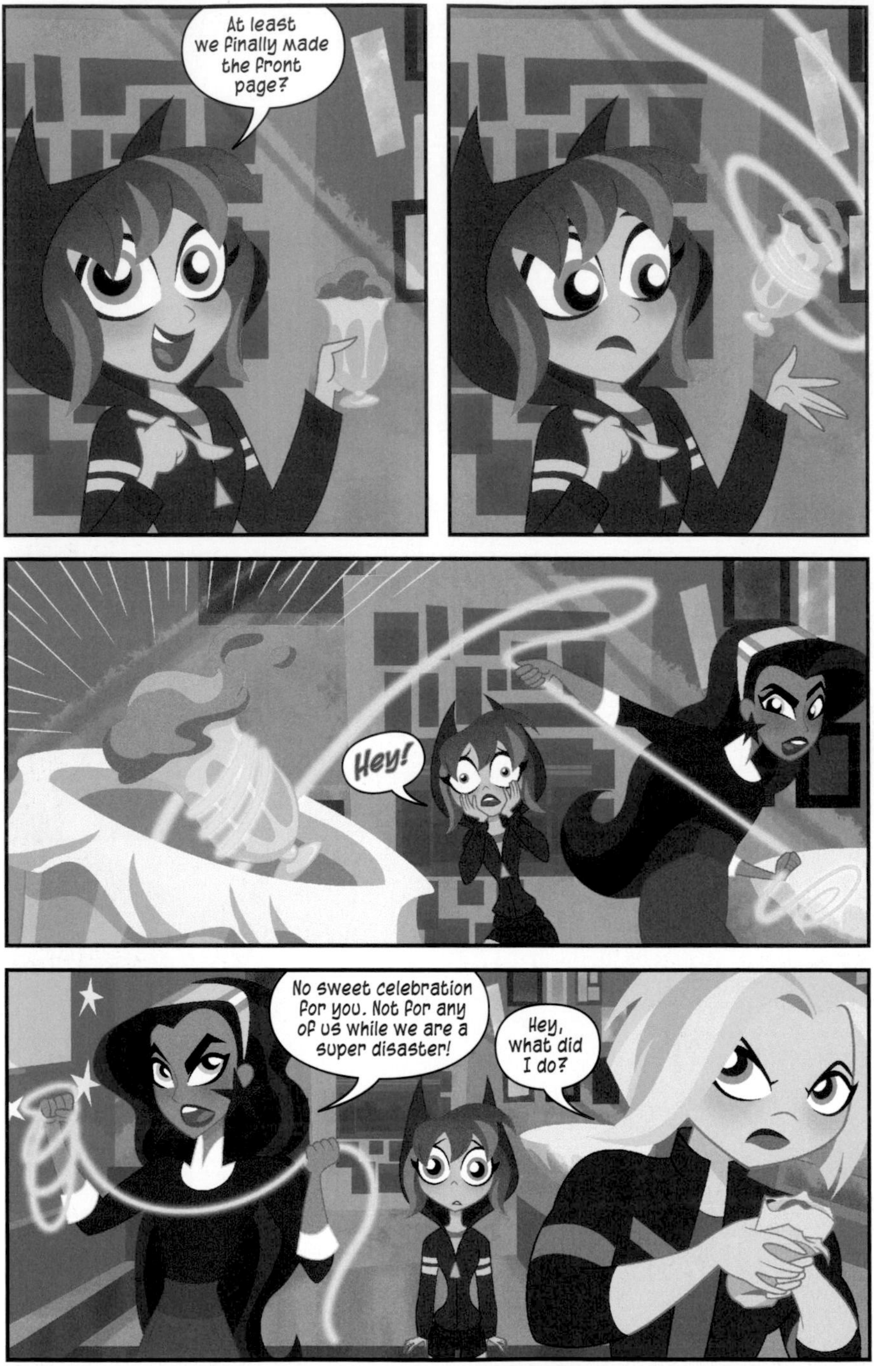
At least we finally made the front page?
Hey!
No sweet celebration for you. Not for any of us while we are a super disaster!
Hey, what did I do?

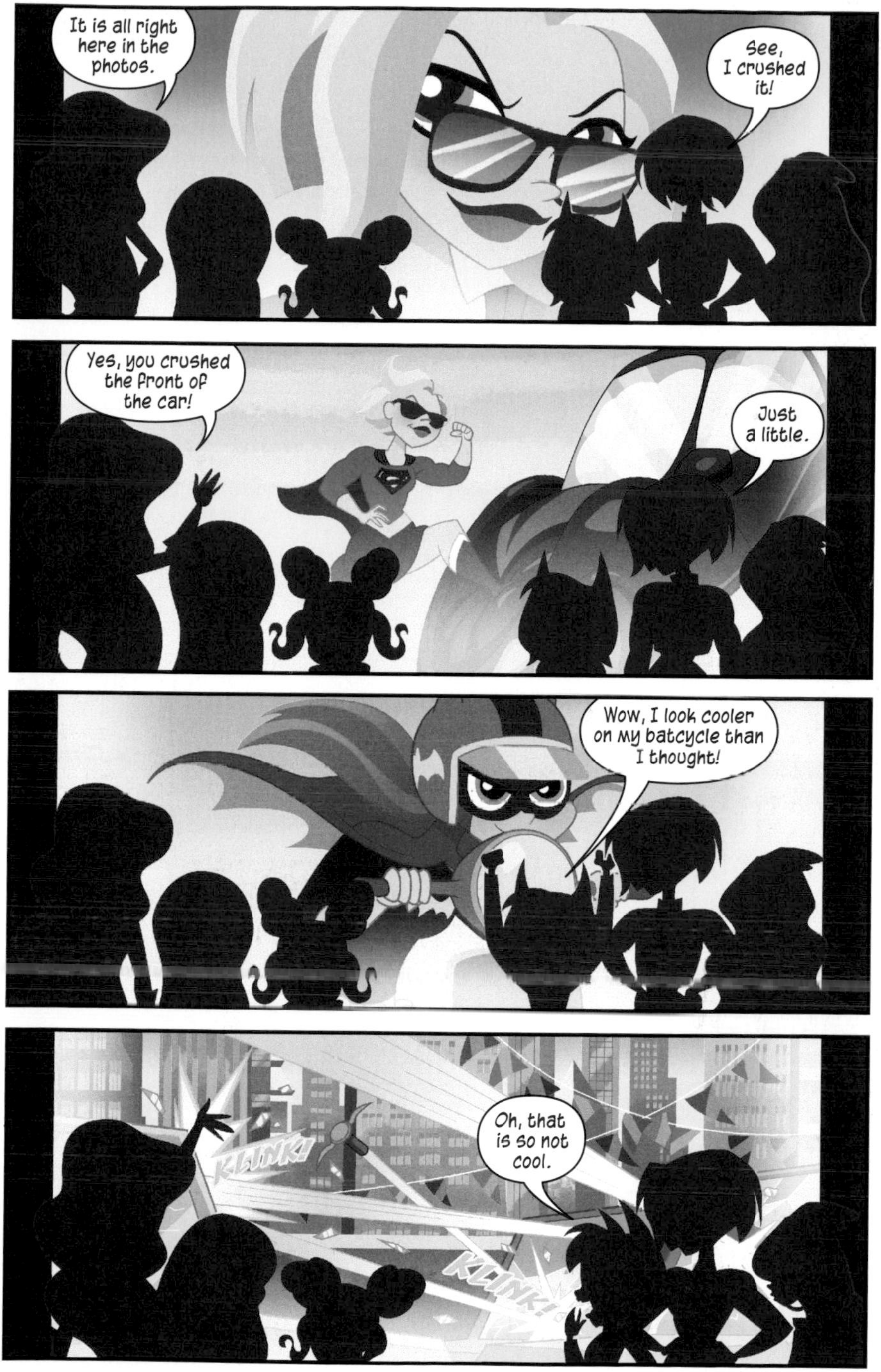
It is all right here in the photos.
See, I crushed it!
Yes, you crushed the front of the car!
Just a little.
Wow, I look cooler on my batcycle than I thought!
KLINK!
Oh, that is so not cool.
KLINK!

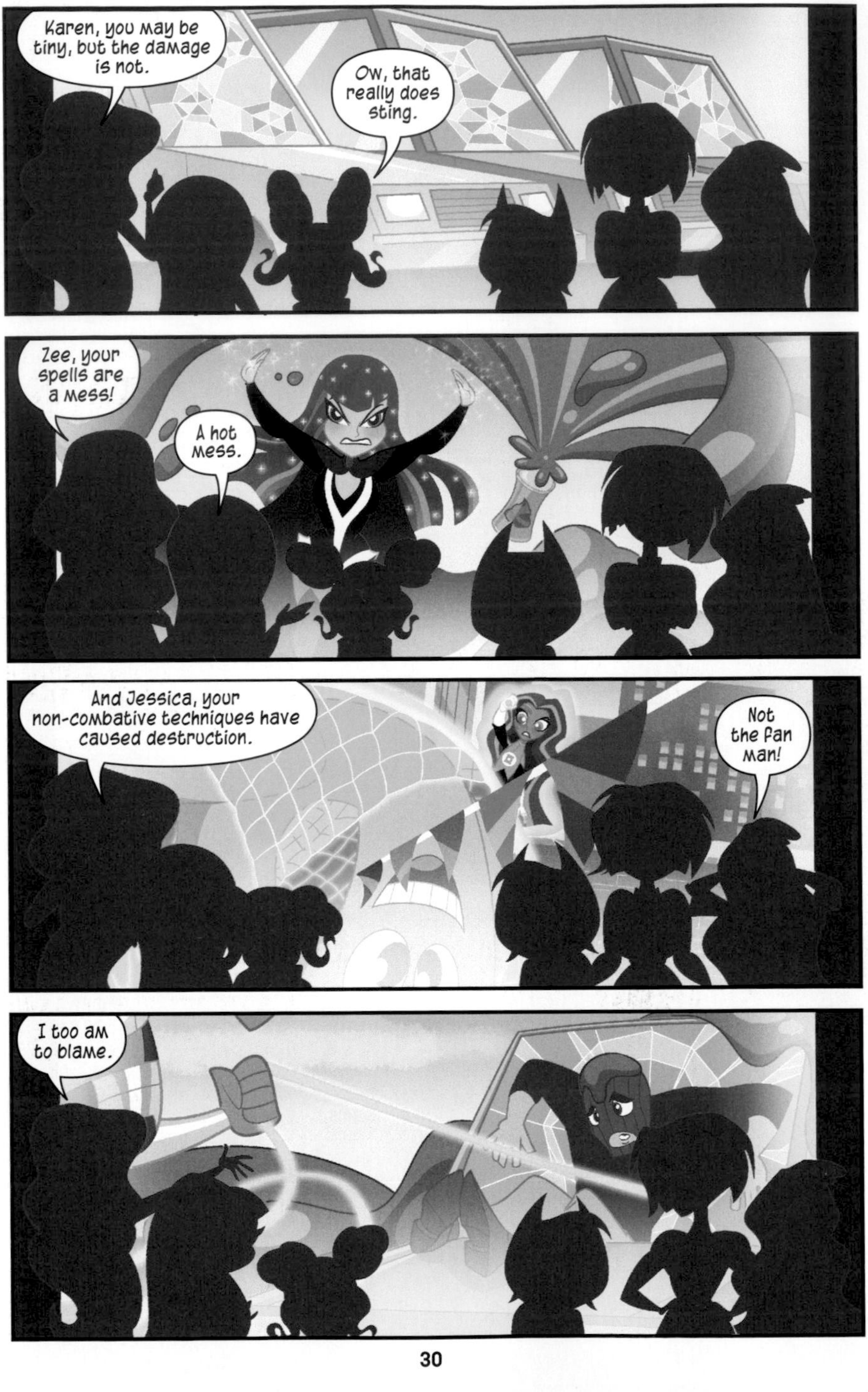
Karen, you may be tiny, but the damage is not.
Ow, that really does sting.
Zee, your spells are a mess!
A hot mess.
And Jessica, your non-combative techniques have caused destruction.
Not the fan man!
I too am to blame.

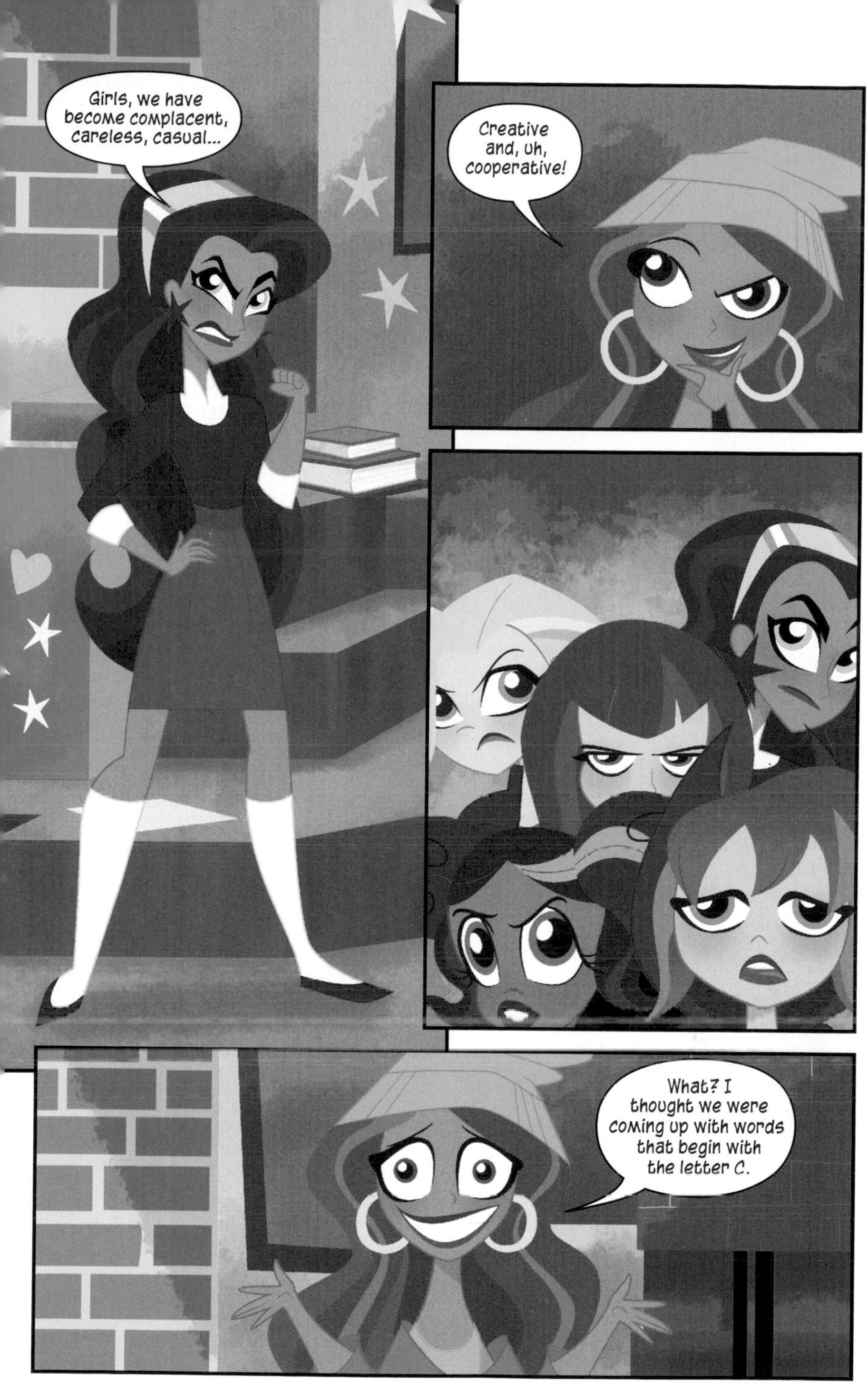
Girls, we have become complacent, careless, casual...
Creative and, uh, cooperative!
What? I thought we were coming up with words that begin with the letter C.

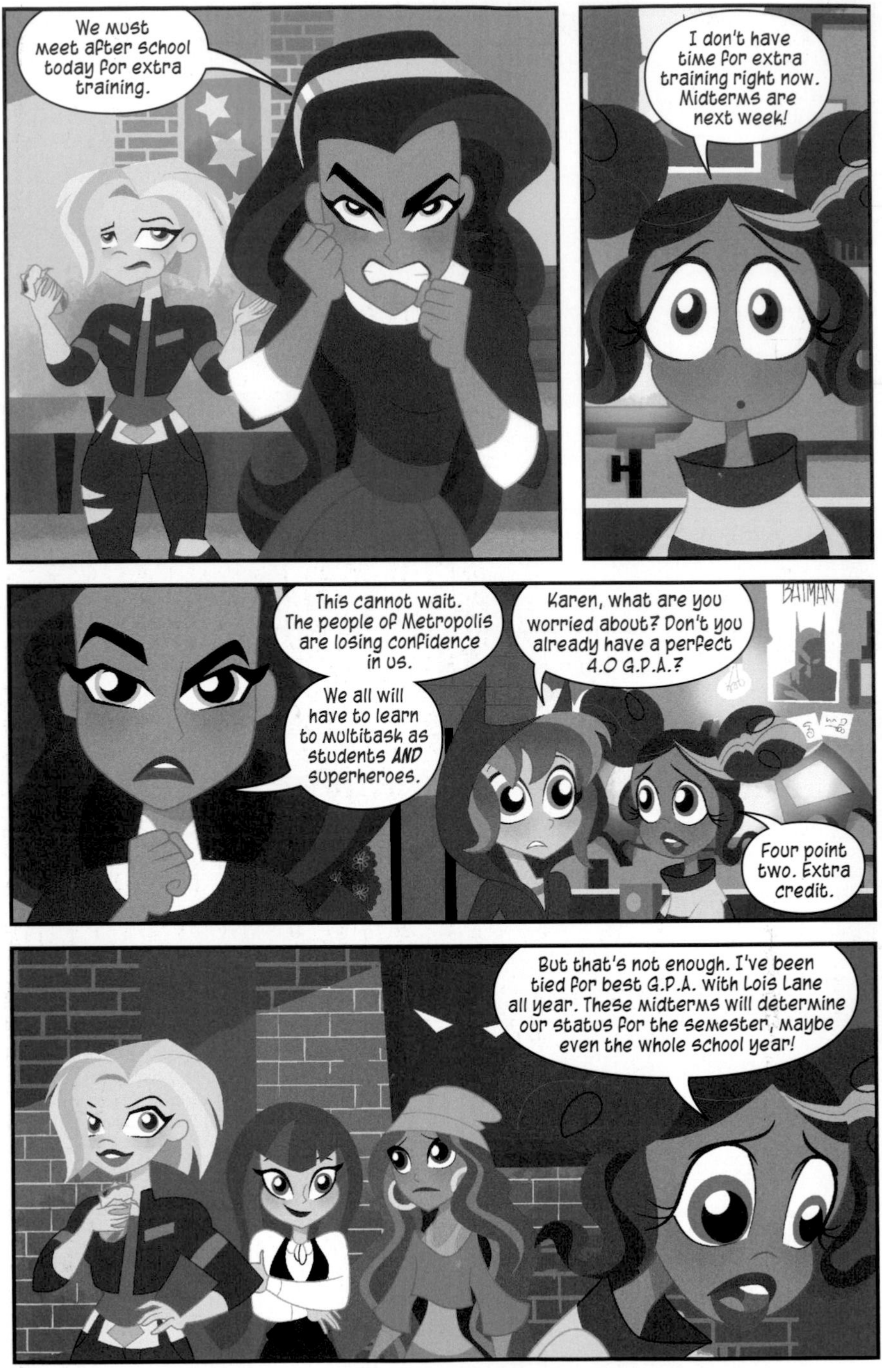
We must meet after school today for extra training.
I don't have time for extra training right now. Midterms are next week!
This cannot wait. The people of Metropolis are losing confidence in us.
We all will have to learn to multitask as students *AND* superheroes.
Karen, what are you worried about? Don't you already have a perfect 4.0 G.P.A.?
BATMAN
Four point two. Extra credit.
But that's not enough. I've been tied for best G.P.A. with Lois Lane all year. These midterms will determine our status for the semester, maybe even the whole school year!

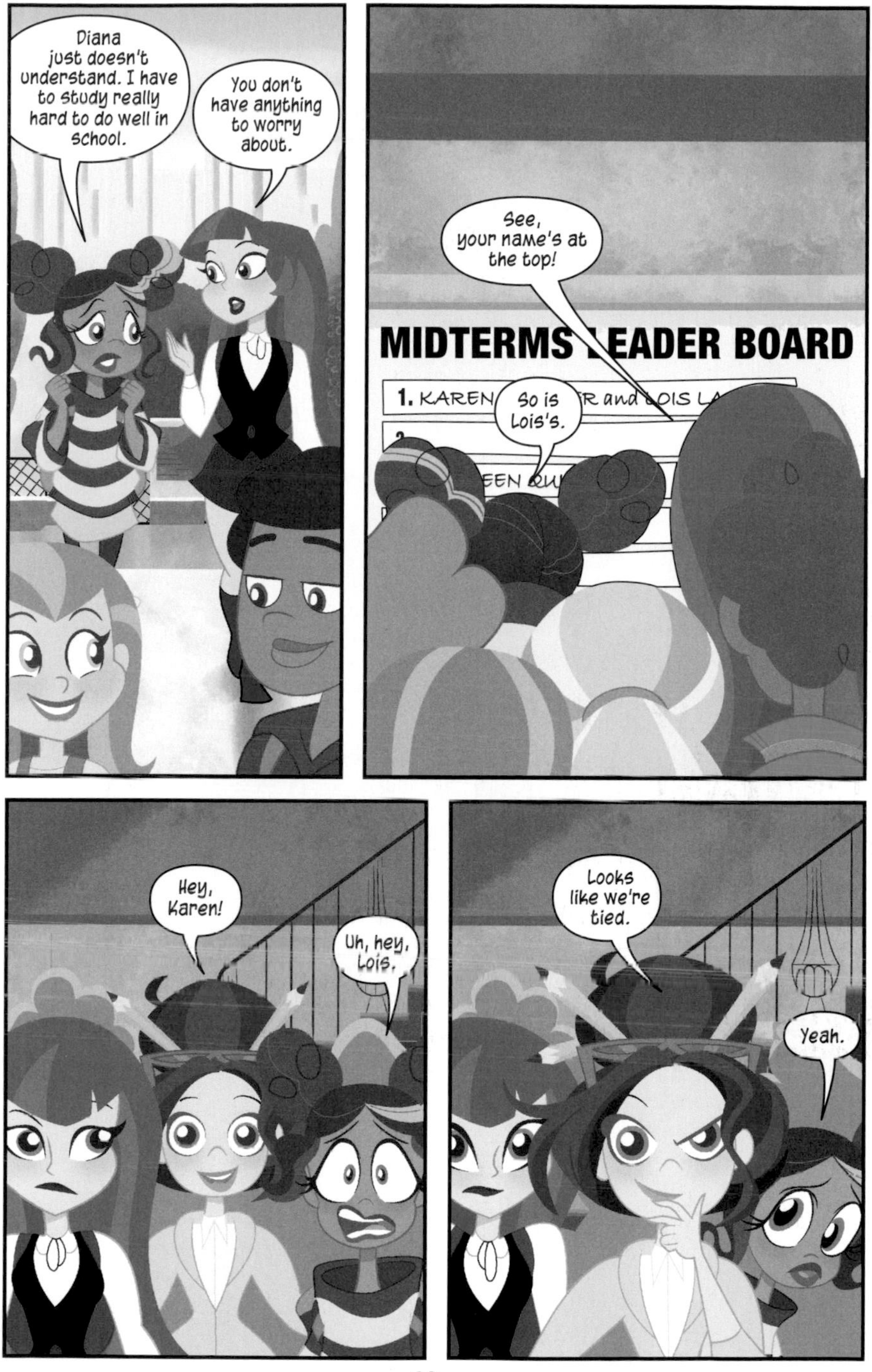
Diana just doesn't understand. I have to study really hard to do well in school.
You don't have anything to worry about.
See, your name's at the top!
MIDTERMS LEADER BOARD
1. KAREN
So is Lois's.
Hey, Karen!
Uh, hey, Lois.
Looks like we're tied.
Yeah.

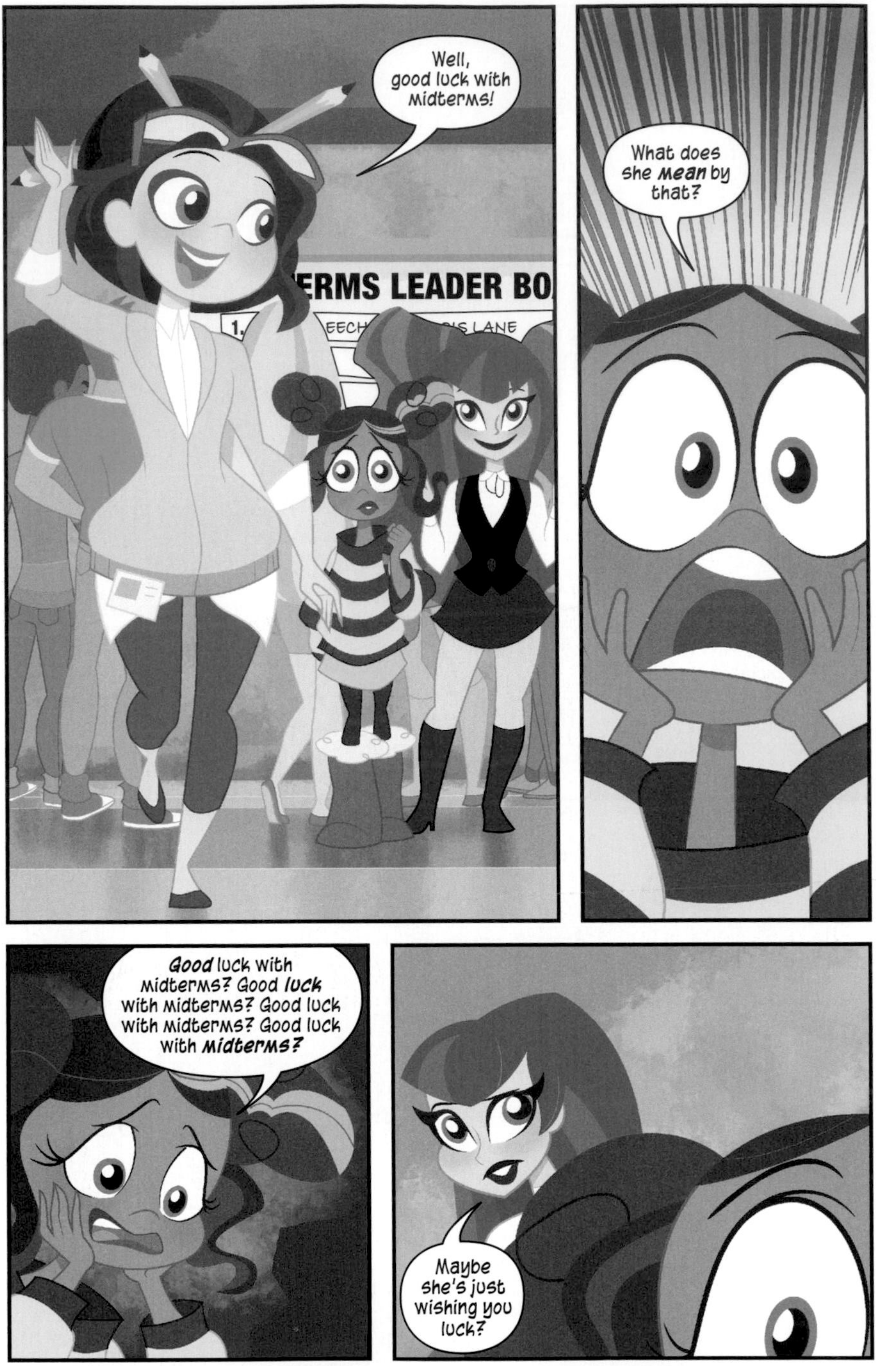
Well, good luck with midterms!
What does she *mean* by that?
***Good*** luck with midterms? Good ***luck*** with midterms? Good luck with midterms? Good luck with ***midterms?***
Maybe she's just wishing you luck?

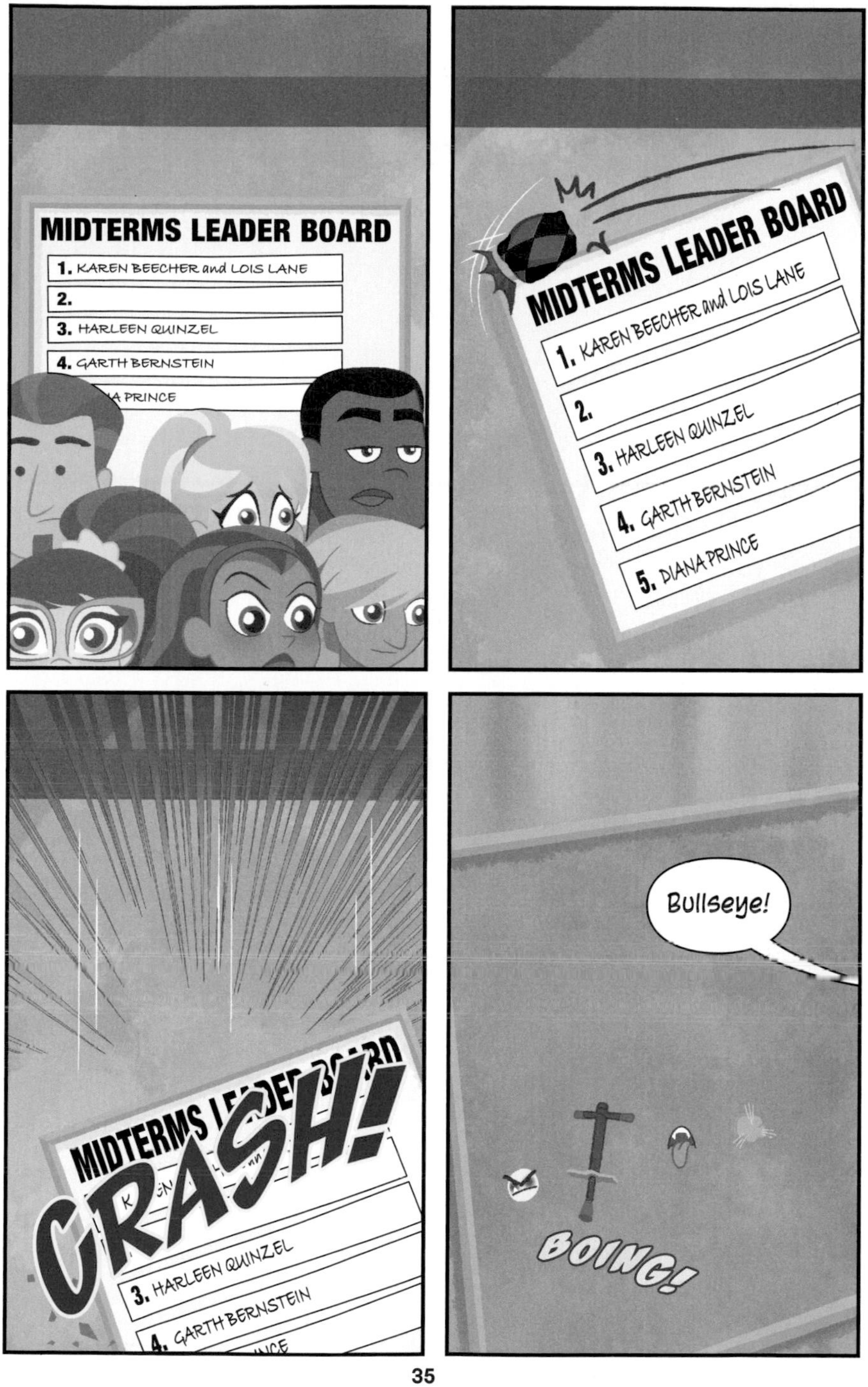
MIDTERMS LEADER BOARD
1. KAREN BEECHER and LOIS LANE
2.
3. HARLEEN QUINZEL
4. GARTH BERNSTEIN
MIDTERMS LEADER BOARD
1. KAREN BEECHER and LOIS LANE
2.
3. HARLEEN QUINZEL
4. GARTH BERNSTEIN
5. DIANA PRINCE
CRASH!
3. HARLEEN QUINZEL
4. GARTH BERNSTEIN
Bullseye!
BOING!

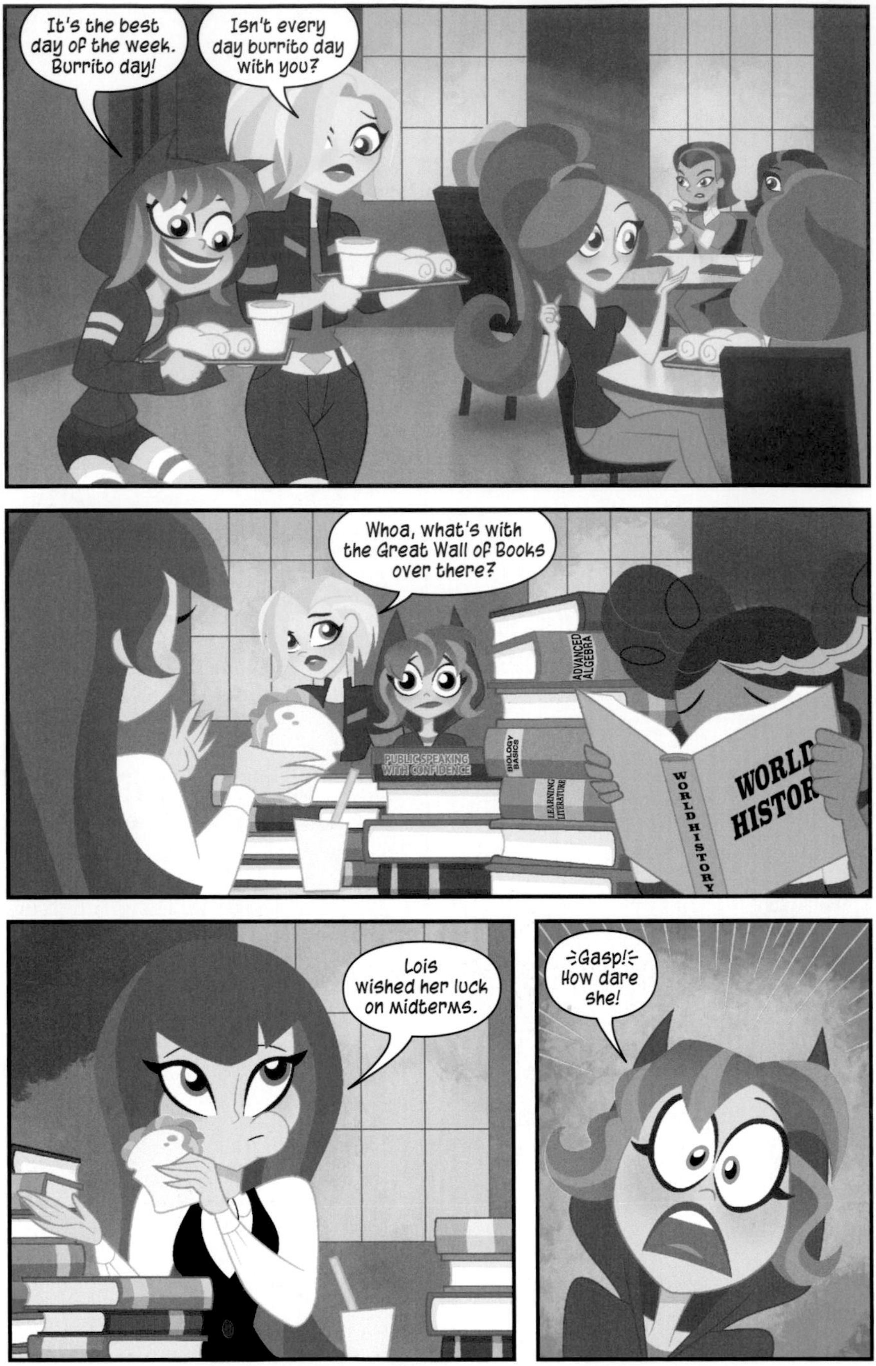
It's the best day of the week. Burrito day!
Isn't every day burrito day with you?
Whoa, what's with the Great Wall of Books over there?
ADVANCED ALGEBRA
PUBLIC SPEAKING WITH CONFIDENCE
BIOLOGY BASICS
LEARNING LITERATURE
WORLD HISTORY
WORLD HISTOR
Lois wished her luck on midterms.
Gasp! How dare she!

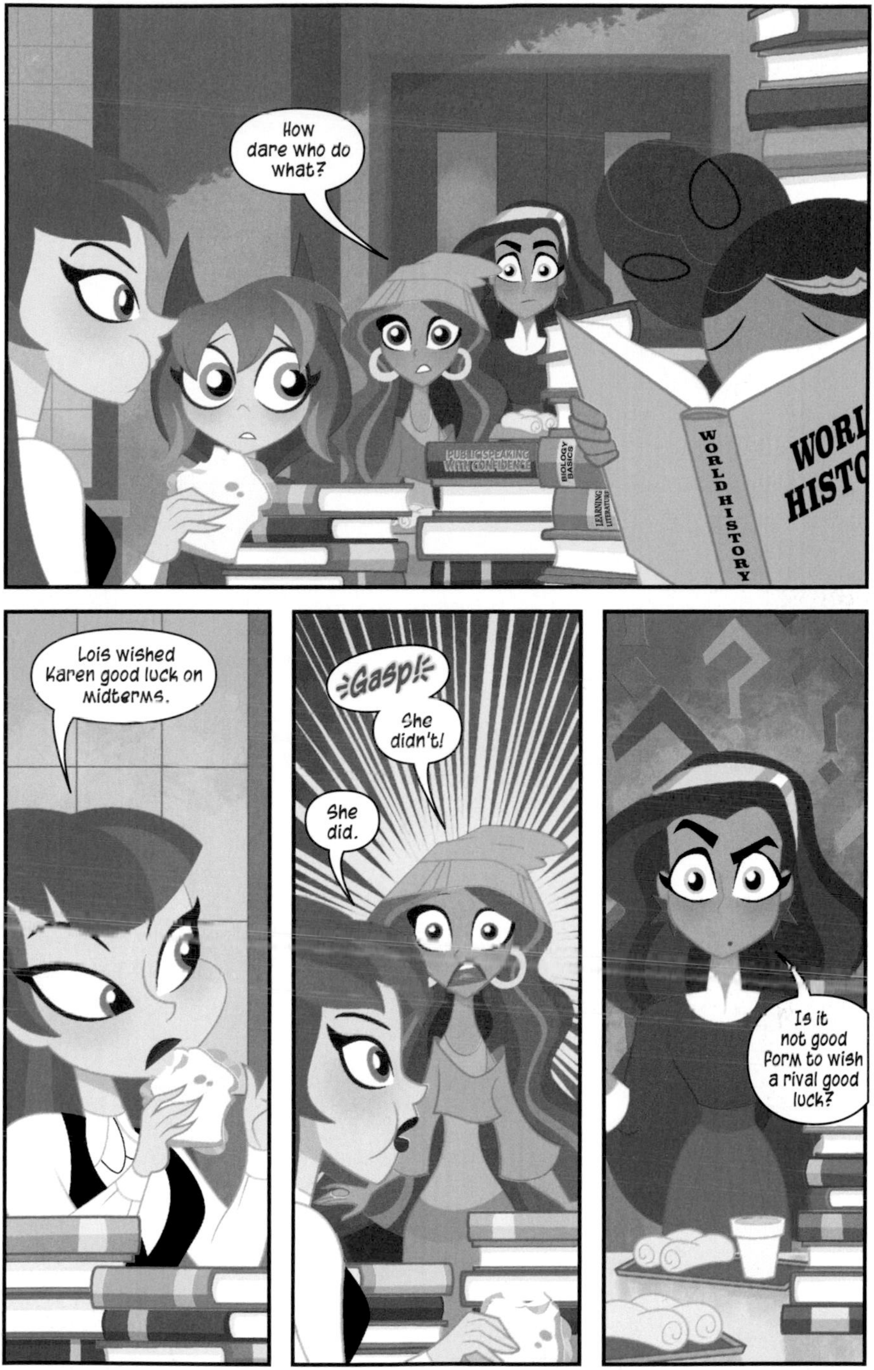
How dare who do what?
PUBLIC SPEAKING WITH CONFIDENCE
BIOLOGY BASICS
LEARNING LITERATURE
WORLD HISTORY
Lois wished Karen good luck on midterms.
Gasp!
She didn't!
She did.
Is it not good form to wish a rival good luck?

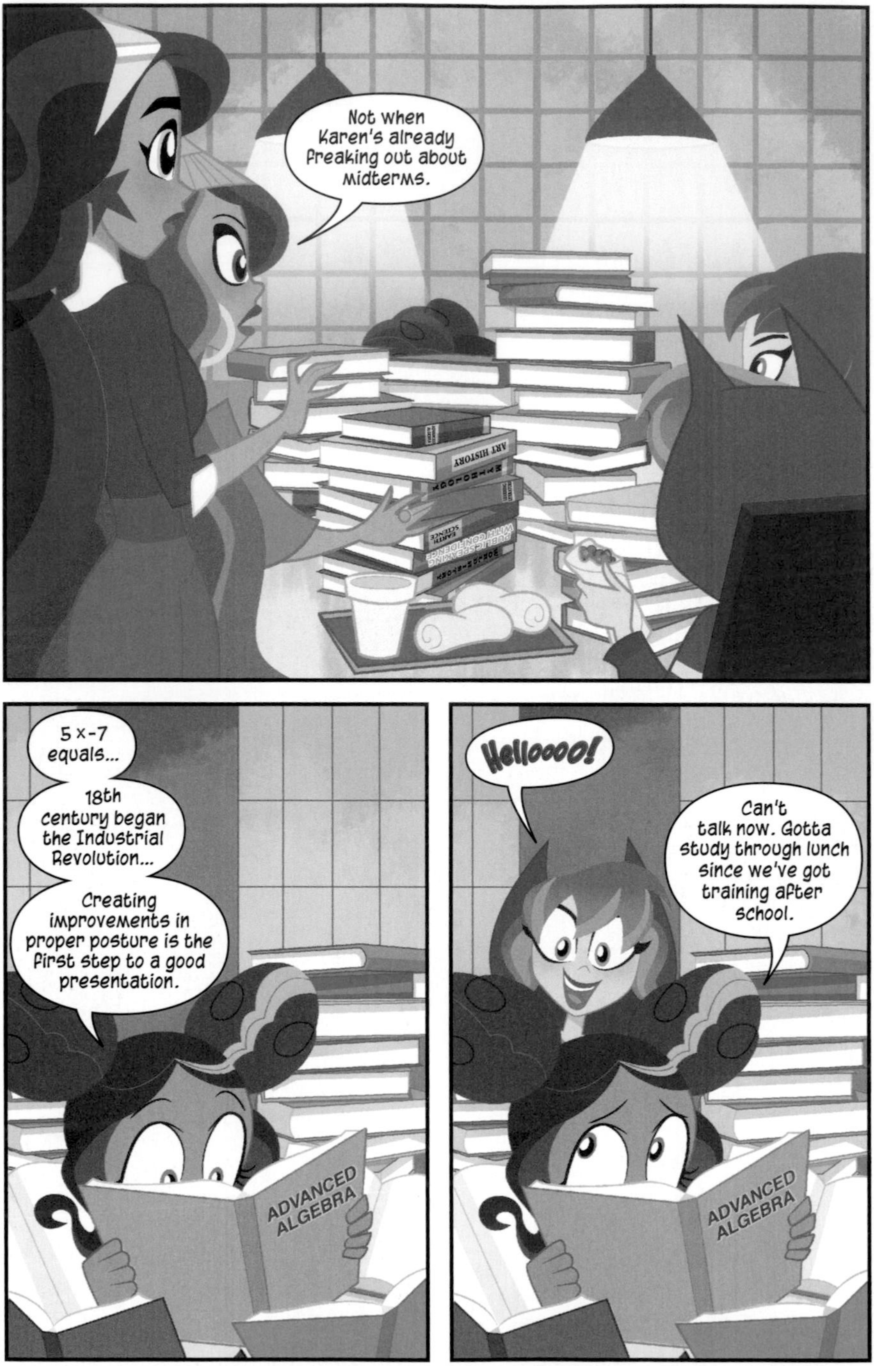
Not when Karen's already freaking out about midterms.
ART HISTORY
MYTHOLOGY
PUBLIC SPEAKING WITH CONFIDENCE
EARTH SCIENCE
5 x -7 equals...
18th century began the Industrial Revolution...
Creating improvements in proper posture is the first step to a good presentation.
ADVANCED ALGEBRA
Helloooo!
Can't talk now. Gotta study through lunch since we've got training after school.
ADVANCED ALGEBRA

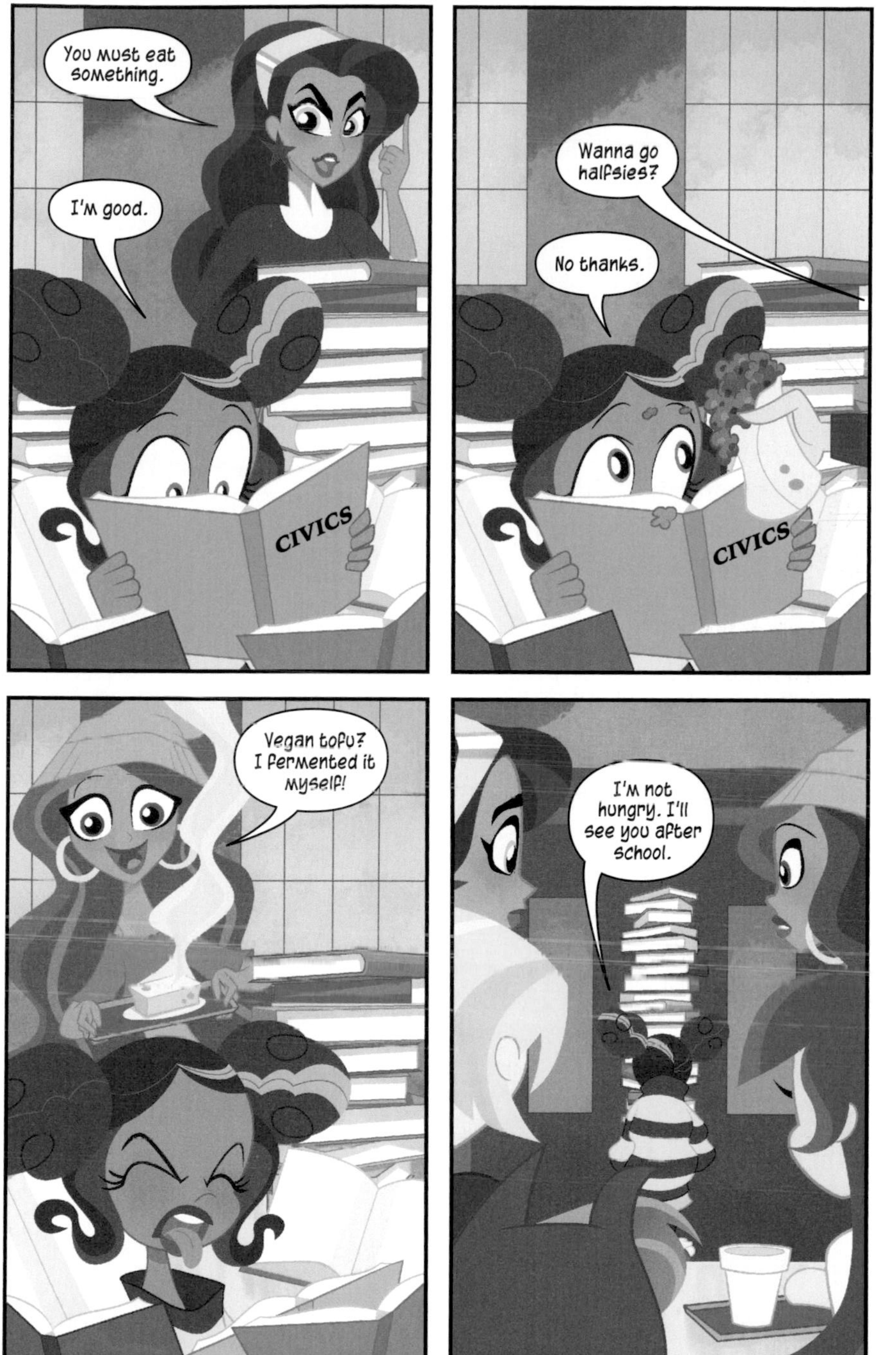
You must eat something.
I'm good.
CIVICS
Wanna go halfsies?
No thanks.
CIVICS
Vegan tofu? I fermented it myself!
I'm not hungry. I'll see you after school.

# chapter three

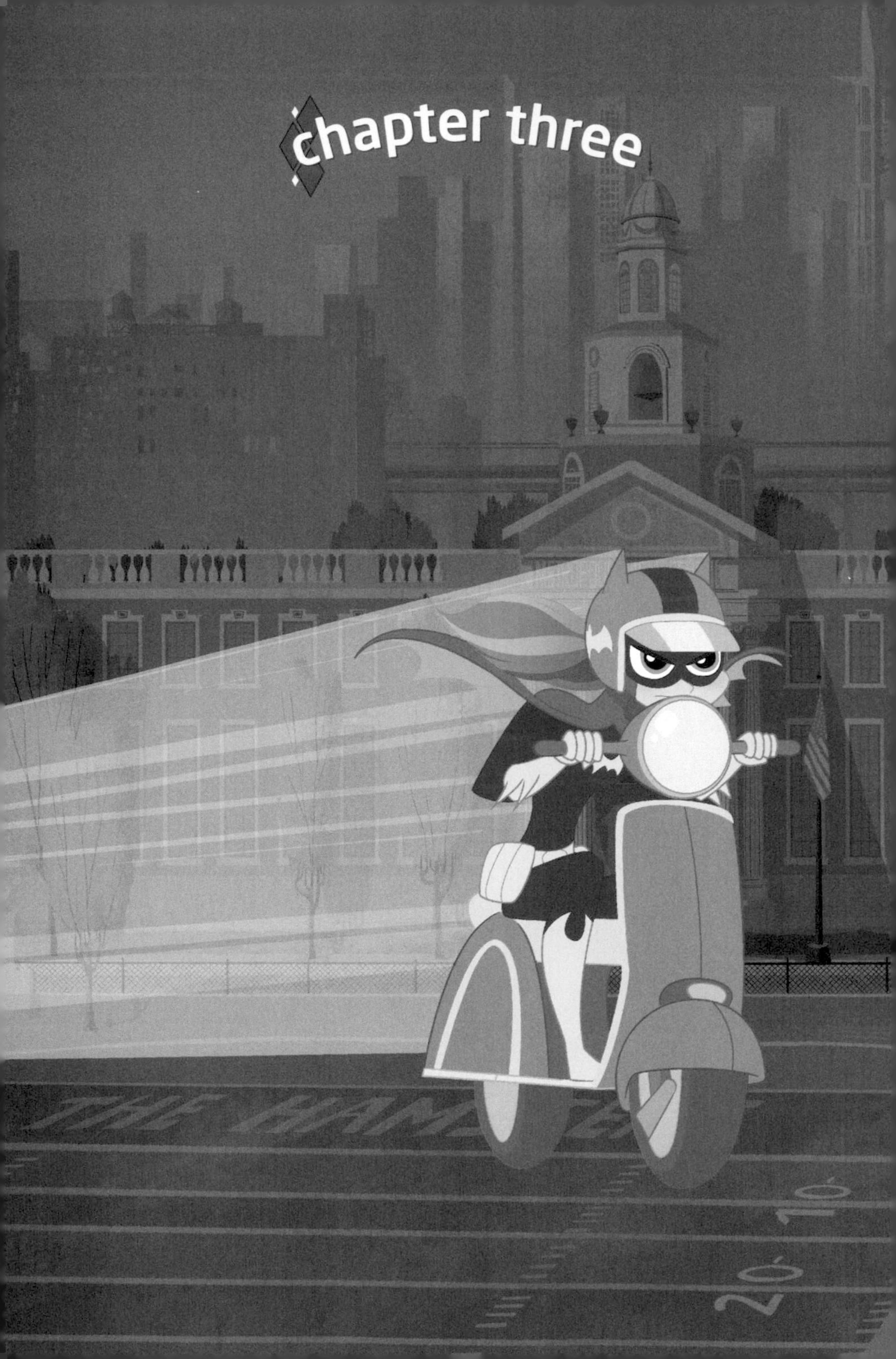

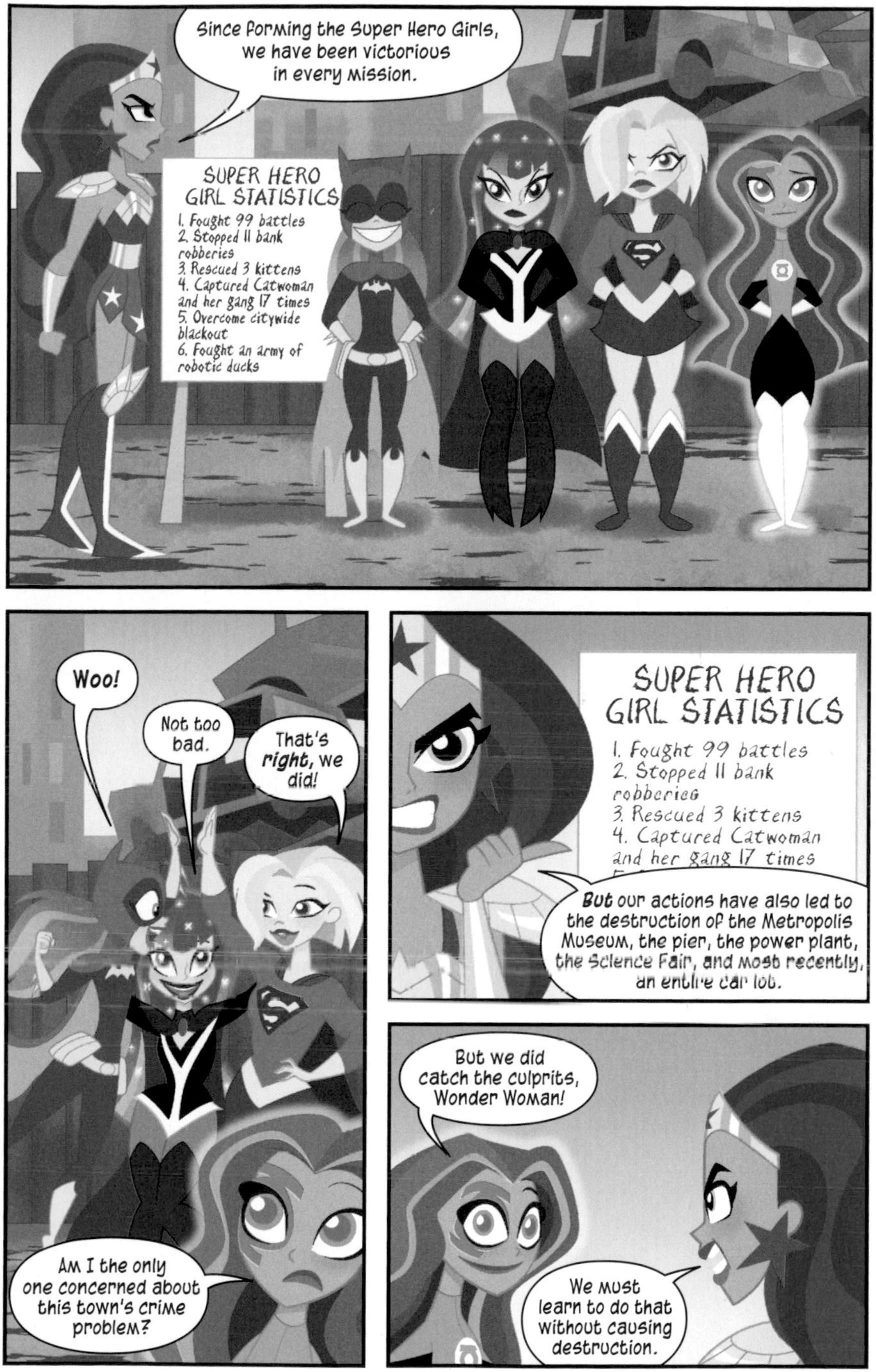

Since forming the Super Hero Girls, we have been victorious in every mission.
SUPER HERO GIRL STATISTICS
1. Fought 99 battles
2. Stopped 11 bank robberies
3. Rescued 3 kittens
4. Captured Catwoman and her gang 17 times
5. Overcome citywide blackout
6. Fought an army of robotic ducks
Woo!
Not too bad.
That's **right**, we did!
Am I the only one concerned about this town's crime problem?
SUPER HERO GIRL STATISTICS
1. Fought 99 battles
2. Stopped 11 bank robberies
3. Rescued 3 kittens
4. Captured Catwoman and her gang 17 times
***But*** our actions have also led to the destruction of the Metropolis Museum, the pier, the power plant, the Science Fair, and most recently, an entire car lot.
But we did catch the culprits, Wonder Woman!
We must learn to do that without causing destruction.

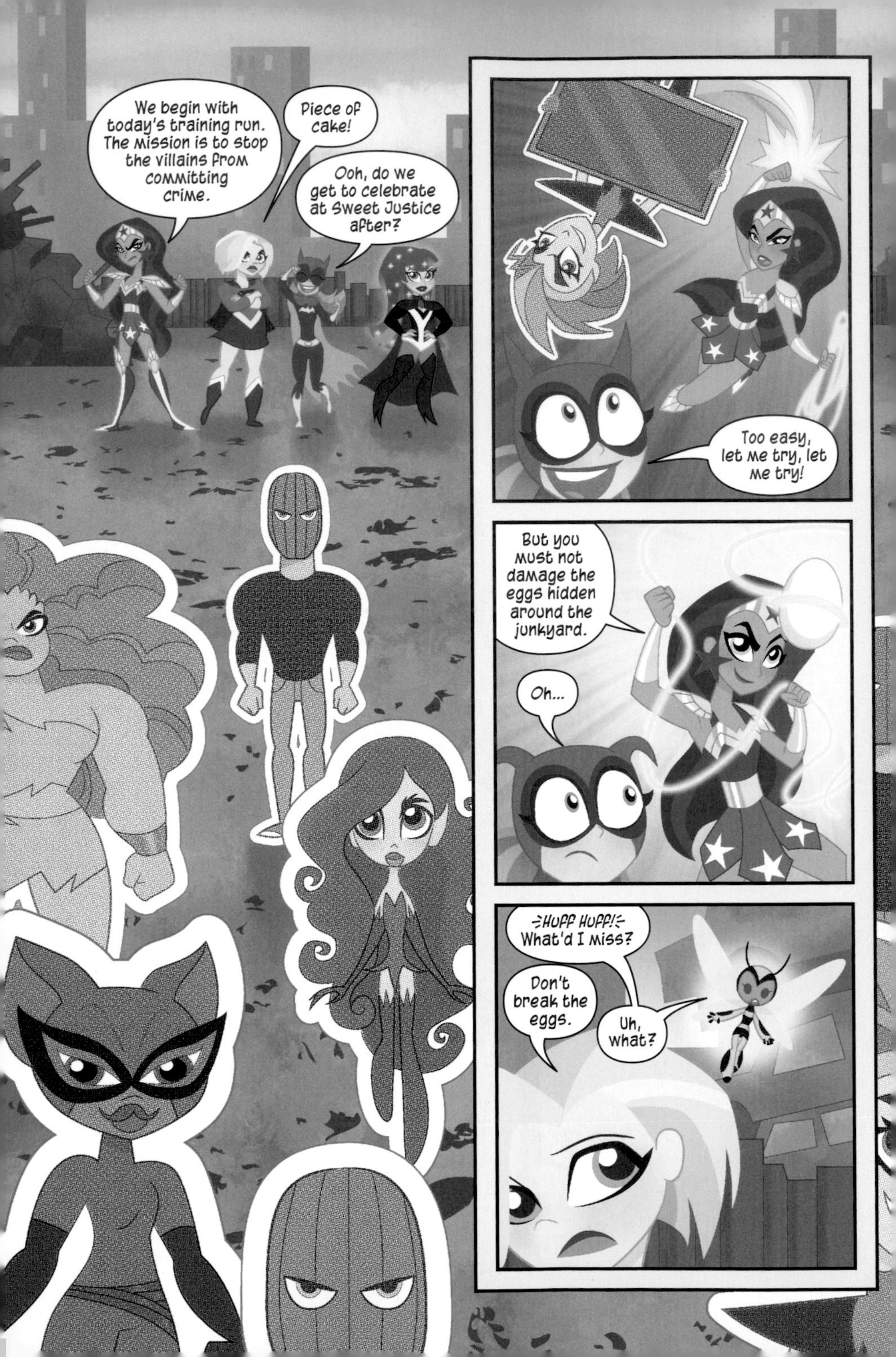
We begin with today's training run. The mission is to stop the villains from committing crime.
Piece of cake!
Ooh, do we get to celebrate at Sweet Justice after?
Too easy, let me try, let me try!
But you must not damage the eggs hidden around the junkyard.
Oh...
HUFF HUFF! What'd I miss?
Don't break the eggs.
Uh, what?

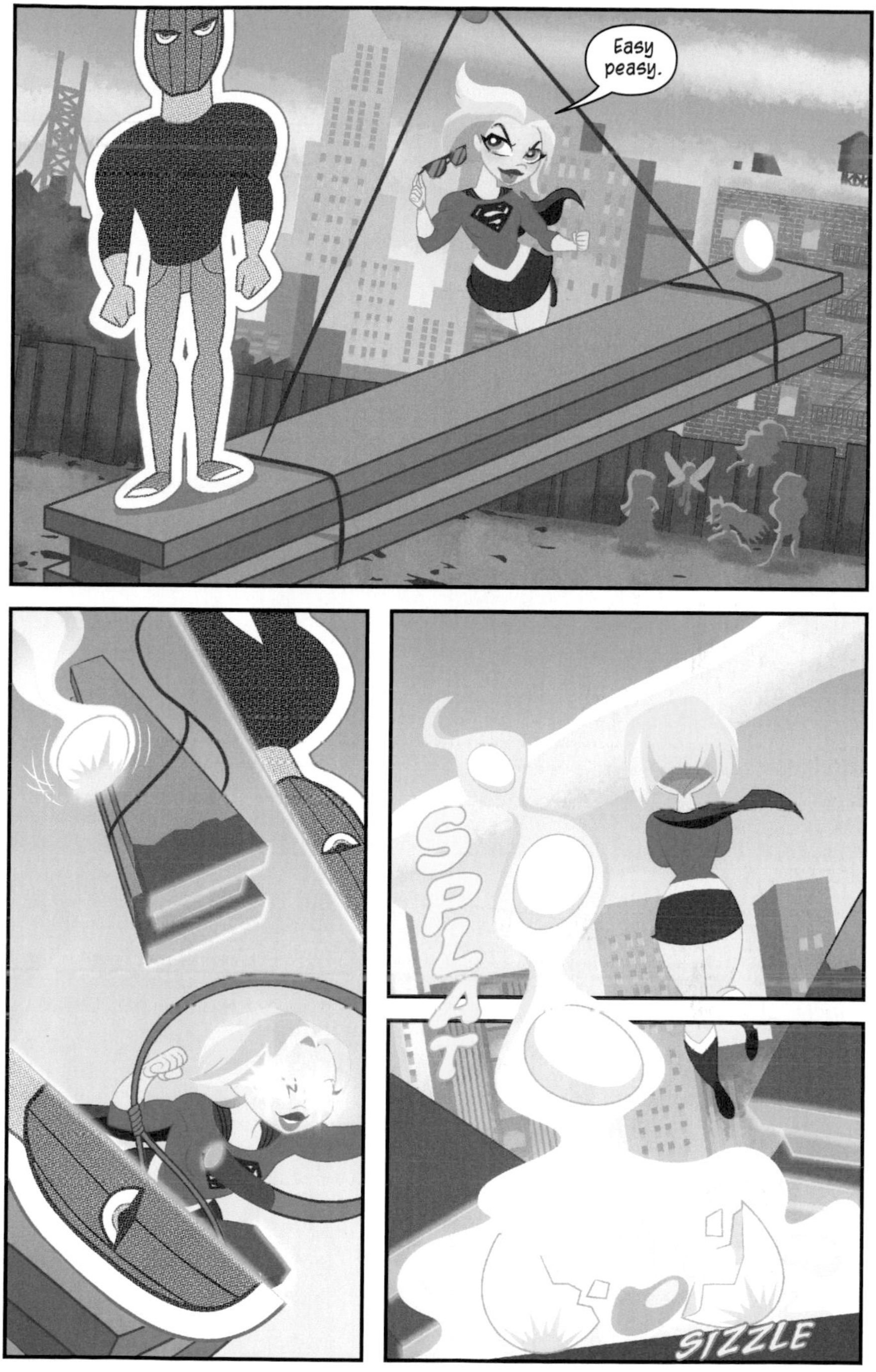
Easy peasy.
SPLAT
SIZZLE

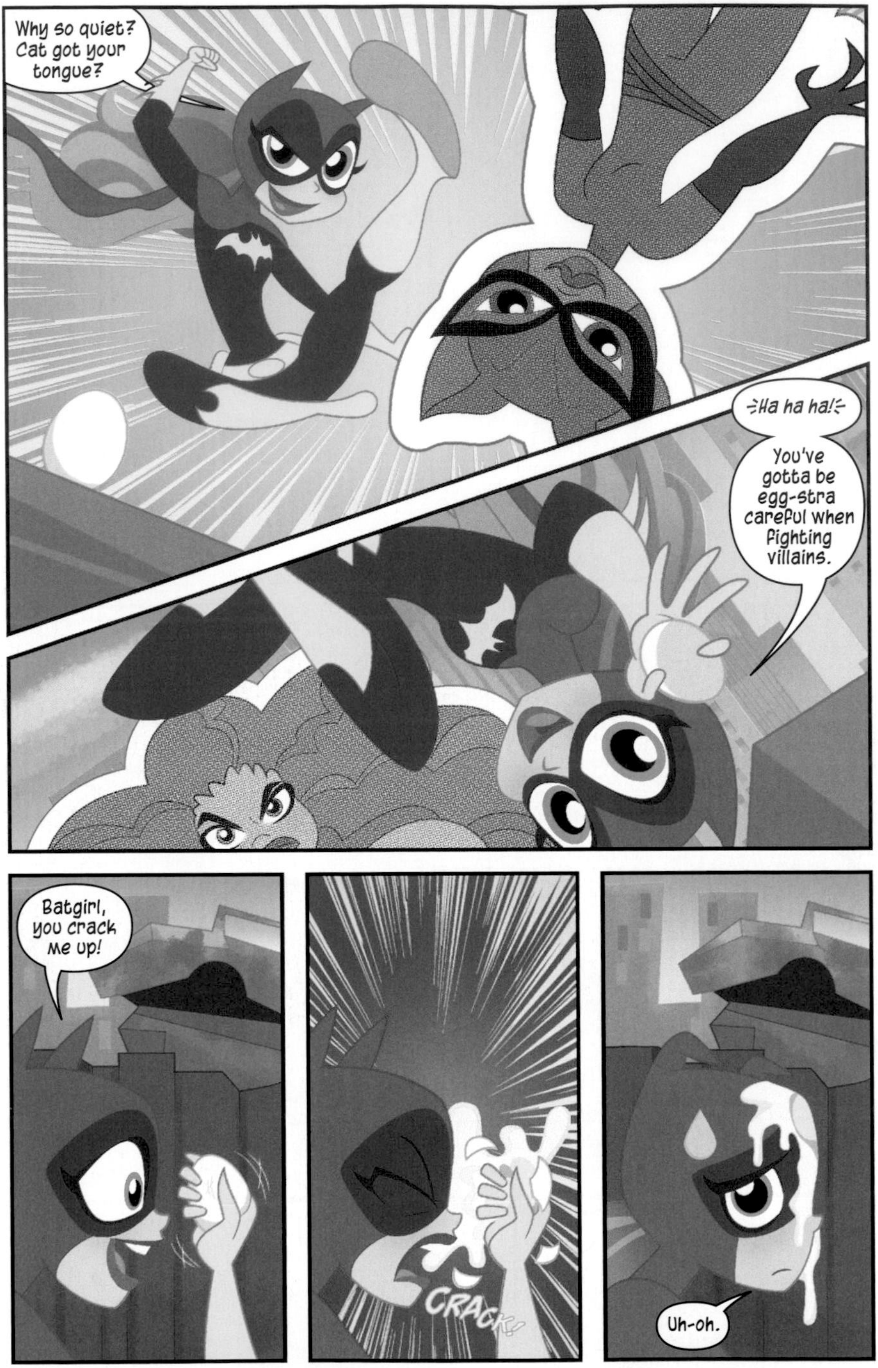
Why so quiet? Cat got your tongue?
Ha ha ha!
You've gotta be egg-stra careful when fighting villains.
Batgirl, you crack me up!
CRACK!
Uh-oh.

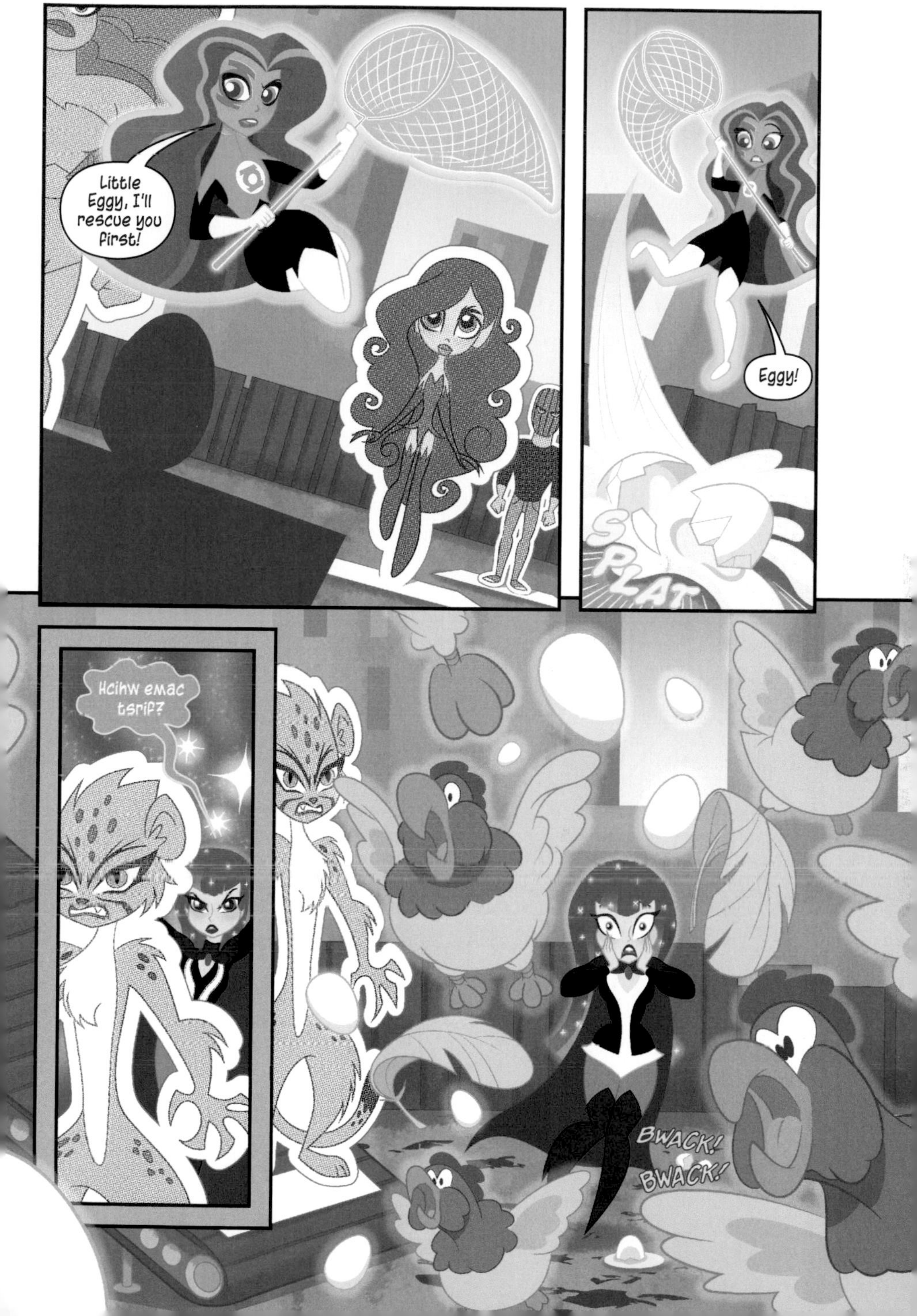

Little Eggy, I'll rescue you first!
Eggy!
SPLAT
Hcihw emac tsrif?
BWACK!
BWACK!

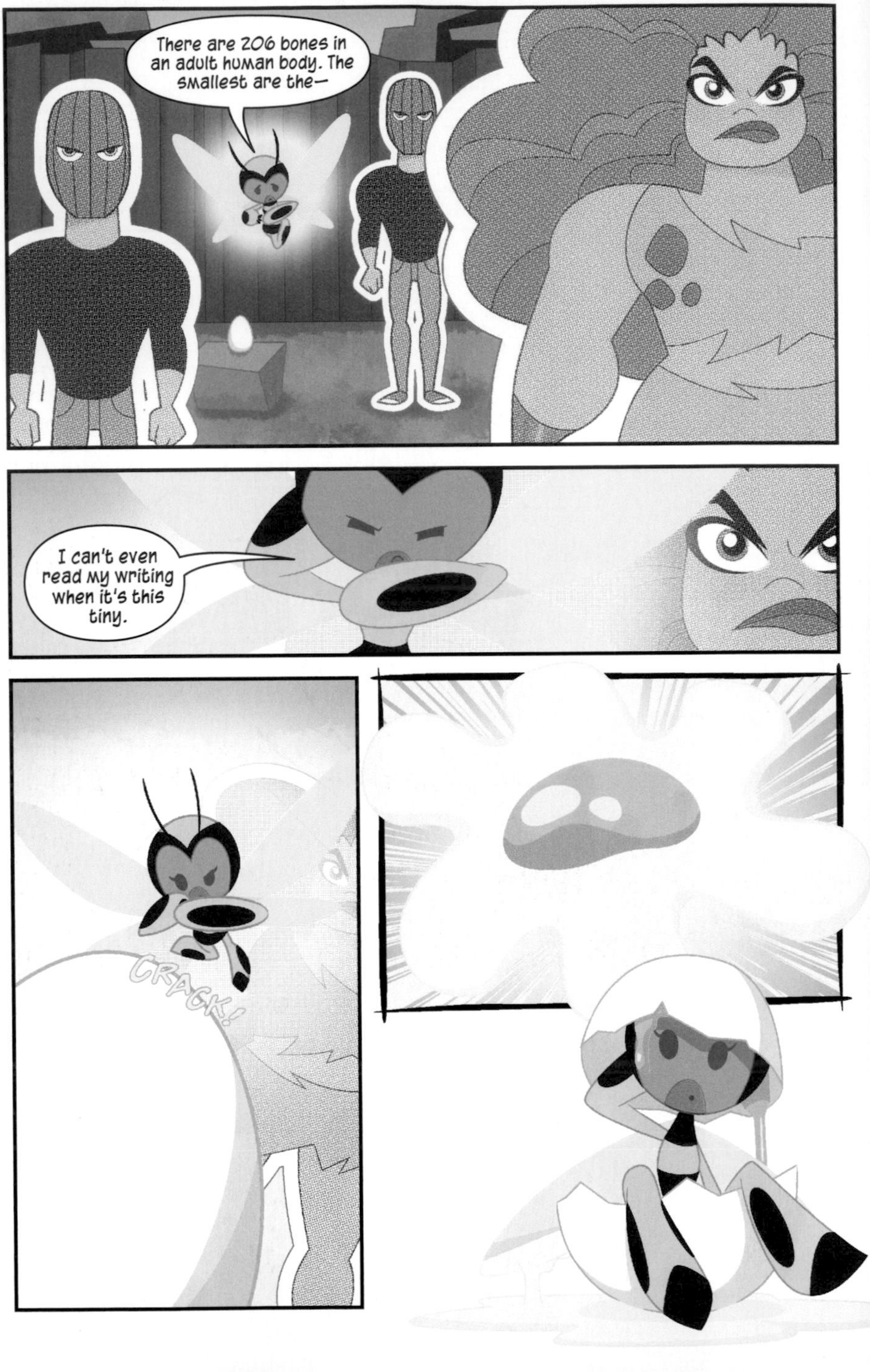

There are 206 bones in an adult human body. The smallest are the—
I can't even read my writing when it's this tiny.
CRACK!

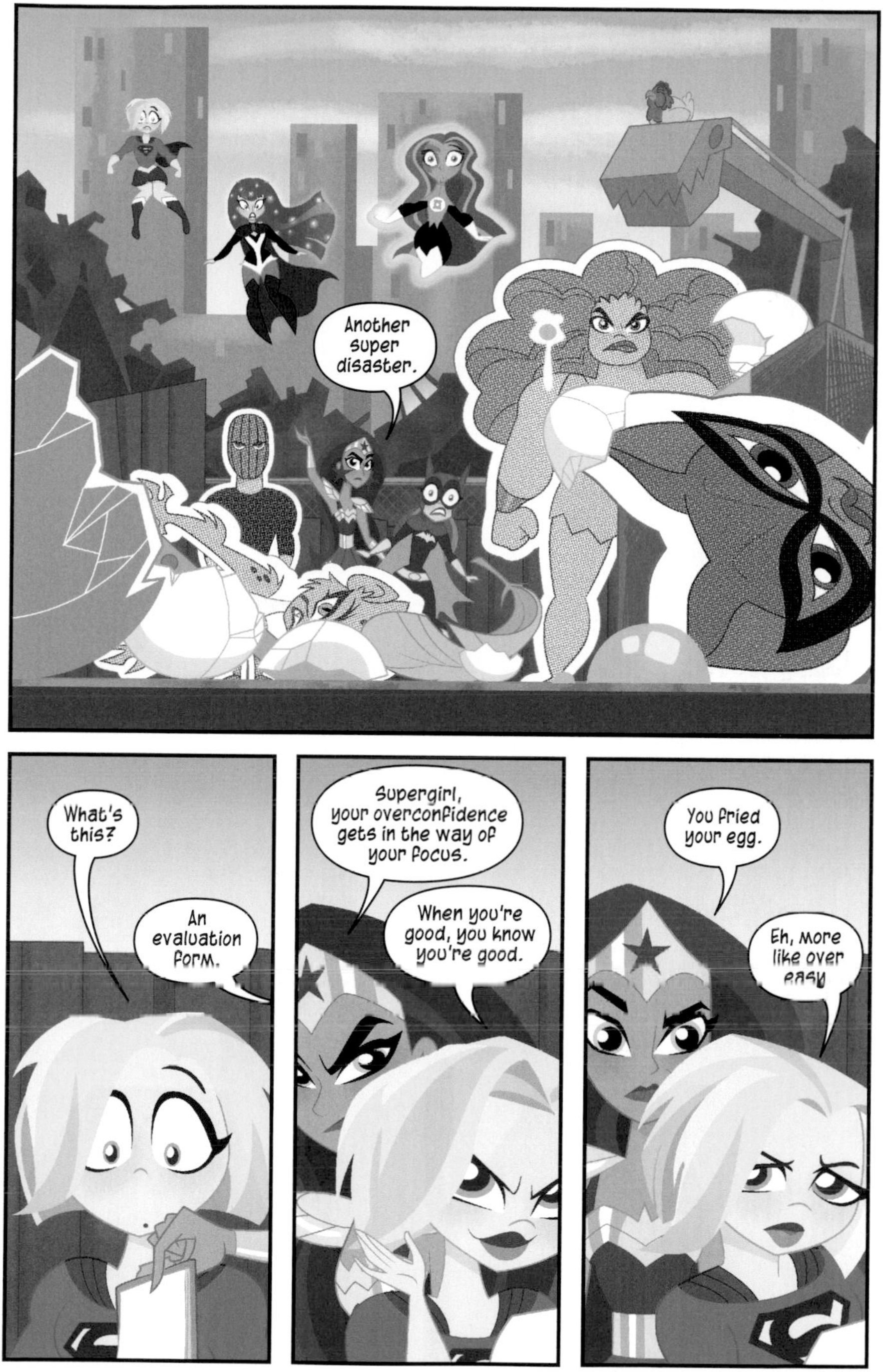
Another super disaster.
What's this?
An evaluation form.
Supergirl, your overconfidence gets in the way of your focus.
When you're good, you know you're good.
You fried your egg.
Eh, more like over easy

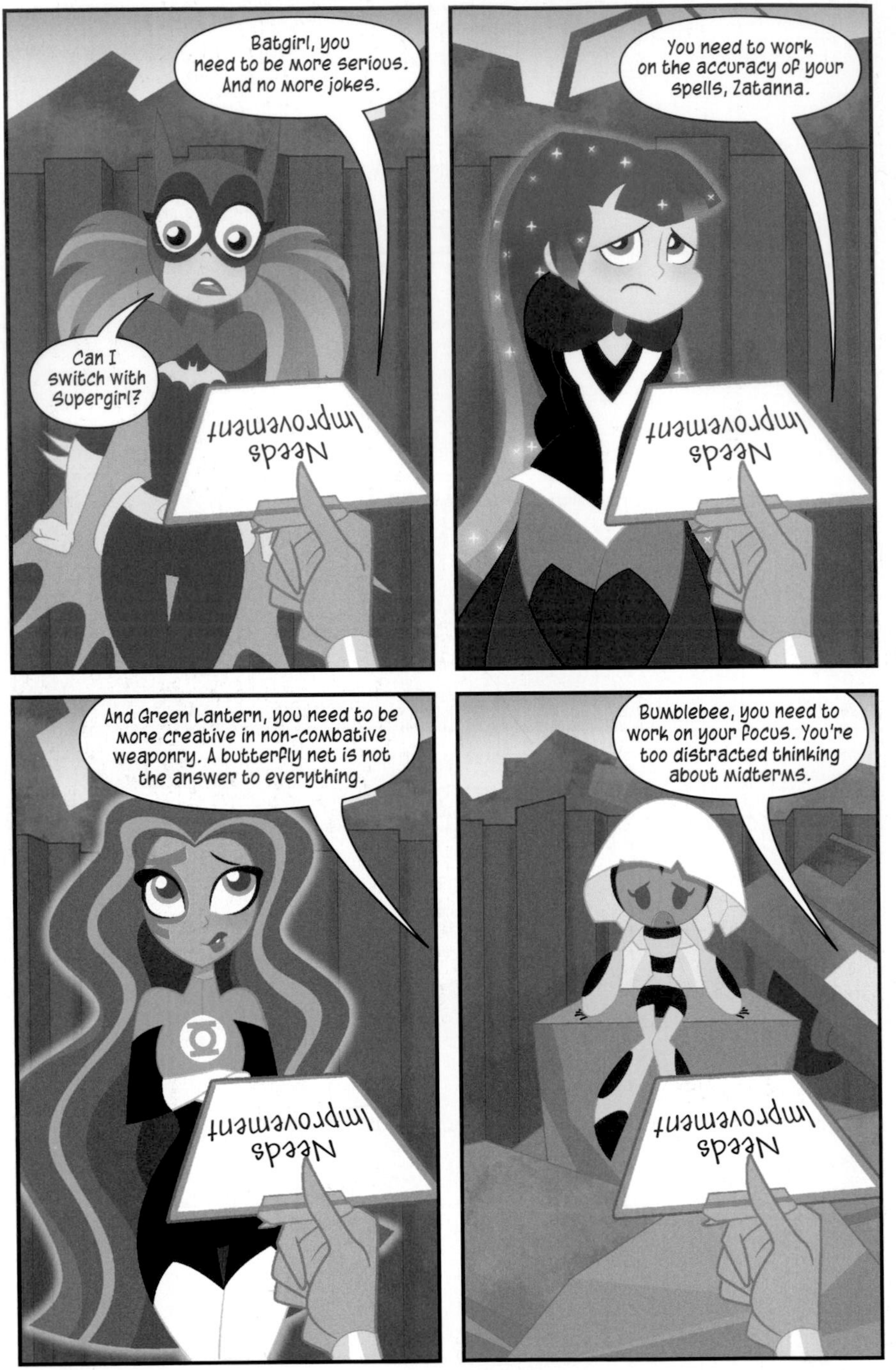

Batgirl, you need to be more serious. And no more jokes.
Can I switch with Supergirl?
Needs Improvement
You need to work on the accuracy of your spells, Zatanna.
Needs Improvement
And Green Lantern, you need to be more creative in non-combative weaponry. A butterfly net is not the answer to everything.
Needs Improvement
Bumblebee, you need to work on your focus. You're too distracted thinking about midterms.
Needs Improvement

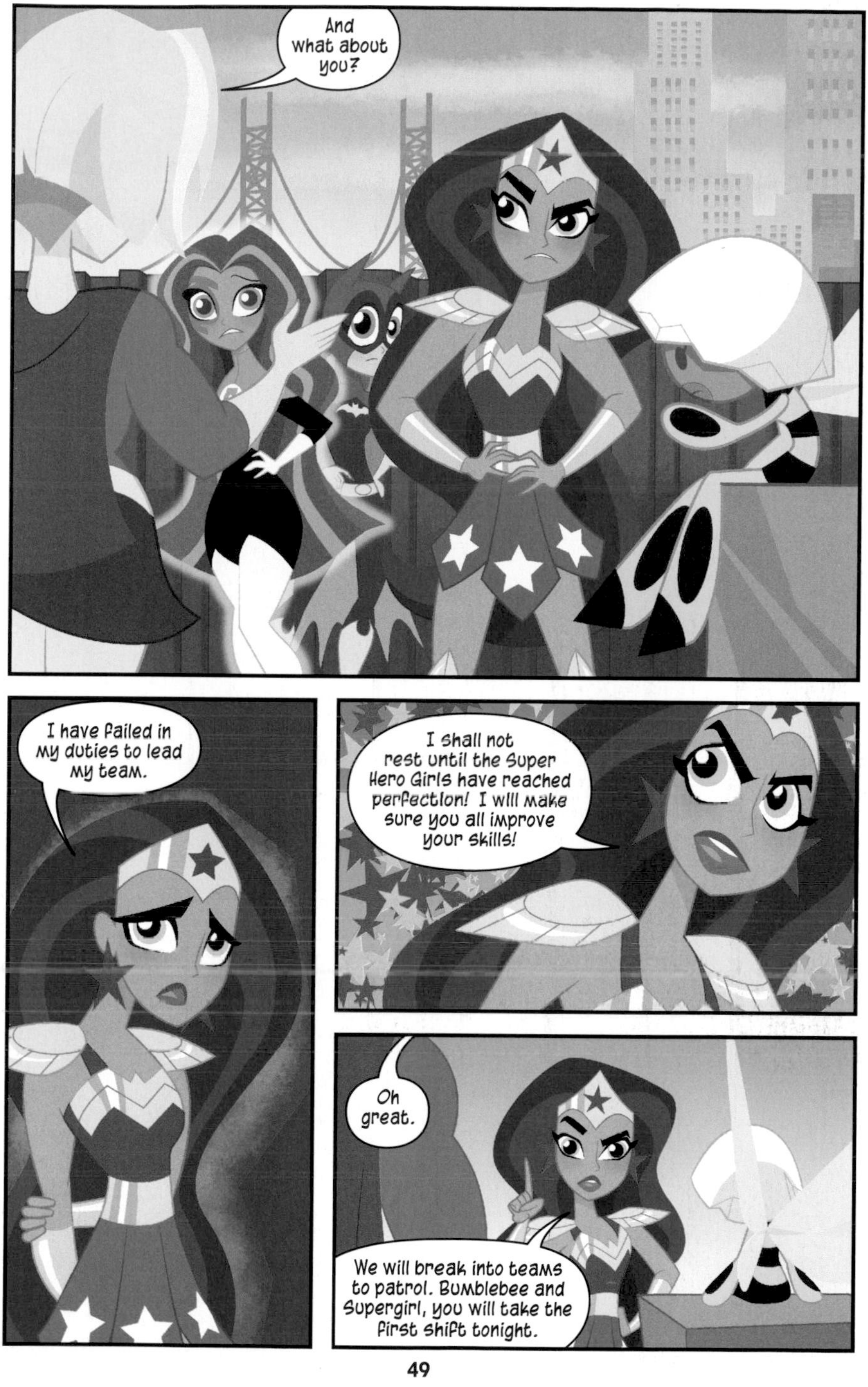
And what about you?
I have failed in my duties to lead my team.
I shall not rest until the Super Hero Girls have reached perfection! I will make sure you all improve your skills!
Oh great.
We will break into teams to patrol. Bumblebee and Supergirl, you will take the first shift tonight.

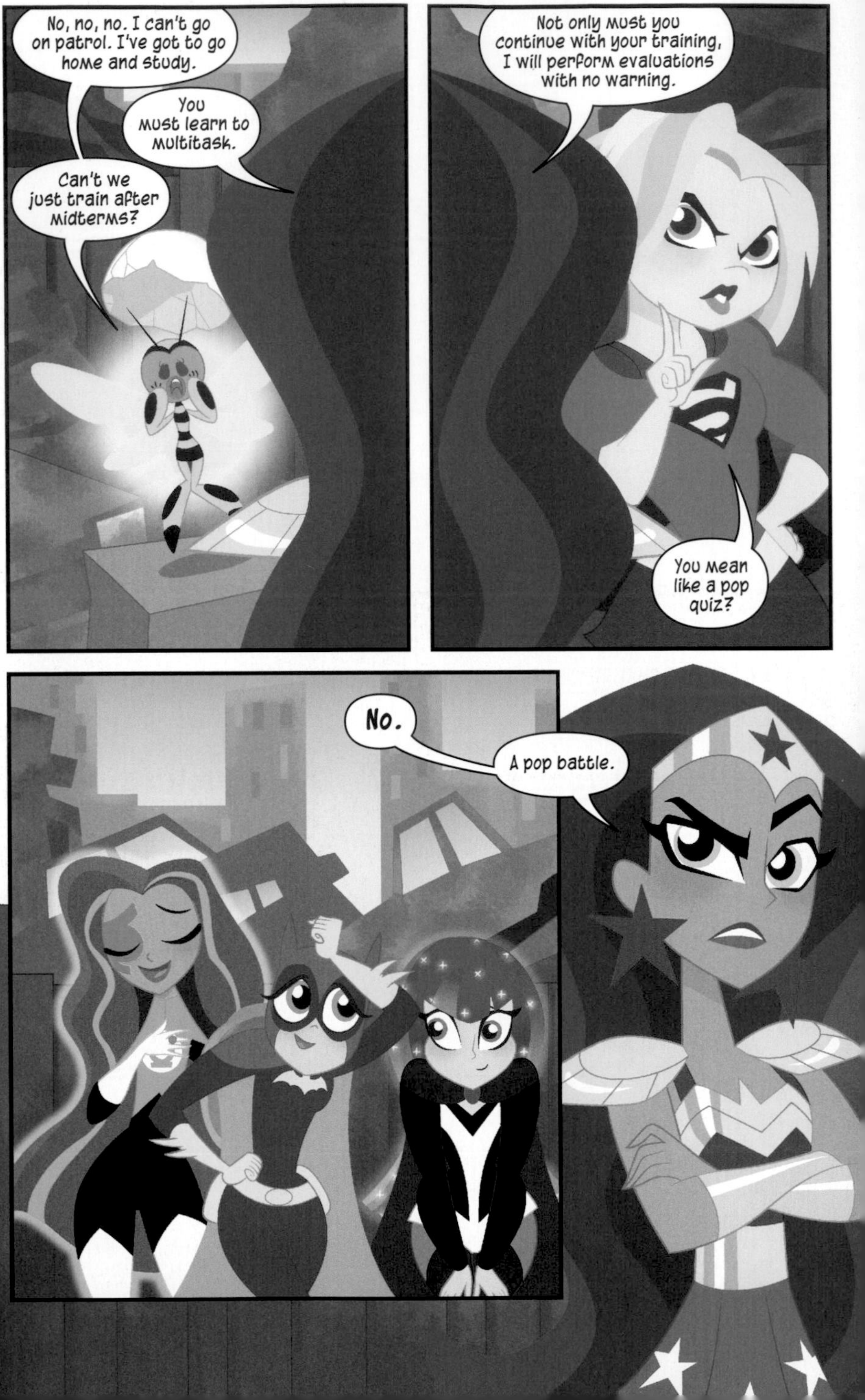
No, no, no. I can't go on patrol. I've got to go home and study.
You must learn to multitask.
Can't we just train after midterms?
Not only must you continue with your training, I will perform evaluations with no warning.
You mean like a pop quiz?
No.
A pop battle.

# chapter four

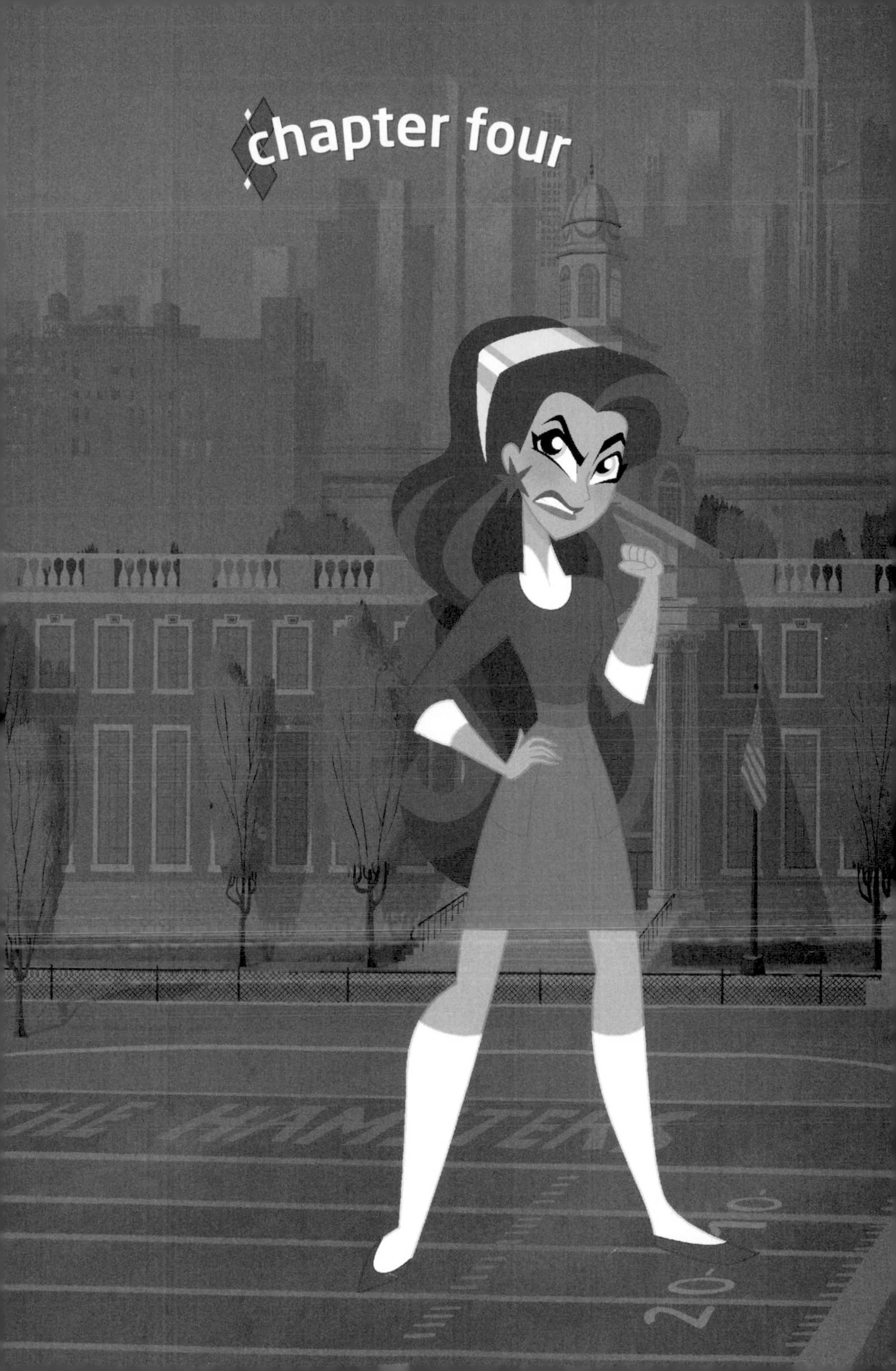

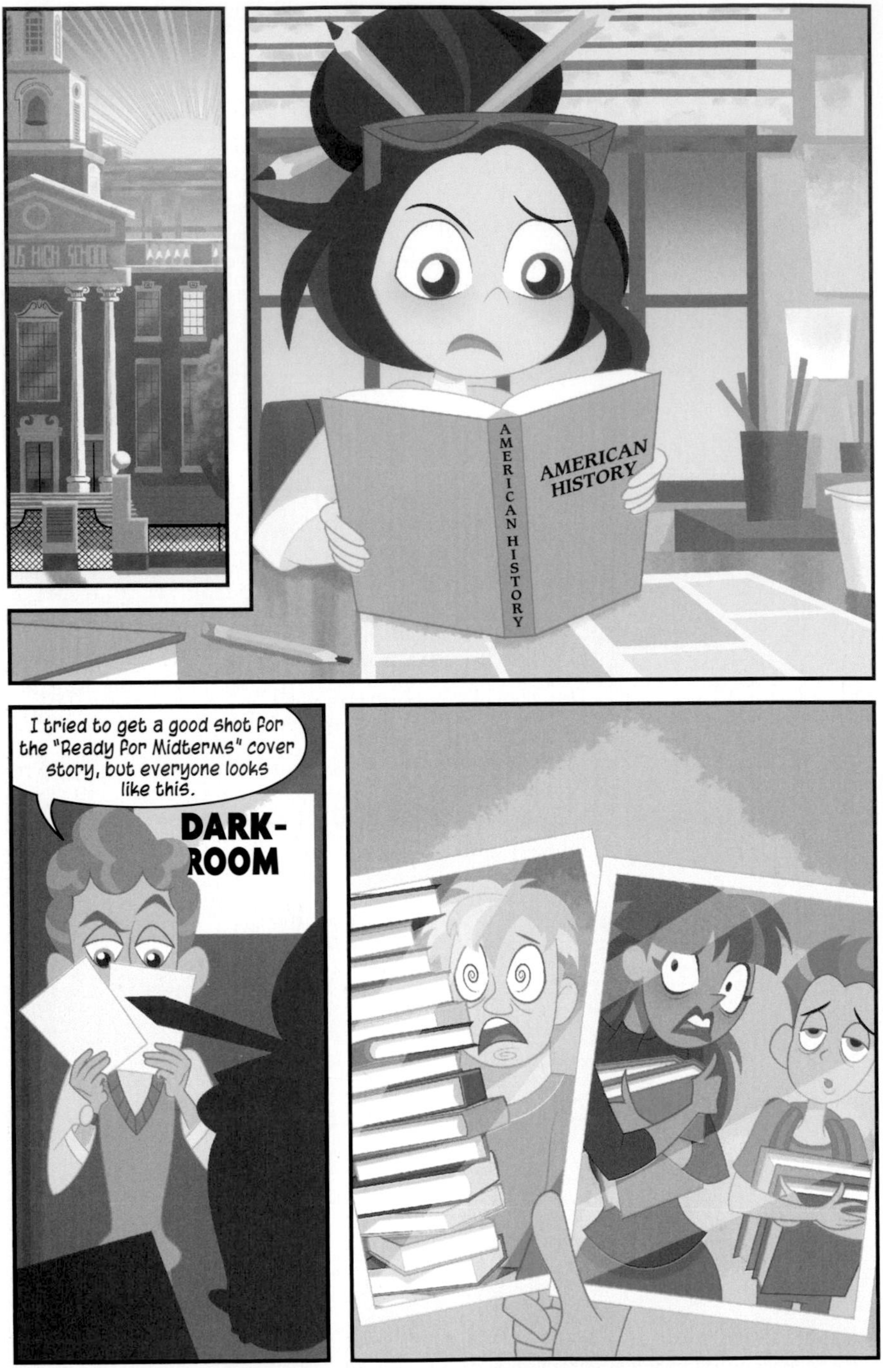
AMERICAN HISTORY
AMERICAN HISTORY
I tried to get a good shot for the "Ready for Midterms" cover story, but everyone looks like this.
DARK-ROOM

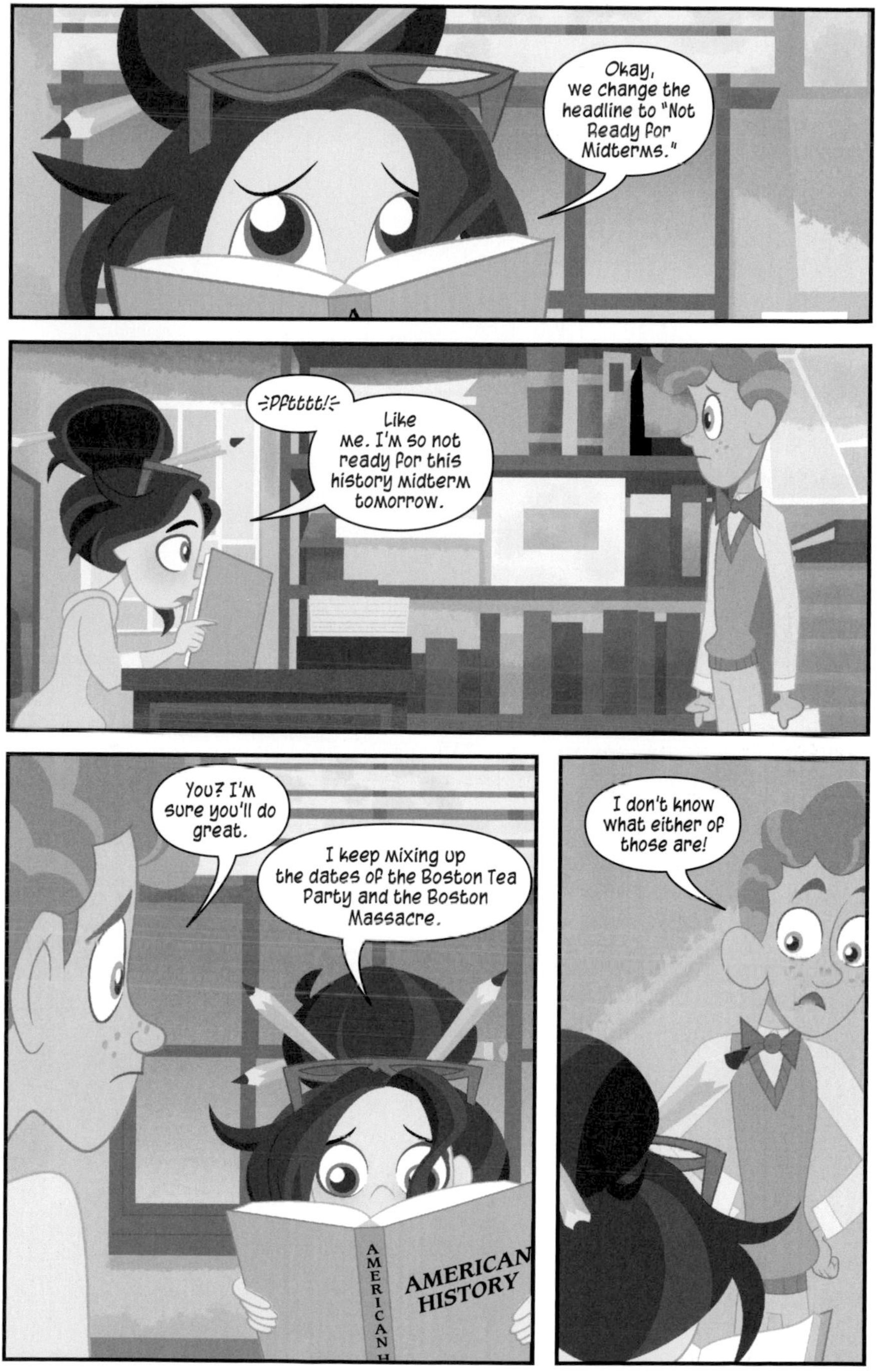
Okay, we change the headline to "Not Ready for Midterms."
PFttttt!
Like me. I'm so not ready for this history midterm tomorrow.
You? I'm sure you'll do great.
I keep mixing up the dates of the Boston Tea Party and the Boston Massacre.
AMERICAN HISTORY
I don't know what either of those are!

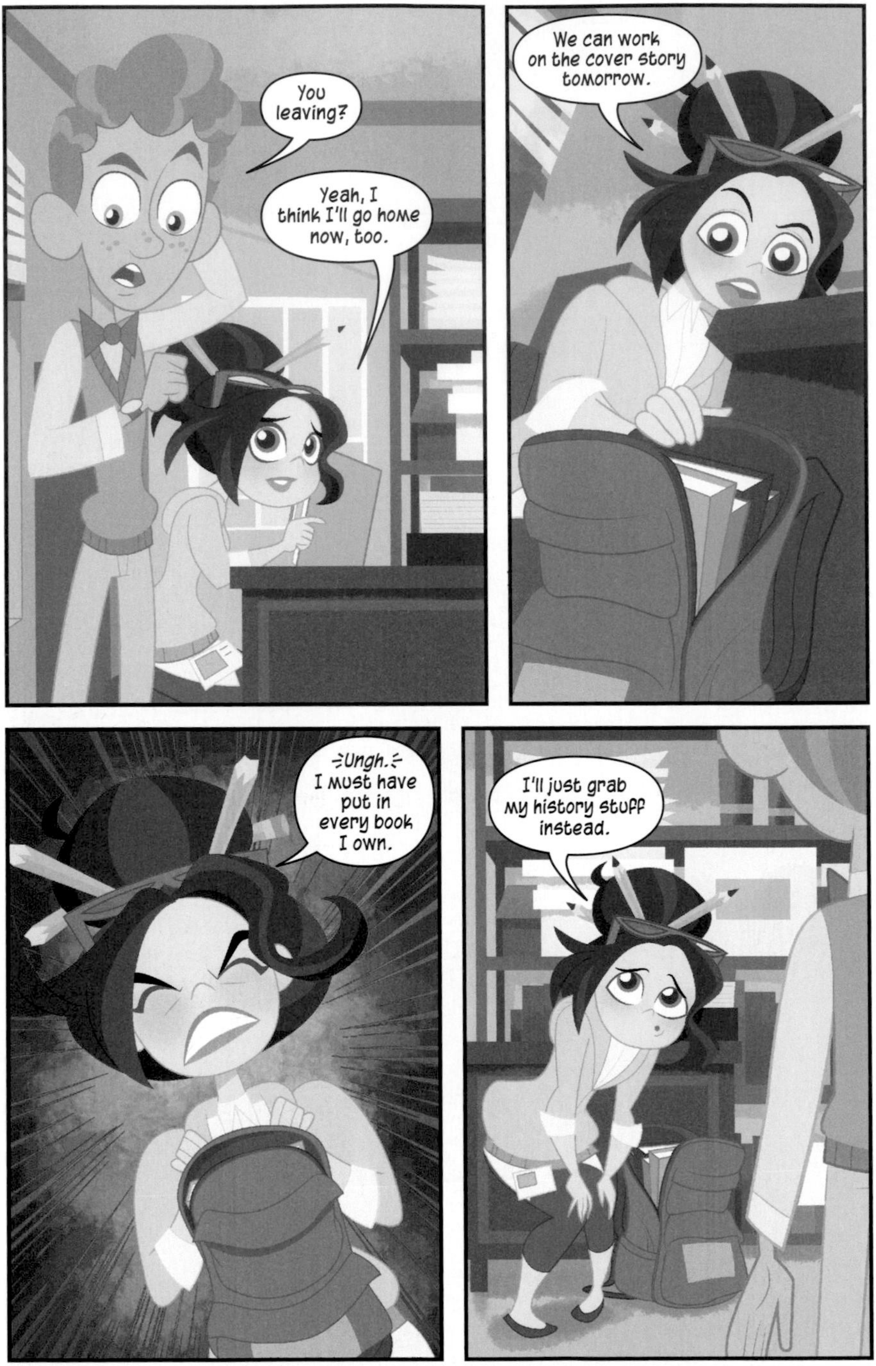
You leaving?
Yeah, I think I'll go home now, too.
We can work on the cover story tomorrow.
=Ungh.= I must have put in every book I own.
I'll just grab my history stuff instead.

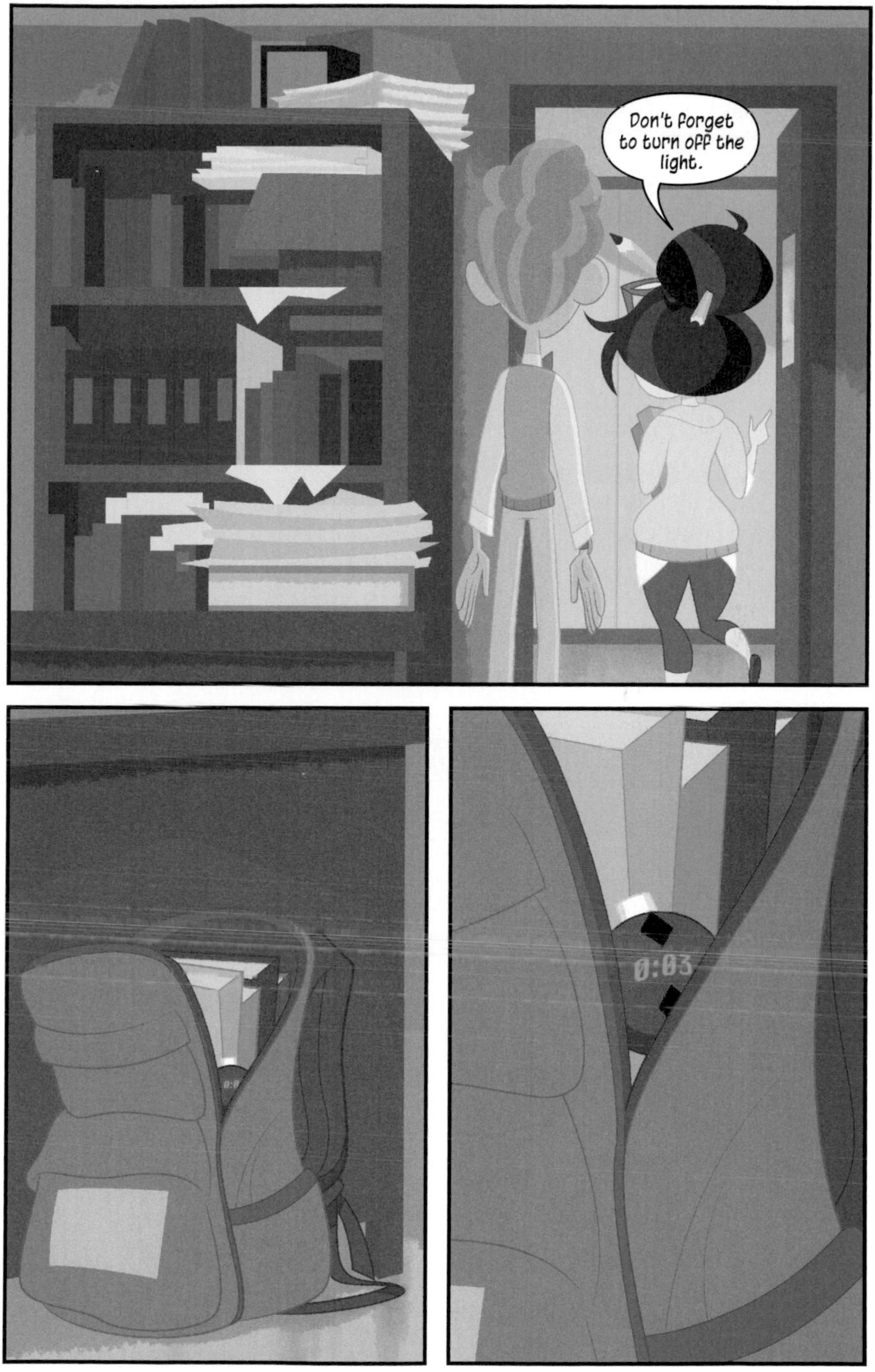
Don't forget to turn off the light.
0:03

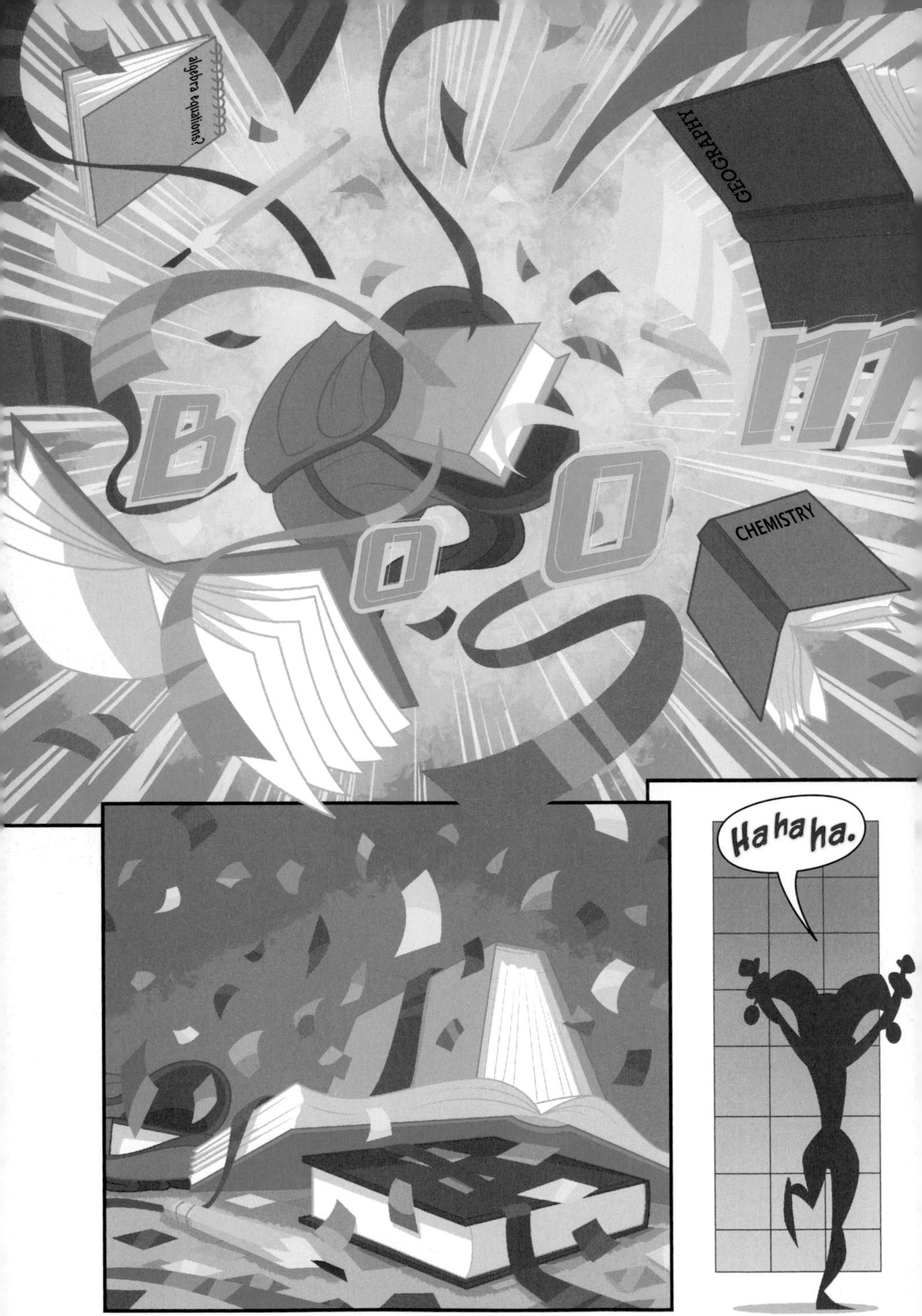
algebra equations?
GEOGRAPHY
BOOM
CHEMISTRY
Hahaha.

# chapter five

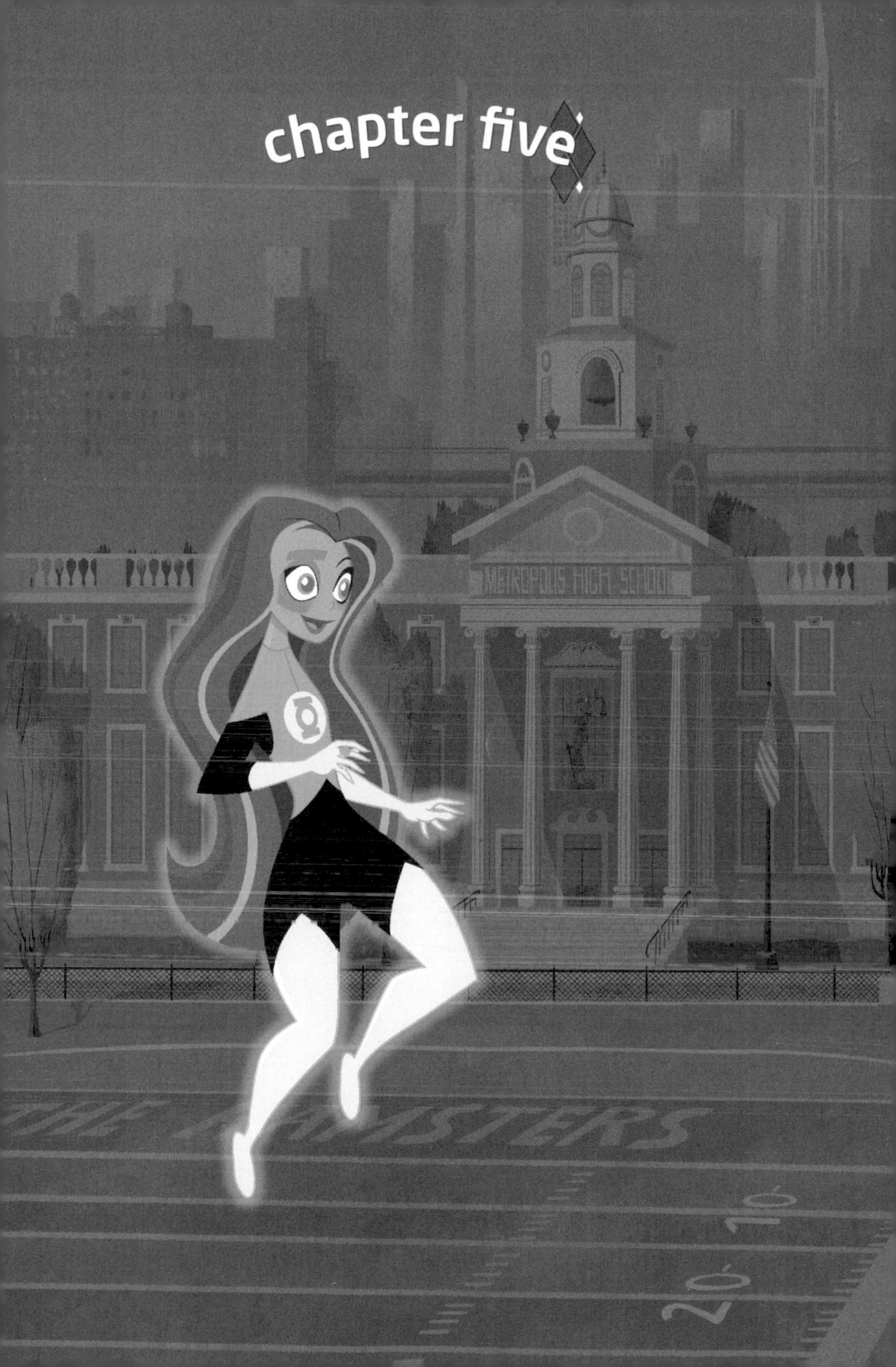
METROPOLIS HIGH SCHOOL

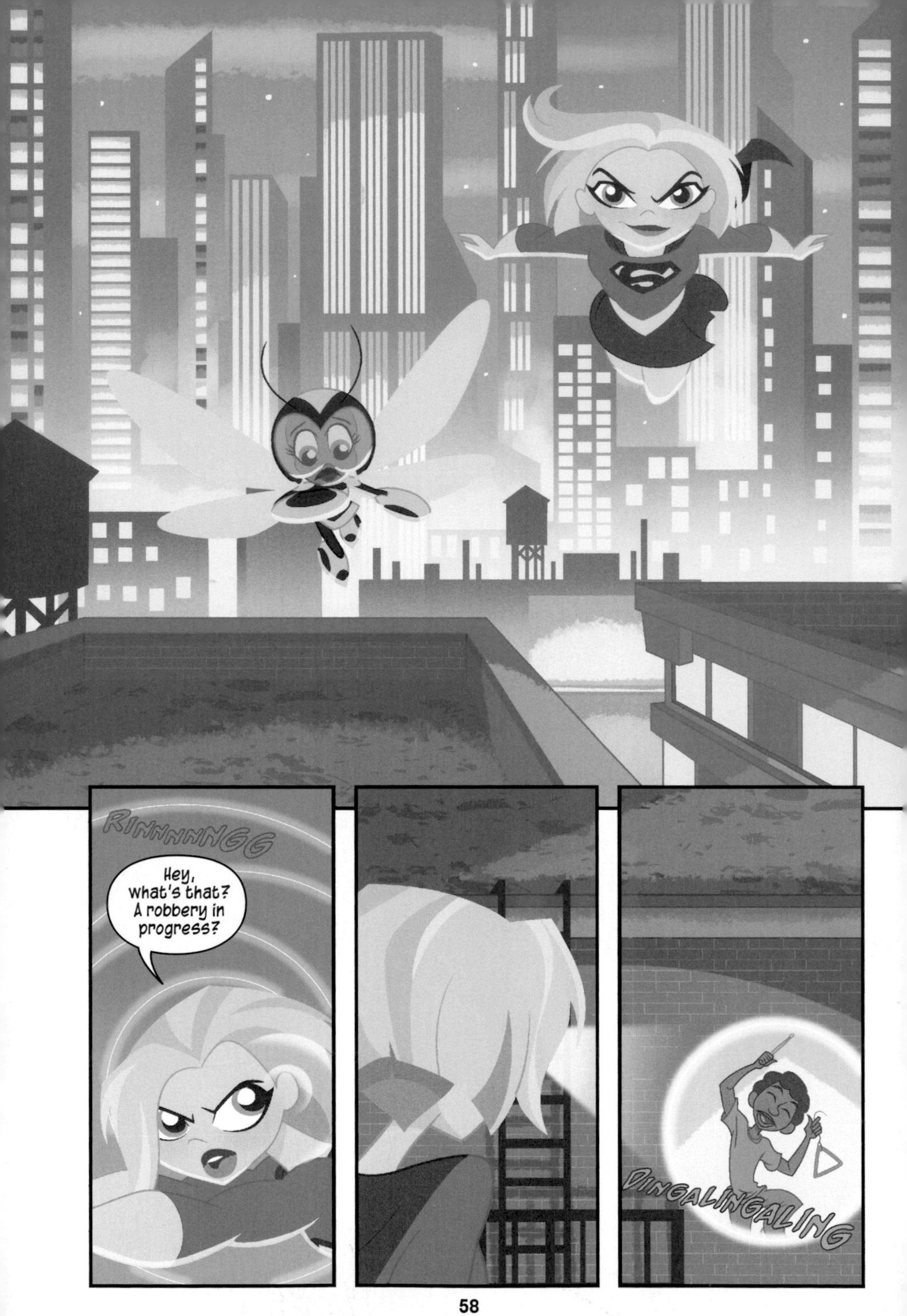
RINNNNNNGG
Hey, what's that? A robbery in progress?
DINGALINGALING

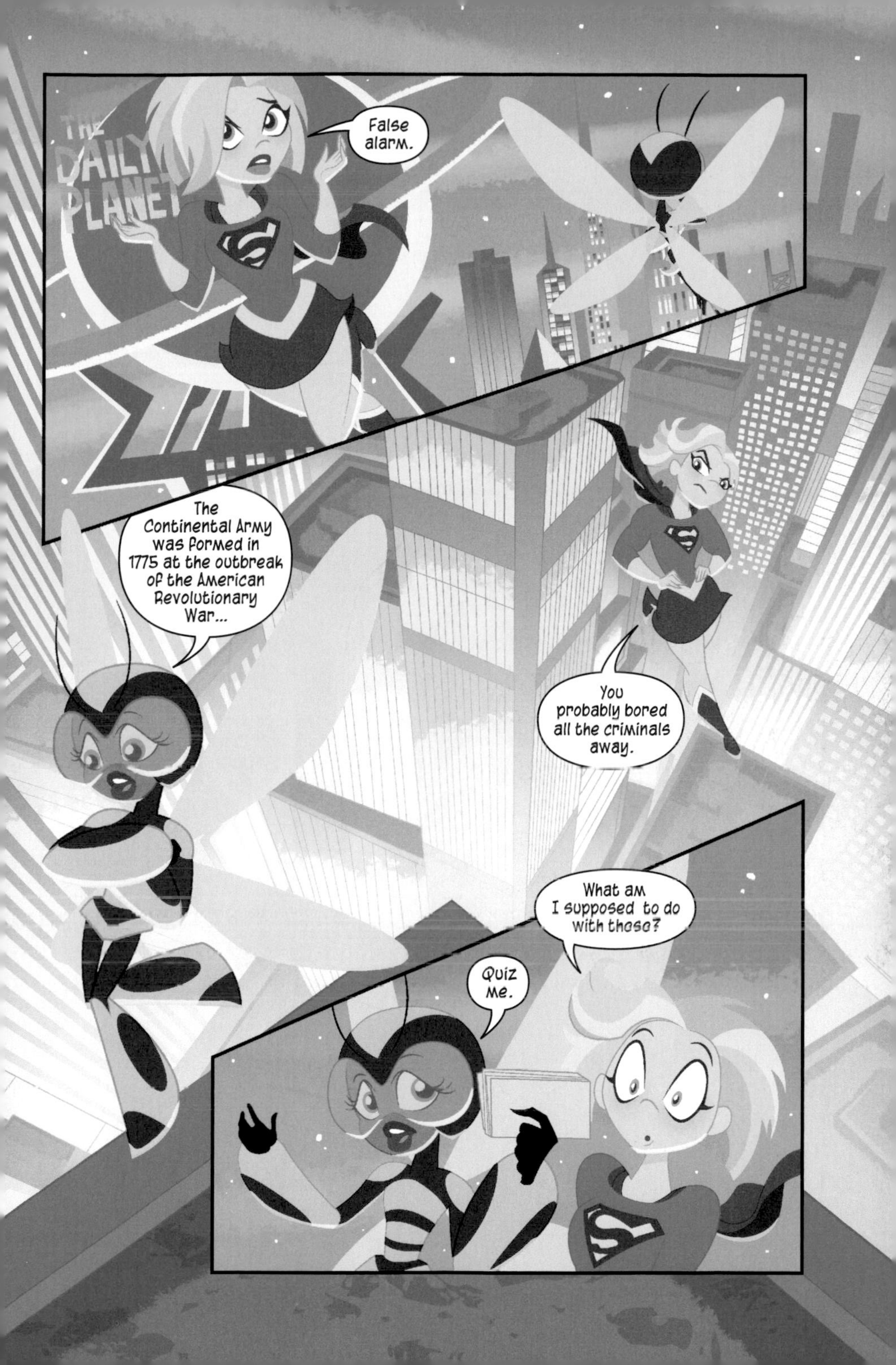
THE DAILY PLANET
False alarm.
The Continental Army was formed in 1775 at the outbreak of the American Revolutionary War...
You probably bored all the criminals away.
What am I supposed to do with those?
Quiz me.

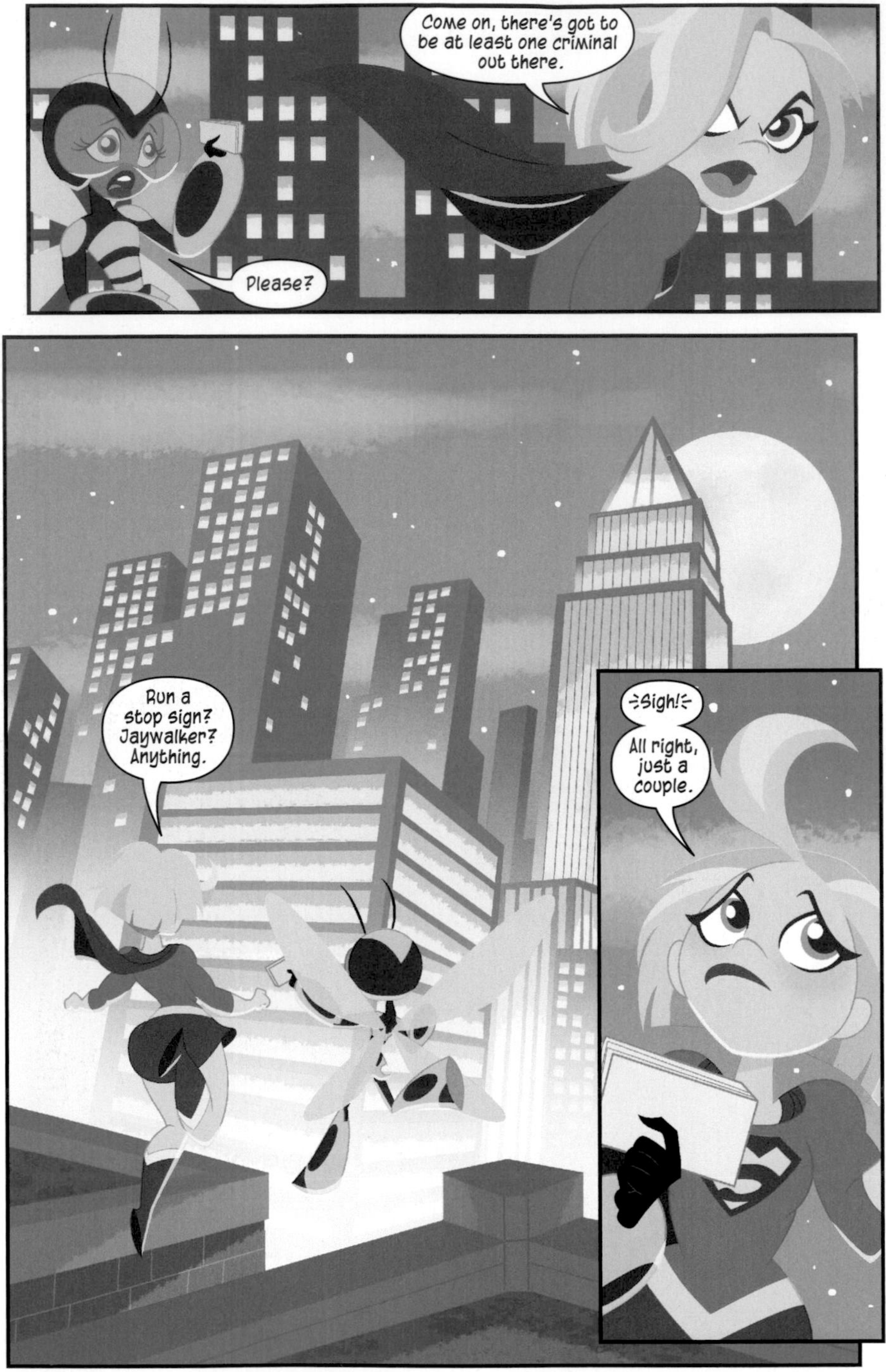
Come on, there's got to be at least one criminal out there.
Please?
Run a stop sign? Jaywalker? Anything.
Sigh!
All right, just a couple.

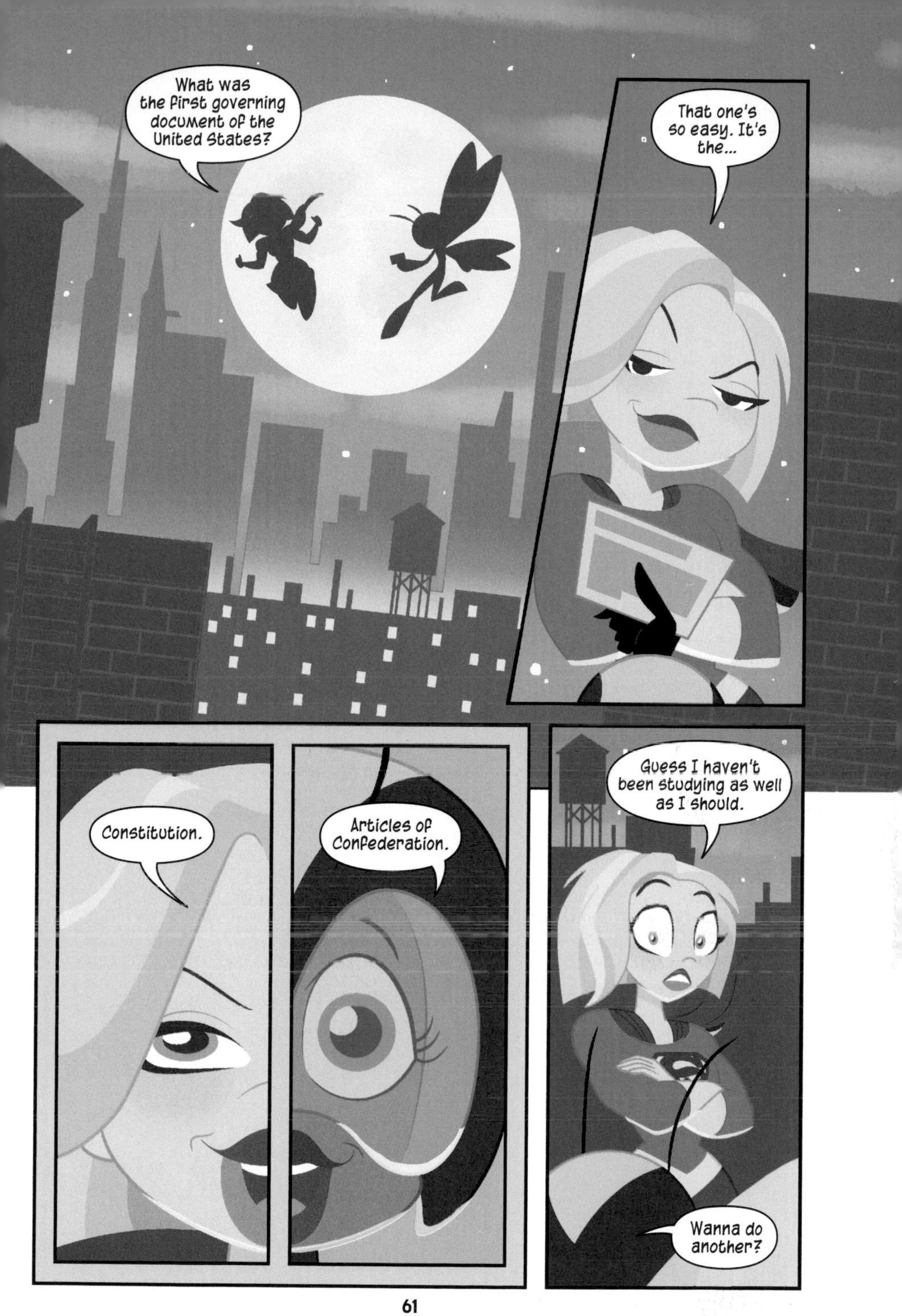
What was the first governing document of the United States?
That one's so easy. It's the...
Constitution.
Articles of Confederation.
Guess I haven't been studying as well as I should.
Wanna do another?

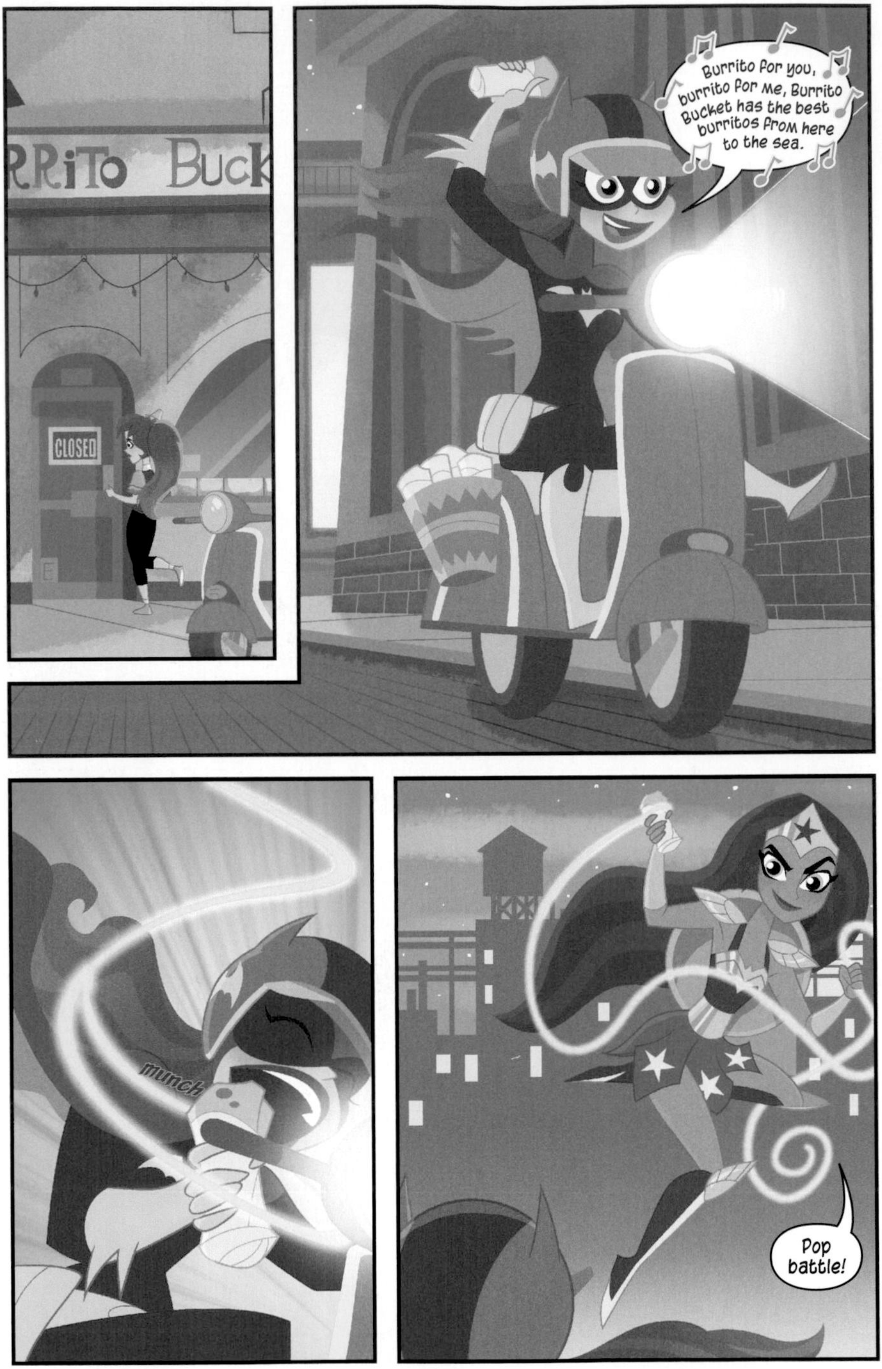
RRITO BUCK
CLOSED
Burrito for you, burrito for me, Burrito Bucket has the best burritos from here to the sea.
munch
Pop battle!

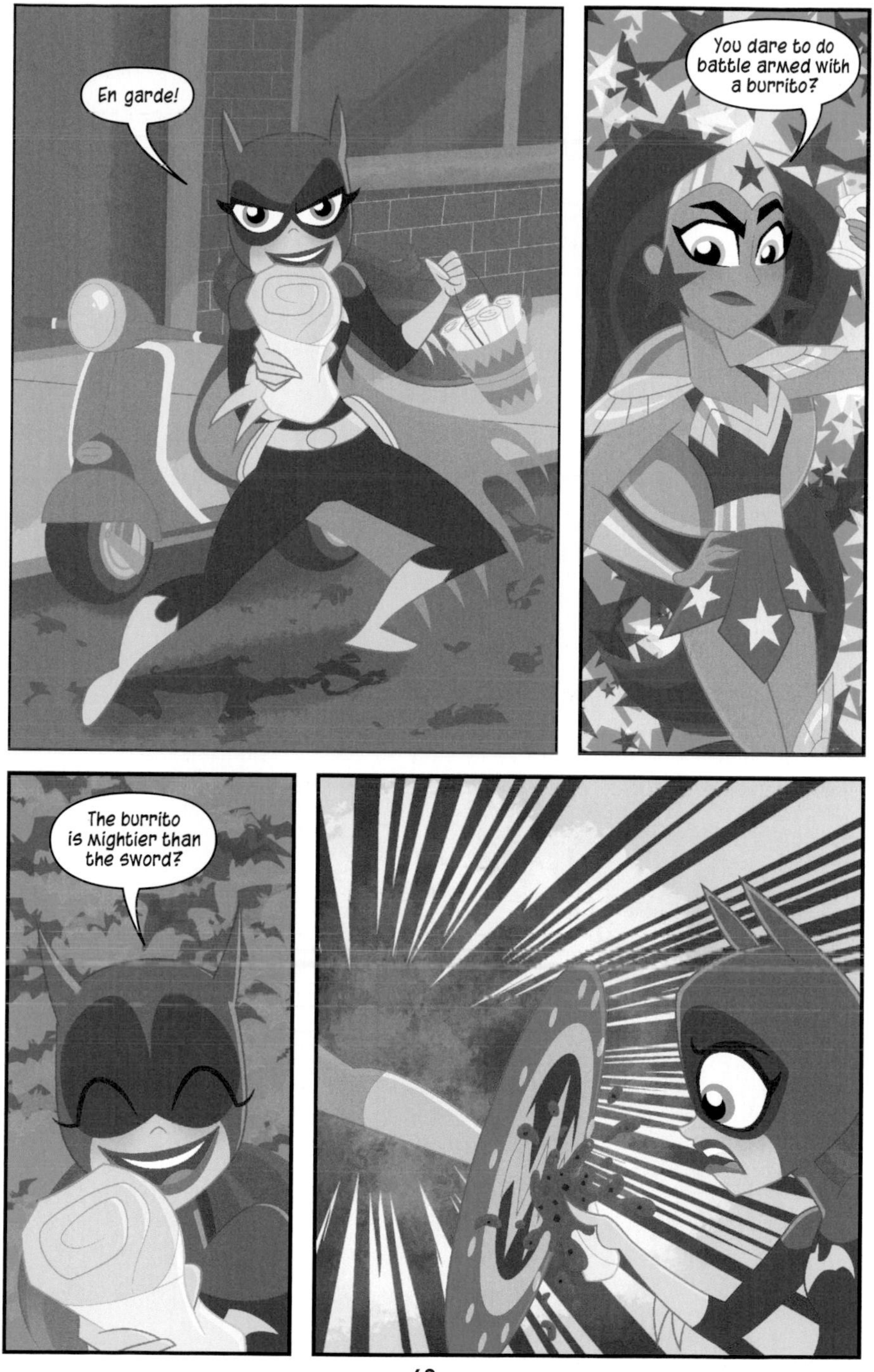
En garde!
You dare to do battle armed with a burrito?
The burrito is mightier than the sword?

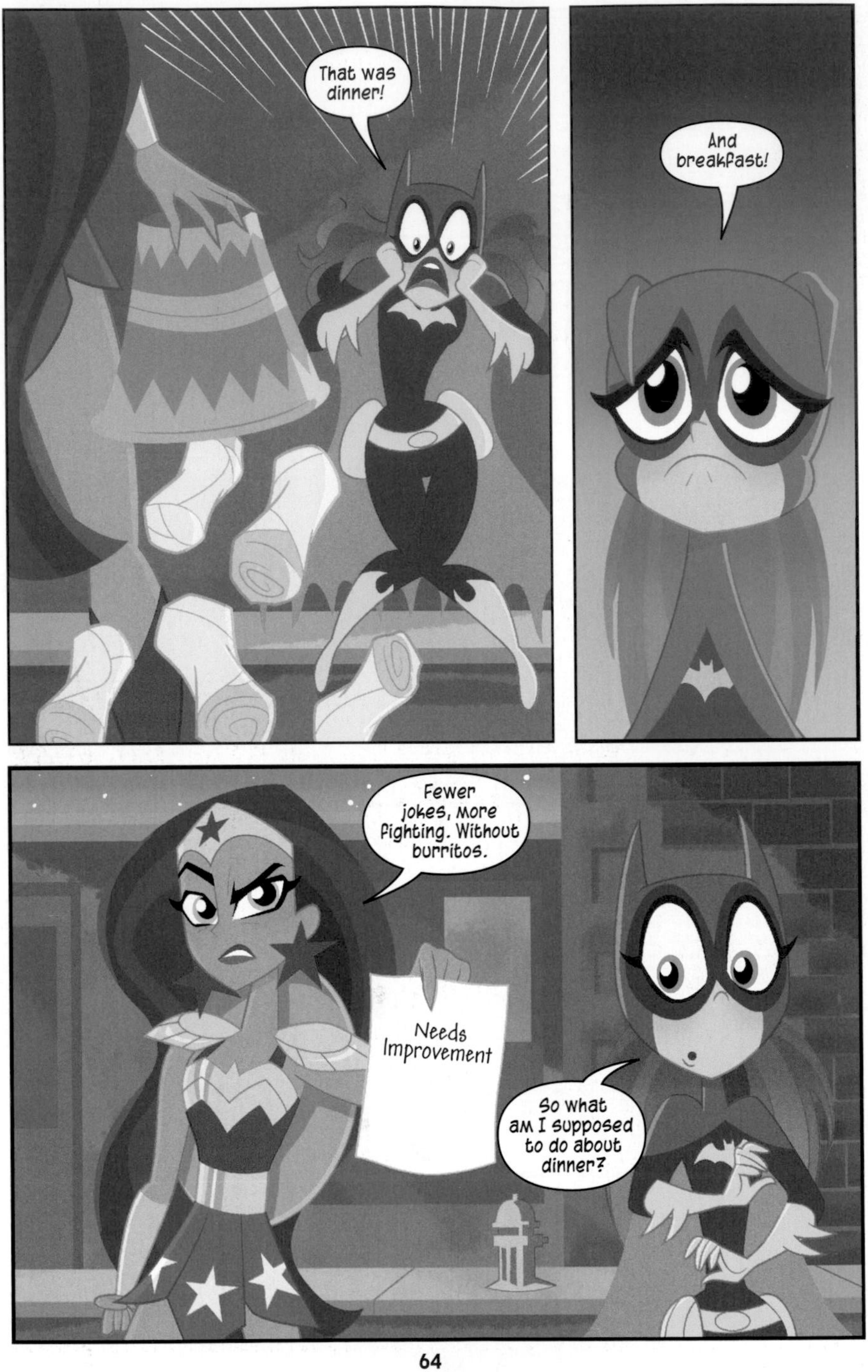
That was dinner!
And breakfast!
Fewer jokes, more fighting. Without burritos.
Needs Improvement
So what am I supposed to do about dinner?

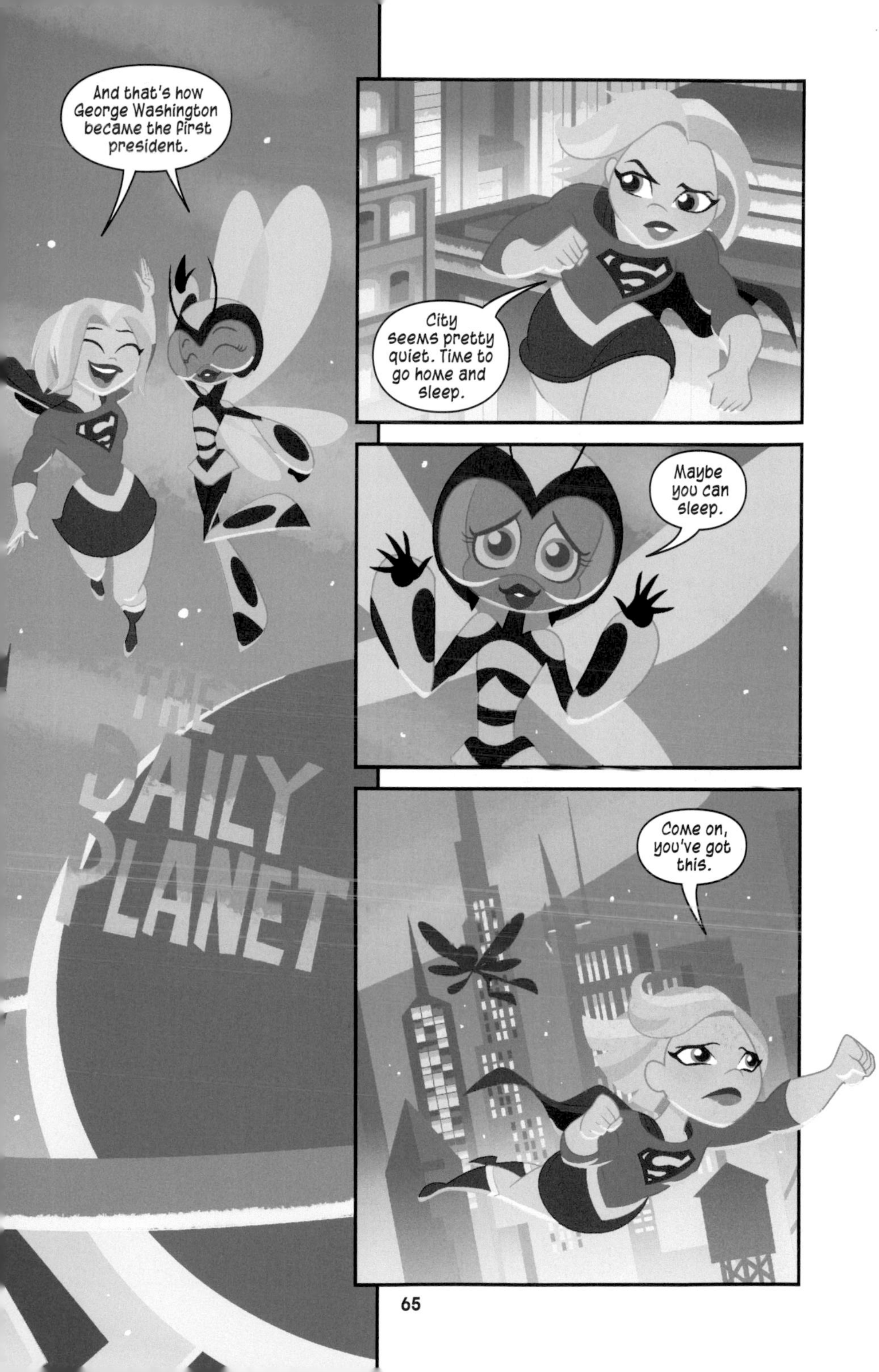
And that's how George Washington became the first president.
THE DAILY PLANET
City seems pretty quiet. Time to go home and sleep.
Maybe you can sleep.
Come on, you've got this.

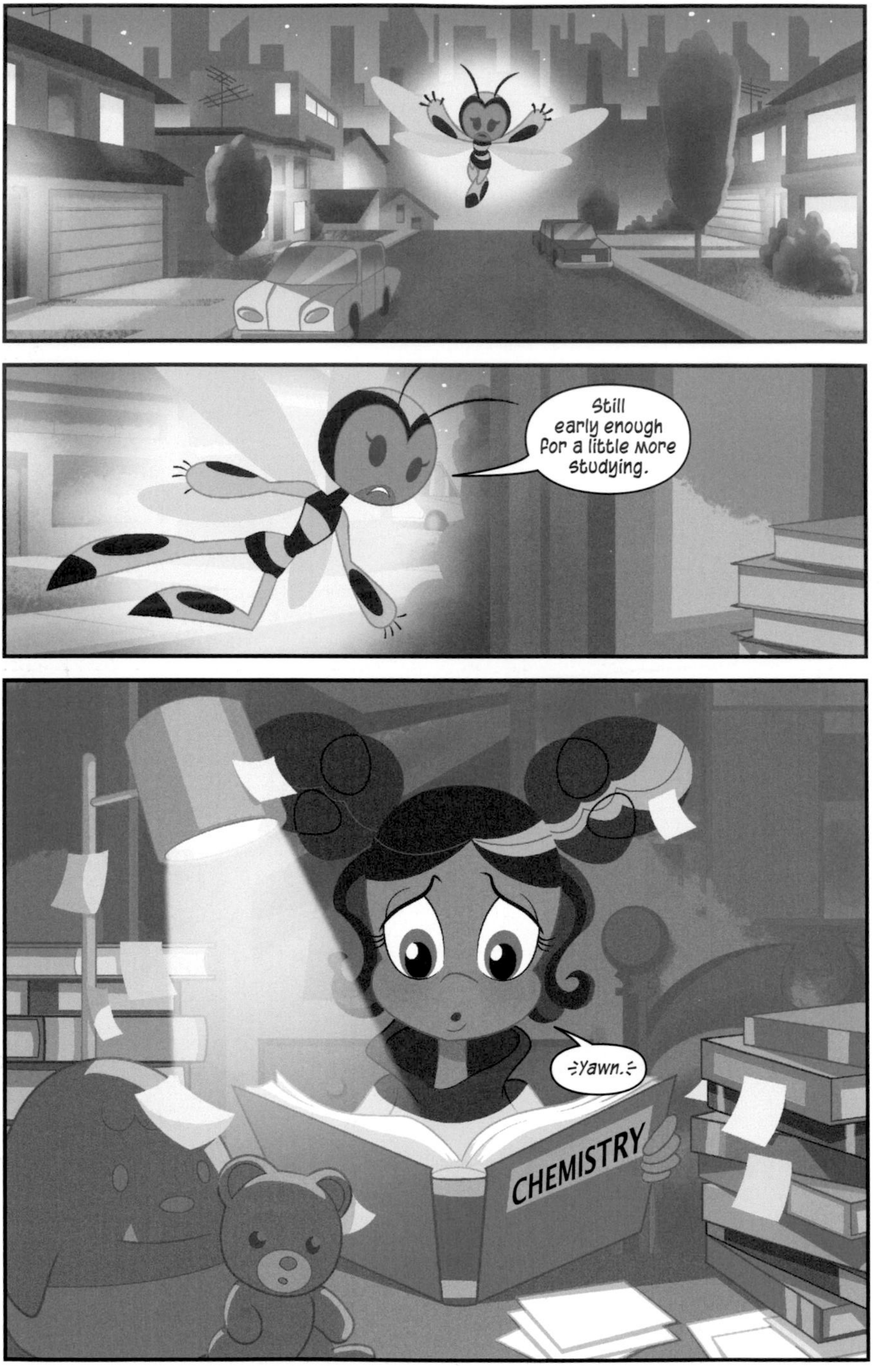
Still early enough for a little more studying.
Yawn.
CHEMISTRY

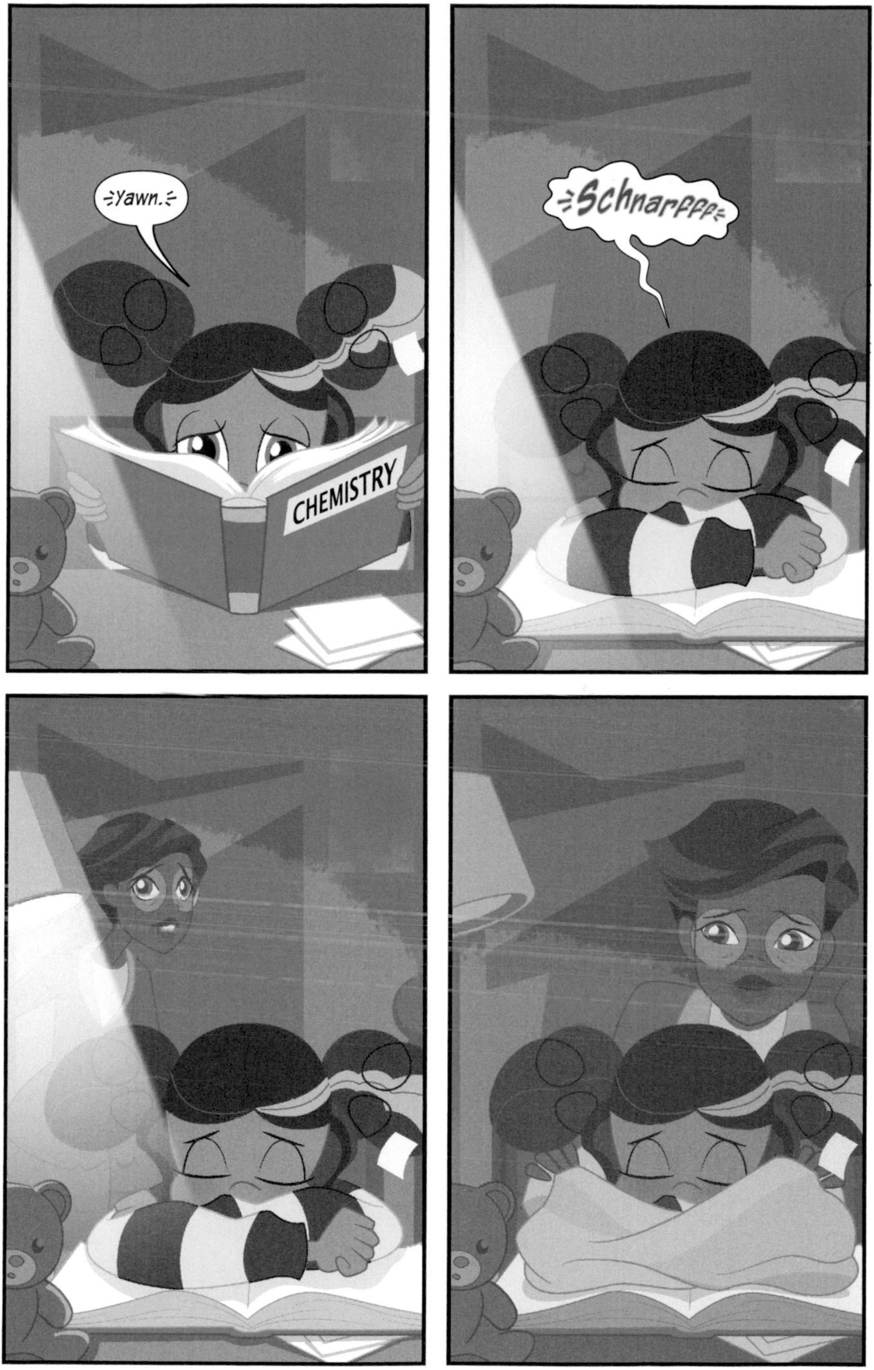
Yawn.
CHEMISTRY
Schnarfff

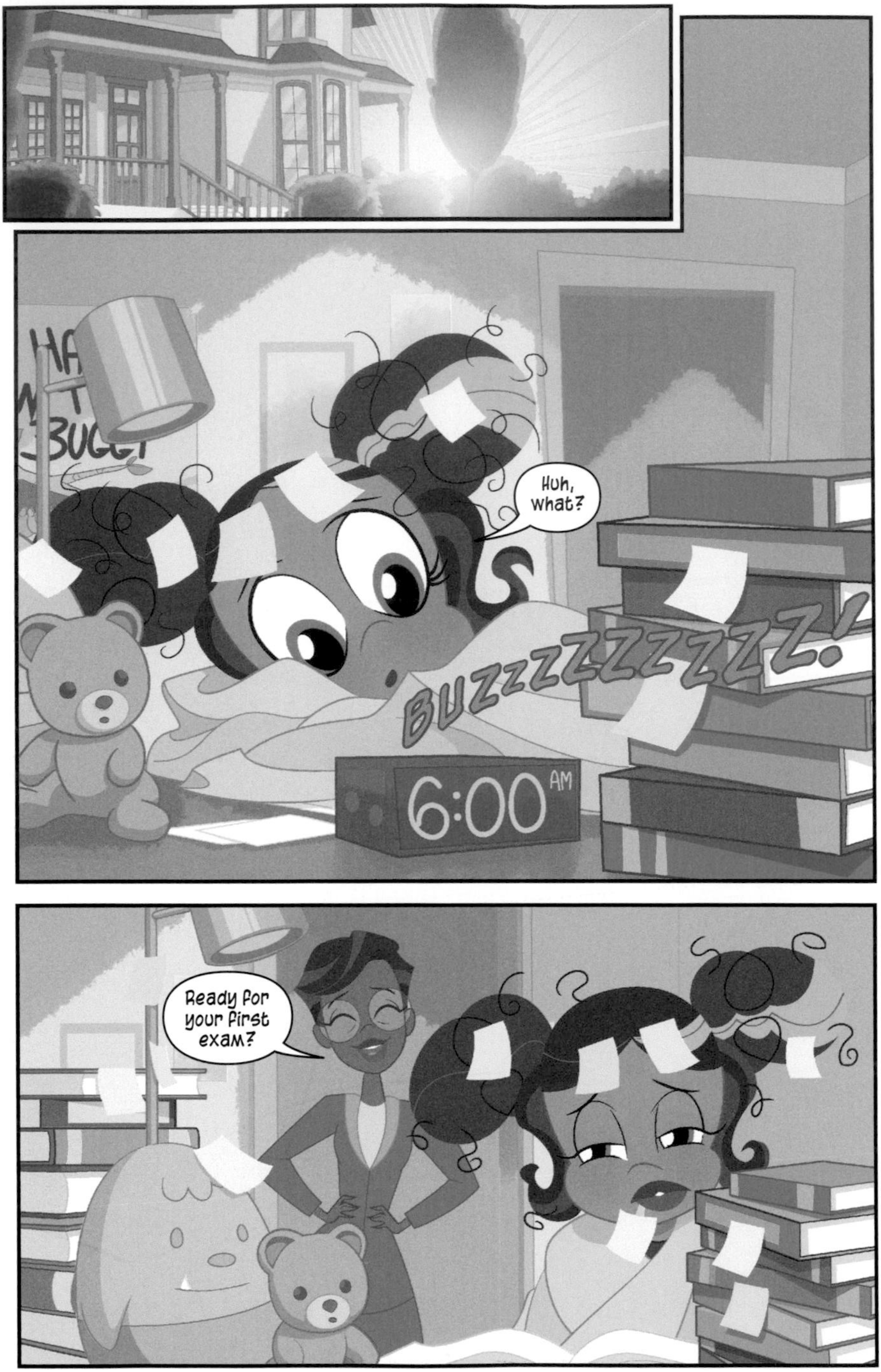
Huh, what?
BUZZZZZZZZZZ!
6:00 AM
Ready for your first exam?

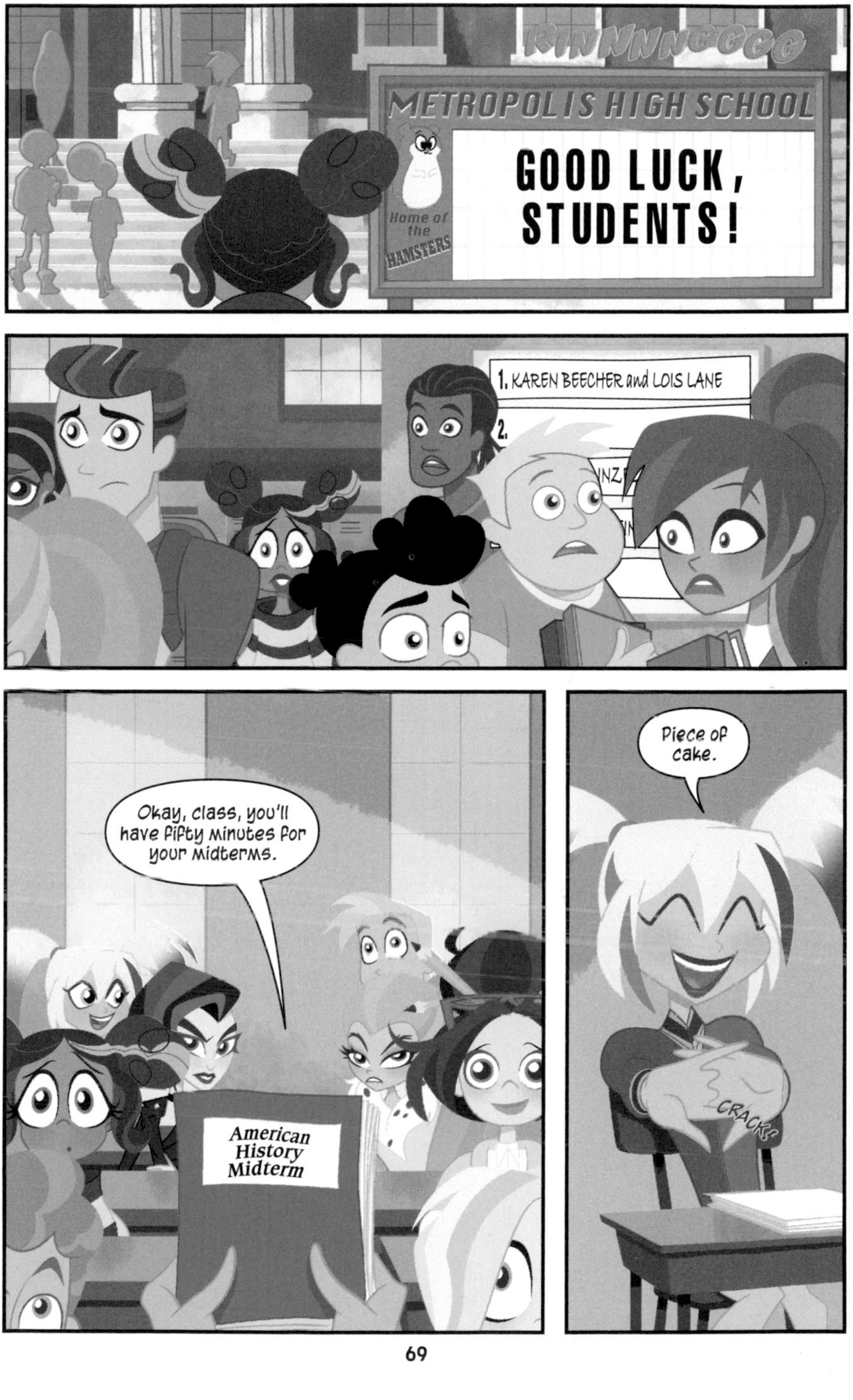
RINNNNGGGG
METROPOLIS HIGH SCHOOL
Home of the HAMSTERS
GOOD LUCK, STUDENTS!
1. KAREN BEECHER and LOIS LANE
2.
Okay, class, you'll have fifty minutes for your midterms.
American History Midterm
Piece of cake.
CRACK!

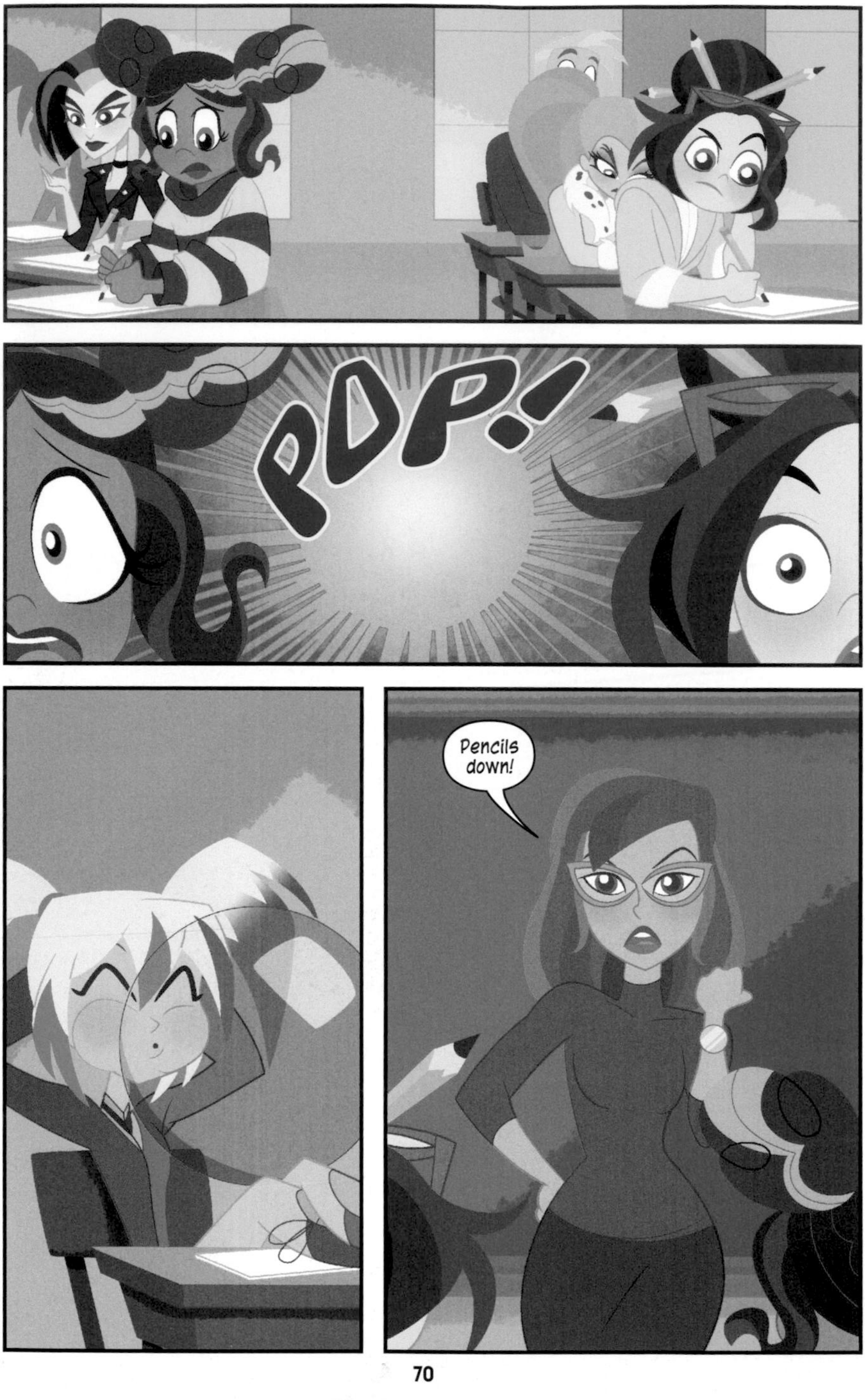
POP!
Pencils down!

# chapter six

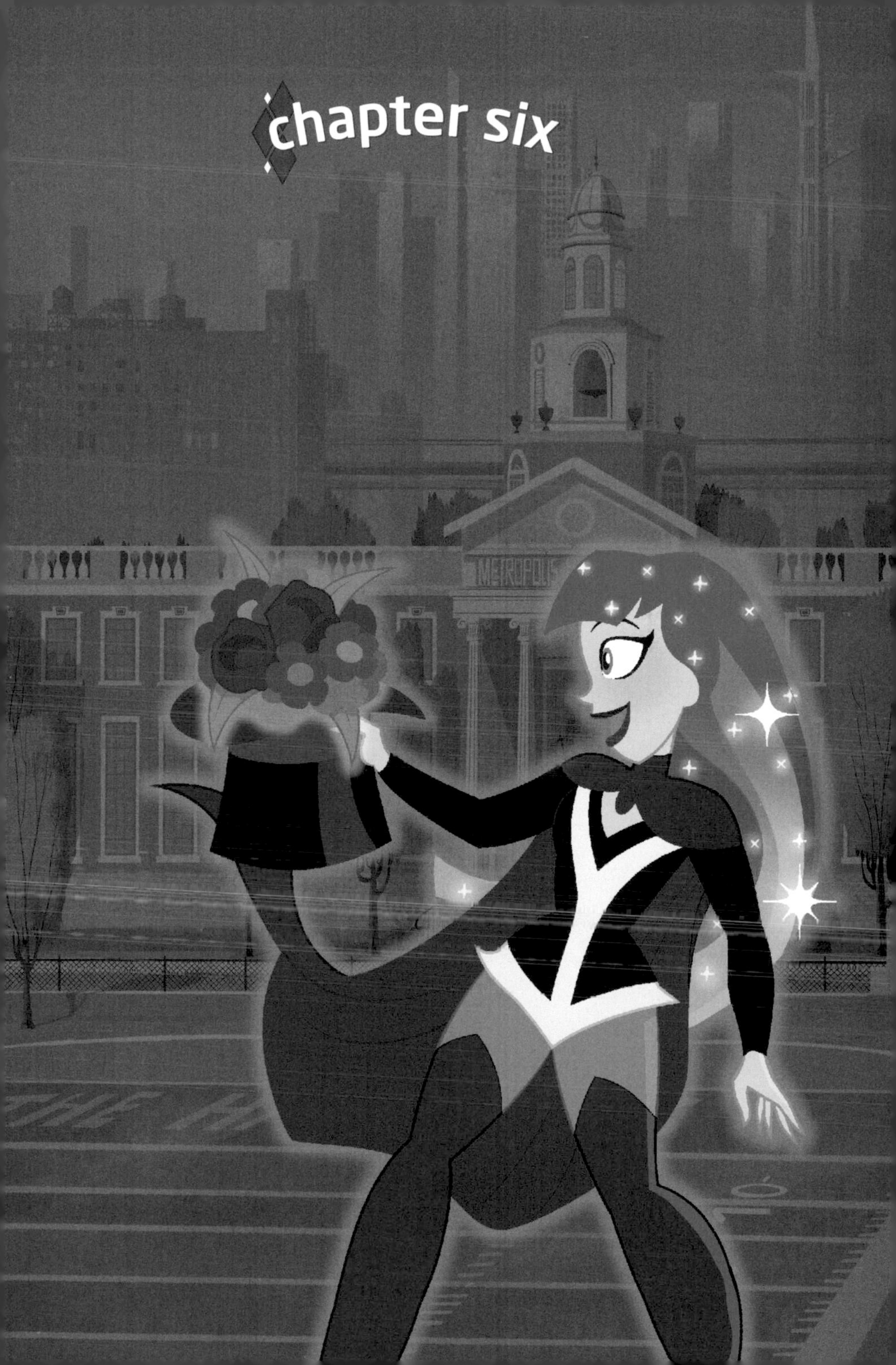

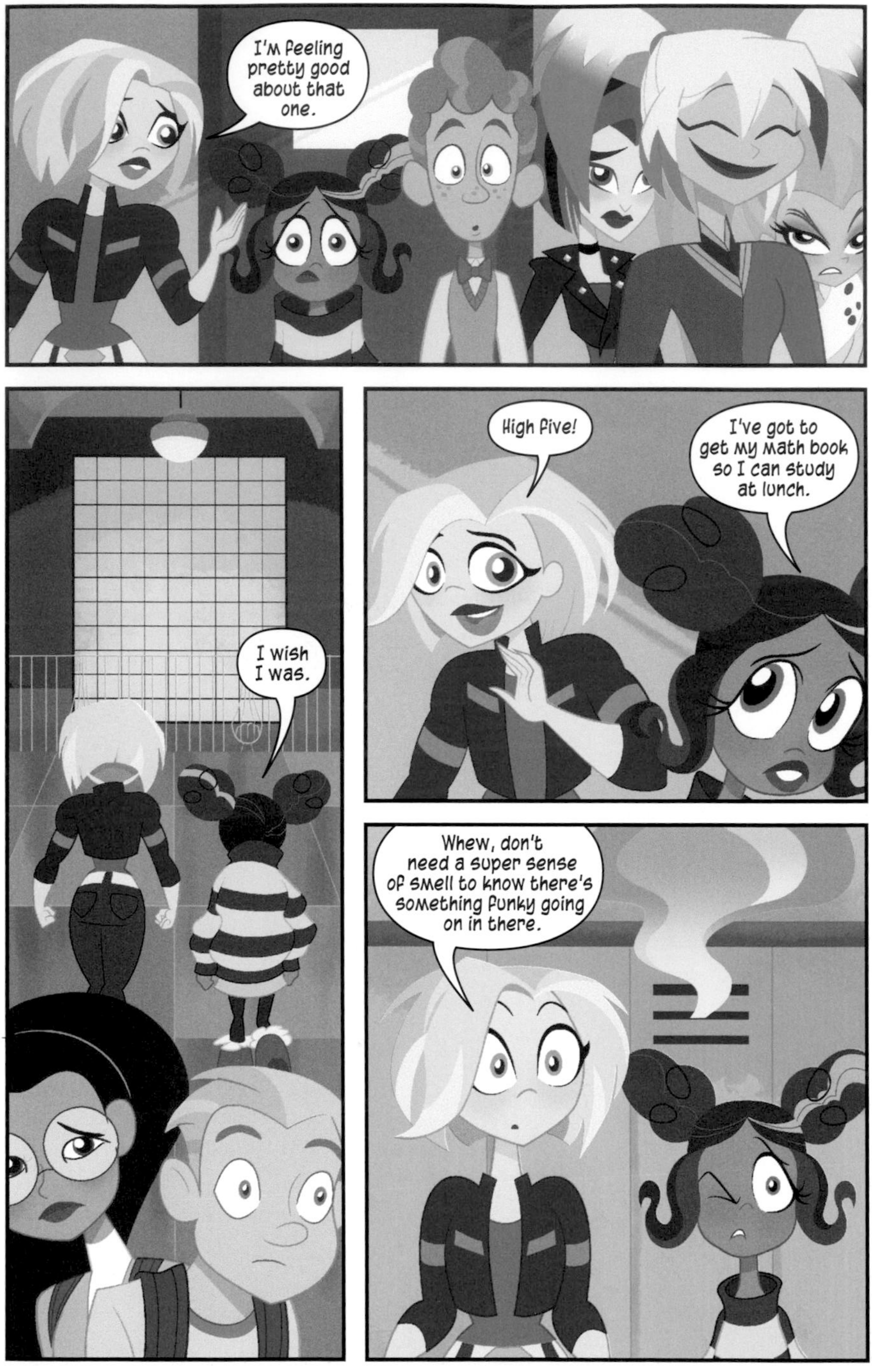
I'm feeling pretty good about that one.
I wish I was.
High five!
I've got to get my math book so I can study at lunch.
Whew, don't need a super sense of smell to know there's something funky going on in there.

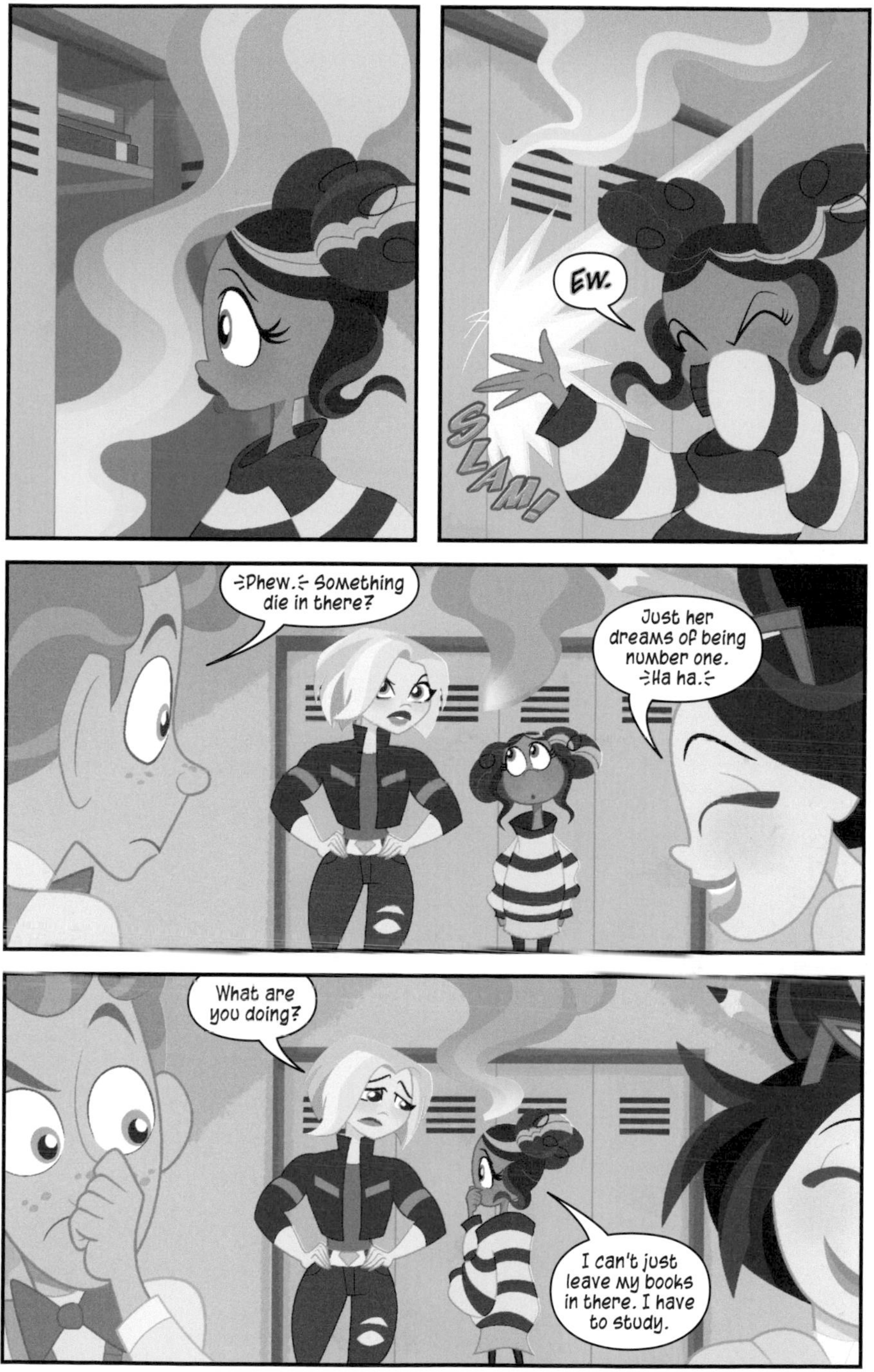
EW.
SLAM!
=Phew.= Something die in there?
Just her dreams of being number one. =Ha ha.=
What are you doing?
I can't just leave my books in there. I have to study.

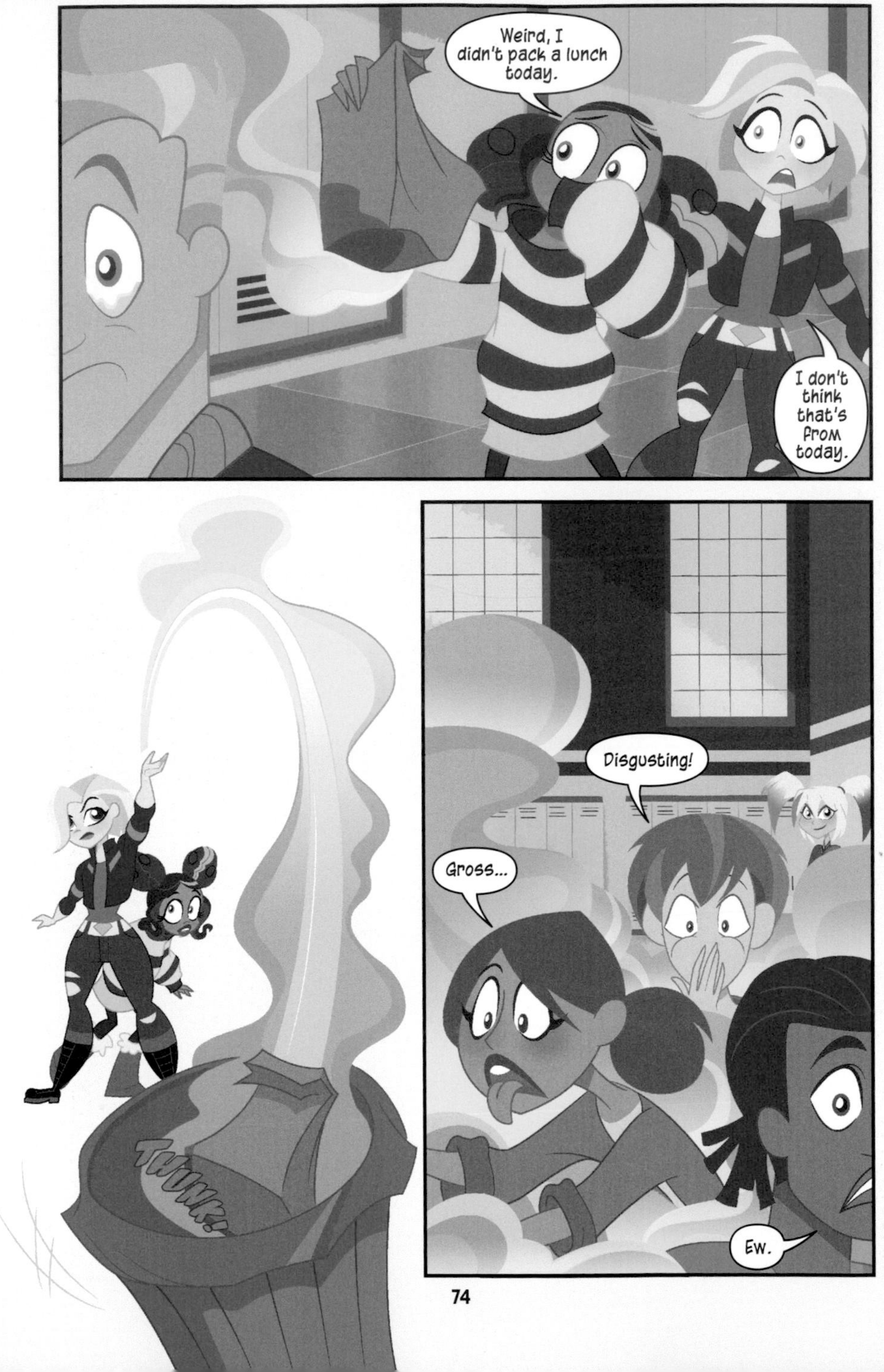
Weird, I didn't pack a lunch today.
I don't think that's from today.
THUNK!
Disgusting!
Gross...
Ew.

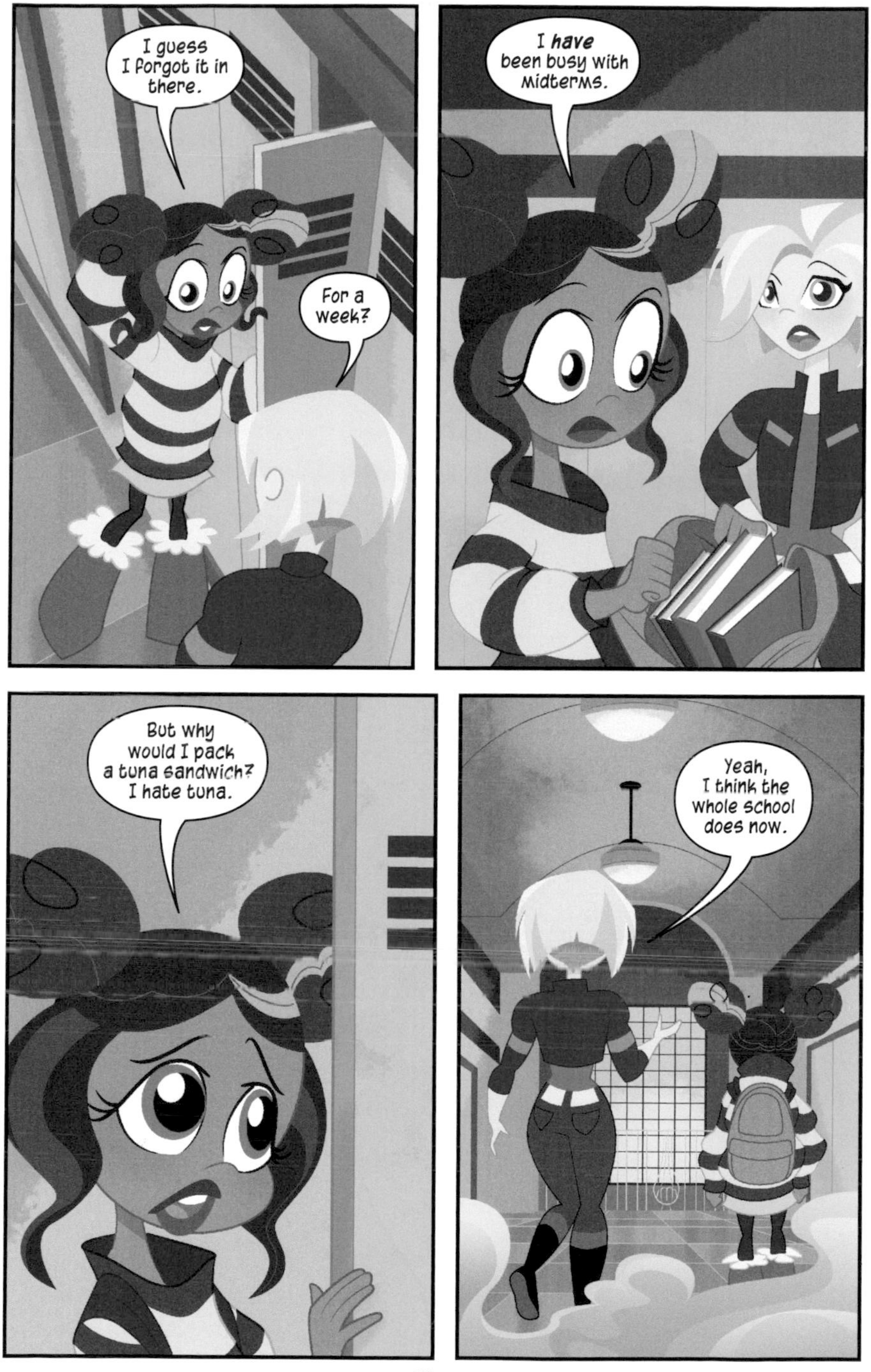
I guess I forgot it in there.
For a week?
I *have* been busy with midterms.
But why would I pack a tuna sandwich? I hate tuna.
Yeah, I think the whole school does now.

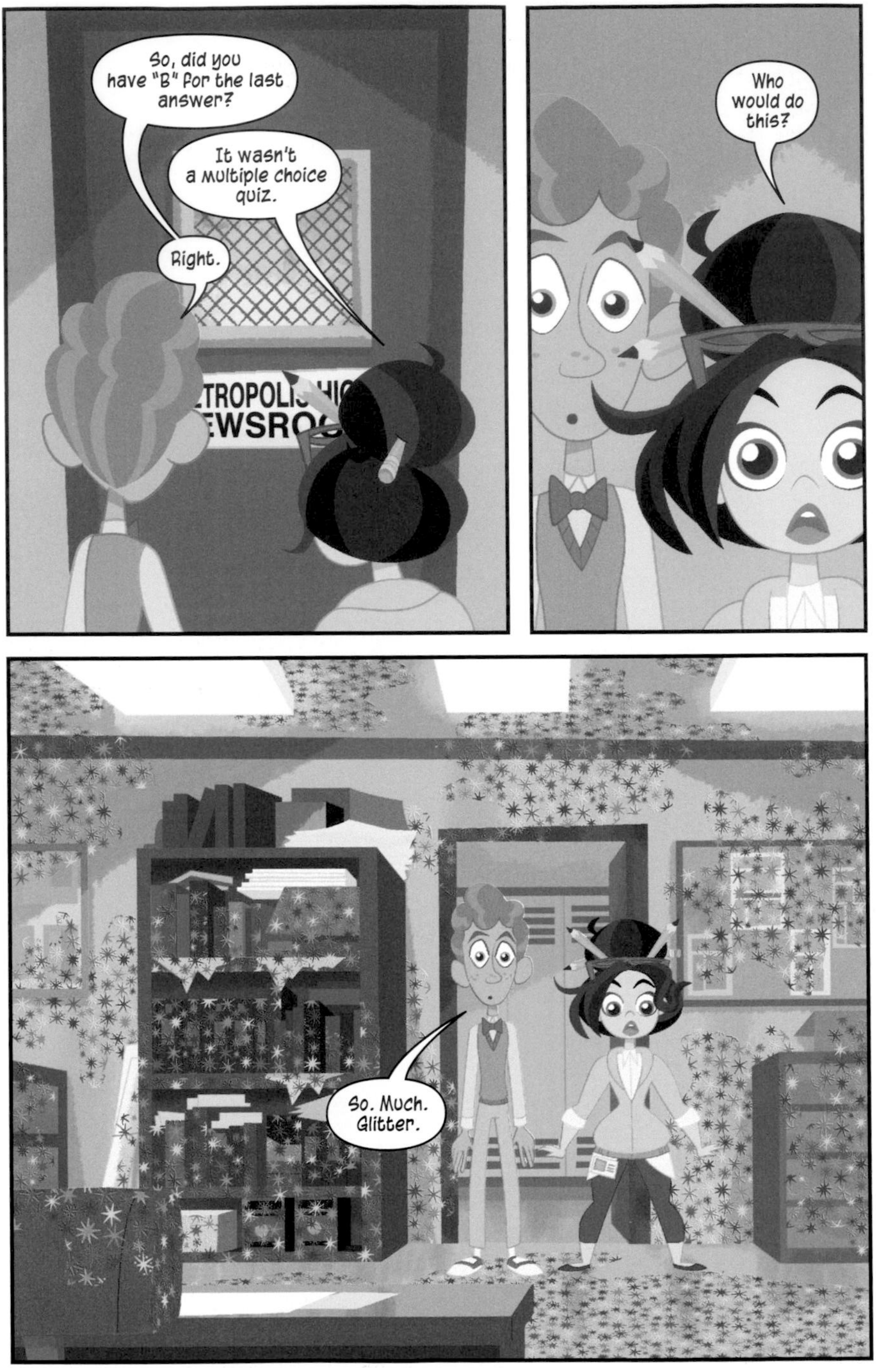
So, did you have "B" for the last answer?
It wasn't a multiple choice quiz.
Right.
Who would do this?
So. Much. Glitter.

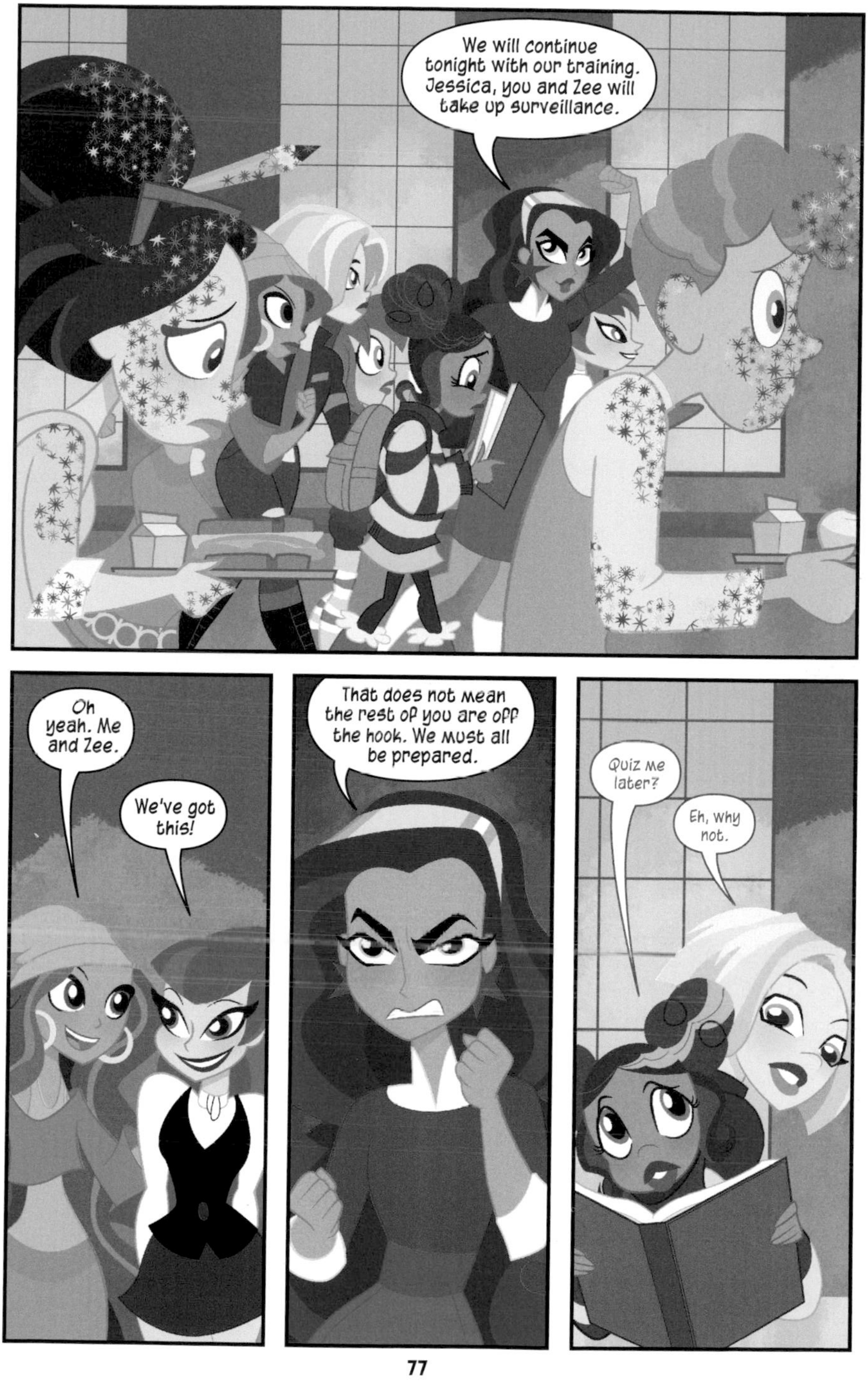
We will continue tonight with our training. Jessica, you and Zee will take up surveillance.
Oh yeah. Me and Zee.
We've got this!
That does not mean the rest of you are off the hook. We must all be prepared.
Quiz me later?
Eh, why not.

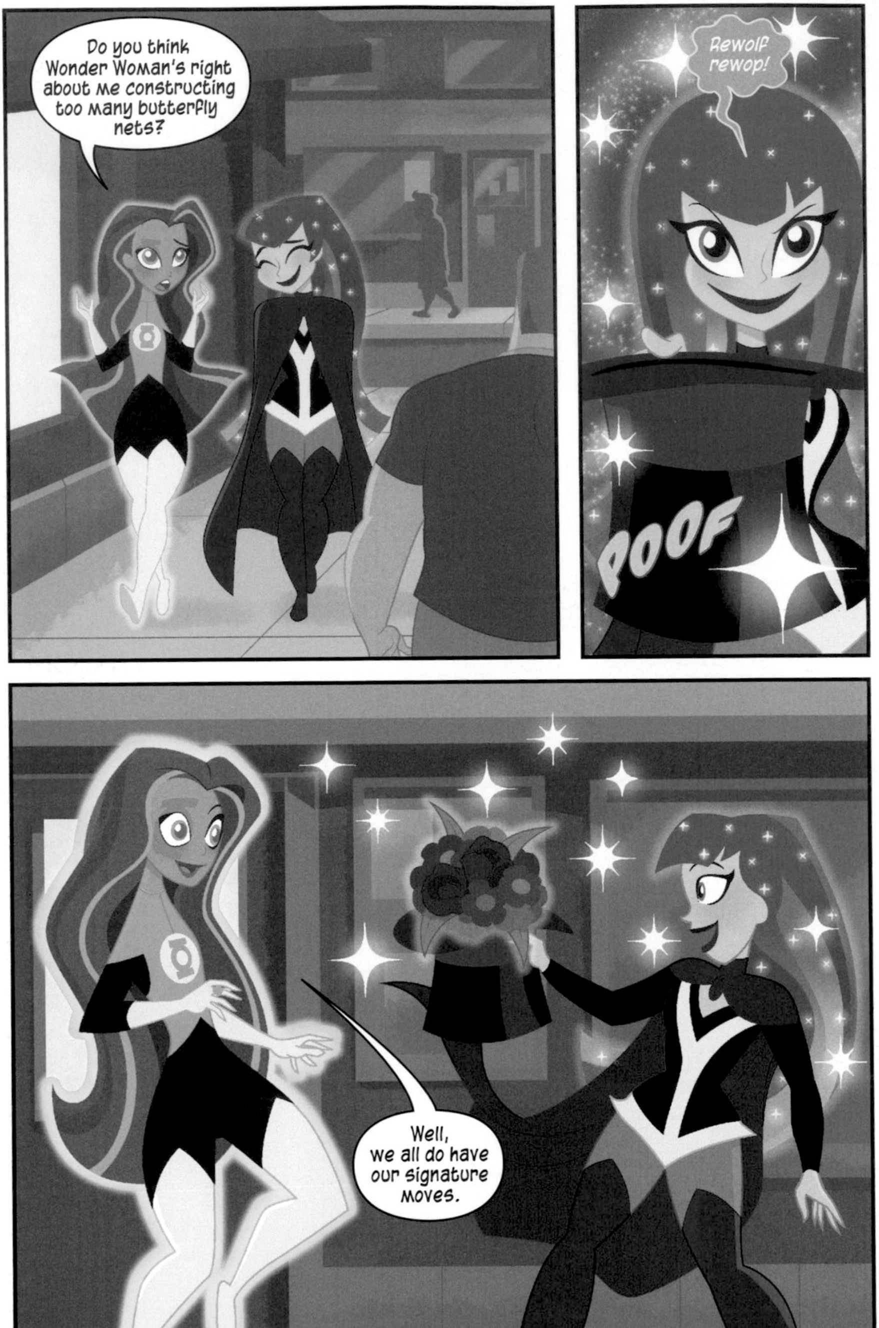
Do you think Wonder Woman's right about me constructing too many butterfly nets?
Rewolf rewop!
POOF
Well, we all do have our signature moves.

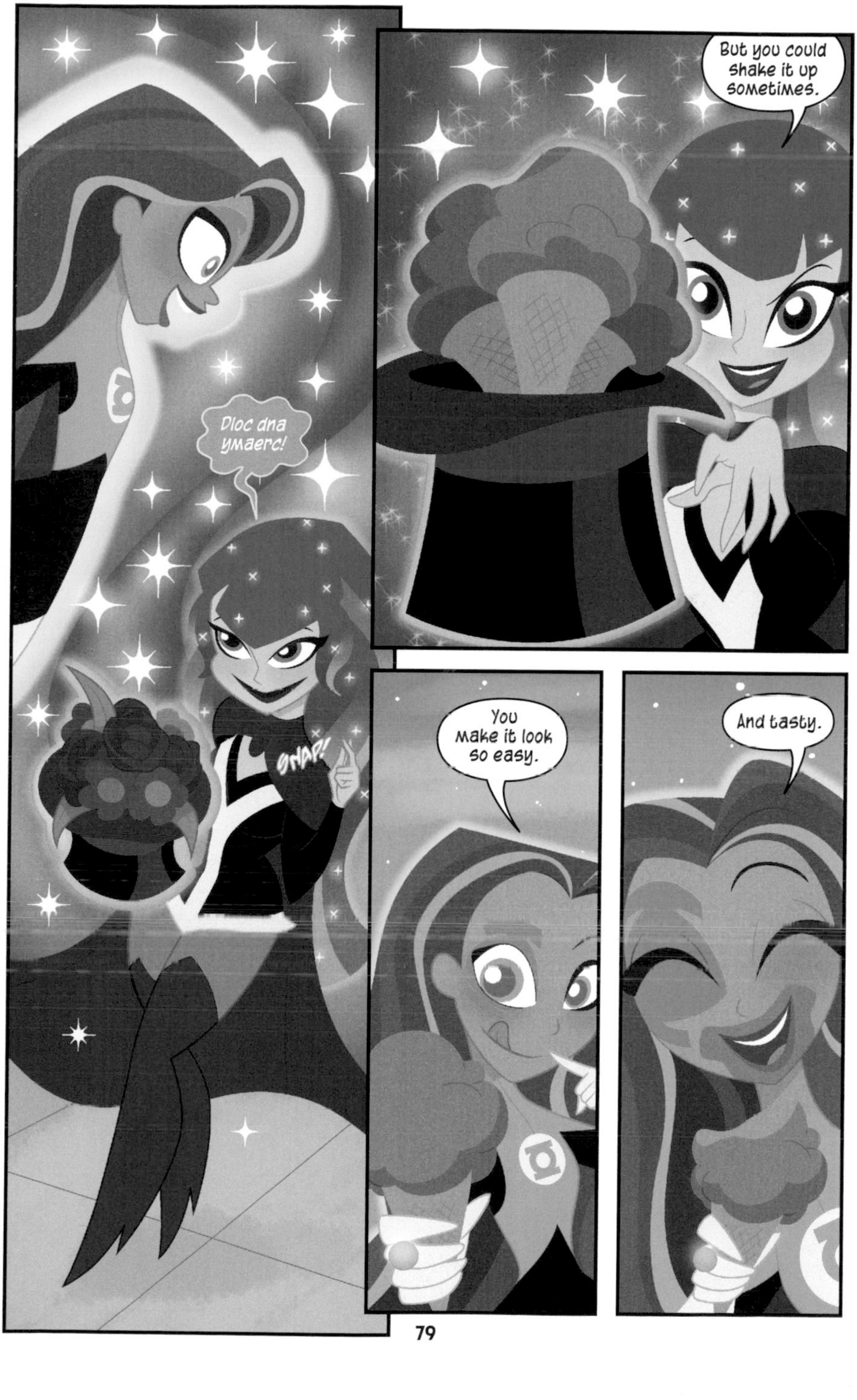
Dloc dna
ymaerc!
SNAP!
But you could
shake it up
sometimes.
You
make it look
so easy.
And tasty.

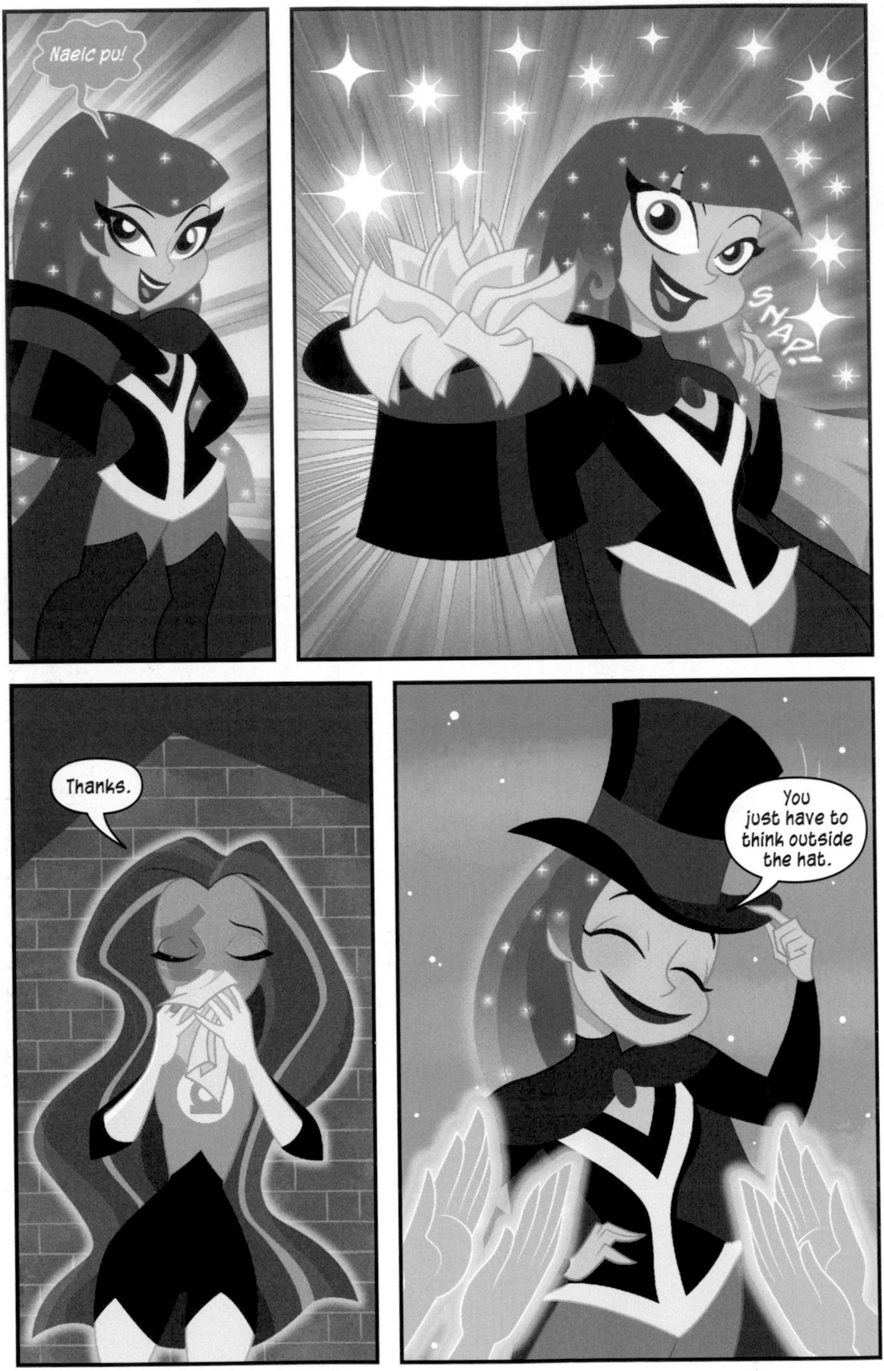
Naelc pu!
SNAP!
Thanks.
You just have to think outside the hat.

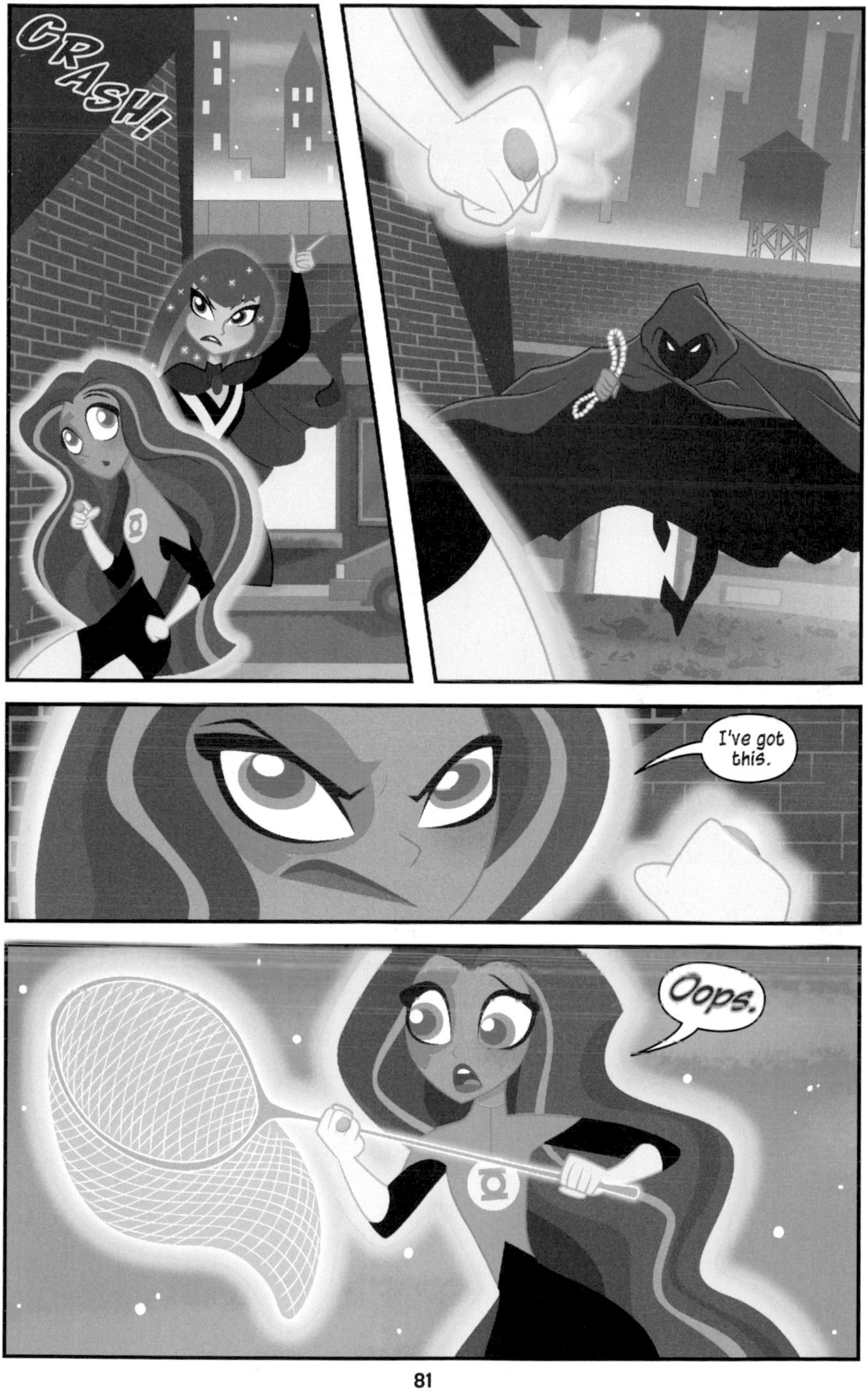
CRASH!
I've got this.
Oops.

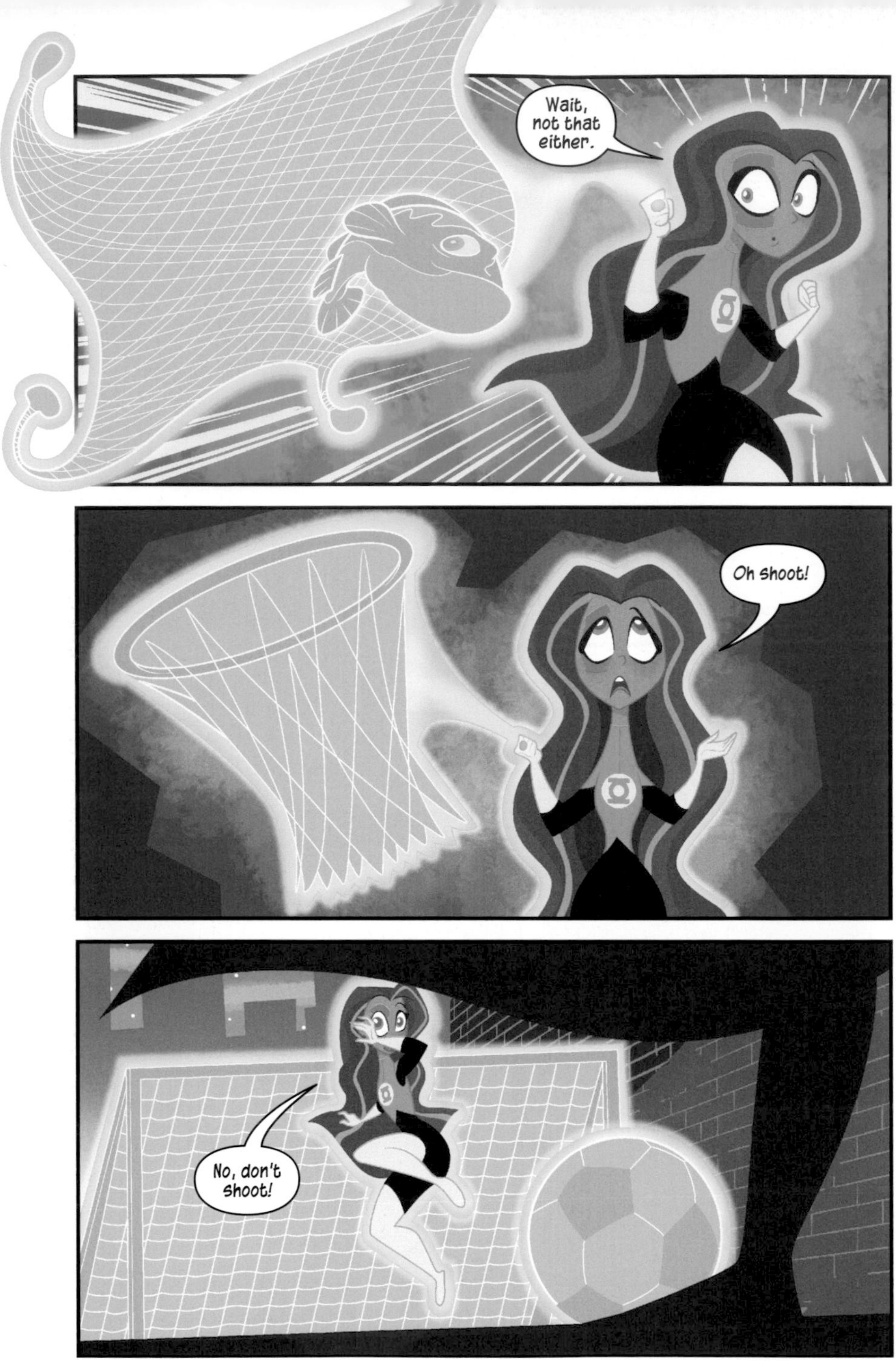
Wait, not that either.
Oh shoot!
No, don't shoot!

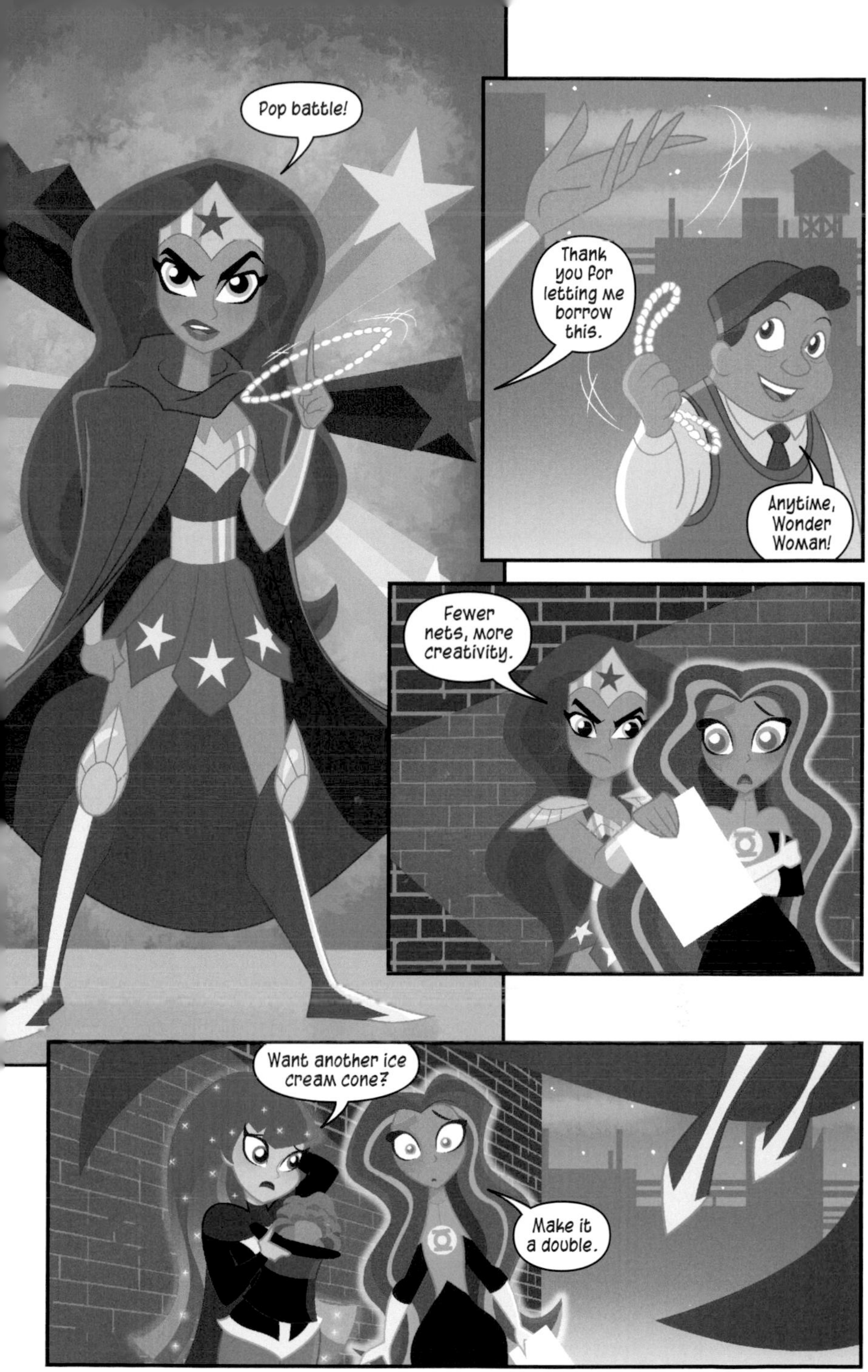
Pop battle!
Thank you for letting me borrow this.
Anytime, Wonder Woman!
Fewer nets, more creativity.
Want another ice cream cone?
Make it a double.

# chapter seven

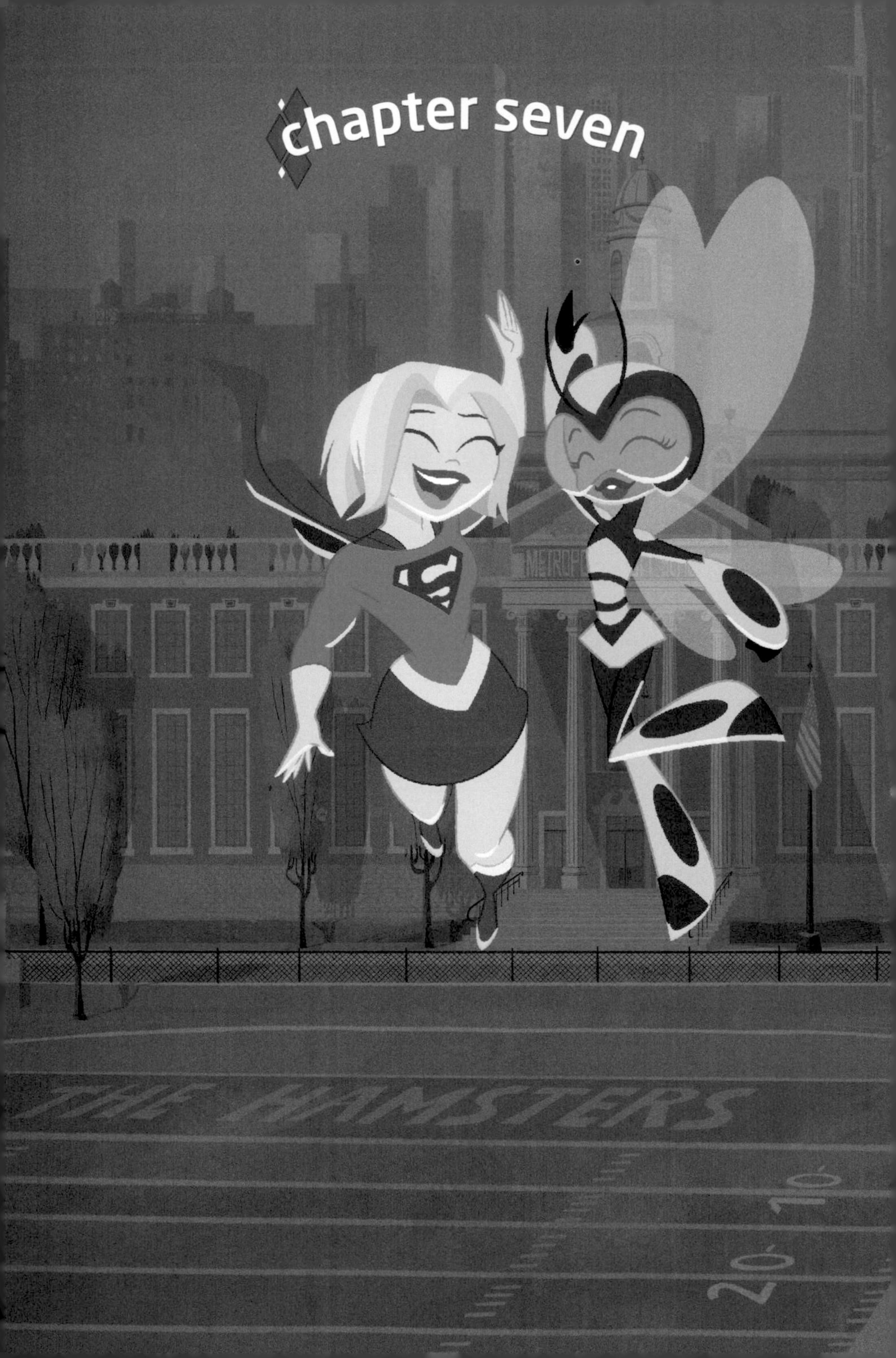
THE HAMSTERS

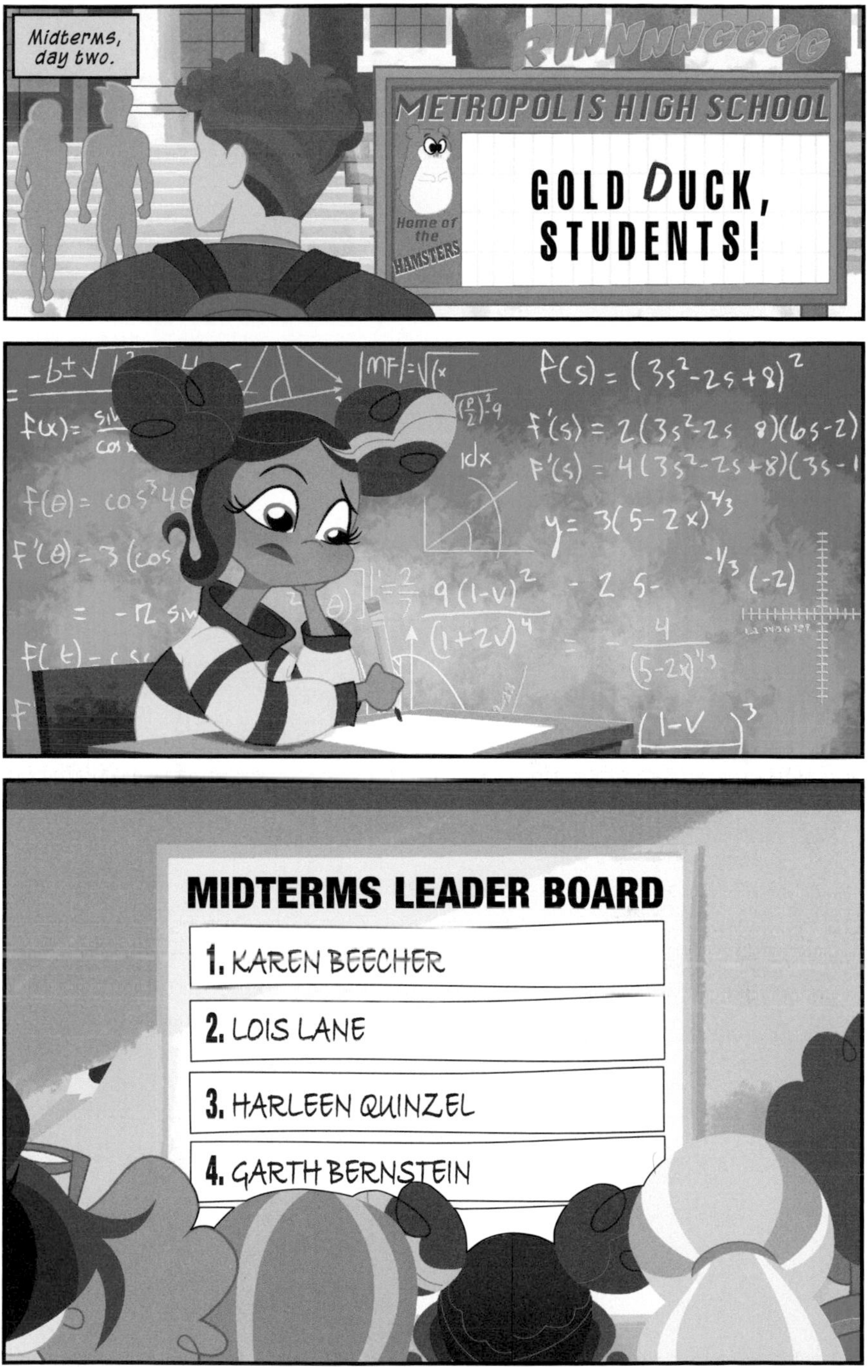
Midterms, day two.
RINNNNGGGG
METROPOLIS HIGH SCHOOL
Home of the HAMSTERS
GOLD DUCK, STUDENTS!
MIDTERMS LEADER BOARD
1. KAREN BEECHER
2. LOIS LANE
3. HARLEEN QUINZEL
4. GARTH BERNSTEIN

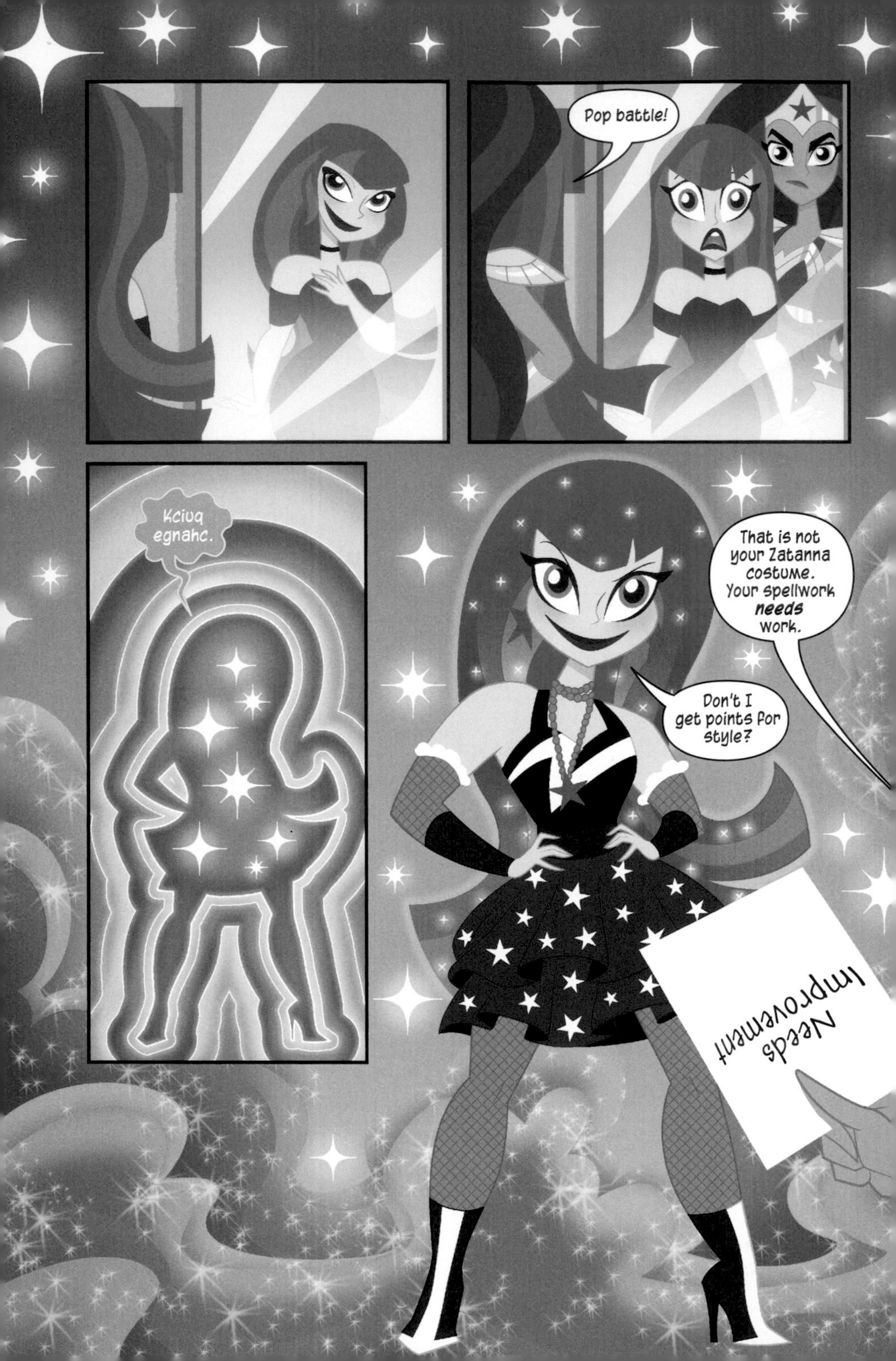
Pop battle!
Kciuq egnahc.
That is not your Zatanna costume. Your spellwork *needs* work.
Don't I get points for style?
Needs Improvement

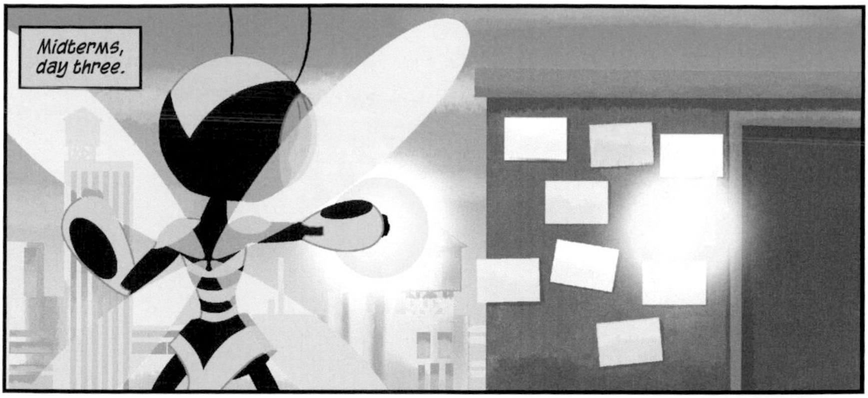
Midterms, day three.

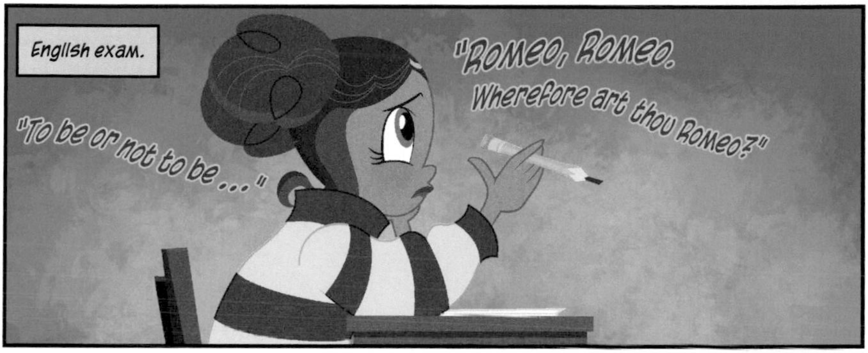
English exam.
"To be or not to be . . ."
"Romeo, Romeo. Wherefore art thou Romeo?"

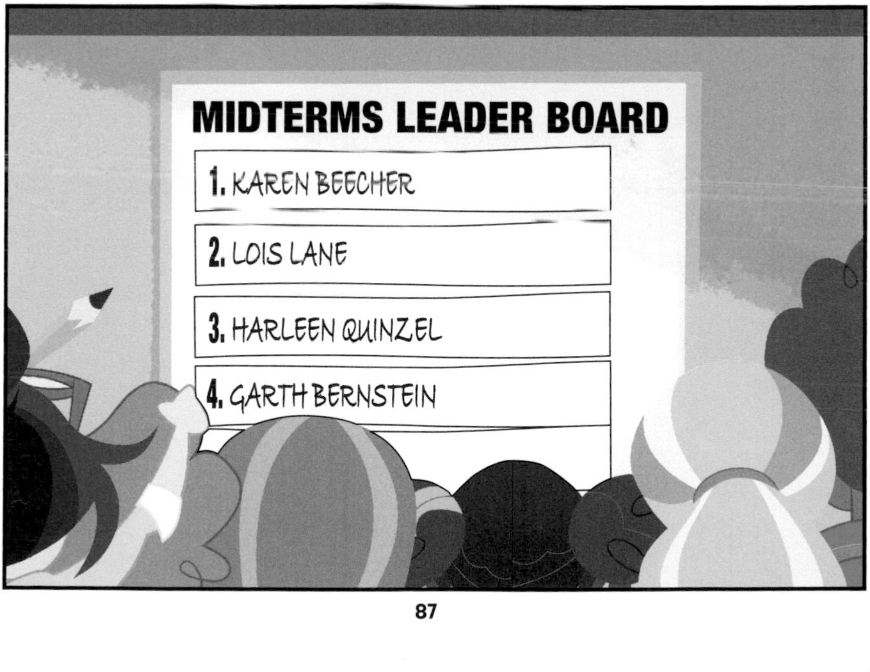
MIDTERMS LEADER BOARD
1. KAREN BEECHER
2. LOIS LANE
3. HARLEEN QUINZEL
4. GARTH BERNSTEIN

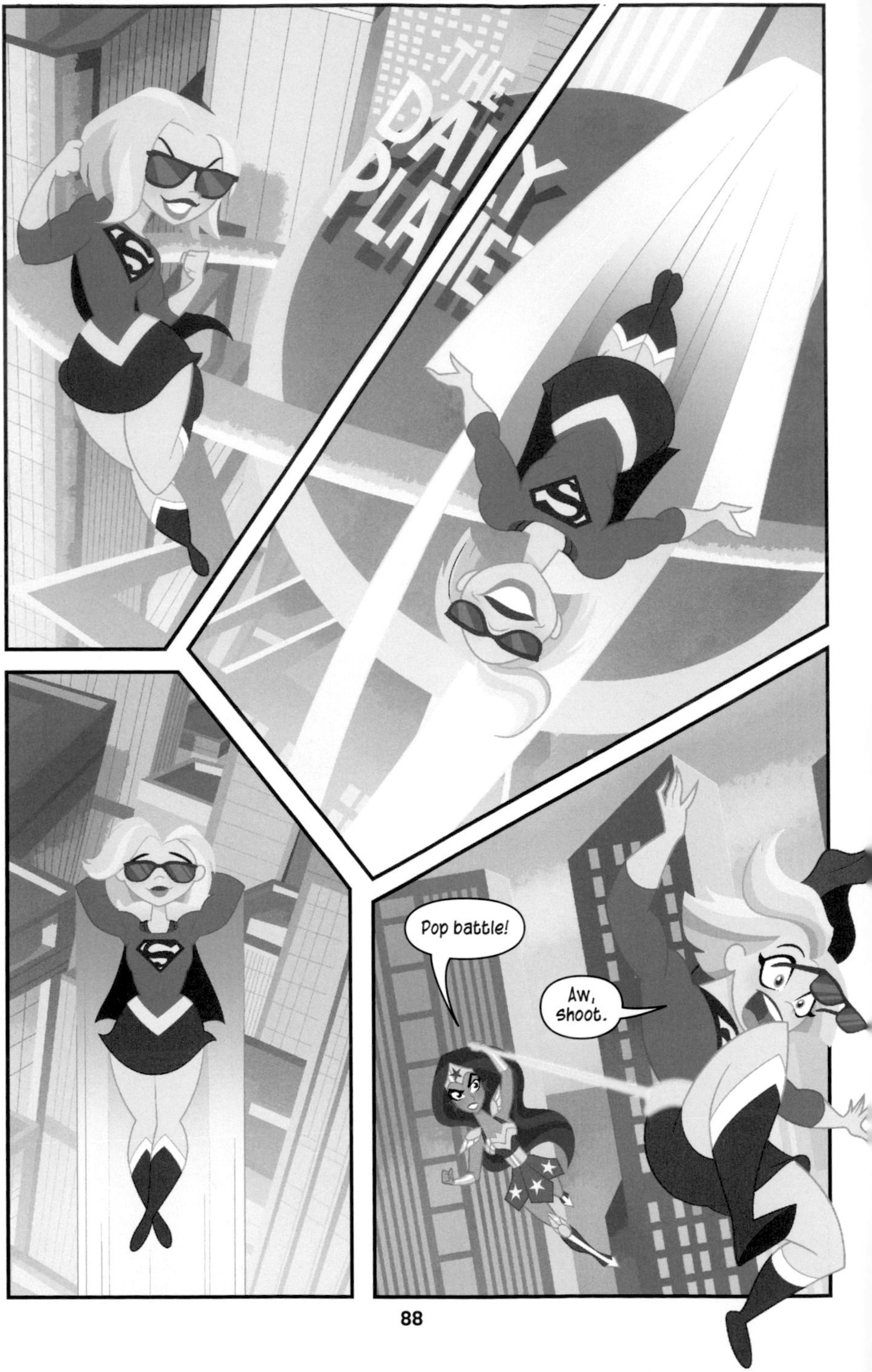
THE DAILY PLANET
Pop battle!
Aw, shoot.

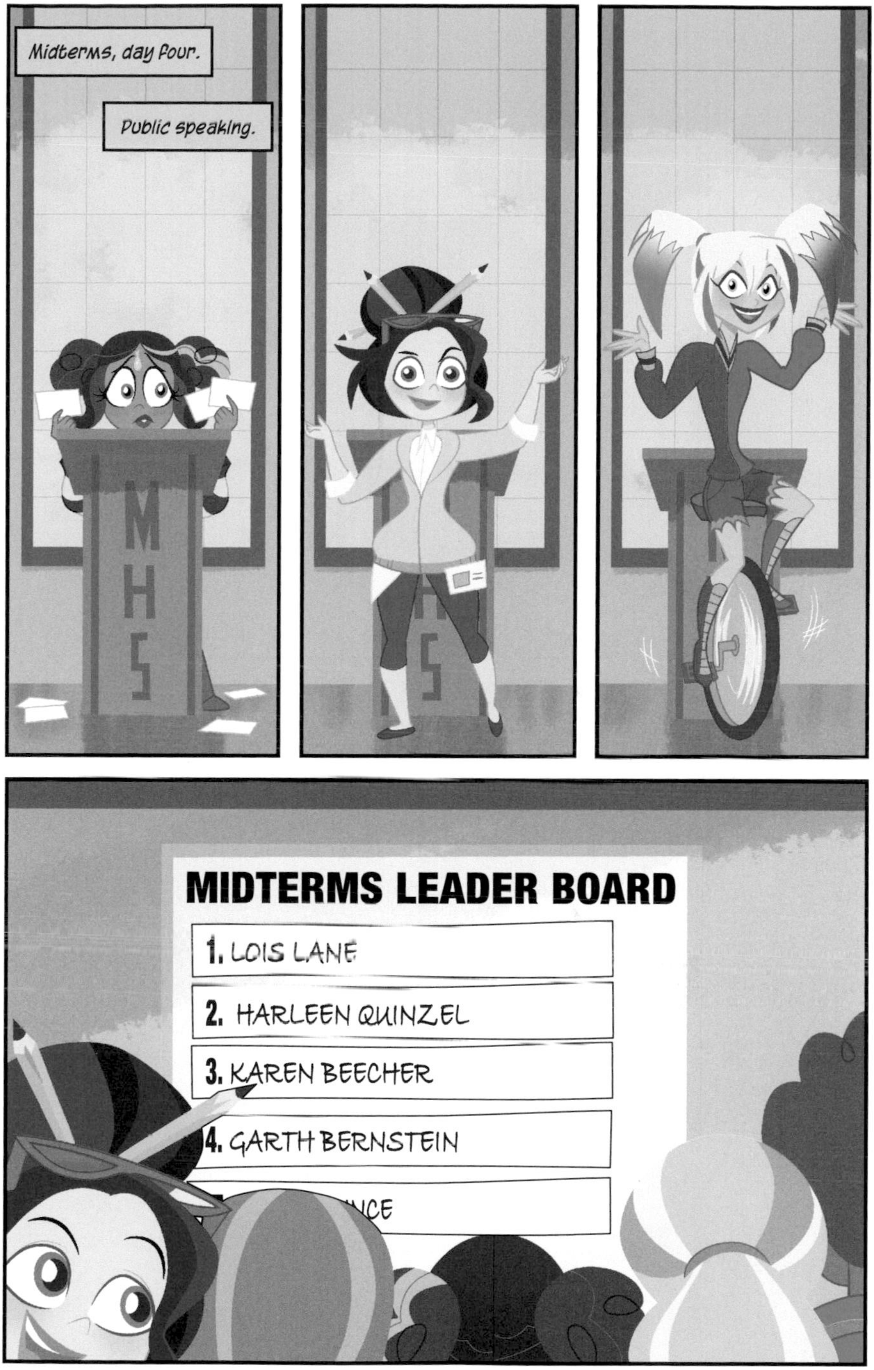
Midterms, day four.
Public speaking.
MHS
MIDTERMS LEADER BOARD
1. LOIS LANE
2. HARLEEN QUINZEL
3. KAREN BEECHER
4. GARTH BERNSTEIN

MIDTERMS LEADER BOARD

1. LOIS LANE

...EN QUINZEL

...EN BEECHER

...TEIN

I never should have picked "How to give a speech without sweating" as my topic for public speaking.

You're doing better than I am.

Better than *all* of us.

But not better than Lois. Or Harleen.

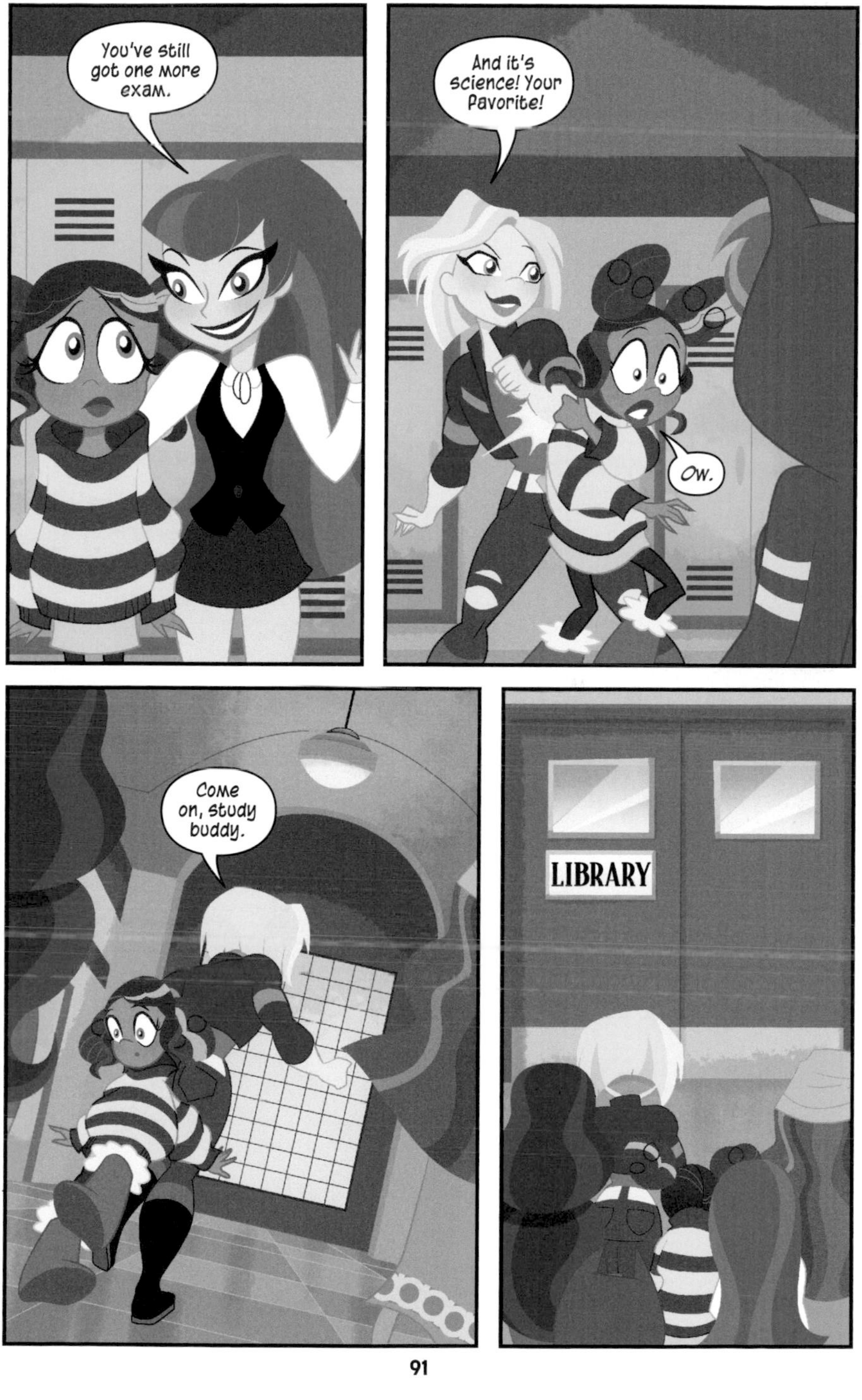
You've still got one more exam.
And it's science! Your favorite!
Ow.
Come on, study buddy.
LIBRARY

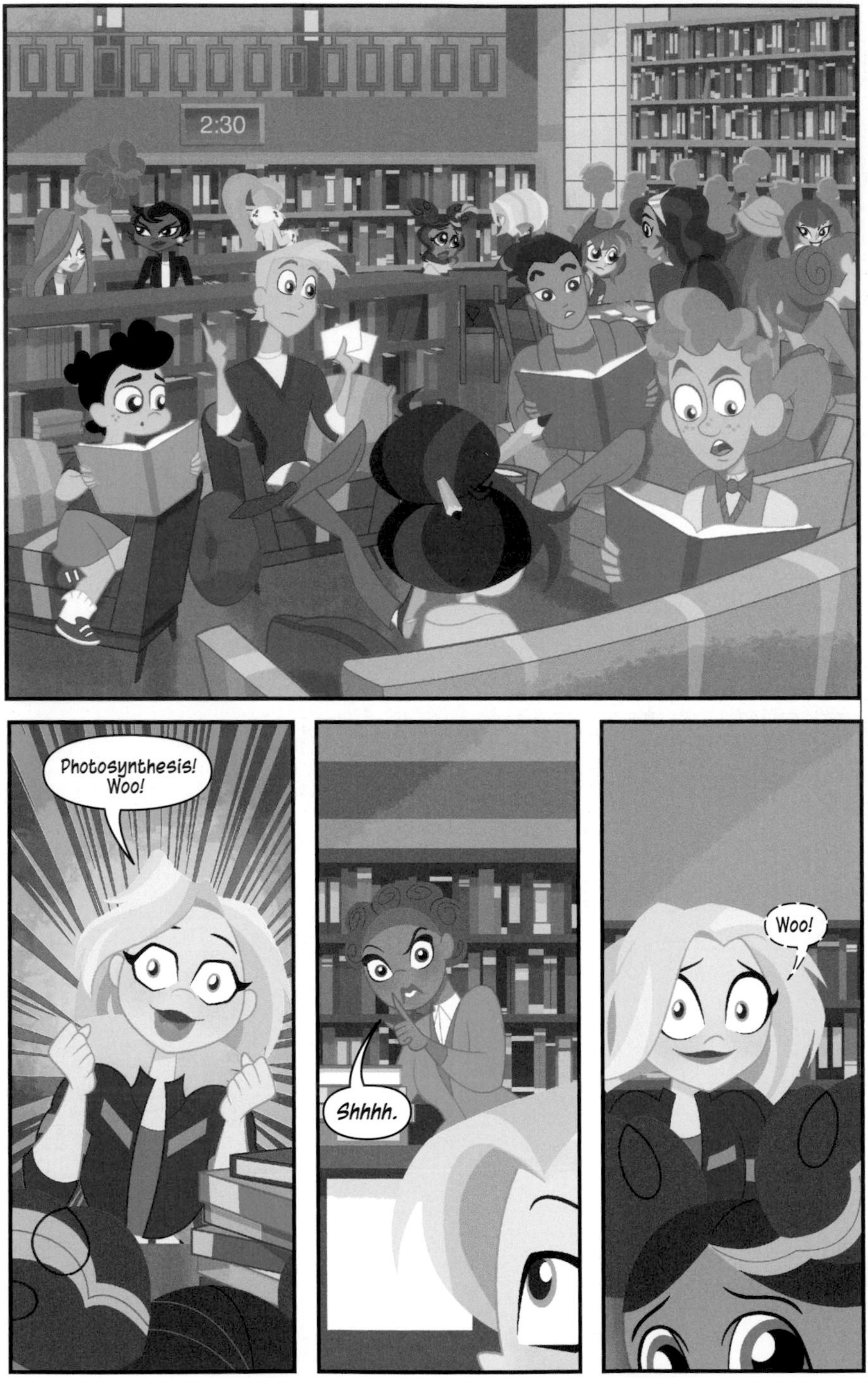
2:30
Photosynthesis! Woo!
Shhhh.
Woo!

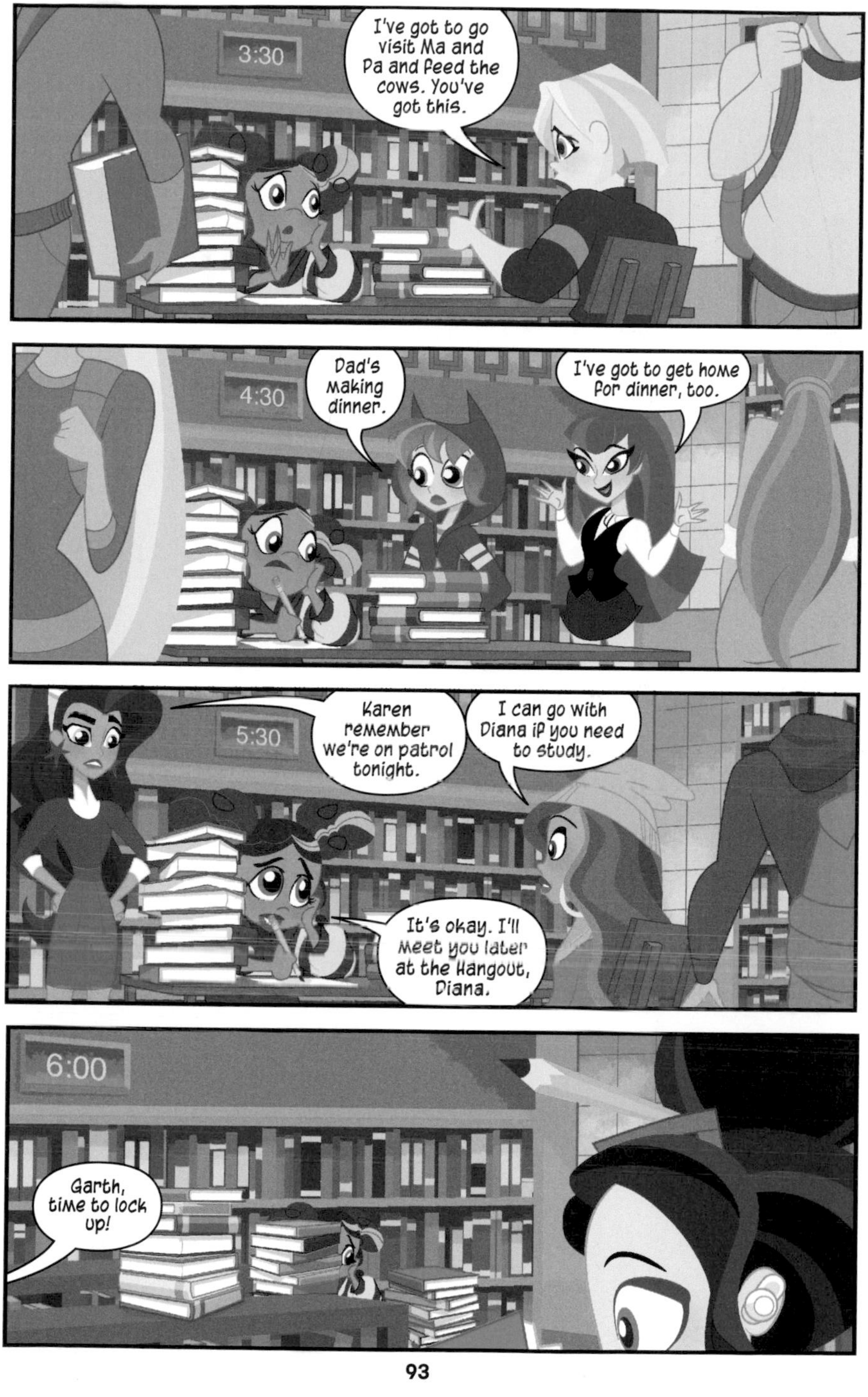
3:30
I've got to go visit Ma and Pa and feed the cows. You've got this.
4:30
Dad's making dinner.
I've got to get home for dinner, too.
5:30
Karen remember we're on patrol tonight.
I can go with Diana if you need to study.
It's okay. I'll meet you later at the Hangout, Diana.
6:00
Garth, time to lock up!

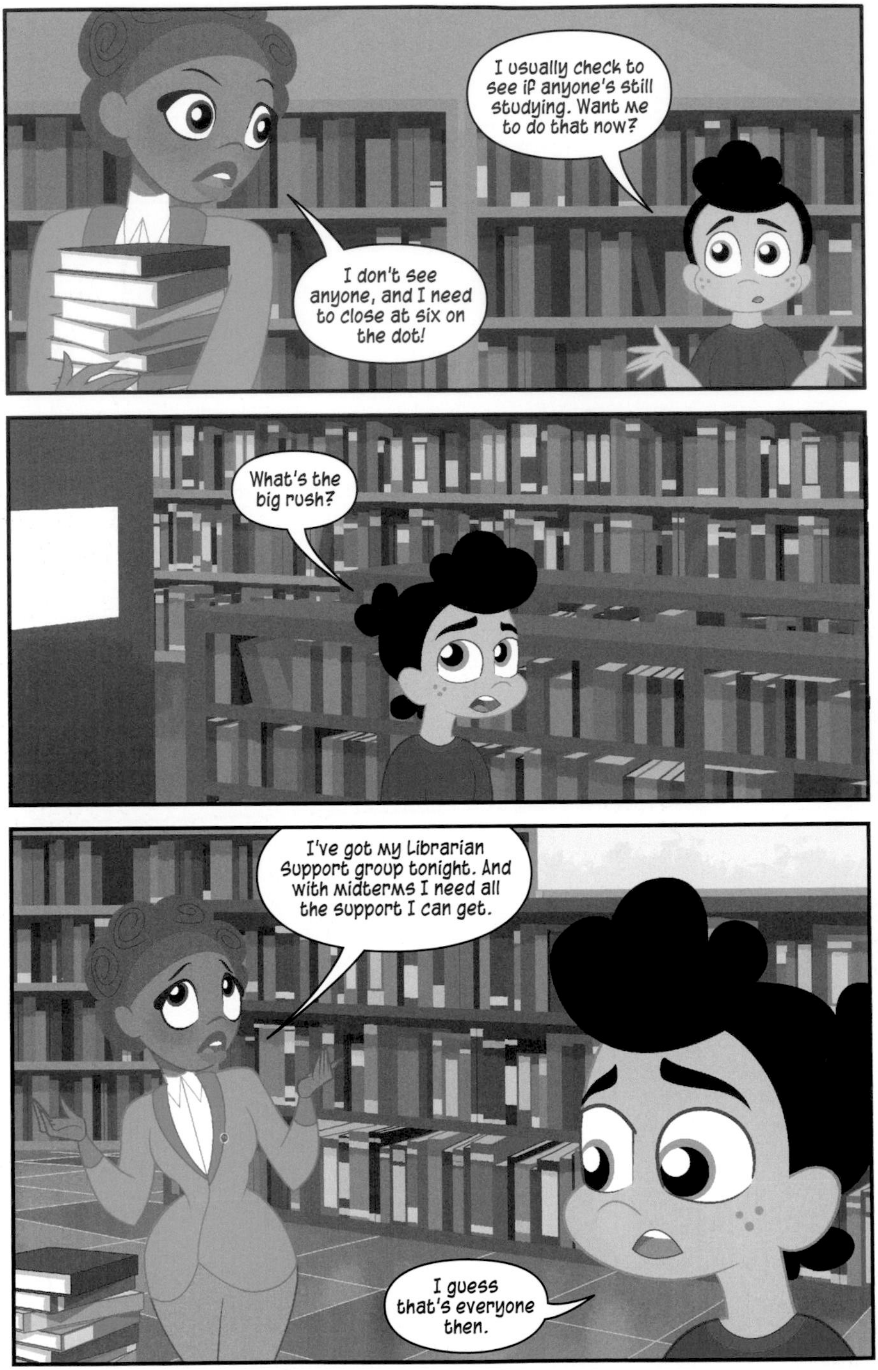
I usually check to see if anyone's still studying. Want me to do that now?
I don't see anyone, and I need to close at six on the dot!
What's the big rush?
I've got my Librarian Support group tonight. And with midterms I need all the support I can get.
I guess that's everyone then.

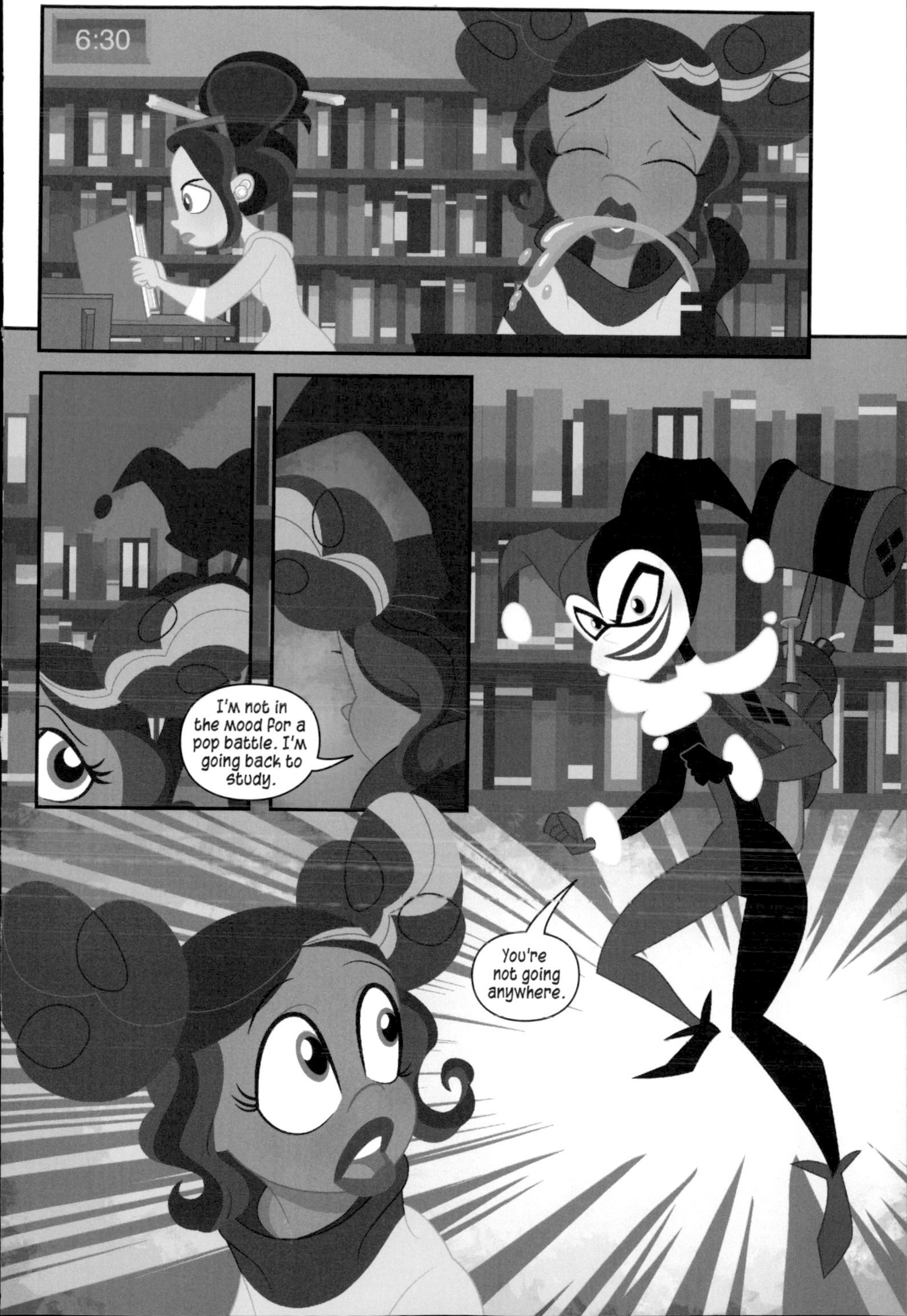
6:30
I'm not in the mood for a pop battle. I'm going back to study.
You're not going anywhere.

# chapter eight

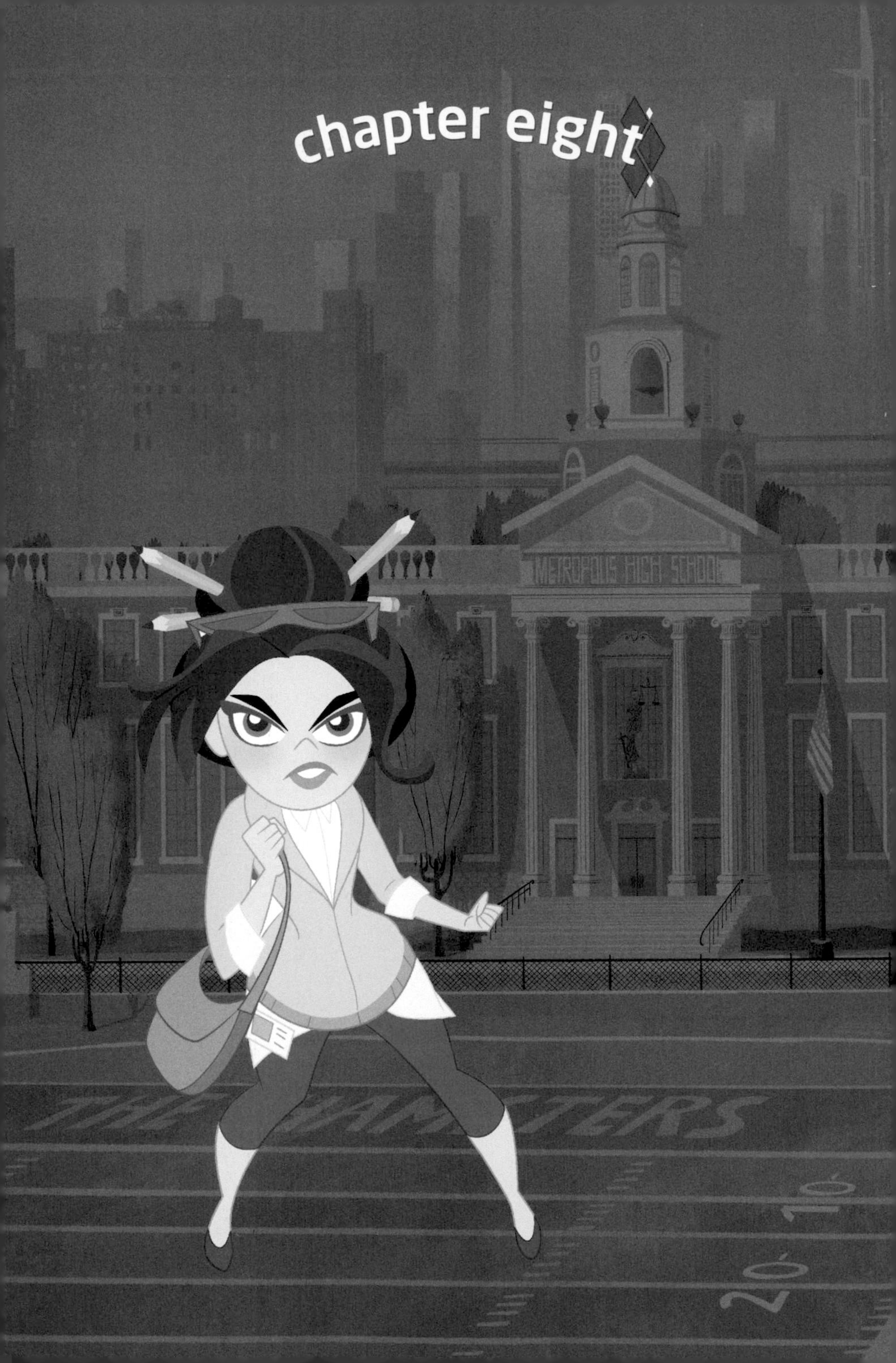
METROPOLIS HIGH SCHOOL

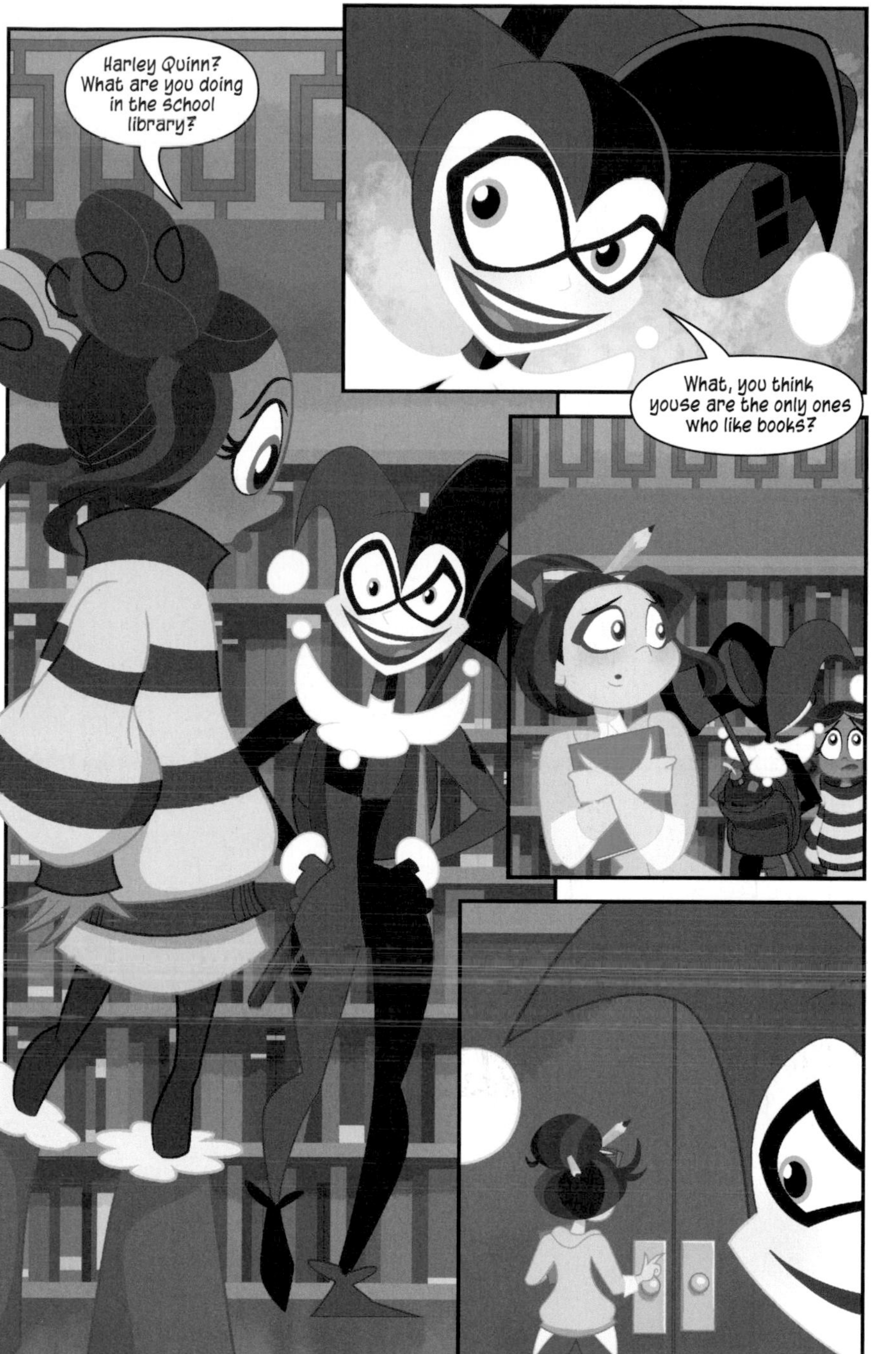
Harley Quinn? What are you doing in the school library?
What, you think youse are the only ones who like books?

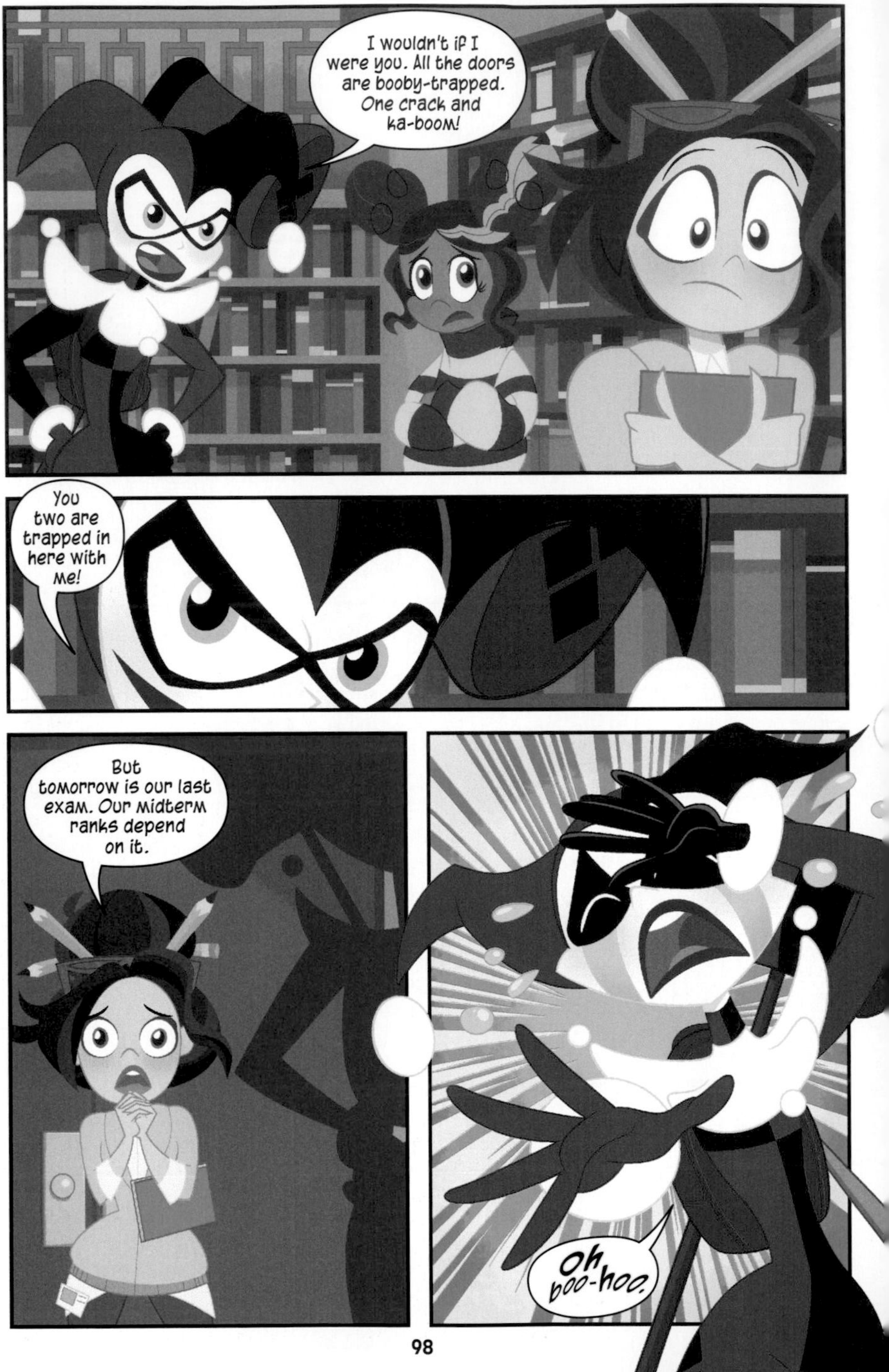
I wouldn't if I were you. All the doors are booby-trapped. One crack and ka-boom!
You two are trapped in here with me!
But tomorrow is our last exam. Our midterm ranks depend on it.
Oh boo-hoo.

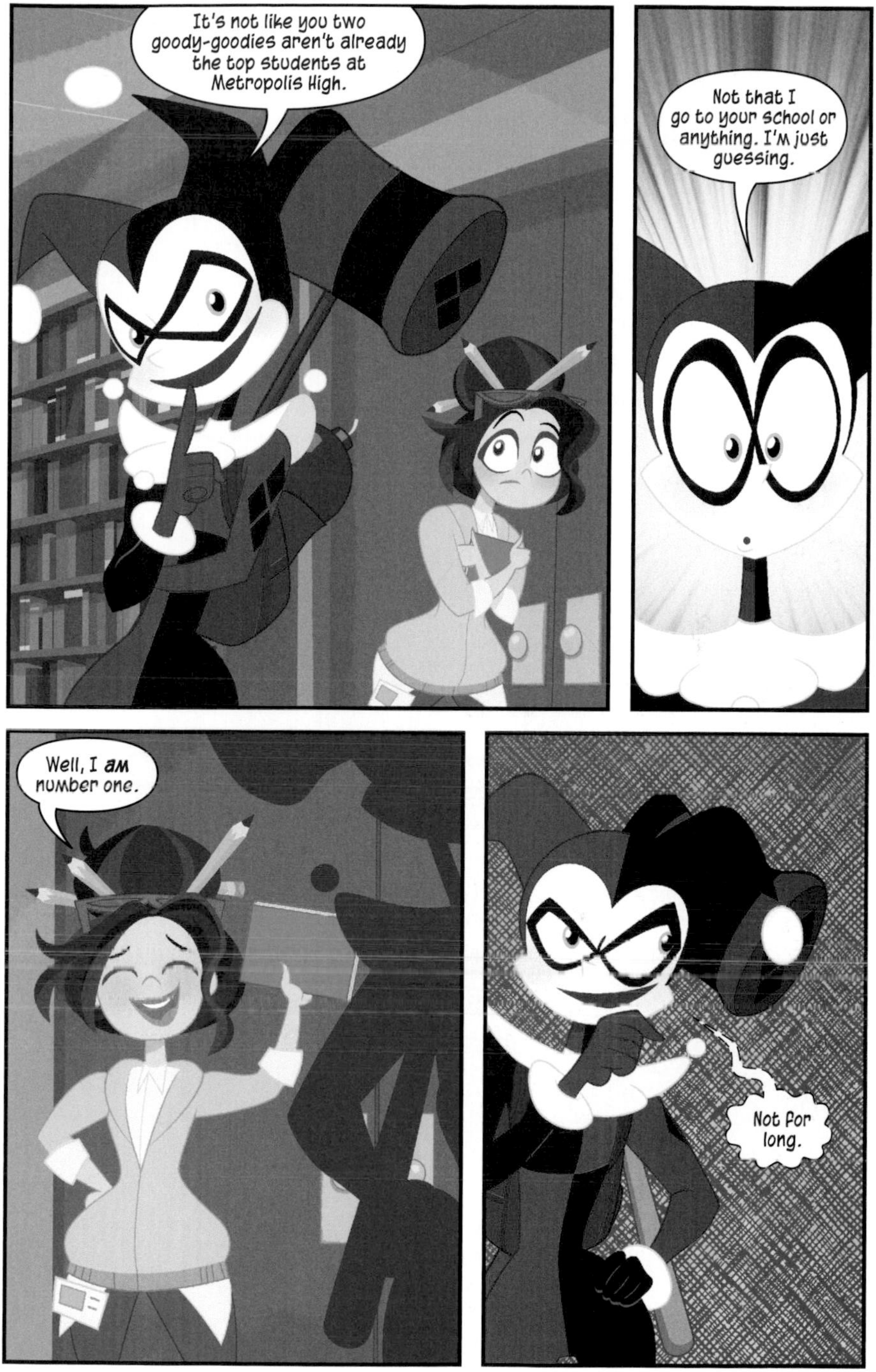
It's not like you two goody-goodies aren't already the top students at Metropolis High.
Not that I go to your school or anything. I'm just guessing.
Well, I am number one.
Not for long.

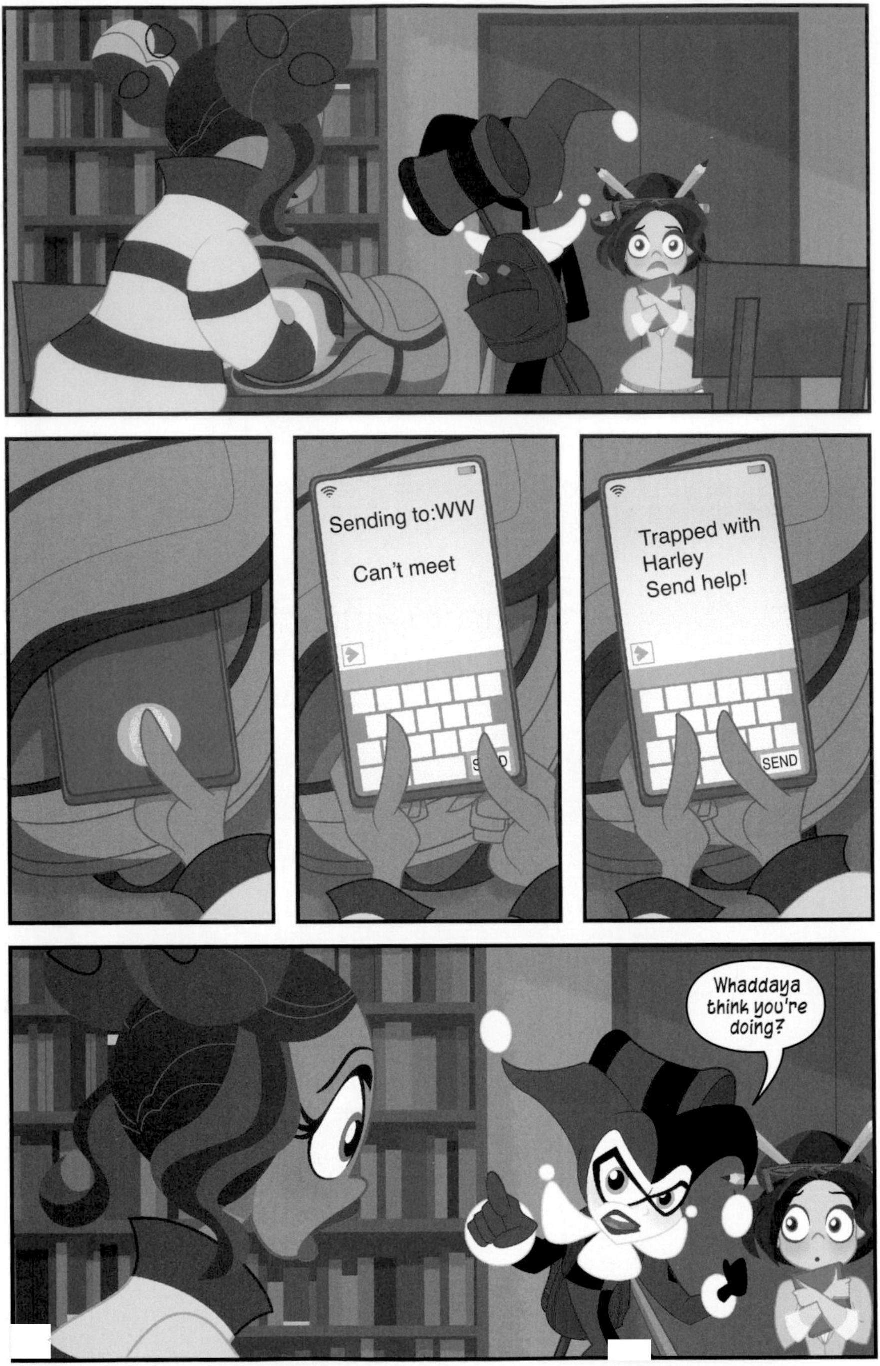
Sending to:WW
Can't meet
SEND
Trapped with
Harley
Send help!
SEND
Whaddaya think you're doing?

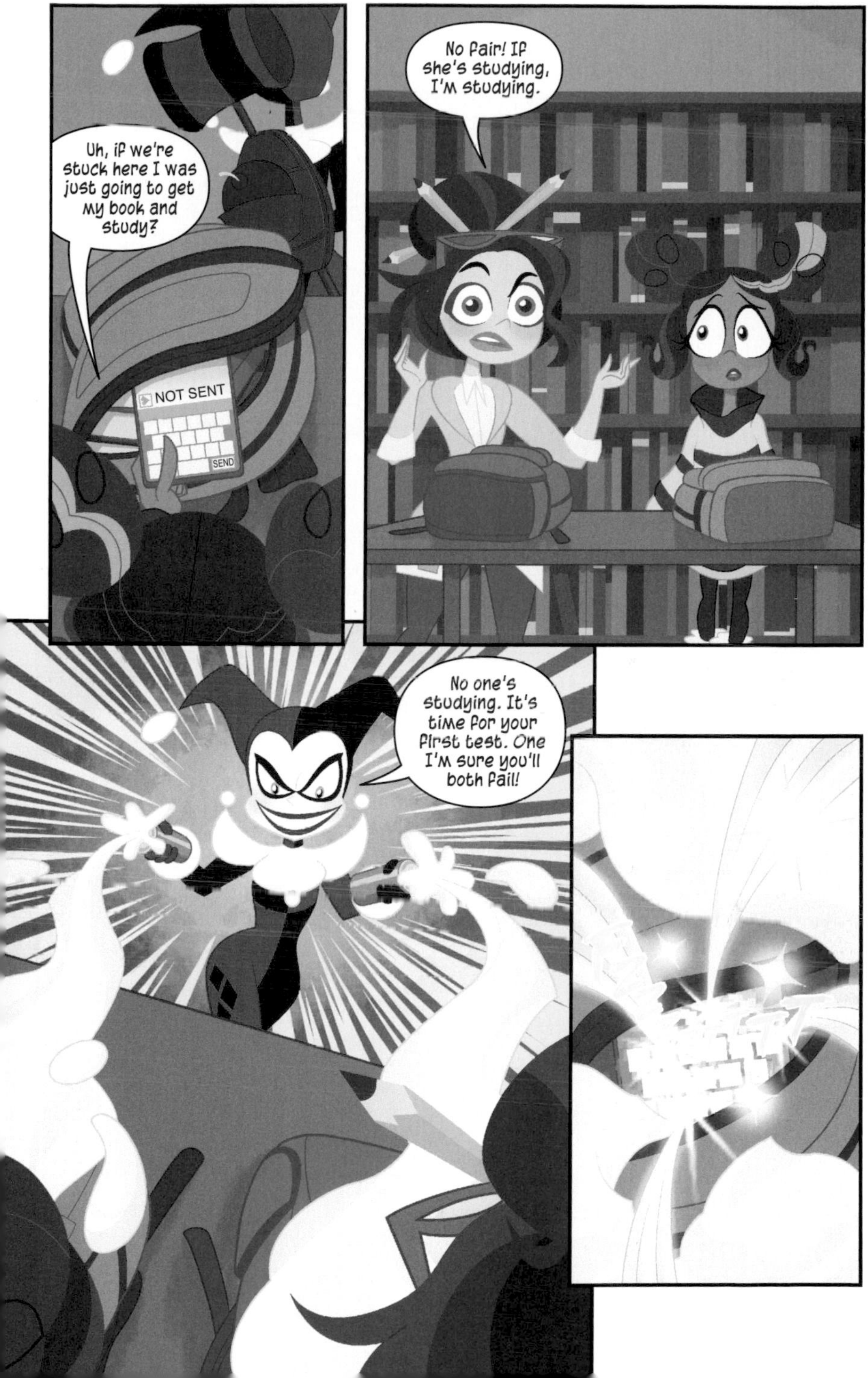
Uh, if we're stuck here I was just going to get my book and study?
NOT SENT
SEND
No fair! If she's studying, I'm studying.
No one's studying. It's time for your first test. One I'm sure you'll both fail!

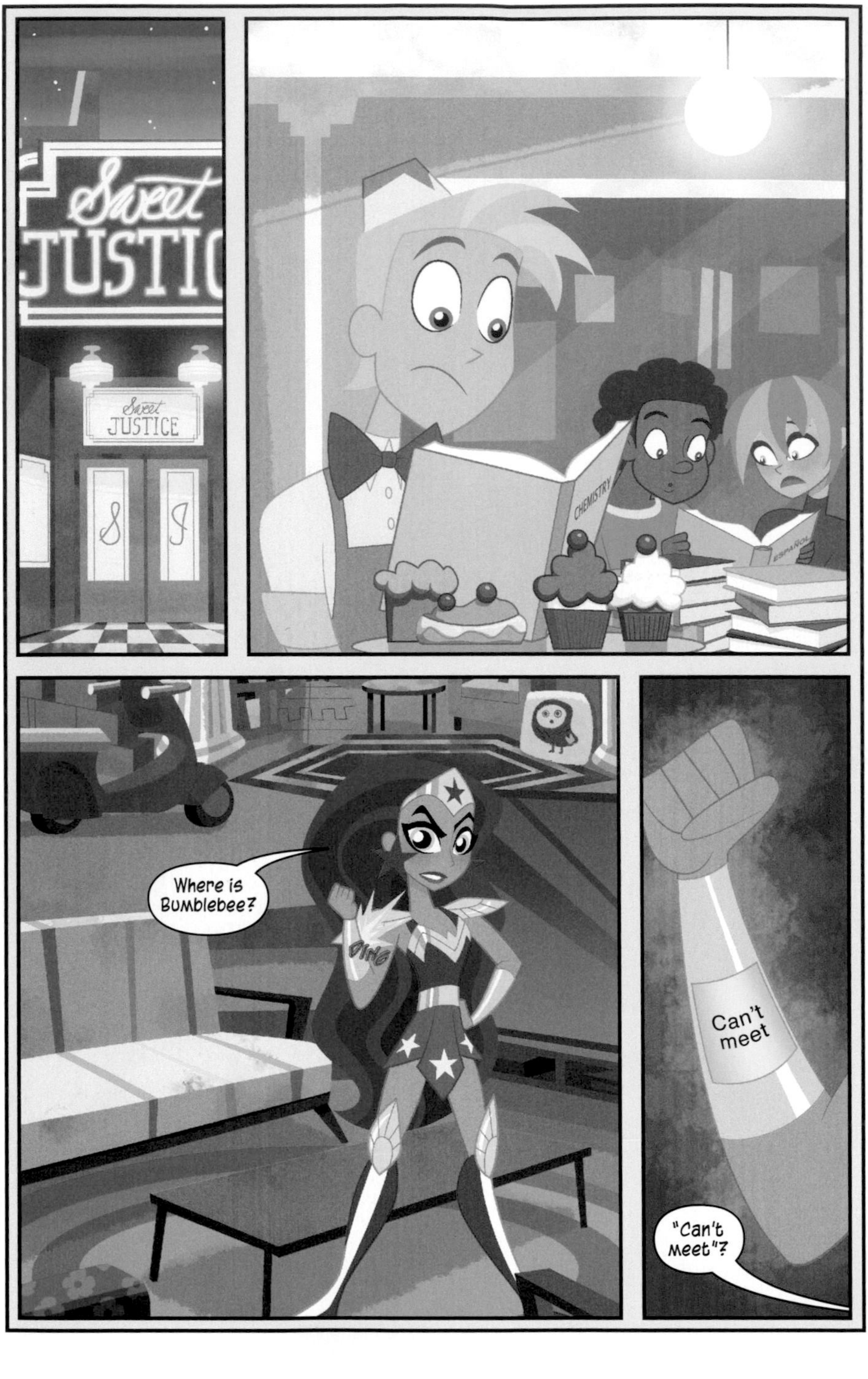
Sweet
JUSTICE
Sweet
JUSTICE
S J
CHEMISTRY
ESPAÑOL
Where is Bumblebee?
DING
Can't meet
"Can't Meet"?

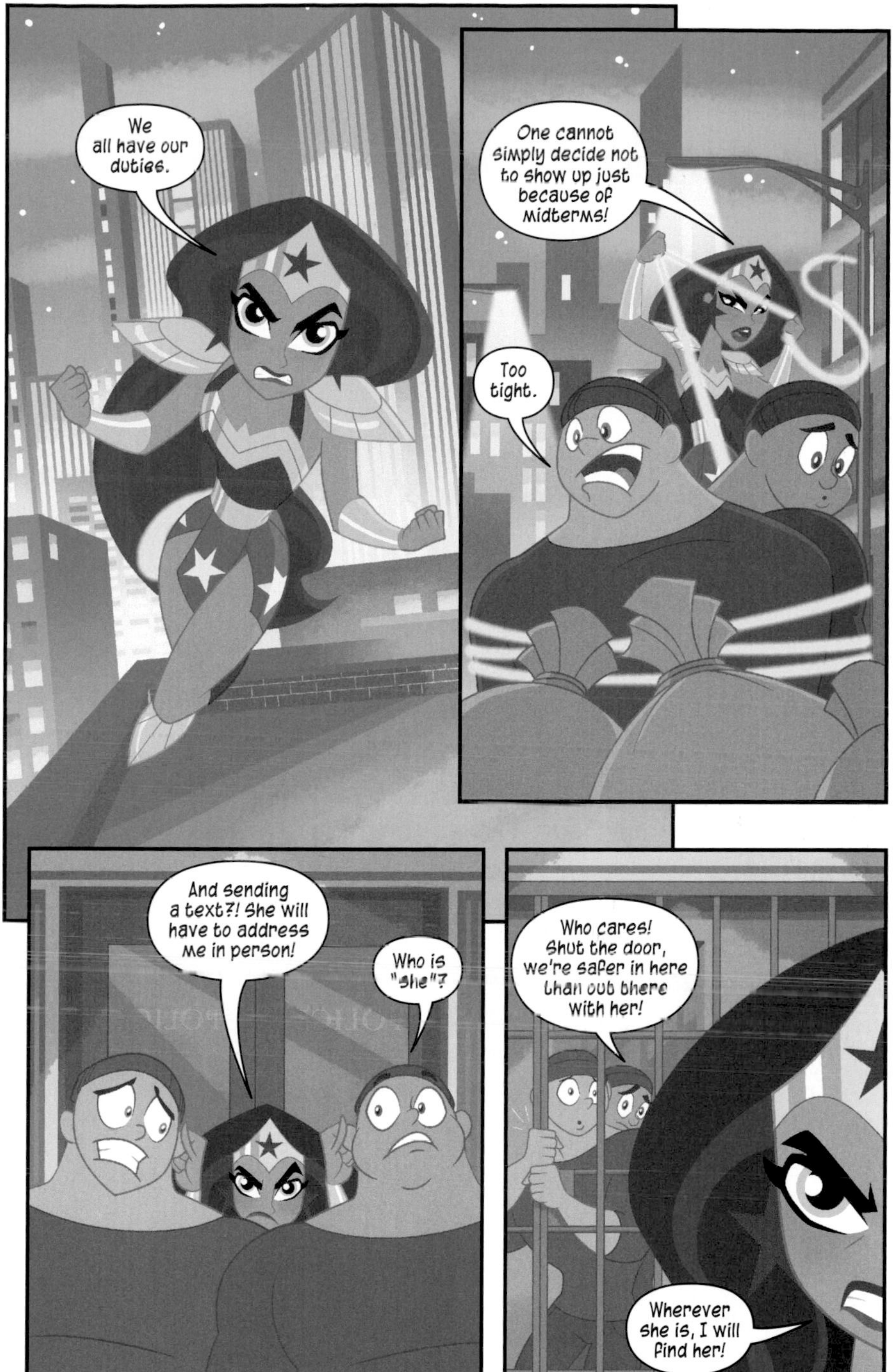

We all have our duties.
One cannot simply decide not to show up just because of midterms!
Too tight.
And sending a text?! She will have to address me in person!
Who is "she"?
Who cares! Shut the door, we're safer in here than out there with her!
Wherever she is, I will find her!

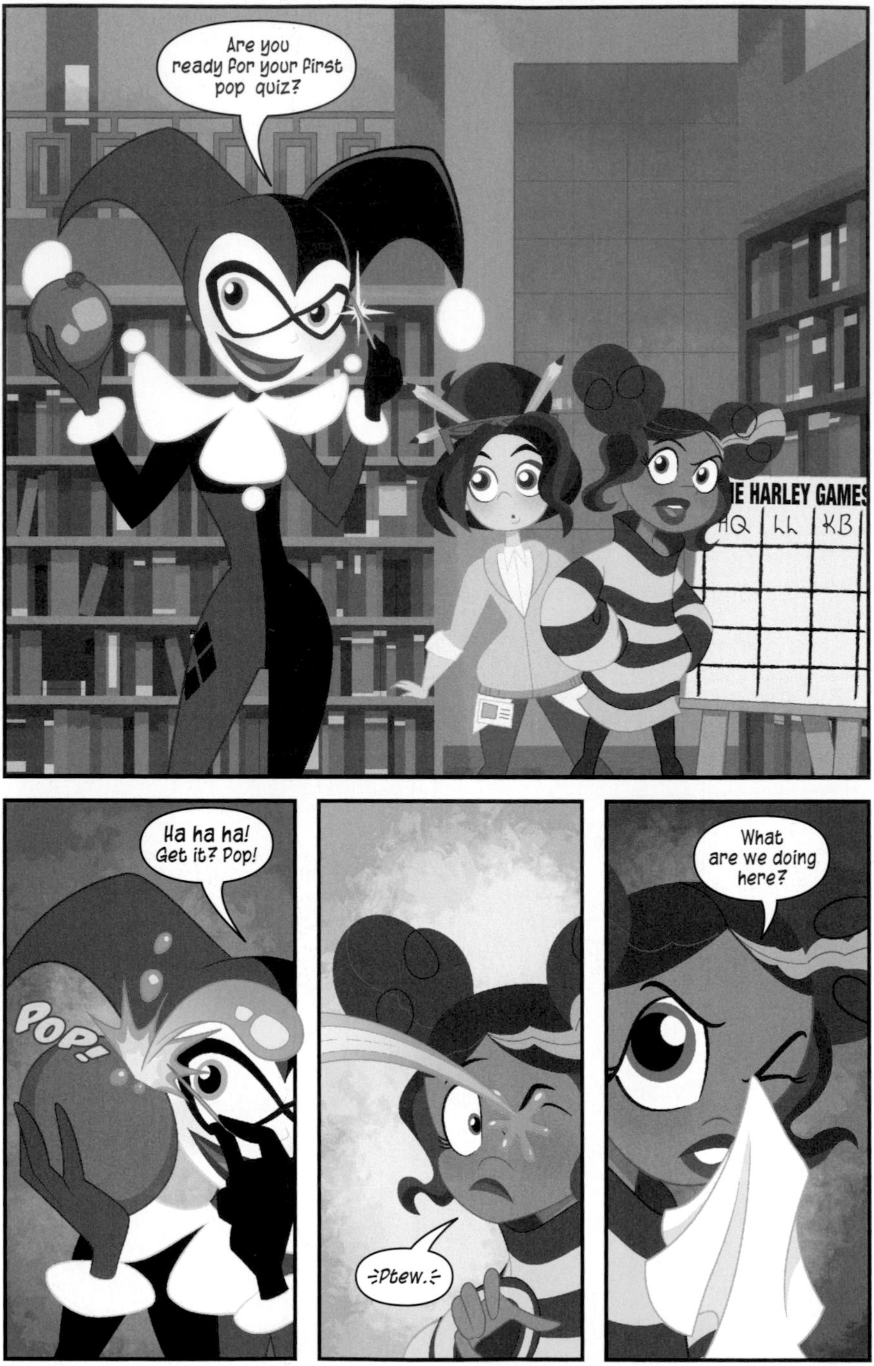
Are you ready for your first pop quiz?
THE HARLEY GAMES
HQ
LL
KB
Ha ha ha! Get it? Pop!
POP!
Ptew.
What are we doing here?

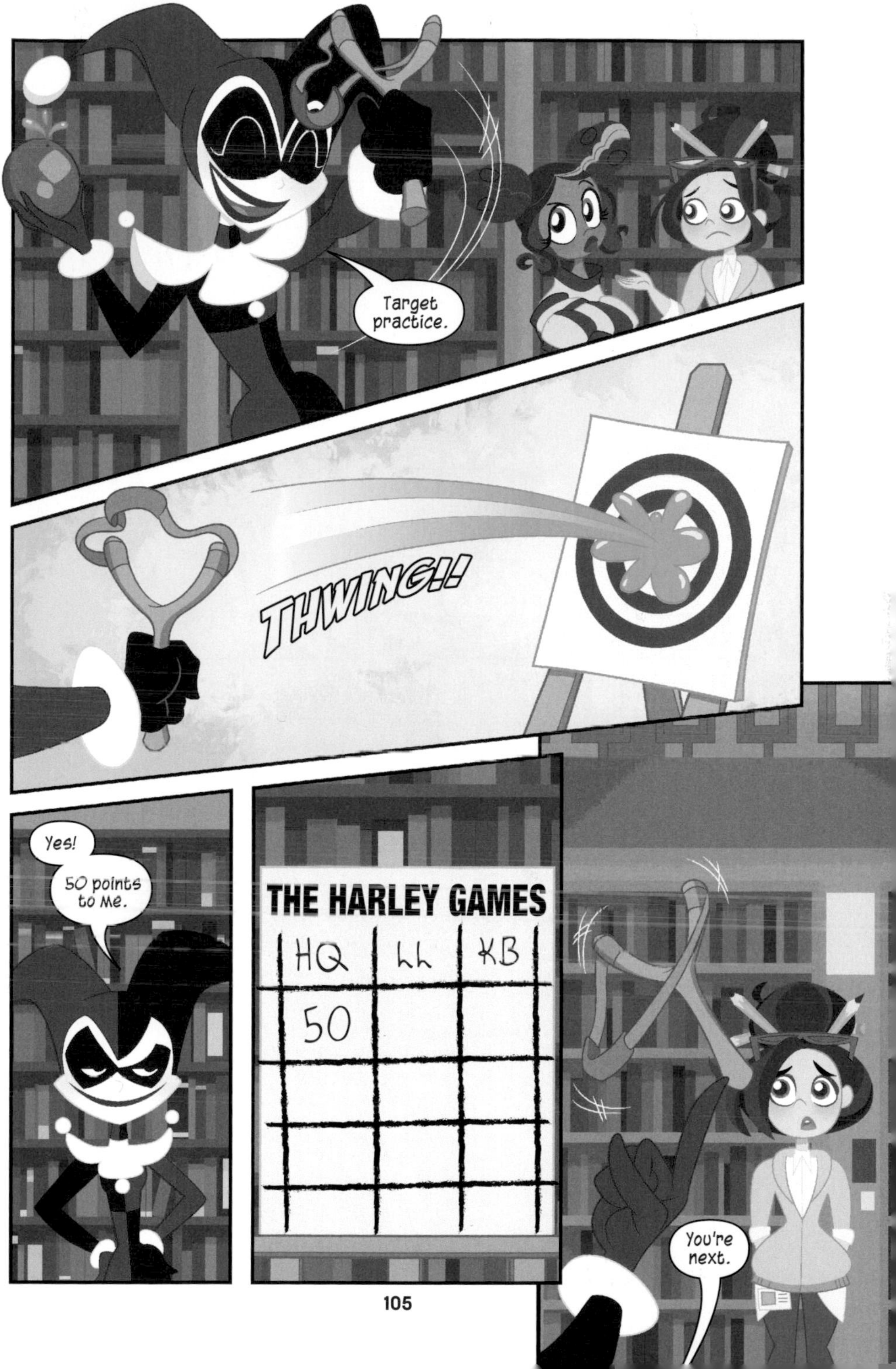
Target practice.
THWING!!
Yes!
50 points to me.
THE HARLEY GAMES
HQ
LL
KB
50
You're next.

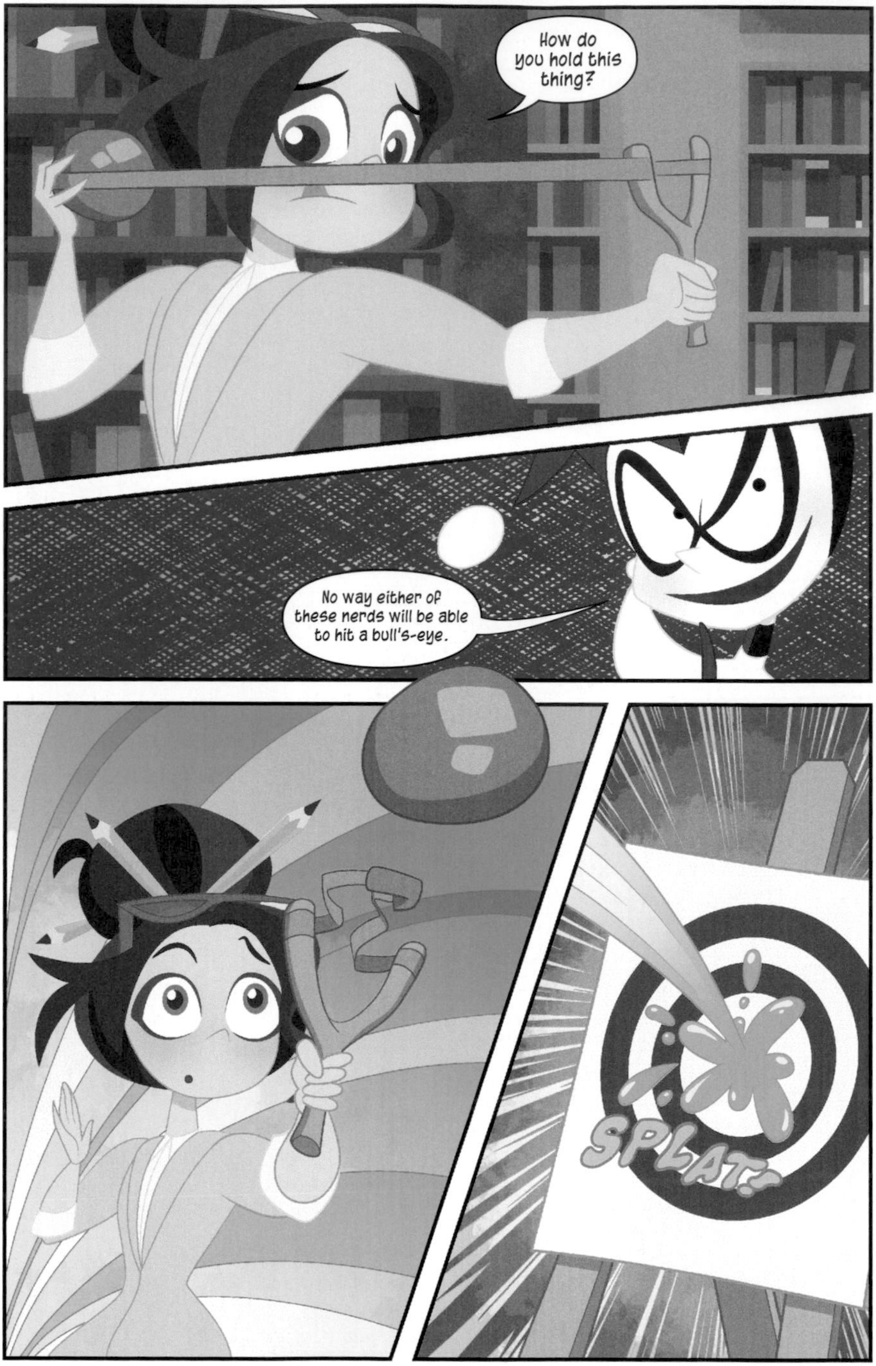
How do you hold this thing?
No way either of these nerds will be able to hit a bull's-eye.
SPLAT!

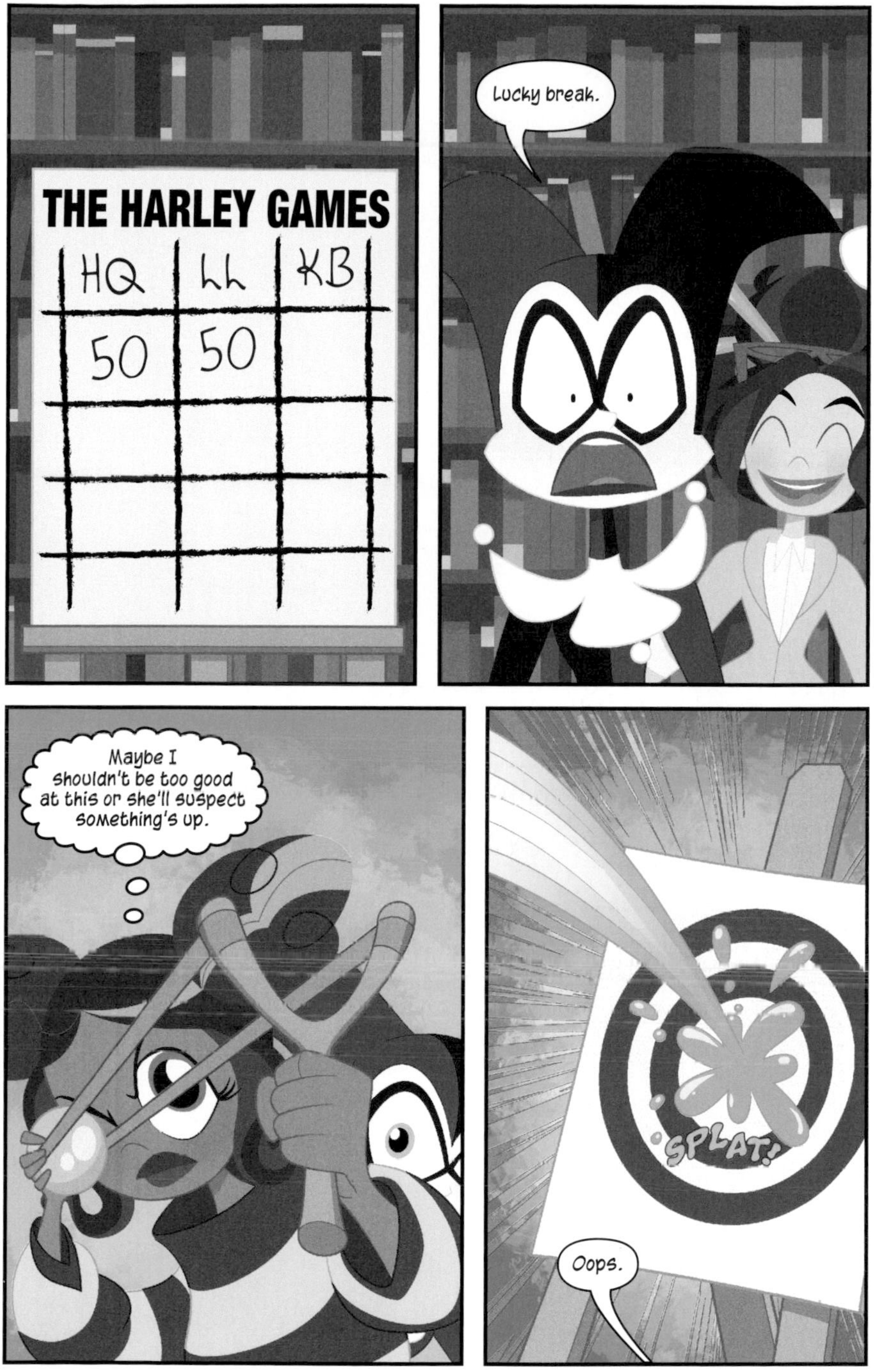
THE HARLEY GAMES
HQ
hh
KB
50
50
Lucky break.
Maybe I shouldn't be too good at this or she'll suspect something's up.
SPLAT!
Oops.

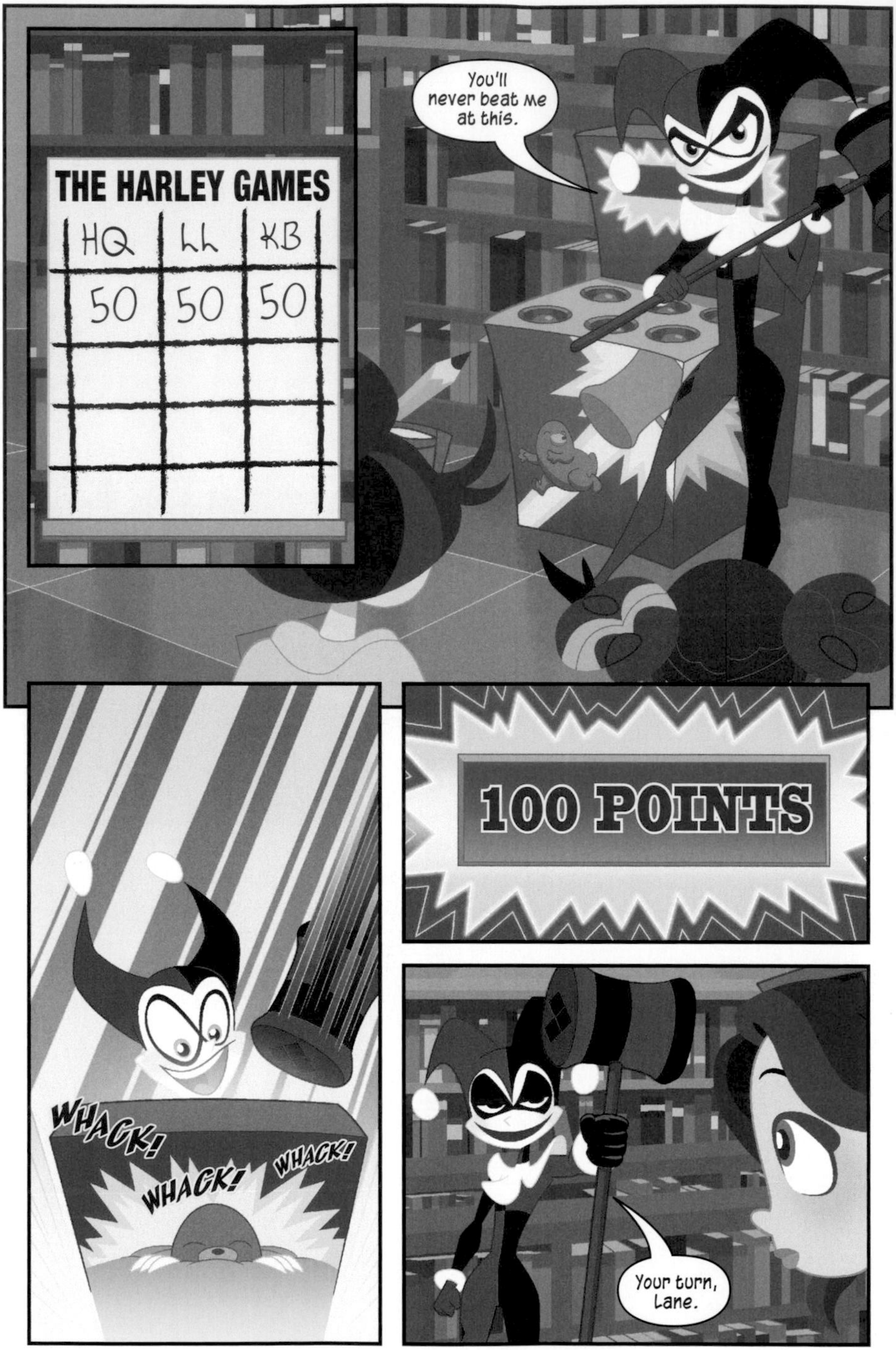
THE HARLEY GAMES
HQ | LL | KB
50 | 50 | 50
You'll never beat me at this.
WHACK!
WHACK!
WHACK!
100 POINTS
Your turn, Lane.

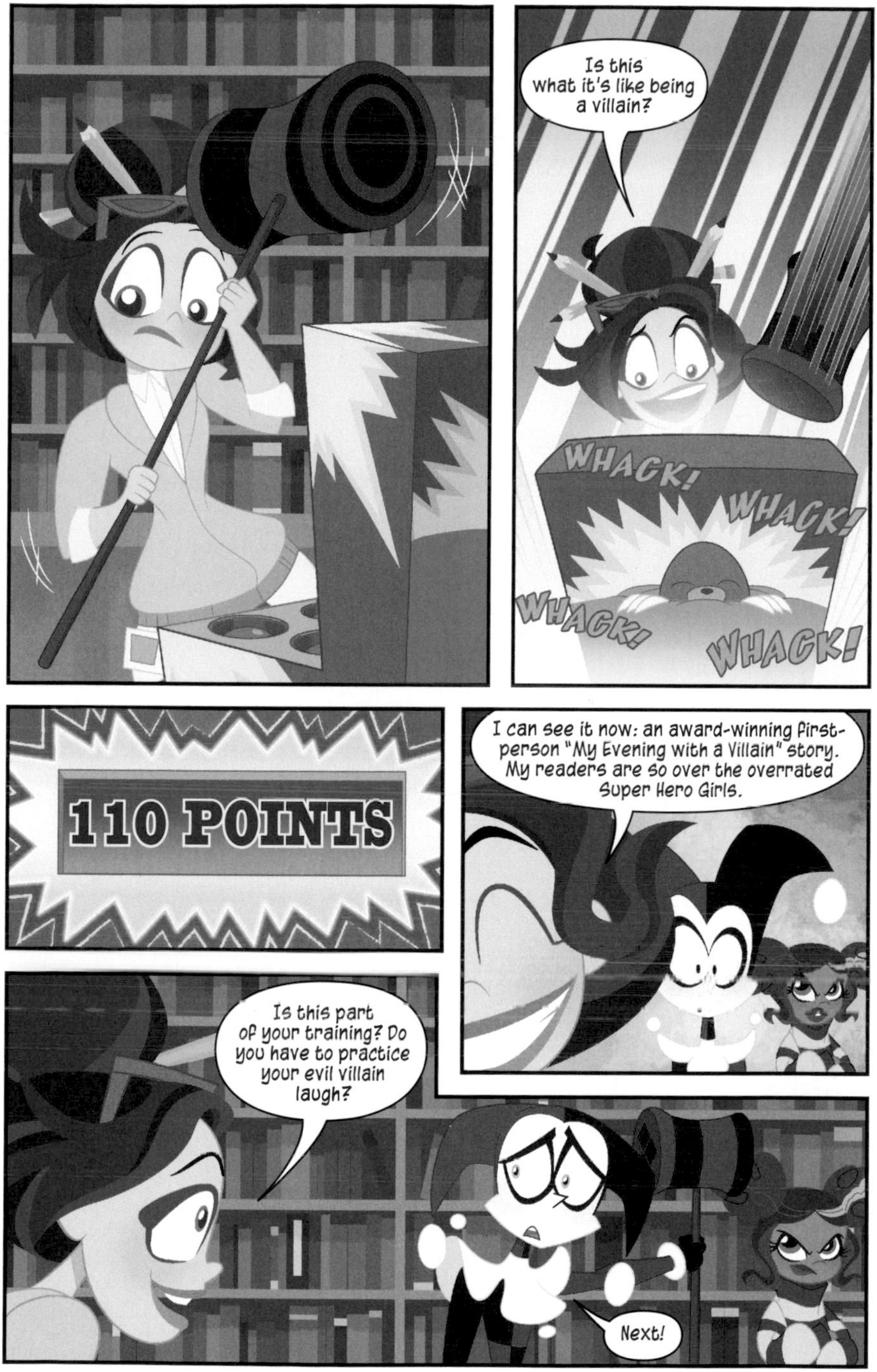

Is this what it's like being a villain?
WHACK!
WHACK!
WHACK!
WHACK!
110 POINTS
I can see it now: an award-winning first-person "My Evening with a Villain" story. My readers are so over the overrated Super Hero Girls.
Is this part of your training? Do you have to practice your evil villain laugh?
Next!

THE HARLEY GAMES

| HQ | LL | KB |
|-----|-----|-----|
| 50 | 50 | 50 |
| 100 | 110 | 120 |
| | | |
| 150 | 160 | 170 |

It's okay, I've got more tests.

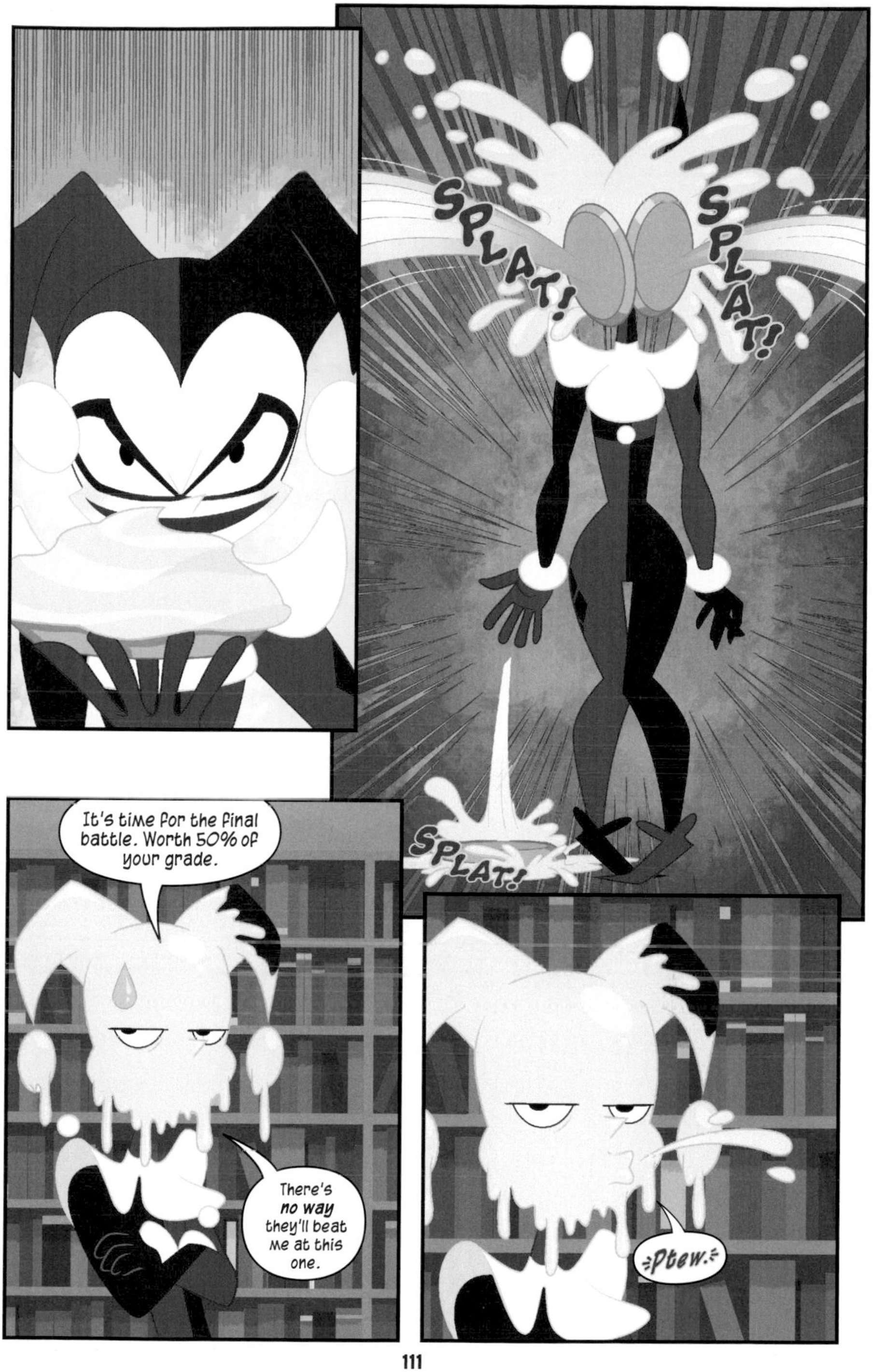
SPLAT!
SPLAT!
SPLAT!
It's time for the final battle. Worth 50% of your grade.
There's **no way** they'll beat me at this one.
Ptew.

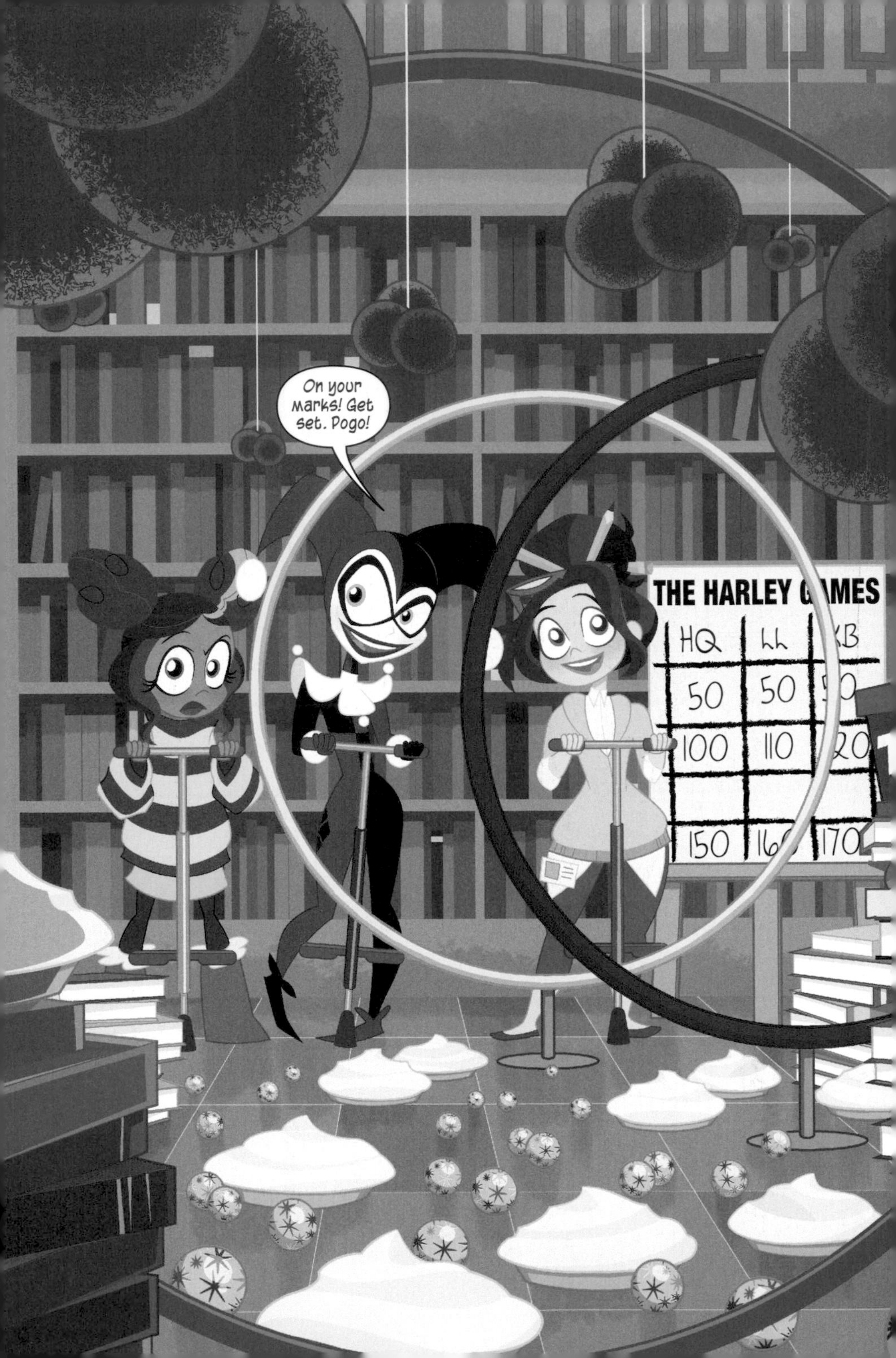
On your Marks! Get set. Pogo!
HQ

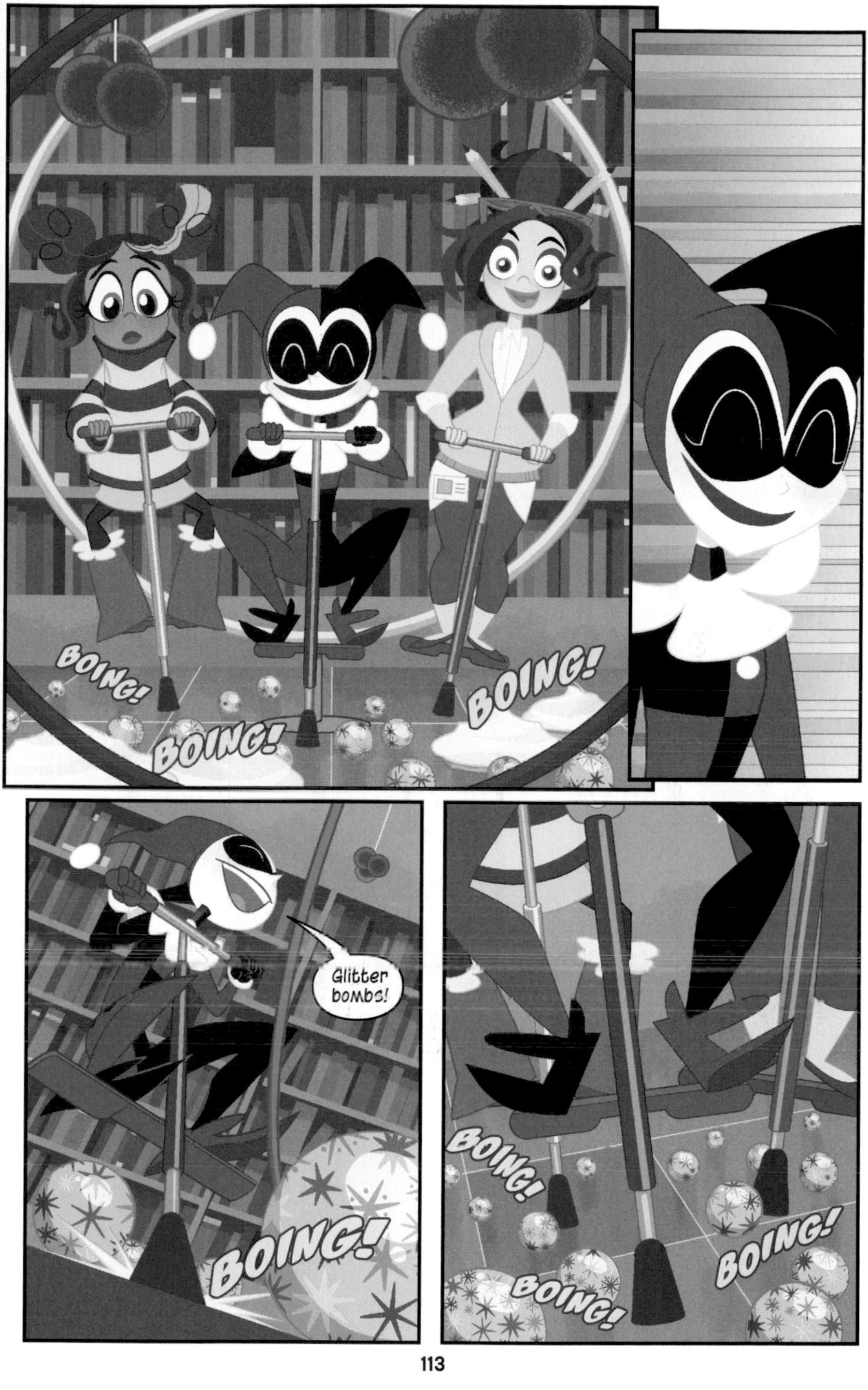
BOING!
BOING!
BOING!
Glitter bombs!
BOING!
BOING!
BOING!
BOING!

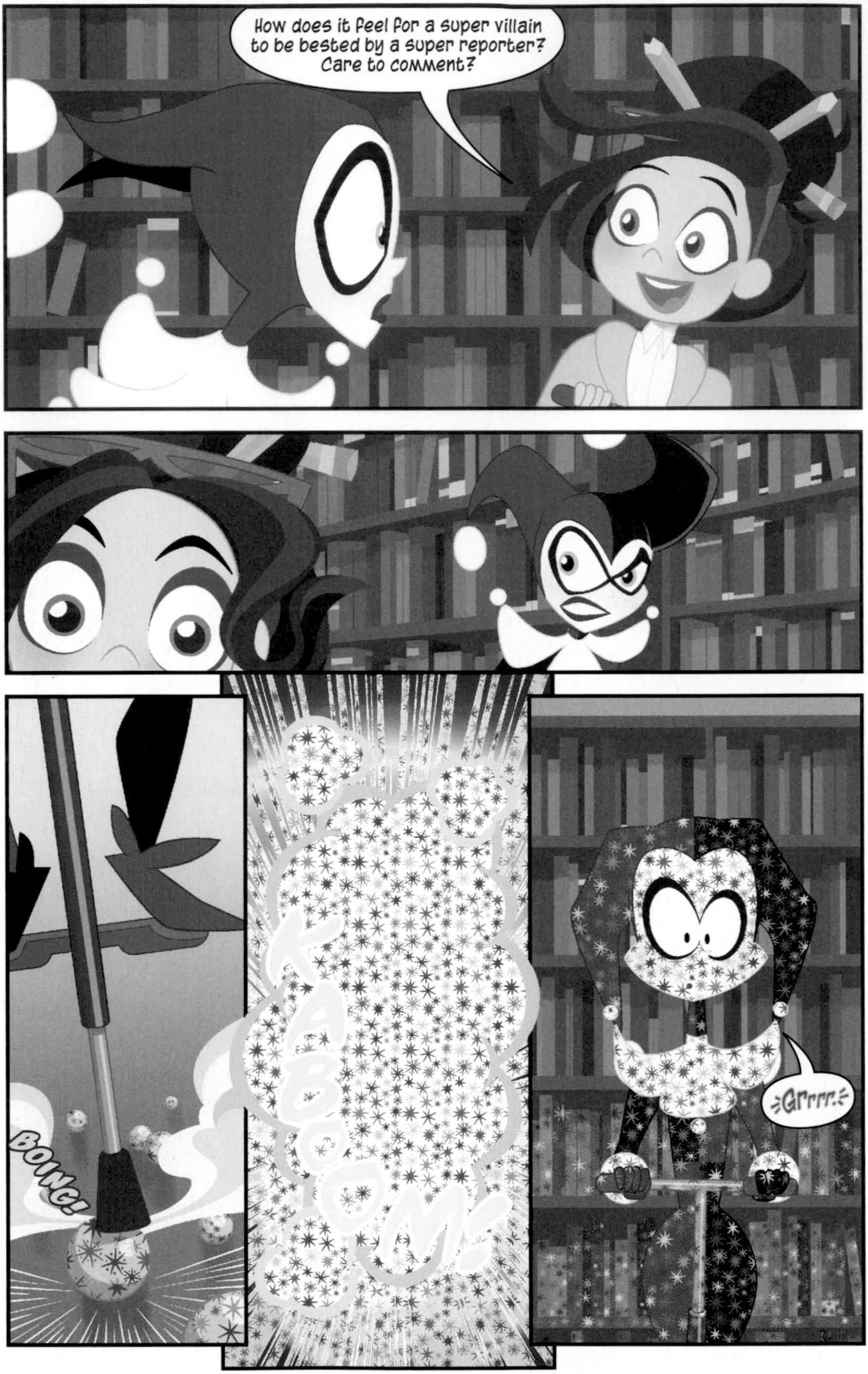
How does it feel for a super villain to be bested by a super reporter? Care to comment?
BOING!
KABOOM!
GRrrr.

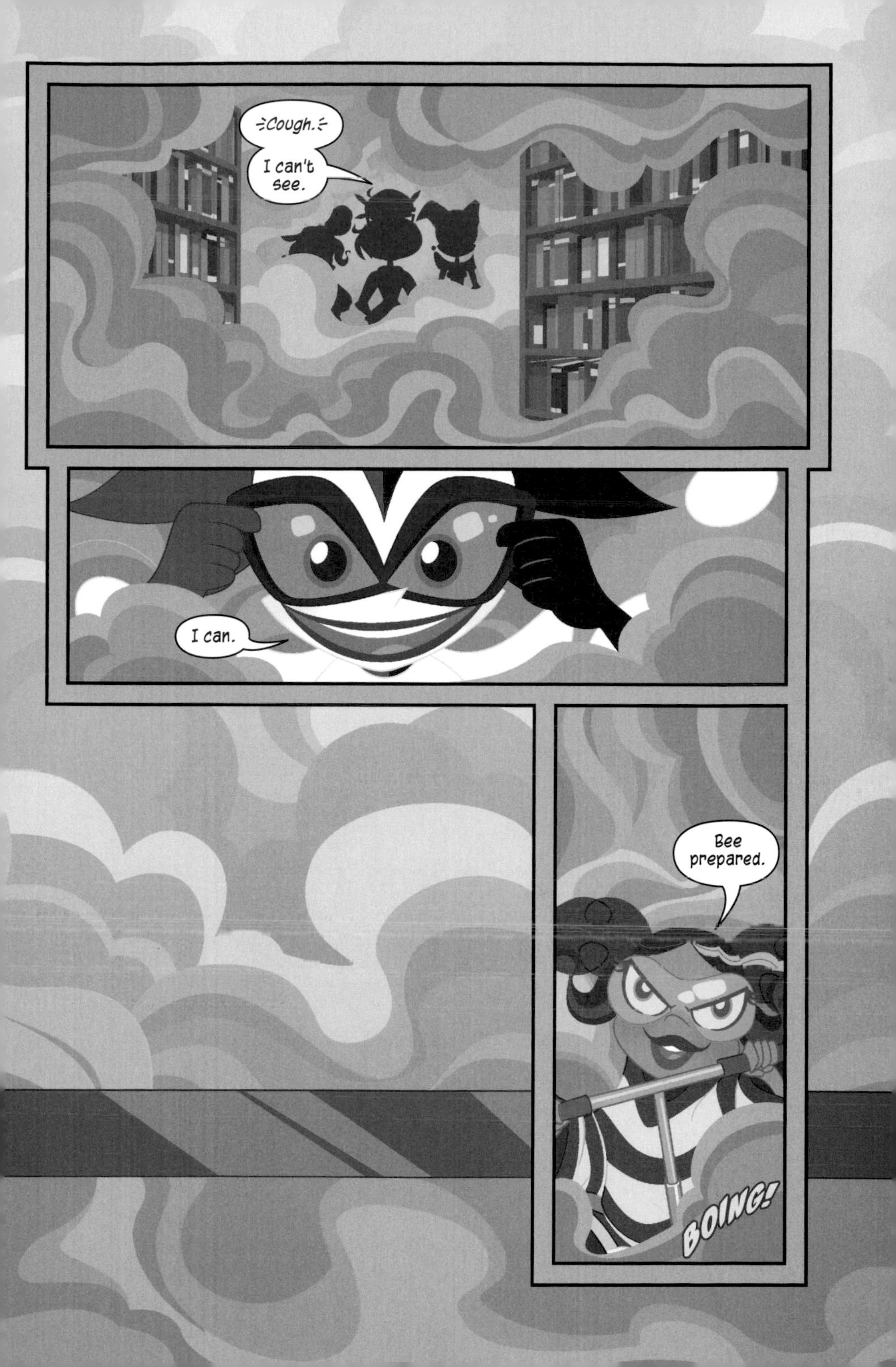

Cough.
I can't see.
I can.
Bee prepared.
BOING!

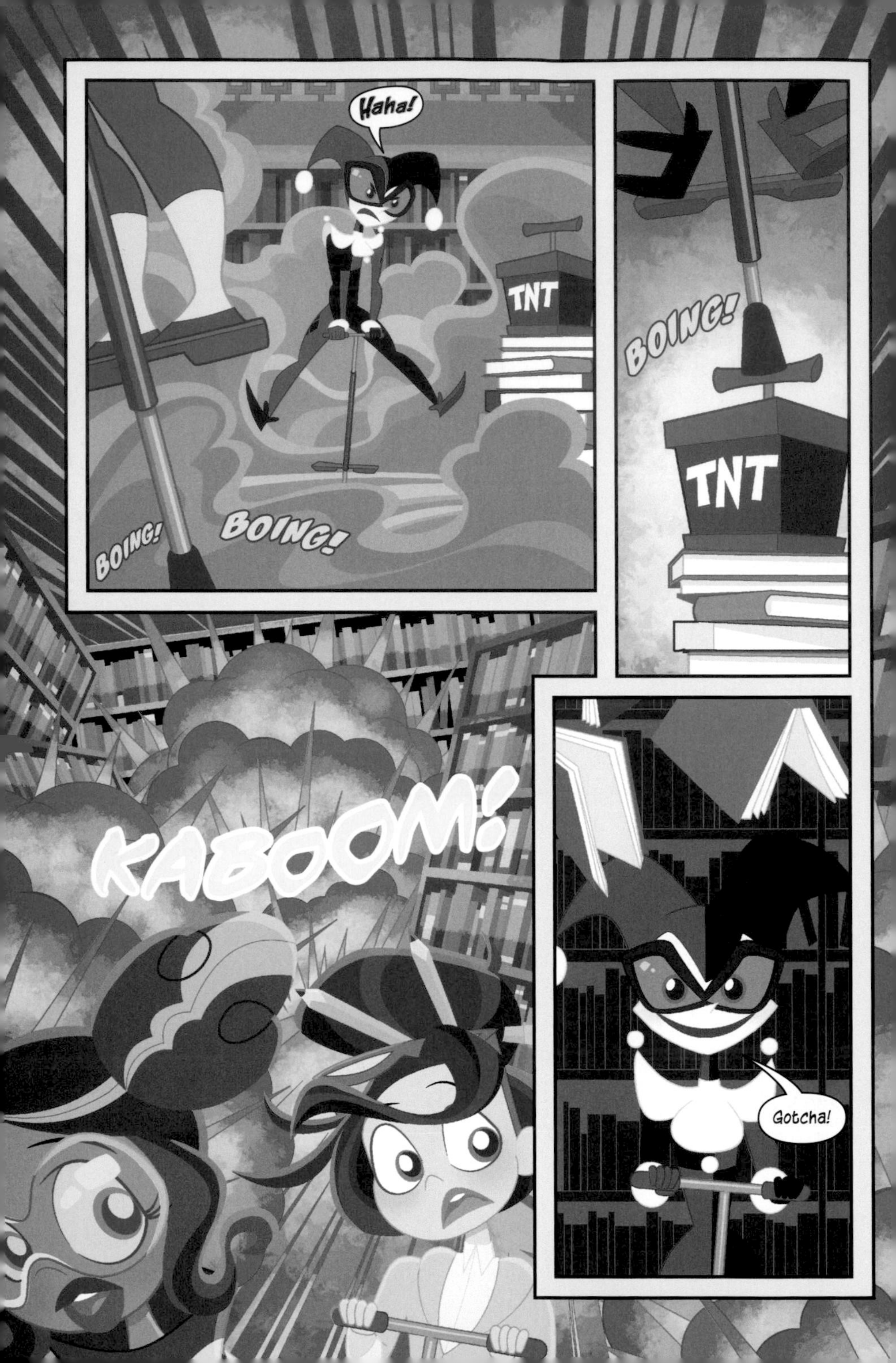
Haha!
BOING!
BOING!
BOING!
KABOOM!
Gotcha!

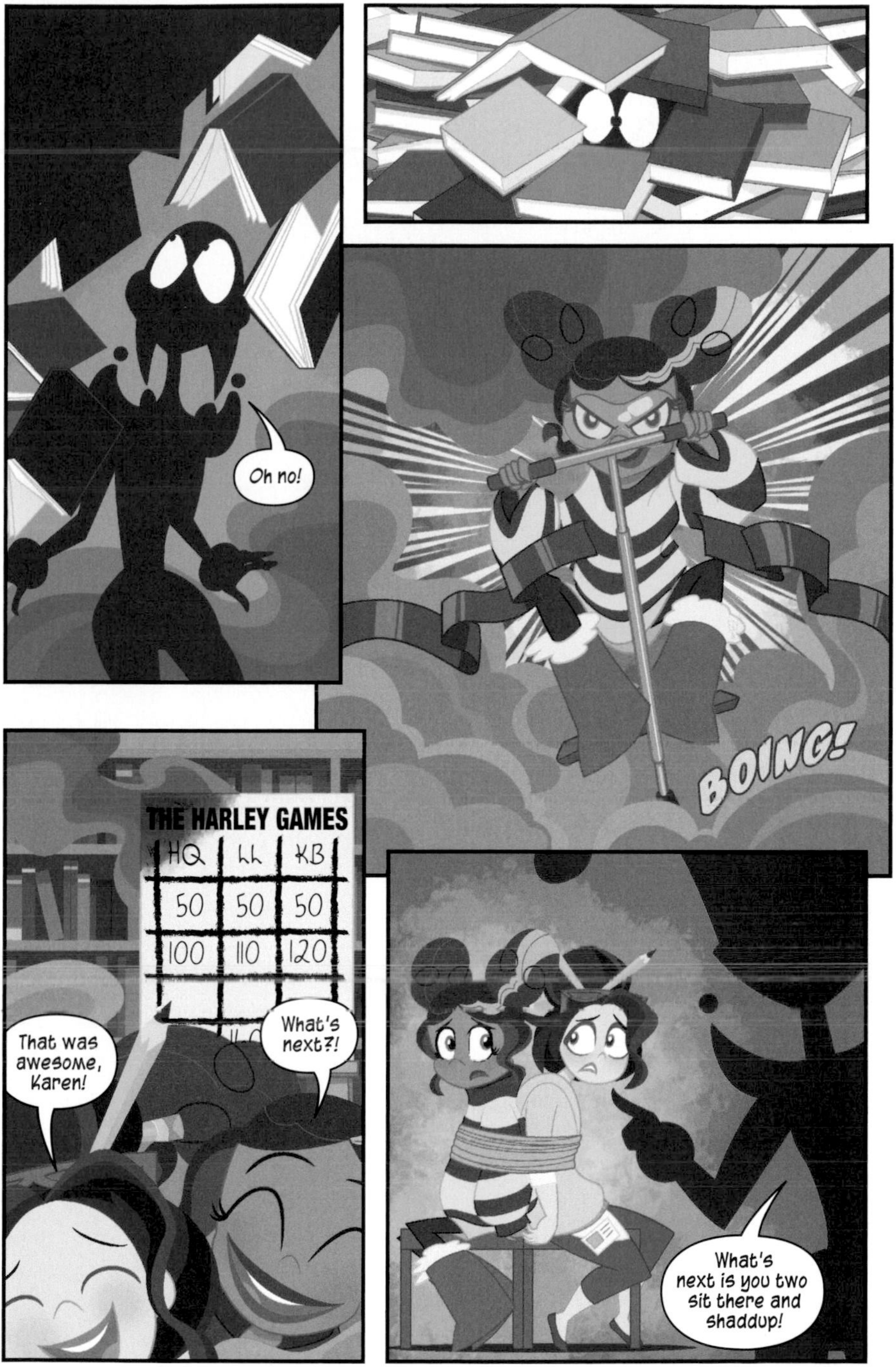
Oh no!
BOING!
THE HARLEY GAMES
HQ LL KB
50 50 50
100 110 120
That was awesome, Karen!
What's next?!
What's next is you two sit there and shaddup!

# chapter nine

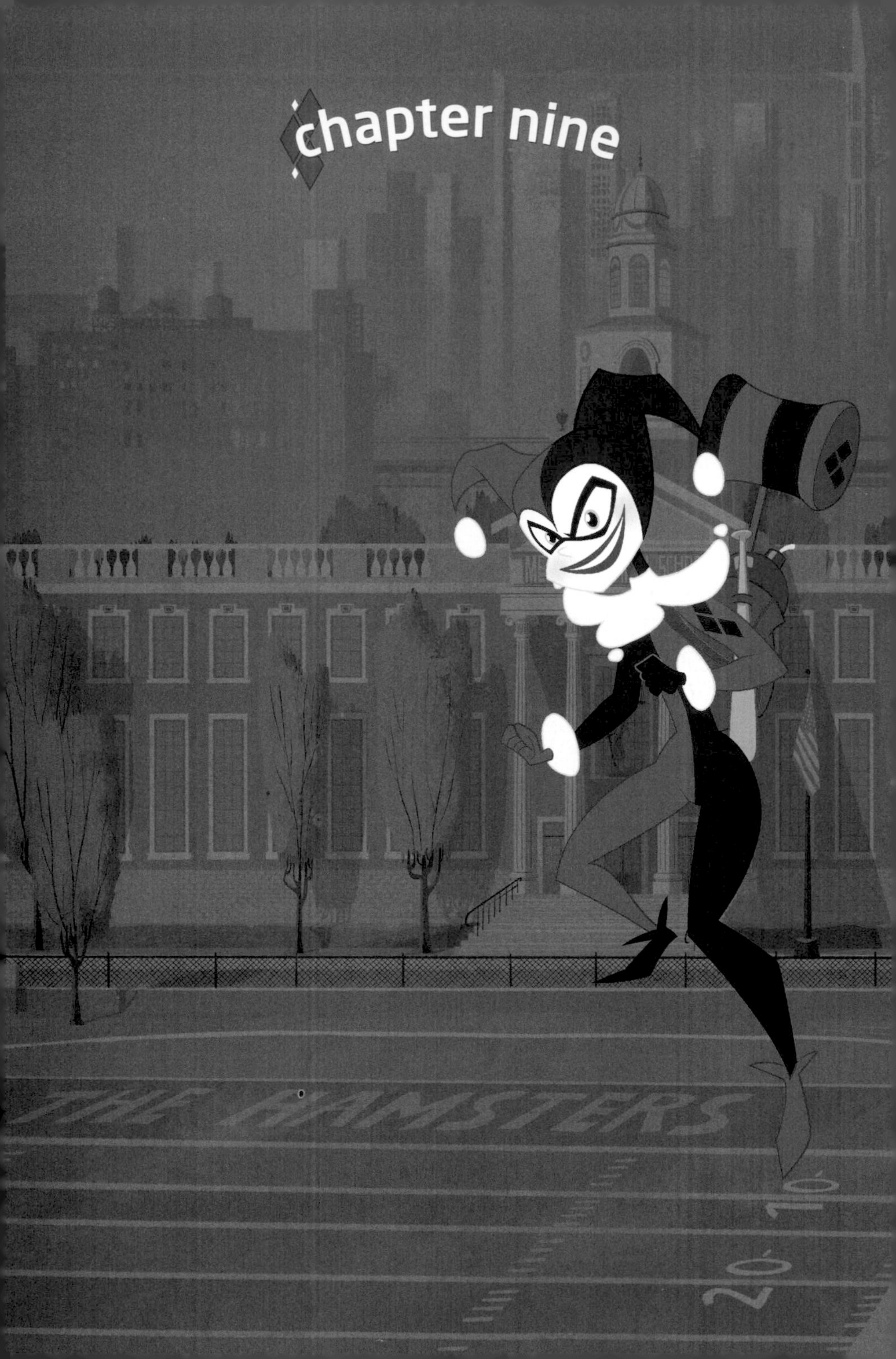
THE HAMSTERS

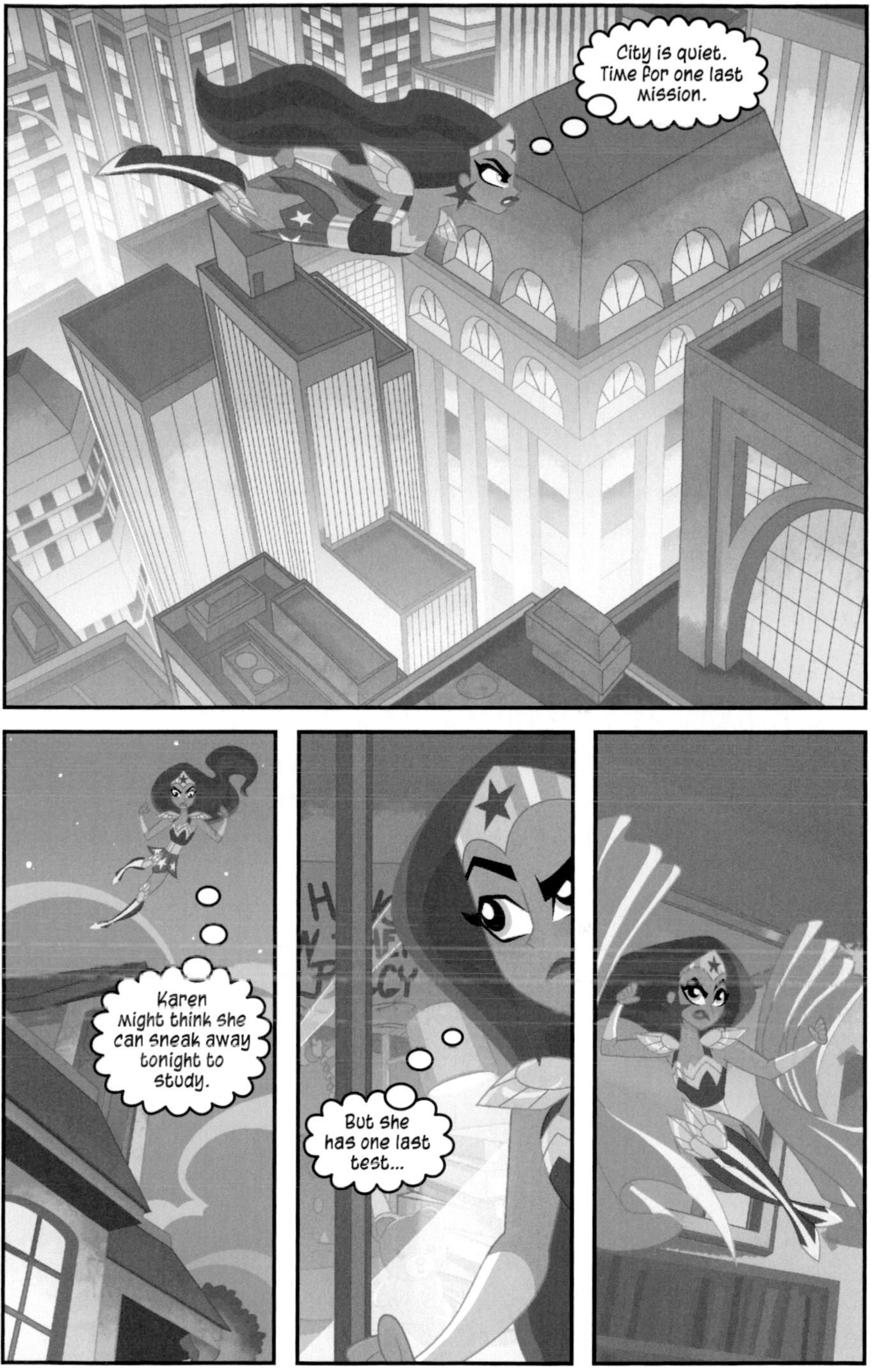
City is quiet. Time for one last mission.
Karen might think she can sneak away tonight to study.
But she has one last test...

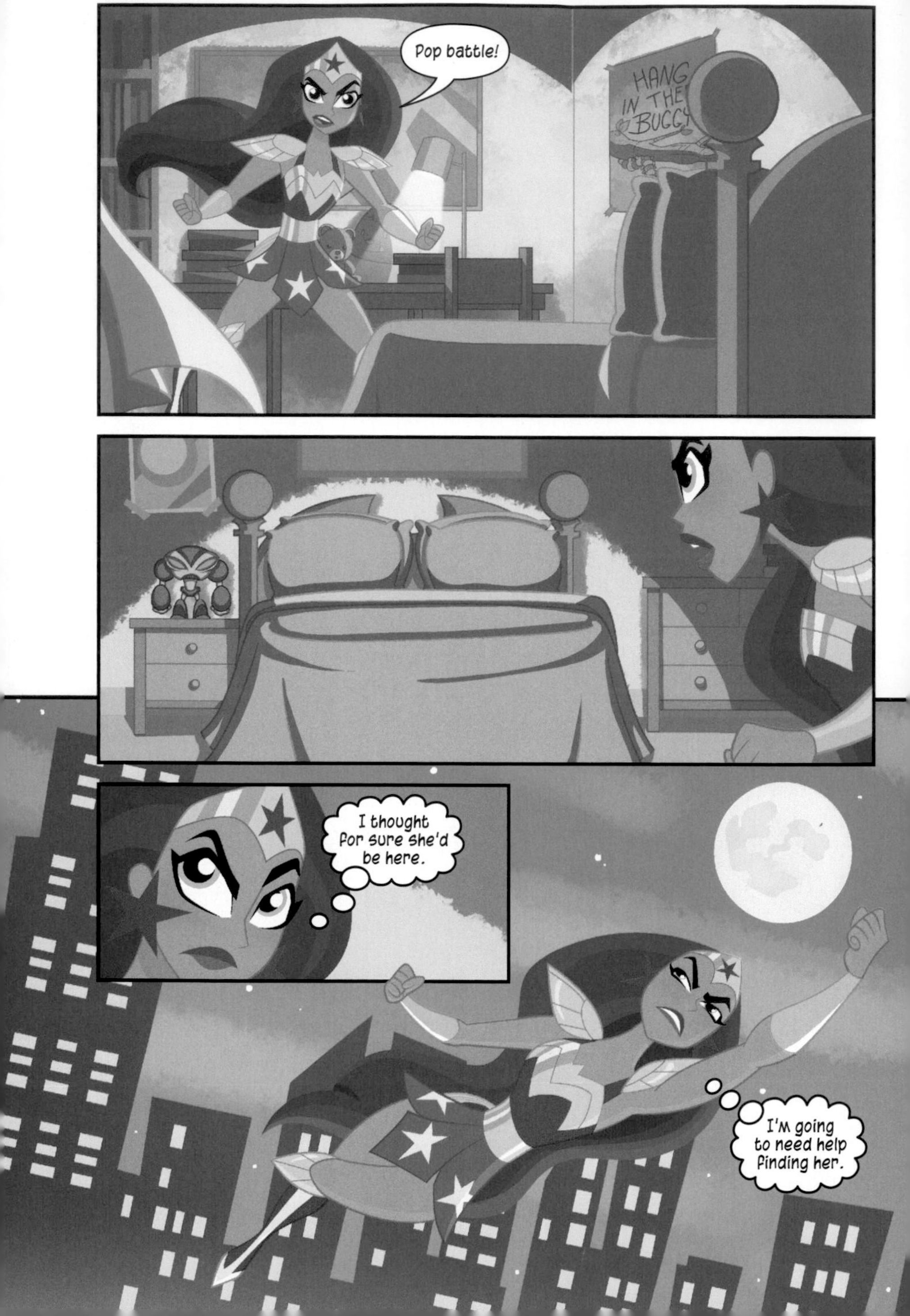
Pop battle!
HANG IN THERE BUGGY
I thought for sure she'd be here.
I'm going to need help finding her.

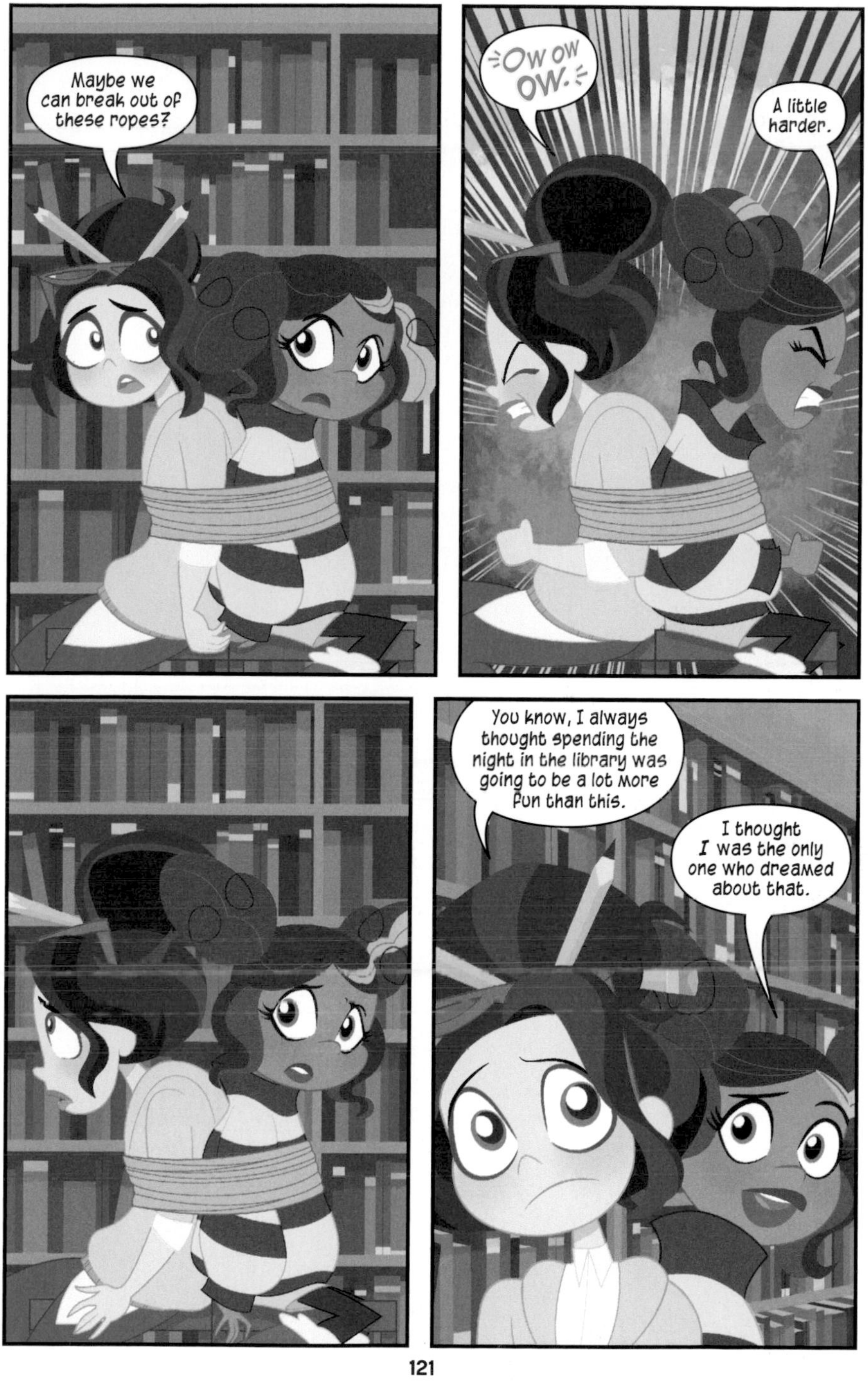
Maybe we can break out of these ropes?
OW OW OW.
A little harder.
You know, I always thought spending the night in the library was going to be a lot more fun than this.
I thought I was the only one who dreamed about that.

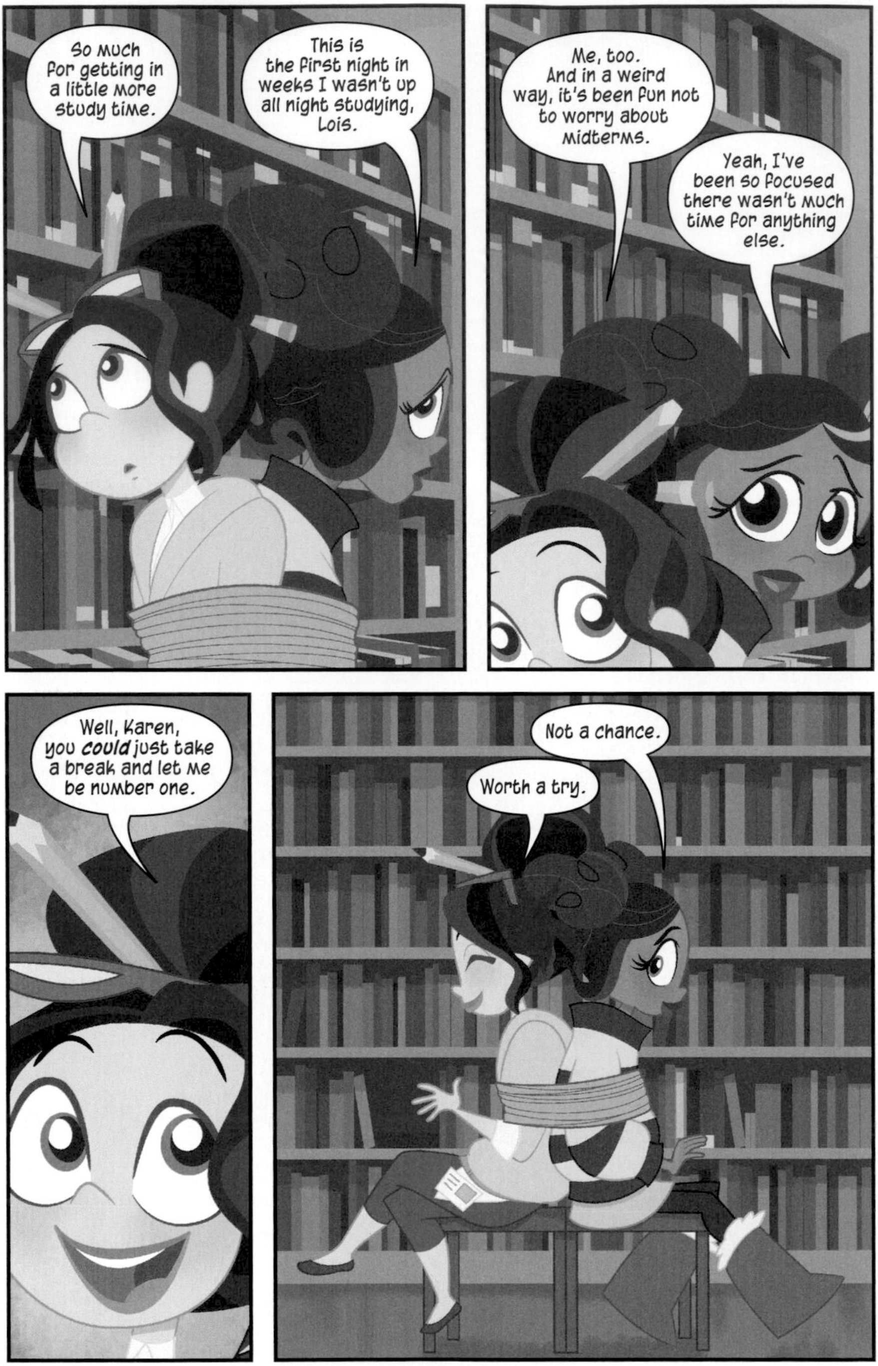
So much for getting in a little more study time.
This is the first night in weeks I wasn't up all night studying, Lois.
Me, too. And in a weird way, it's been fun not to worry about midterms.
Yeah, I've been so focused there wasn't much time for anything else.
Well, Karen, you *could* just take a break and let me be number one.
Not a chance.
Worth a try.

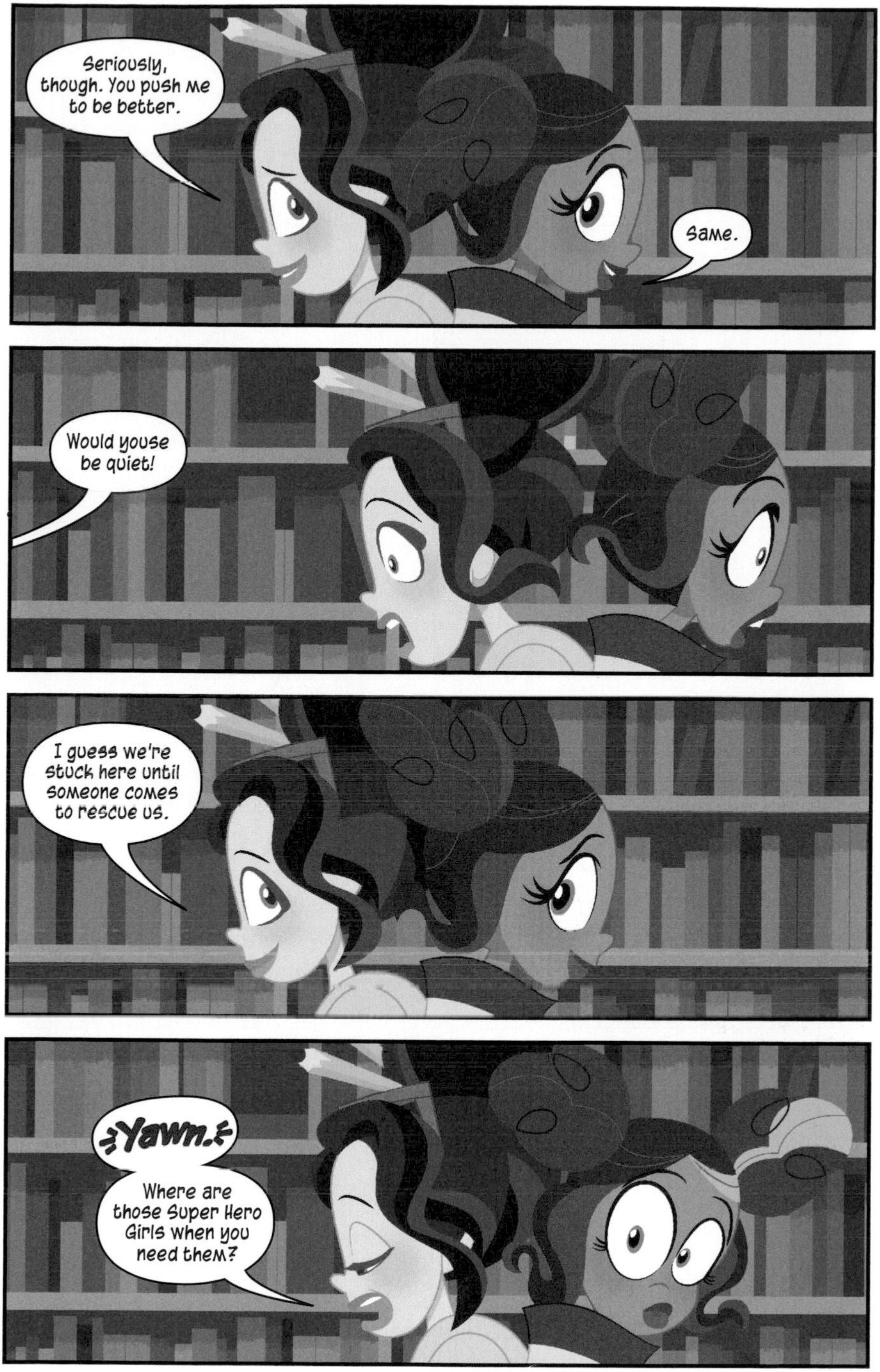
Seriously, though. You push me to be better.
Same.
Would youse be quiet!
I guess we're stuck here until someone comes to rescue us.
Yawn.
Where are those Super Hero Girls when you need them?

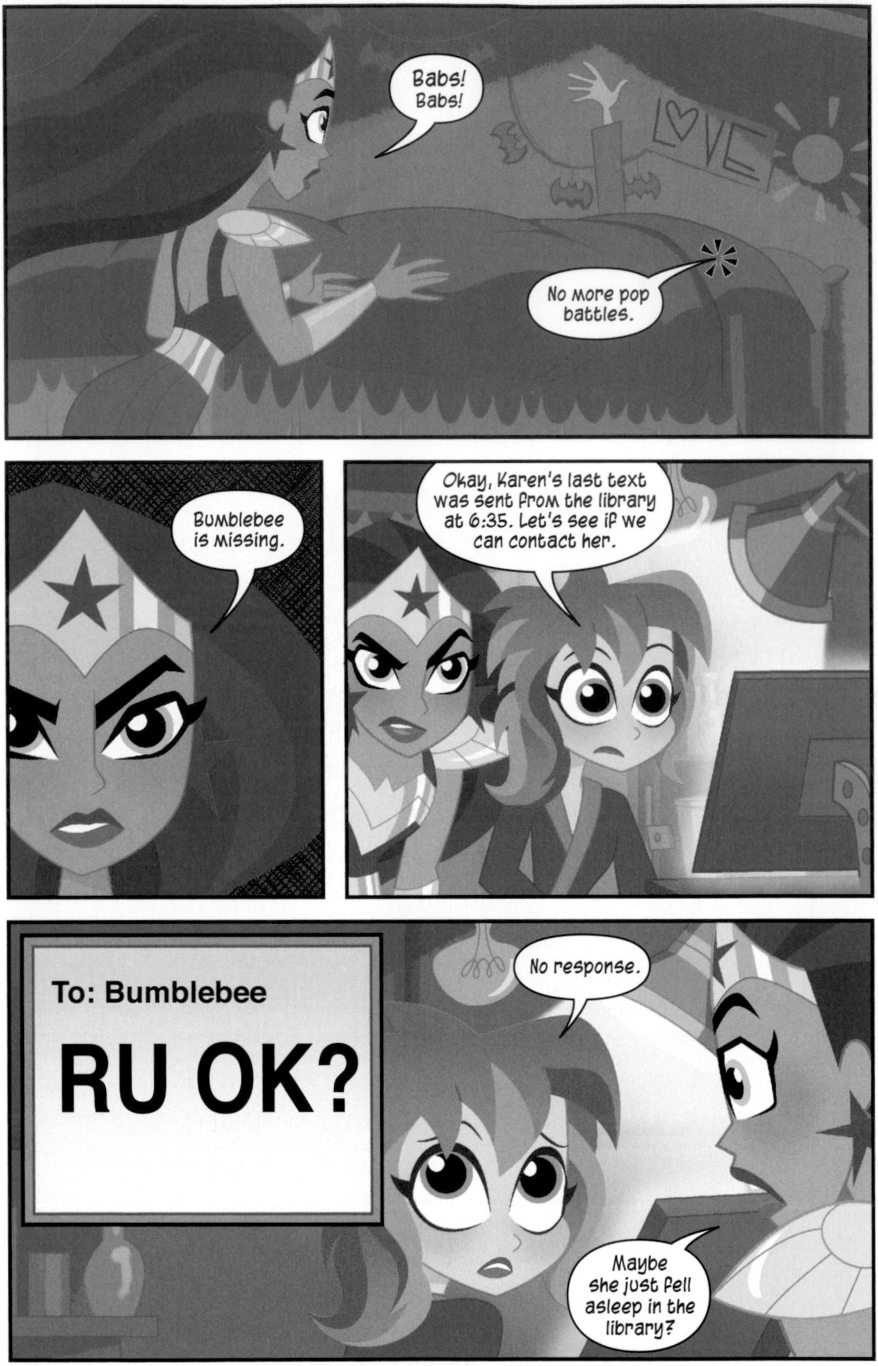
Babs! Babs!
No more pop battles.
Bumblebee is missing.
Okay, Karen's last text was sent from the library at 6:35. Let's see if we can contact her.
To: Bumblebee
RU OK?
No response.
Maybe she just fell asleep in the library?

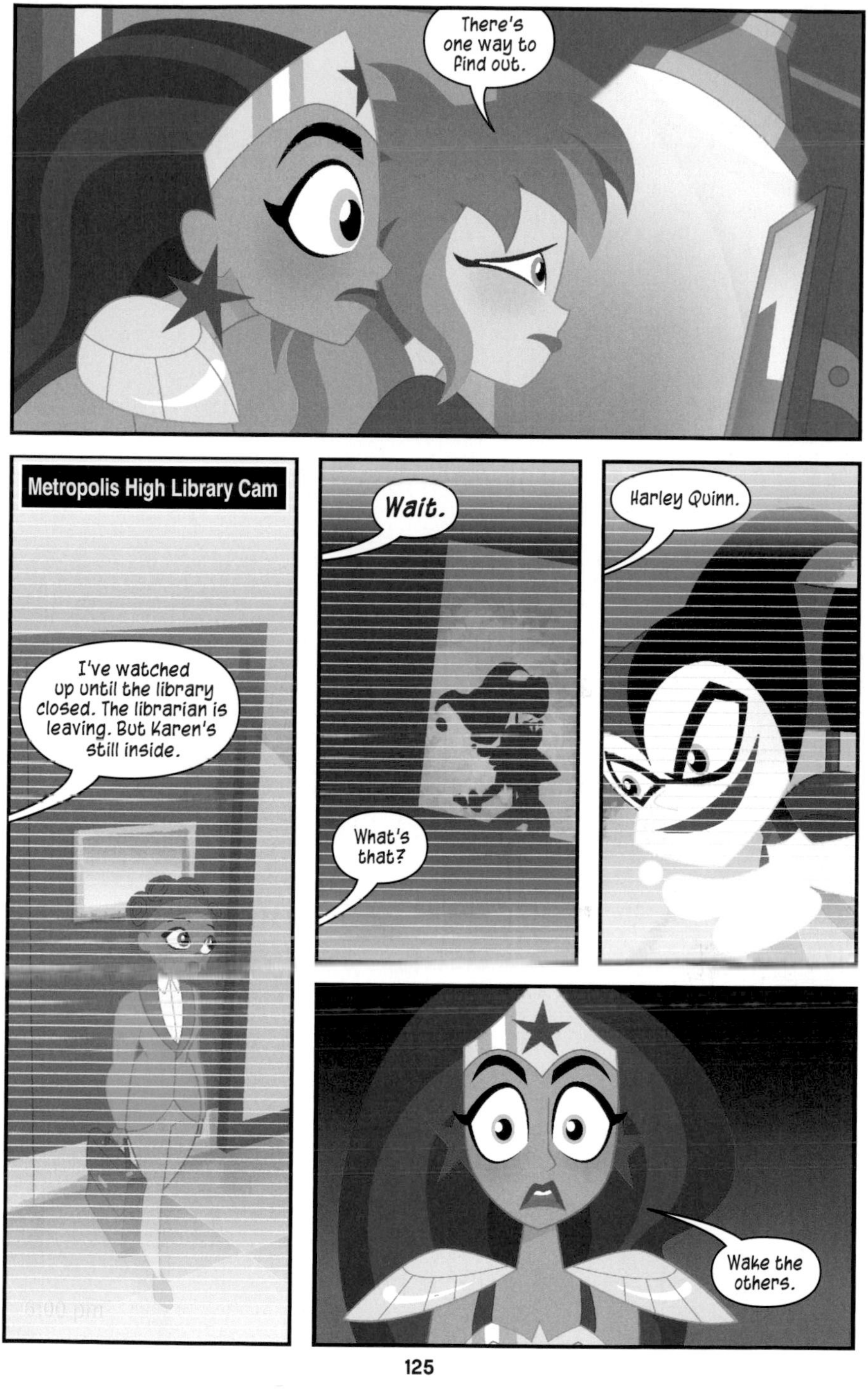
There's one way to find out.
Metropolis High Library Cam
I've watched up until the library closed. The librarian is leaving. But Karen's still inside.
Wait.
What's that?
Harley Quinn.
Wake the others.

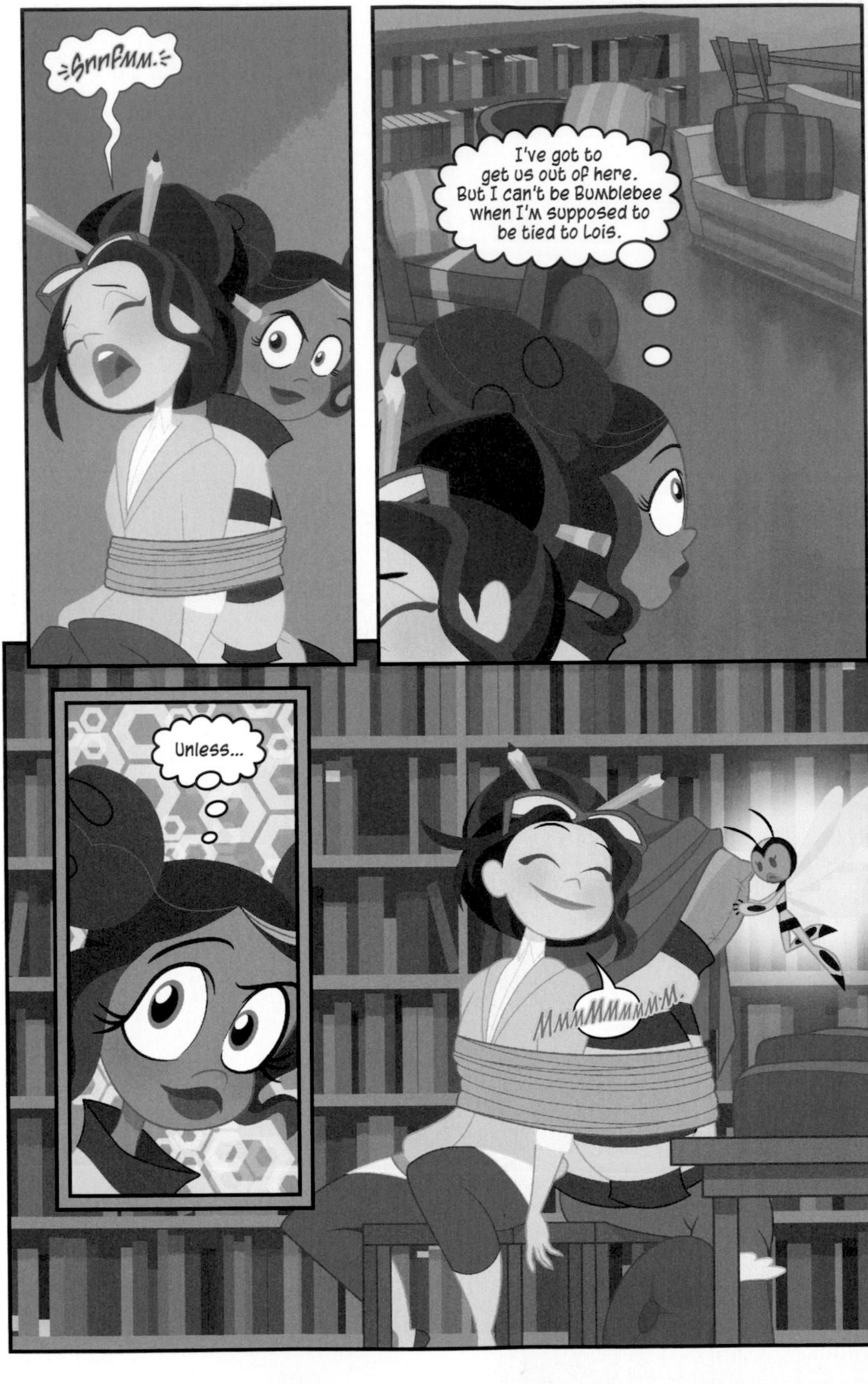
SnnFMM.
I've got to get us out of here. But I can't be Bumblebee when I'm supposed to be tied to Lois.
Unless...
MmmMMmmmM.

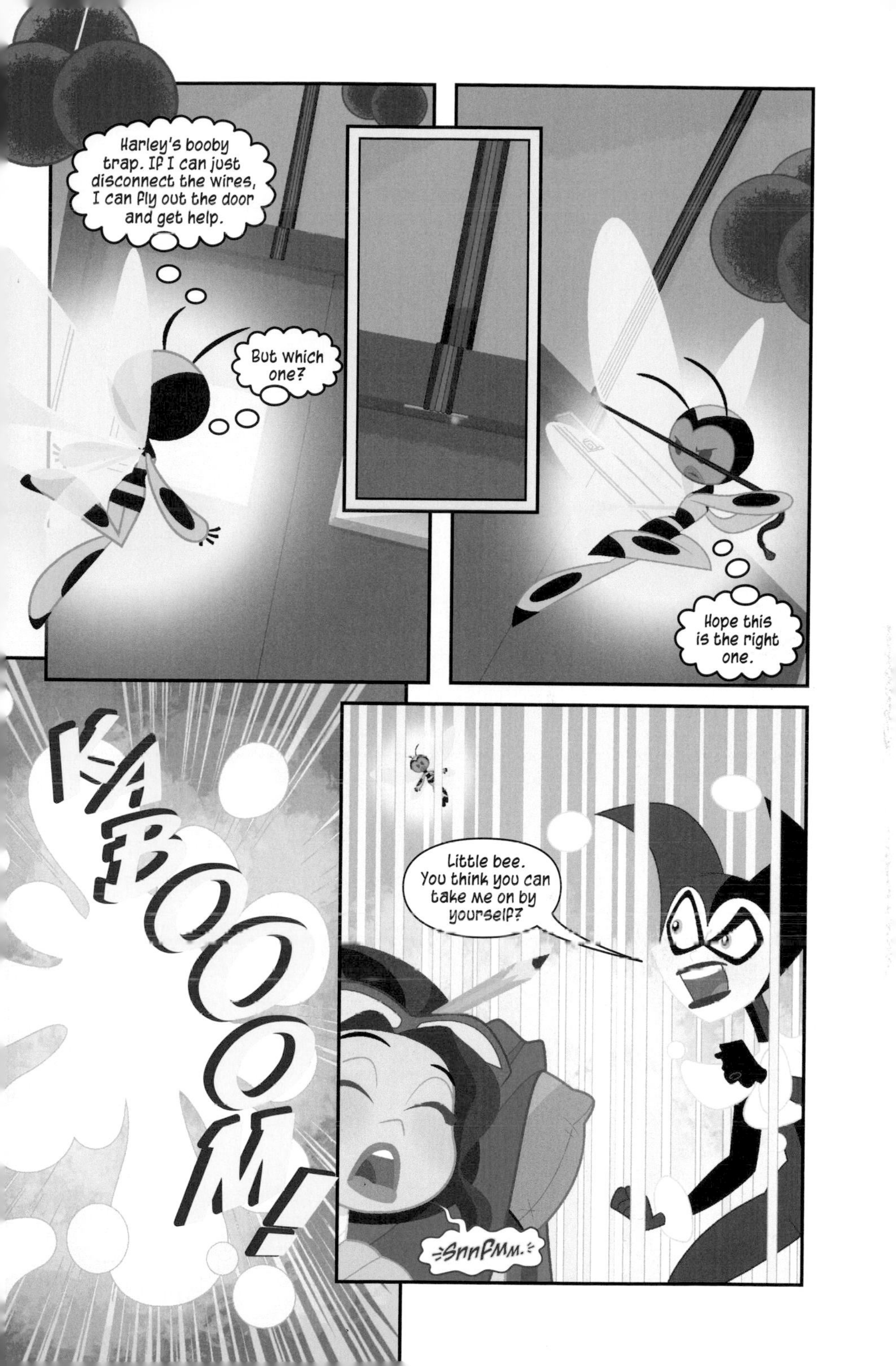
Harley's booby trap. If I can just disconnect the wires, I can fly out the door and get help.
But which one?
Hope this is the right one.
KABOOOOM!
Little bee. You think you can take me on by yourself?
SnnFMM.

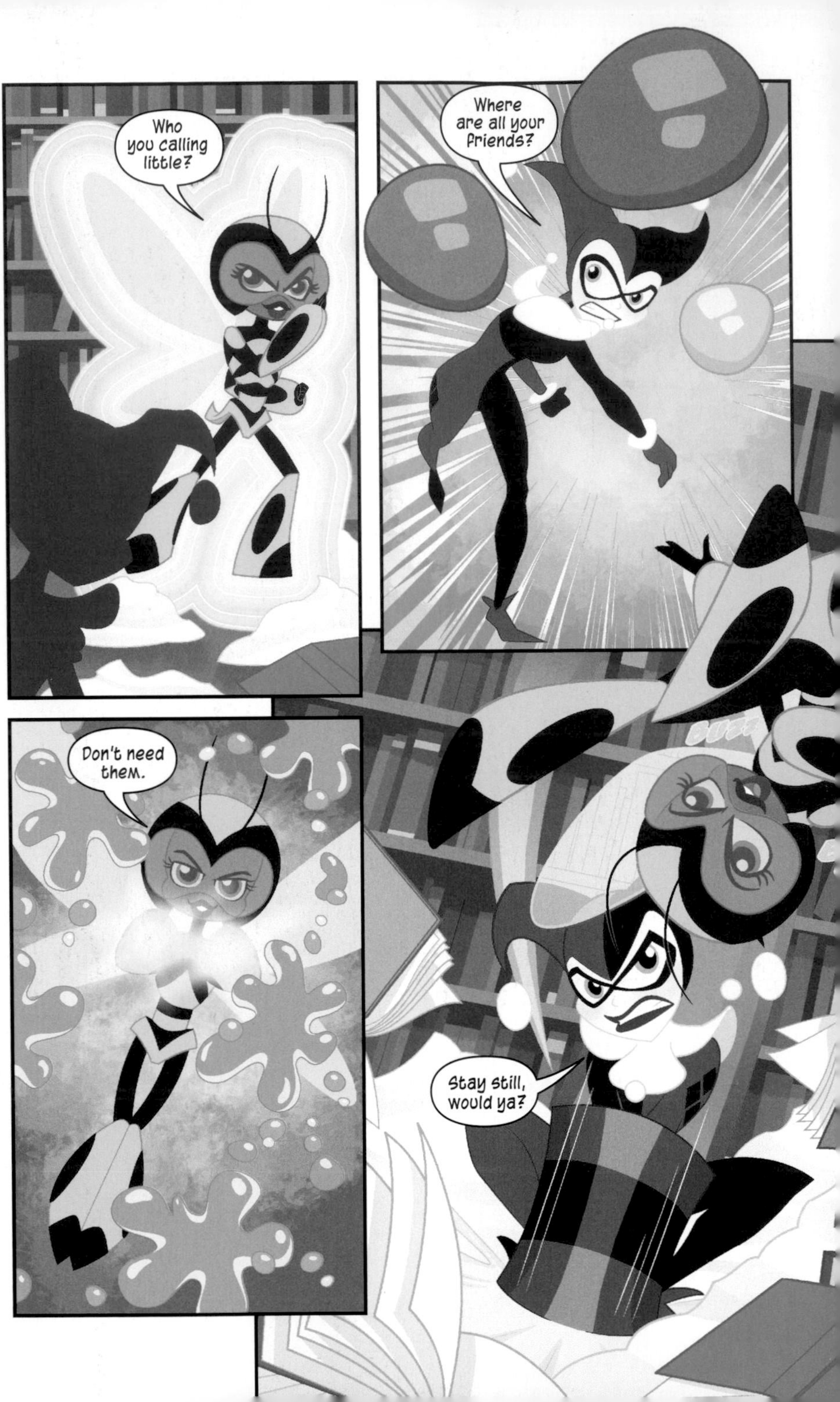
Who you calling little?
Where are all your friends?
Don't need them.
Stay still, would ya?

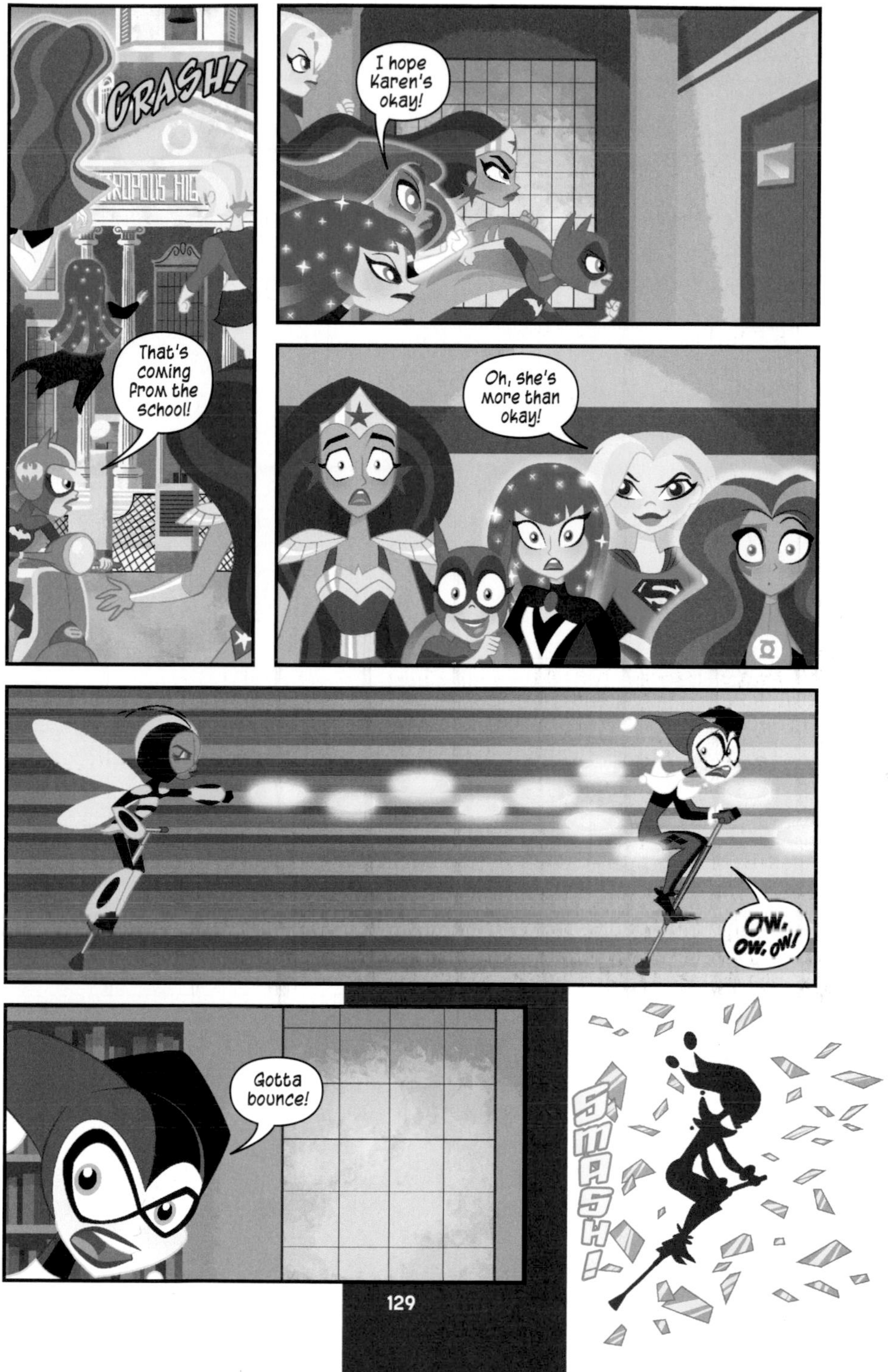
CRASH!
METROPOLIS HIG
That's coming from the school!
I hope Karen's okay!
Oh, she's more than okay!
OW. OW. OW!
Gotta bounce!
SMASH!

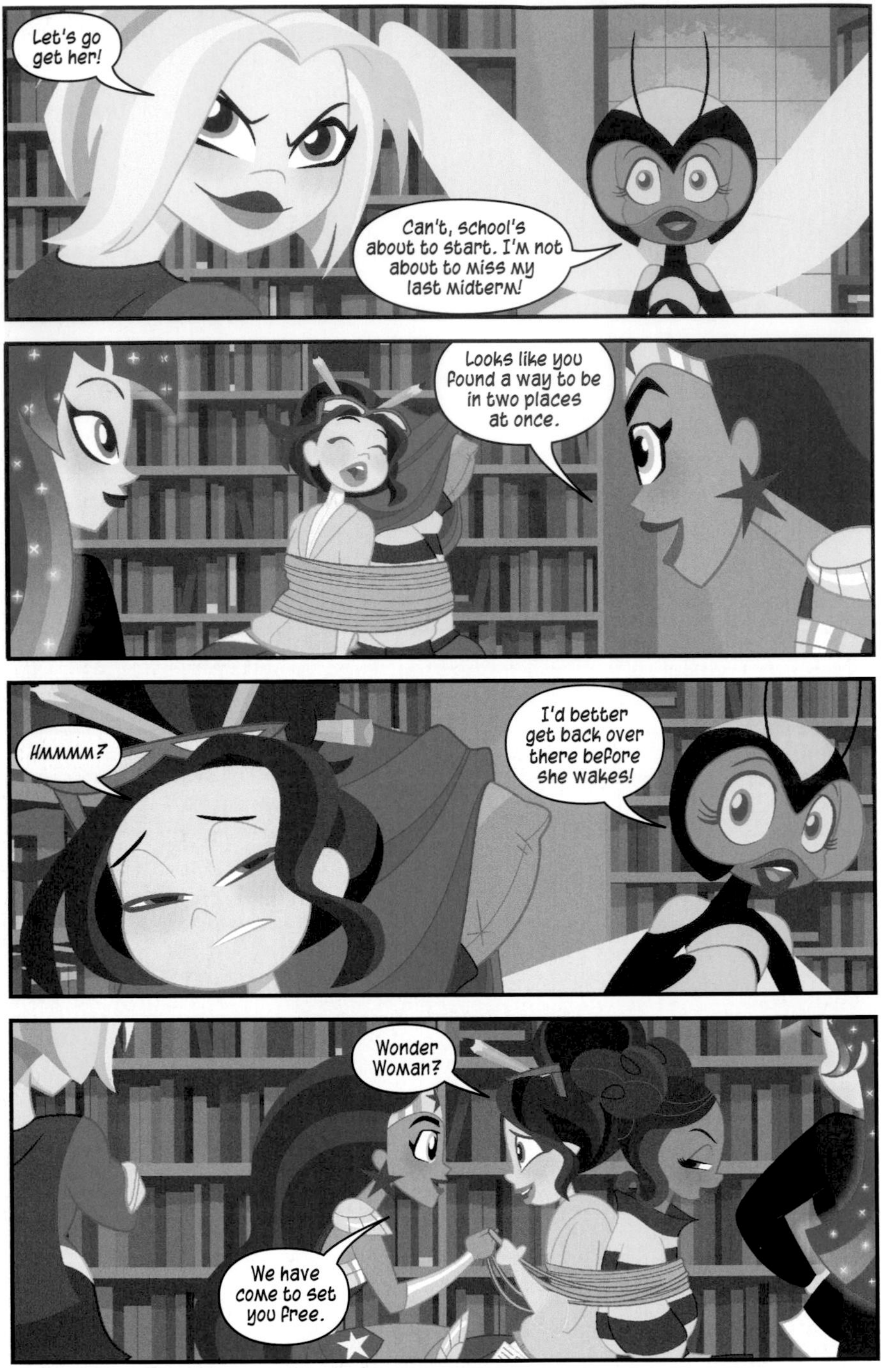

Let's go get her!
Can't, school's about to start. I'm not about to miss my last midterm!
Looks like you found a way to be in two places at once.
HMMMM?
I'd better get back over there before she wakes!
Wonder Woman?
We have come to set you free.

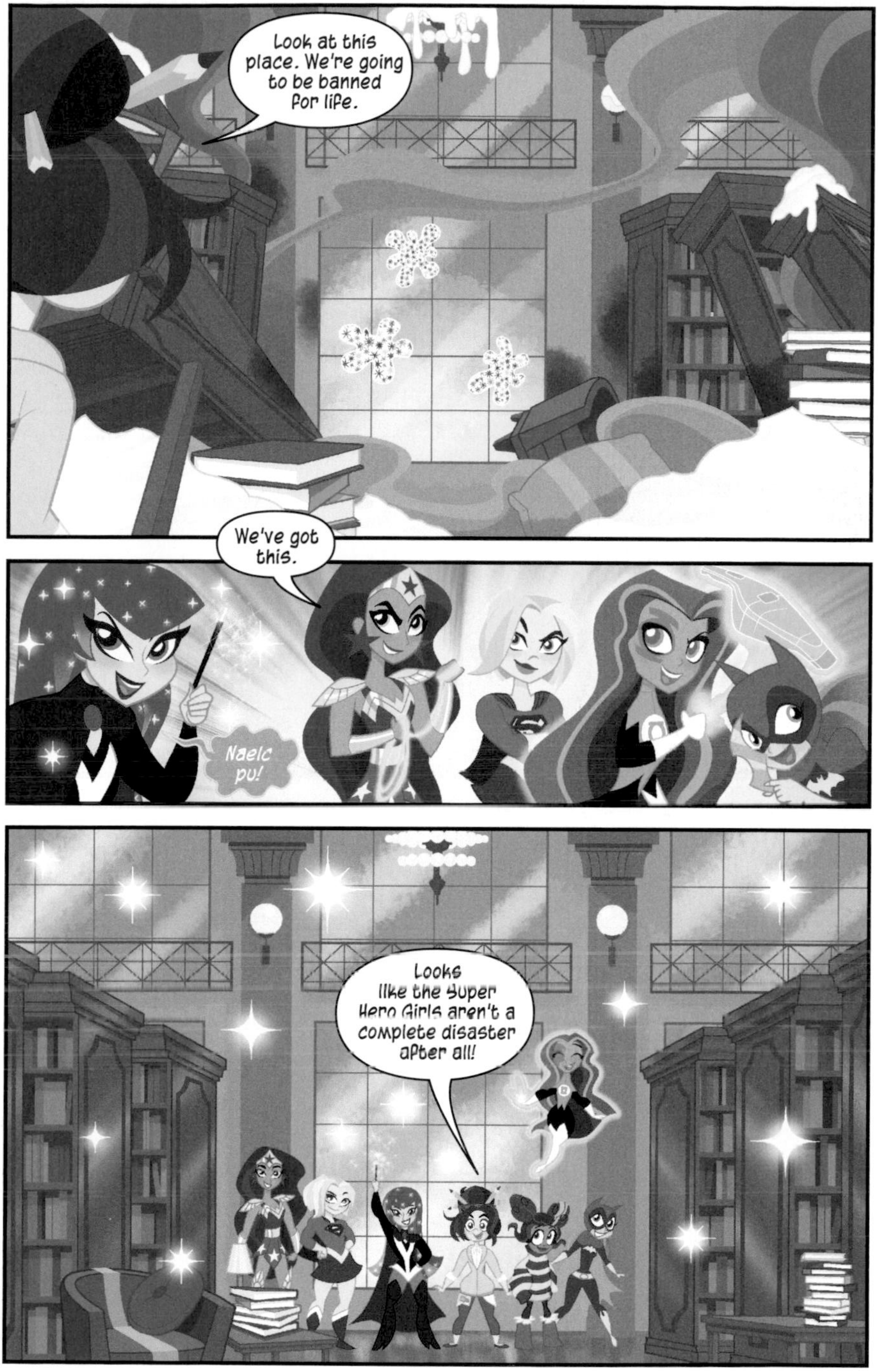
Look at this place. We're going to be banned for life.
We've got this.
Naelc pu!
Looks like the Super Hero Girls aren't a complete disaster after all!

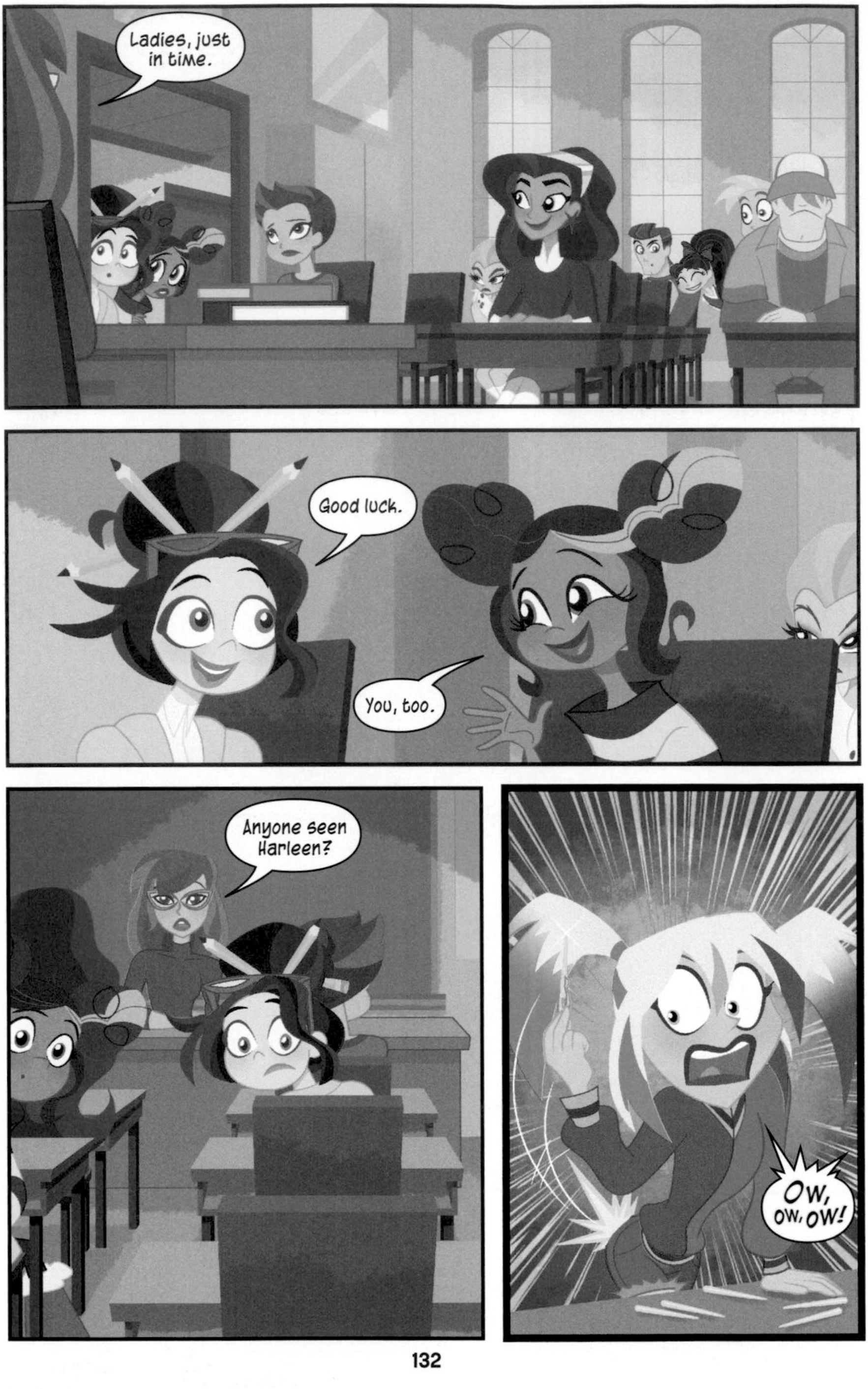

Ladies, just in time.
Good luck.
You, too.
Anyone seen Harleen?
OW, OW, OW!

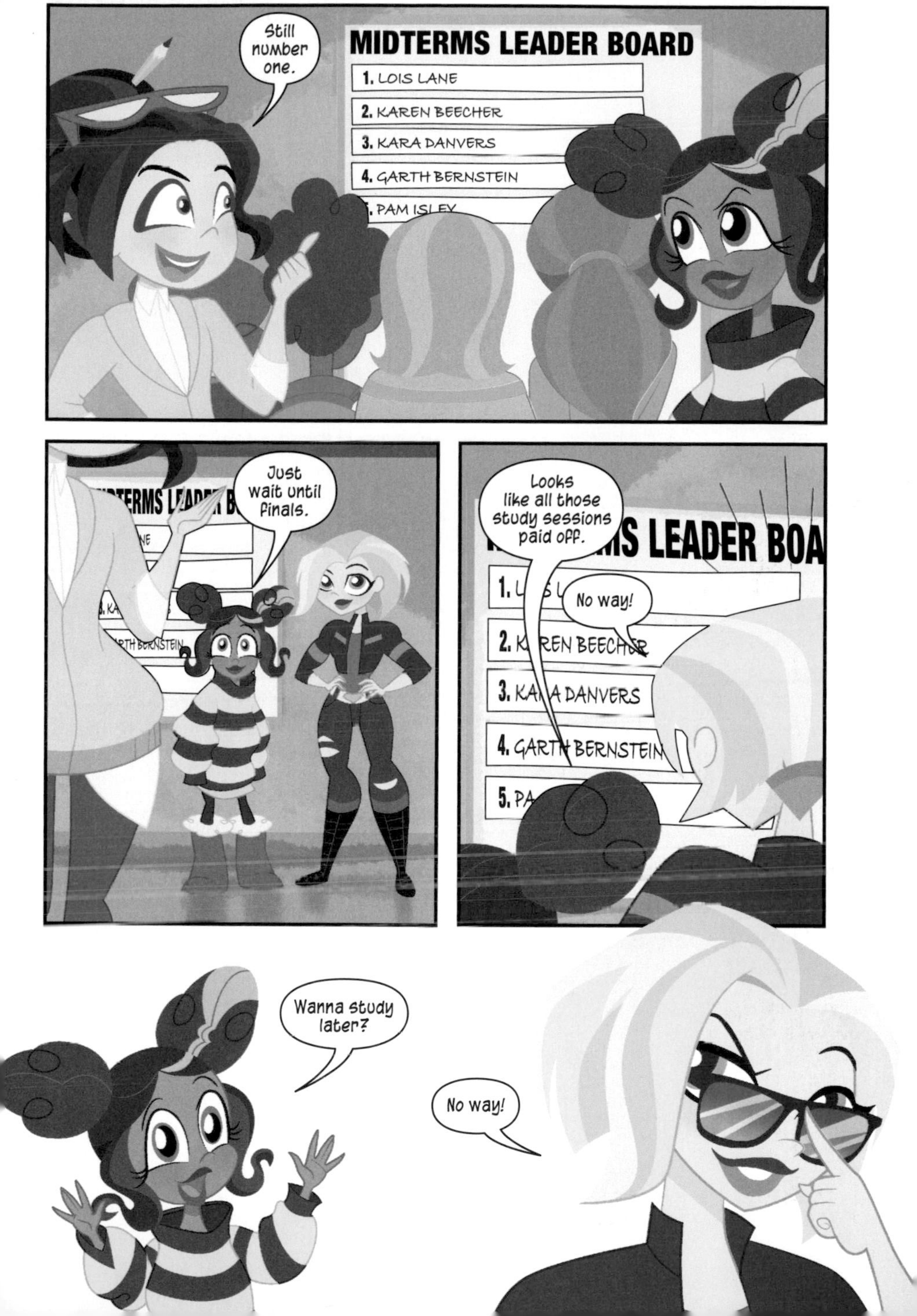
Still number one.
MIDTERMS LEADER BOARD
1. LOIS LANE
2. KAREN BEECHER
3. KARA DANVERS
4. GARTH BERNSTEIN
PAM ISLEY
Just wait until finals.
Looks like all those study sessions paid off.
No way!
Wanna study later?
No way!

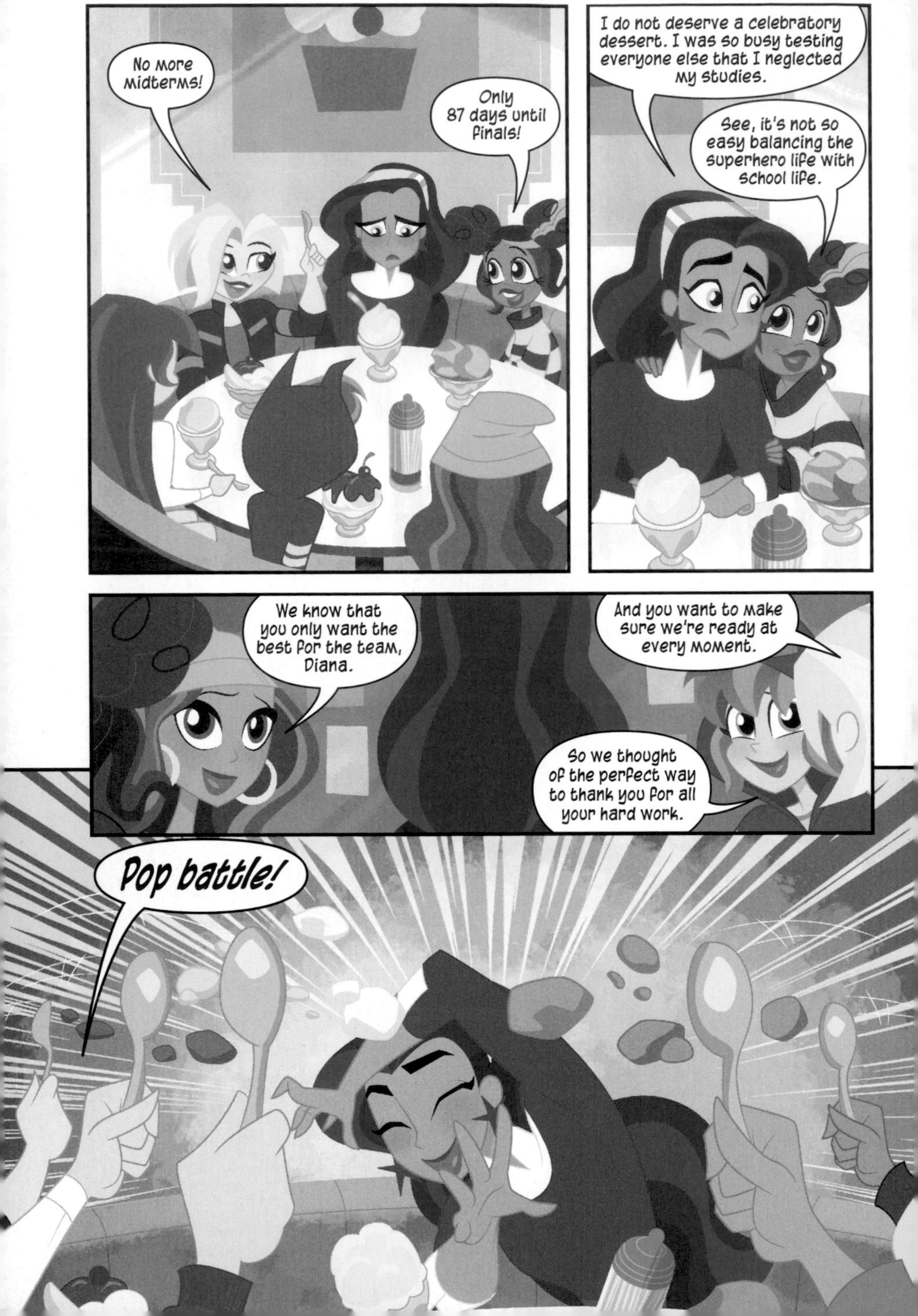
No more midterms!
Only 87 days until finals!
I do not deserve a celebratory dessert. I was so busy testing everyone else that I neglected my studies.
See, it's not so easy balancing the superhero life with school life.
We know that you only want the best for the team, Diana.
And you want to make sure we're ready at every moment.
So we thought of the perfect way to thank you for all your hard work.
Pop battle!

**Amy Wolfram** is an Emmy-nominated writer for television, movies, and comic books. She is super excited to be writing *DC Super Hero Girls* graphic novels! If she had to pick a favorite Super Hero Girl—she'd pick them all! Best known for writing for Teen Titans for both television (*Teen Titans, Teen Titans Go!*) and comics (*Teen Titans: Year One, Teen Titans Go!*), Amy has also had fun writing for many of her favorite characters: Barbie, Stuart Little, Ben 10, Thunderbirds Are Go, and Scooby-Doo. When not busy writing, she enjoys crafting and quilting.

**Yancey Labat** is the bestselling illustrator of the original *DC Super Hero Girls* graphic novel series. He got his start at Marvel Comics before moving on to illustrate children's books from *Hello Kitty* to *Peanuts* for Scholastic, as well as books for Chronicle Books, ABC Mouse, and others. His book *How Many Jelly Beans?* with writer Andrea Menotti won the 2013 Cook Prize for best STEM (Science, Technology, Education, Math) picture book from Bank Street College of Education.

**Carrie Strachan** is an award-awaiting colorist who has worked on *Hellblazer, Smallville: Season 11, MAD Magazine,* and *MAD Spy vs. Spy: An Explosive Celebration.* She currently lives in San Diego with her husband, Matt, where she's hard at work on more *DC Super Hero Girls.*

# ROLL THE DICE ON A NEW GAME OF BASEMENTS AND BASILISKS!

Robin's reminding his teammates of all the fun they had on their last B&B quest, and he's sure that this time, they won't get sucked into any alternate dimensions. But do their imaginations count?

Heather Nuhfer, P.C. Morrissey, and Sandy Jarrell return to the game they created, and Agnes Garbowska joins them for a tabletop adventure of epic proportions.

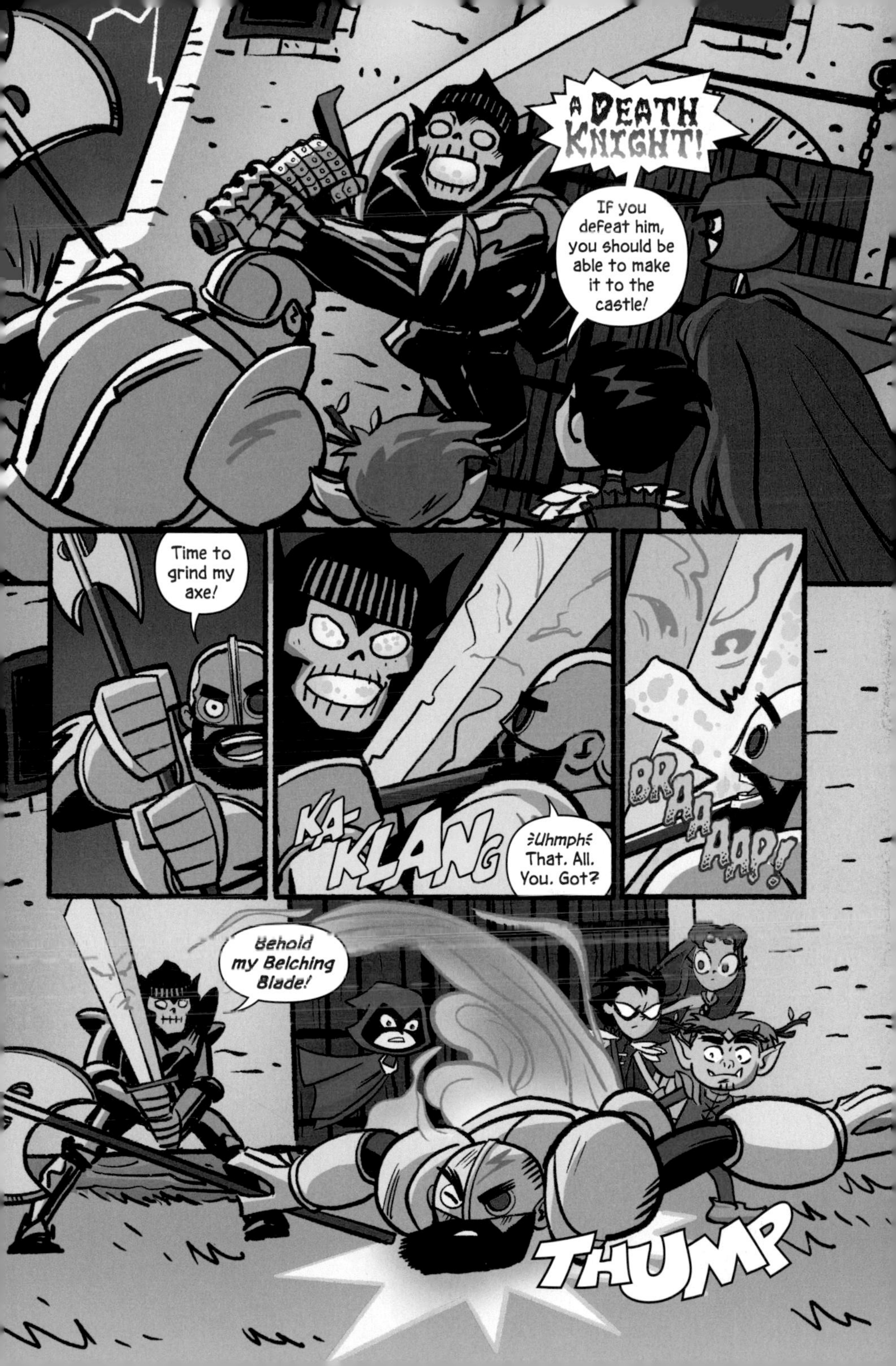
A DEATH KNIGHT!
If you defeat him, you should be able to make it to the castle!
Time to grind my axe!
KA-KLANG
Uhmph
That. All. You. Got?
BRAAAAAP!
Behold my Belching Blade!
THUMP

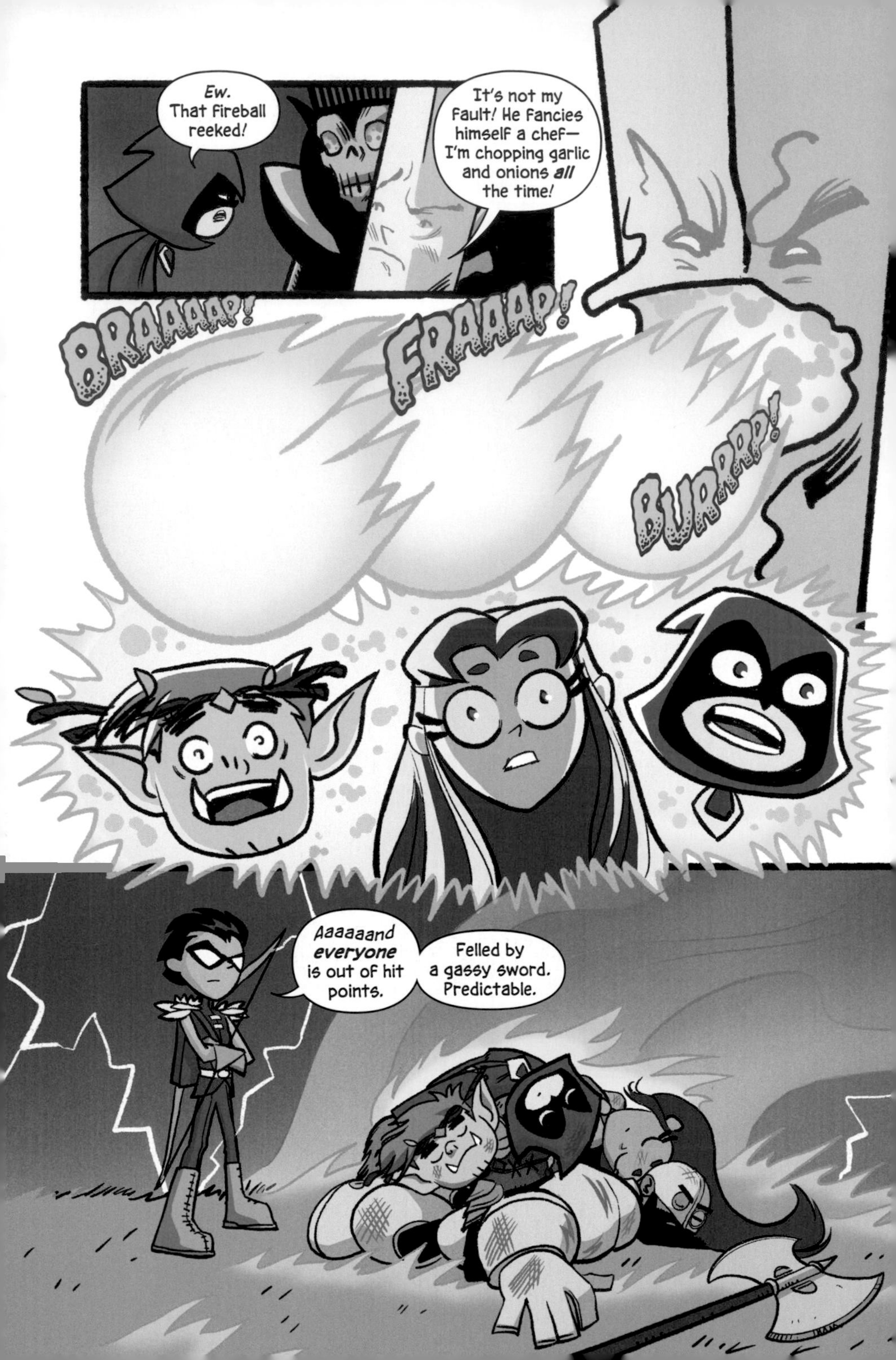
Ew. That fireball reeked!
It's not my fault! He fancies himself a chef—I'm chopping garlic and onions *all* the time!
BRAAAAAP!
FRAAAP!
BURRRP!
Aaaaaand *everyone* is out of hit points.
Felled by a gassy sword. Predictable.

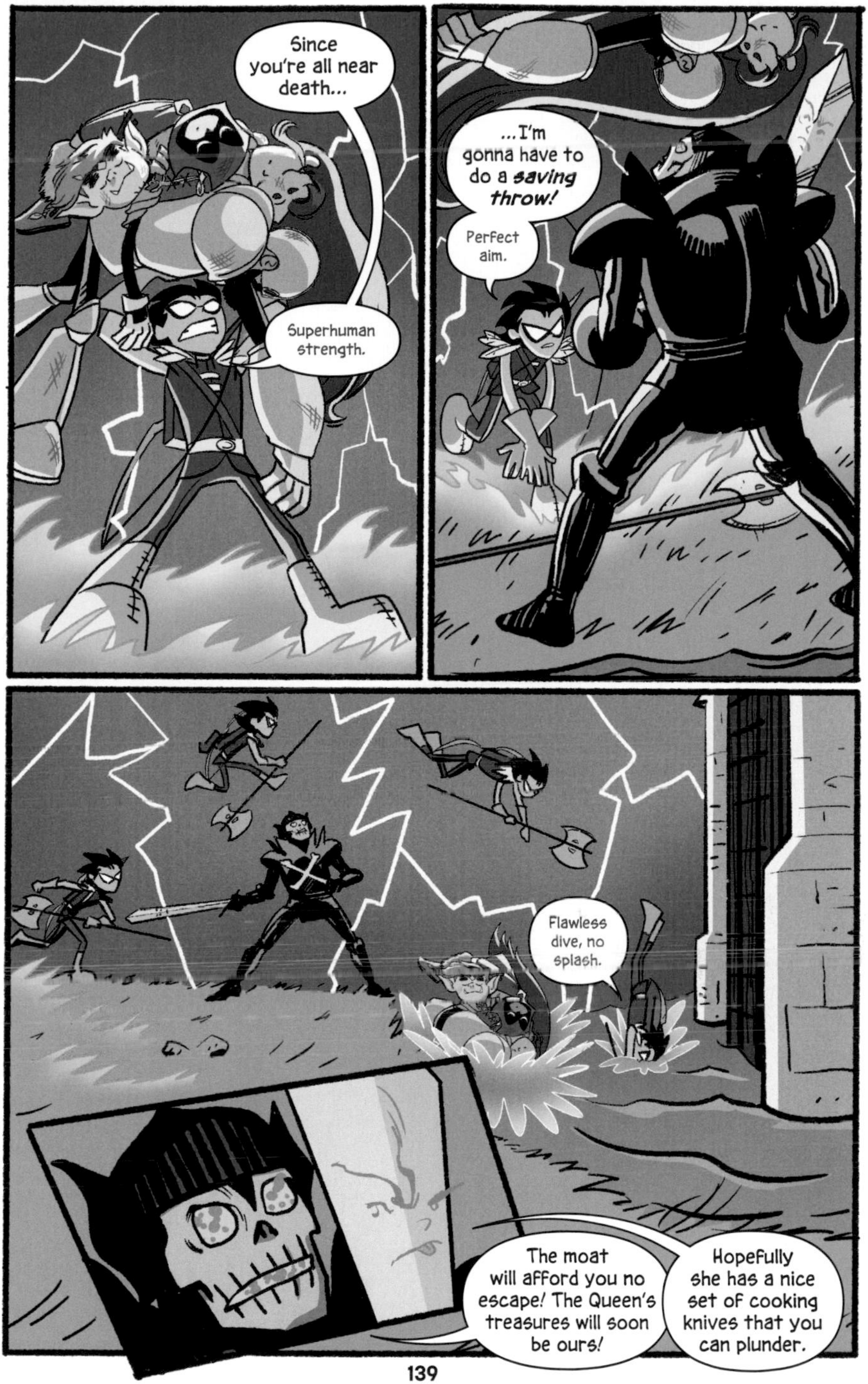
Since you're all near death...
Superhuman strength.
...I'm gonna have to do a saving throw!
Perfect aim.
Flawless dive, no splash.
The moat will afford you no escape! The Queen's treasures will soon be ours!
Hopefully she has a nice set of cooking knives that you can plunder.

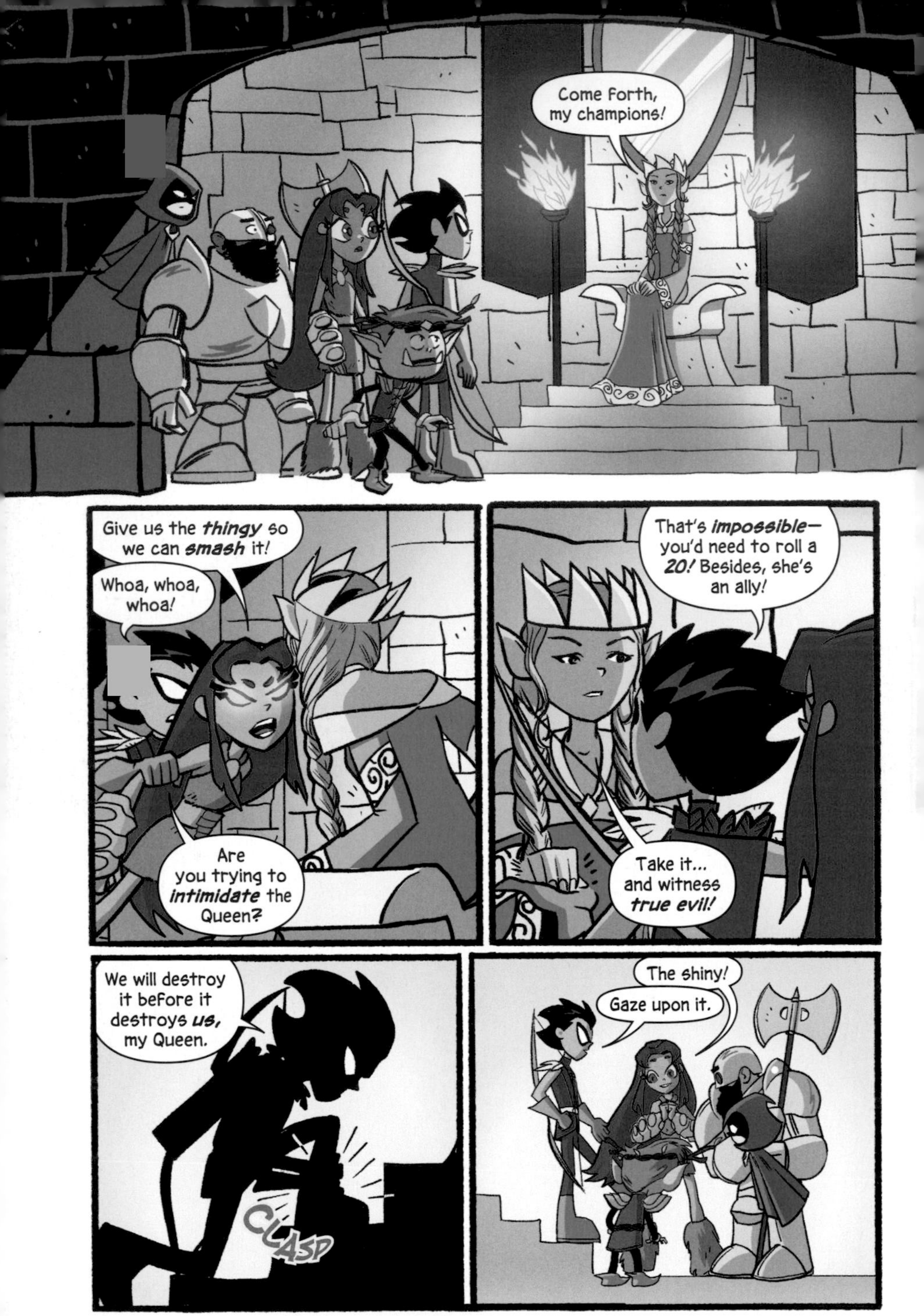
Come forth, my champions!
Give us the *thingy* so we can *smash* it!
Whoa, whoa, whoa!
Are you trying to *intimidate* the Queen?
That's *impossible*—you'd need to roll a *20!* Besides, she's an ally!
Take it... and witness *true evil!*
We will destroy it before it destroys *us,* my Queen.
CLASP
The shiny!
Gaze upon it.

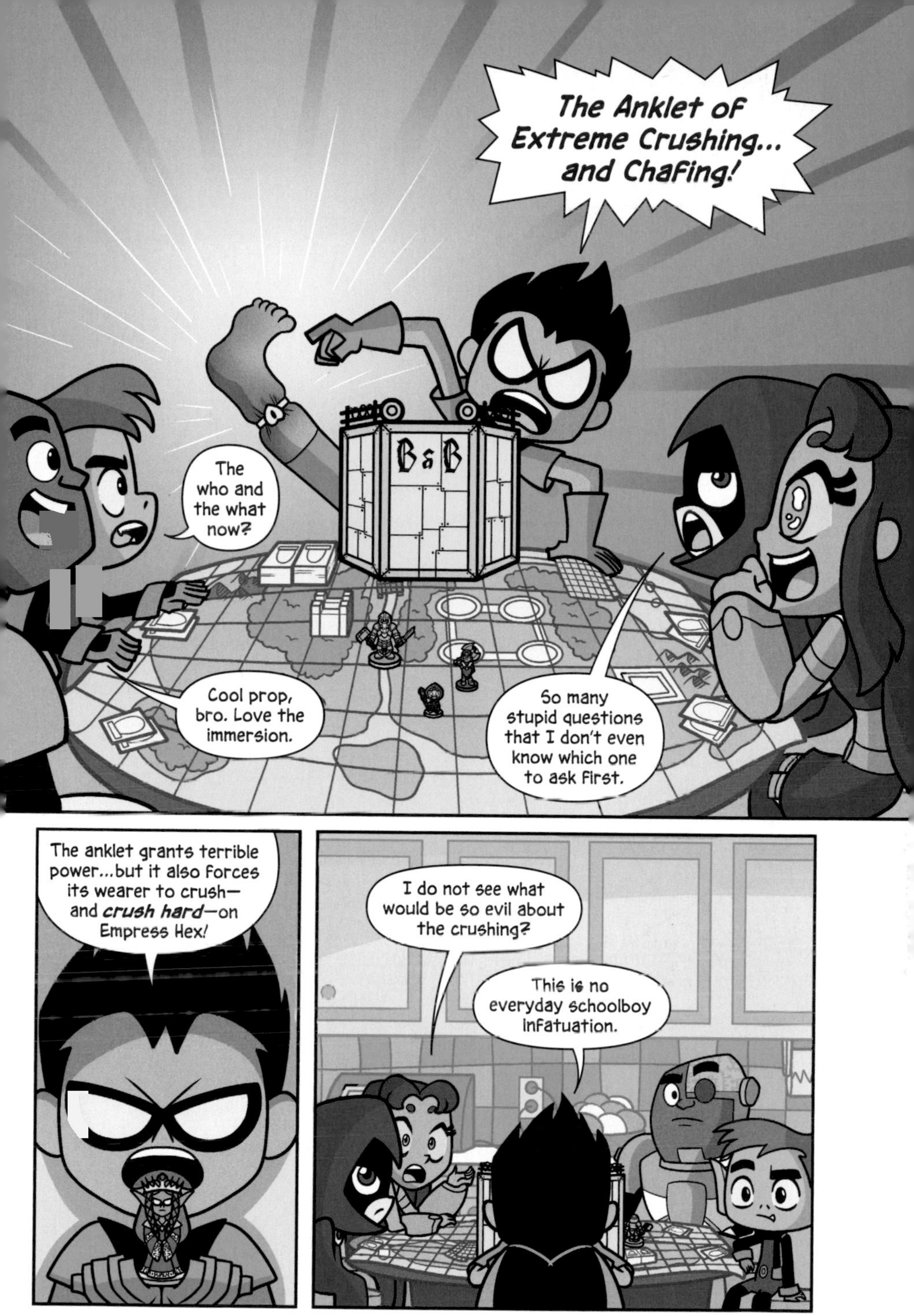
The Anklet of Extreme Crushing... and Chafing!
The who and the what now?
Cool prop, bro. Love the immersion.
So many stupid questions that I don't even know which one to ask first.
The anklet grants terrible power...but it also forces its wearer to crush—and *crush hard*—on Empress Hex!
I do not see what would be so evil about the crushing?
This is no everyday schoolboy infatuation.

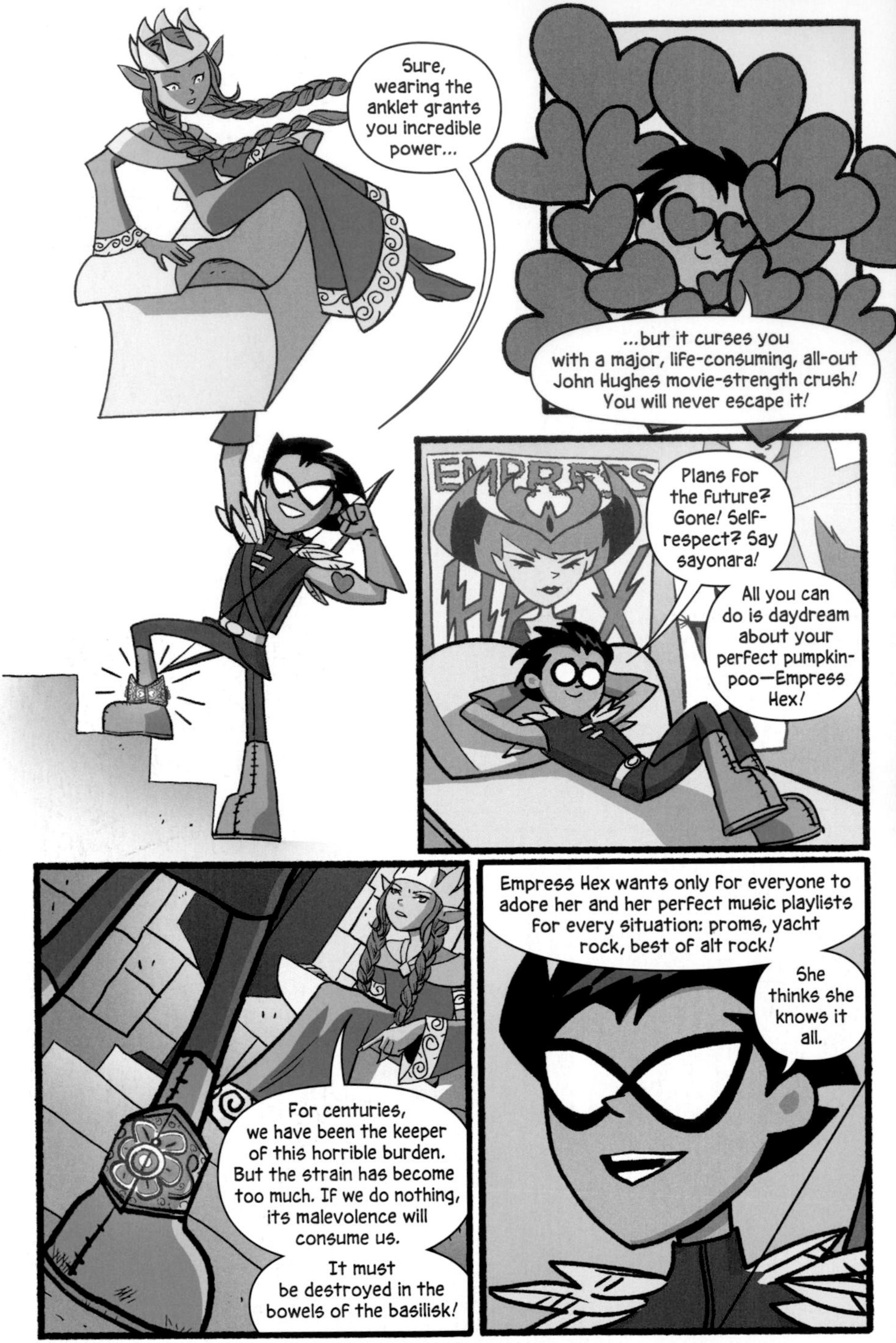
Sure, wearing the anklet grants you incredible power...
...but it curses you with a major, life-consuming, all-out John Hughes movie-strength crush! You will never escape it!
EMPRESS HEX
Plans for the future? Gone! Self-respect? Say sayonara!
All you can do is daydream about your perfect pumpkin-poo—Empress Hex!
For centuries, we have been the keeper of this horrible burden. But the strain has become too much. If we do nothing, its malevolence will consume us.
It must be destroyed in the bowels of the basilisk!
Empress Hex wants only for everyone to adore her and her perfect music playlists for every situation: proms, yacht rock, best of alt rock!
She thinks she knows it all.

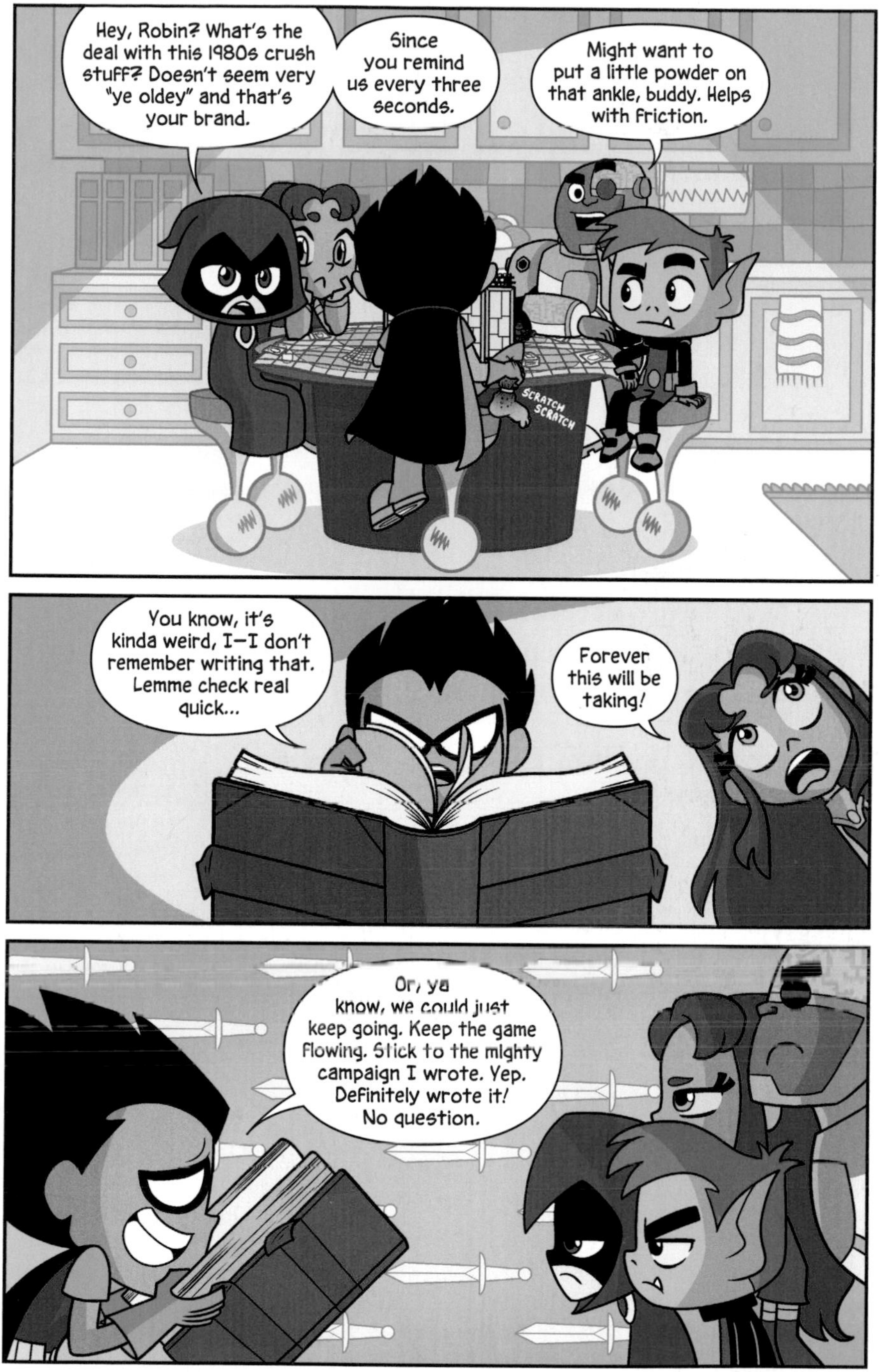
Hey, Robin? What's the deal with this 1980s crush stuff? Doesn't seem very "ye oldey" and that's your brand.
Since you remind us every three seconds.
Might want to put a little powder on that ankle, buddy. Helps with friction.
SCRATCH SCRATCH
You know, it's kinda weird, I—I don't remember writing that. Lemme check real quick...
Forever this will be taking!
Or, ya know, we could just keep going. Keep the game flowing. Stick to the mighty campaign I wrote. Yep. Definitely wrote it! No question.

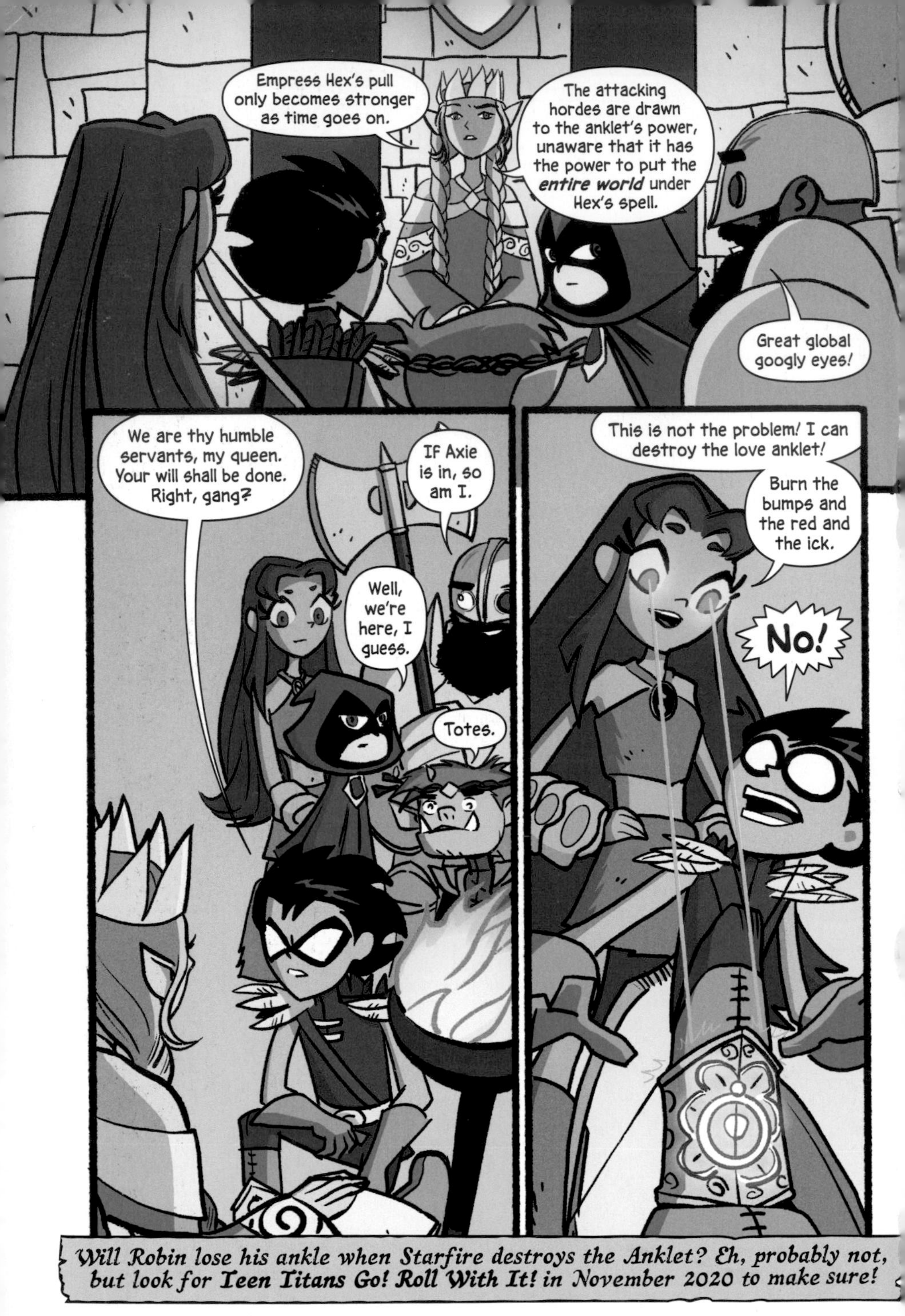
Empress Hex's pull only becomes stronger as time goes on.
The attacking hordes are drawn to the anklet's power, unaware that it has the power to put the entire world under Hex's spell.
Great global googly eyes!
We are thy humble servants, my queen. Your will shall be done. Right, gang?
If Axie is in, so am I.
Well, we're here, I guess.
Totes.
This is not the problem! I can destroy the love anklet!
Burn the bumps and the red and the ick.
No!
Will Robin lose his ankle when Starfire destroys the Anklet? Eh, probably not, but look for Teen Titans Go! Roll With It! in November 2020 to make sure!